Love to
    Laura L. La_____
From Grandm & Grandpa
        Landis

        Christmas
            1974

ALL HORSES GO TO HEAVEN

Hast thou given the horse strength?
Hast thou clothed his neck with thunder?
Canst thou make him afraid as a grasshopper?
The glory of his nostrils is terrible.
He paweth in the valley, and rejoiceth in his strength,
He goeth on to meet the armed men.
He mocketh at fear and is not affrighted;
Neither turneth he back from the sword.
The quiver rattleth against him,
The glittering spear and the shield.
He swalloweth the ground with fierceness and rage:
Neither believeth he that it is the sound of the trumpet.
He saith among the trumpets, Ha, ha,
And he smelleth the battle afar off,
The thunder of the captains, and the shouting.

JOB XXXIX: 19–25

All Horses Go to Heaven

AN ANTHOLOGY OF STORIES ABOUT HORSES

SELECTED BY BETH BROWN

ILLUSTRATED BY FRANK VAUGHN

PUBLISHERS Grosset & Dunlap NEW YORK

Acknowledgments

I deeply appreciate the cooperation of the following authors, publishers, and literary representatives for their kind permission to reprint the stories in this collection:

MAXWELL ALEY ASSOCIATES for "Dark Child" by Edward North Robinson. Copyright © 1947 by Curtis Publishing Company.

AMERICAN-SCANDINAVIAN FOUNDATION for "Skobelef" by Johan Bojer, translated by Sigurd B. Hustvedt. Published originally in the *American-Scandinavian Review*, July, 1922, and reprinted here by permission of the American-Scandinavian Foundation.

APPLETON-CENTURY-CROFTS, INC., for "The Look of Eagles" by John Taintor Foote. Reprinted by permission of the publishers, Appleton-Century-Crofts, Inc., an affiliate of Meredith Press.

JOHN BIGGS, JR., for "Corkran of the Clamstretch" by John Biggs, Jr. Copyright © 1921 by Charles Scribner's Sons; renewal copyright © 1949. Used by permission of the author.

WILLIAM BRANDON for "Chiltipiquin" by William Brandon. Copyright © 1943 by the Curtis Publishing Company. Reprinted from *The Saturday Evening Post* by permission of the author.

BETH BROWN for "All Horses Go to Heaven," by Beth Brown, written especially for this book.

BETH BROWN for "Gypsy," from *Mr. Jolly's Hotel for Dogs*, copyright © 1947. Permission for adaptation by the author.

CANCER RESEARCH FOUNDATION OF AMERICA for "That Colt Pericles" by Henry H. Knibbs. Reprinted with permission of the Cancer Research Foundation of America, 7413 Hawthorne Avenue, Hollywood, California.

GLADYS HASTY CARROLL for "Maudie Tom, Jockey" by Gladys Hasty Carroll. Reprinted by permission of the author.

JACQUES CHAMBRUN, INC., for "Storm Winds" by R. J. Rocklin. Copyright © 1945 by Rock John Rocklin.

CHILTON COMPANY—BOOK DIVISION (Philadelphia) and ANGUS & ROBERTSON LTD. (Australia) for "Valiant Lady" from *Of Men, Dogs and Horses* by J. C. Bendrodt. Copyright © 1952 by Chilton Company, Philadelphia and New York. Reprinted by permission.

CURTIS BROWN LTD. and CHARLOTTE EDWARDS for "Pool of Sand" by Charlotte Edwards. Copyright © 1960 by the Curtis Publishing Company. Reprinted from the November 12, 1960, *Saturday Evening Post*.

iv

DEVIN-ADAIR COMPANY for "Pinto Horse" by Charles Elliott Perkins, published 1960 by the Devin-Adair Company, New York.

BARTHOLD FLES for "Palomino" by Bud Murphy. Copyright © 1945 by *Senior Scholastic*. Used by permission of Barthold Fles, literary agent.

HOLIDAY HOUSE, INC. and PAUL ANNIXTER for "The Runner" by Jane and Paul Annixter, from *The Runner*, copyright © 1956 by Holiday House, Inc. Reprinted through a special arrangement with Holiday House, Inc.

HOLT, RINEHART & WINSTON, INC. and HAMISH HAMILTON, LTD. for "Colt of Destiny" by Alida Malkus. Copyright © 1950 by Alida Malkus; copyright © Alida Malkus, Hamish Hamilton, London, 1953. Reprinted by permission of Holt, Rinehart & Winston, Inc. and Hamish Hamilton, Ltd.

HOLT, RINEHART & WINSTON, INC., publishers of the American edition, and FABER AND FABER, LTD., publishers of the British Commonwealth edition, for "The Ghost Horse" from *Long Lance* by Chief Buffalo Child Long Lance. Copyright © 1928, copyright © renewed 1956, by Holt, Rinehart & Winston, Inc. Reprinted by permission of Holt, Rinehart & Winston, Inc. and Faber and Faber, Ltd.

J. B. LIPPINCOTT and LAURENCE POLLINGER, LTD. (English agent) for "My Friend Flicka" by Mary O'Hara. Copyright © 1941 by Mary O'Hara. Published by J. B. Lippincott Company, Philadelphia, and Eyre & Spottiswode Ltd., London.

WILLIAM MORRIS AGENCY, INC., for "Throw Your Heart Over" by Stuart Cloete. Copyright © 1960 by the Curtis Publishing Company. Reprinted by permission.

HAROLD OBER ASSOCIATES, INC., for "My Kingdom for Jones" by Wilbur Schramm. Copyright © 1944 by Wilbur Schramm. Reprinted by the permission of Harold Ober Associates, Inc.

RAND MCNALLY & COMPANY for "The White Horse Mystery" by Alice Alison Lide, from *Child Life Magazine*. Copyright © 1940 by Rand McNally & Company.

MRS. HERBERT RAVENEL SASS for "Northwind" from *The Way of the Wild* by Herbert Ravenel Sass. Copyright © 1925 by H. R. Sass.

CHARLES SCRIBNER'S SONS, publishers of the American edition, and WILLIAM HEINEMANN, LTD., publishers of the British Commonwealth edition, for "Memories." Reprinted with the permission of Charles Scribner's Sons from *The Inn of Tranquility* by John Galsworthy. Copyright © 1912 by Charles Scribner's Sons; renewal copyright © 1940 by Ada Galsworthy.

CHARLES SCRIBNER'S SONS and CHRISTY & MOORE, LTD., for "The Pacing Mustang" from *Wild Animals I Have Known* by Ernest Thompson Seton. Reprinted with permission of Charles Scribner's Sons and Christy & Moore, Ltd.

CHARLES SCRIBNER'S SONS for "The Seeing Eye," reprinted with the permission of Charles Scribner's Sons from *Horses I Have Known* by Will James. Copyright © 1940, Will James.

CHARLES SCRIBNER'S SONS for "Skipper" from *Horses Nine* by Sewell Ford. Reprinted with permission of Charles Scribner's Sons.

THE VIKING PRESS, INC., publishers of the American edition, and WILLIAM HEINEMANN, LTD., publishers of the British Commonwealth edition, for "The Gift" from *The Red Pony* by John Steinbeck. Copyright © 1937 by John Steinbeck. Reprinted by permission of The Viking Press, Inc. and William Heinemann, Ltd.

GLORIA GODDARD WOOD for "Tzagan" by Clement Wood. Copyright © 1924, 1940, by Clement Wood.

To
GIBSON SCHEAFFER
for
wisdom of the mind

Preface

THERE HAD ALWAYS been dogs in my life.

Ever since I could remember, the moment I emerged on the street the call would go out by animal radar, and out of thin fog all sorts of strays would suddenly materialize—wagging, barking, begging.

One by one, my four-legged brothers would greet me with transports of joy. The battalion would fall into place and wait for the lift of my baton. Then on came the parade, marching toward the free refreshment stand which I had set up for dogdom in a home where only *one* dog was allowed.

The rule was the same for cats. One cat was all my mother would permit on the premises.

But my childhood pen scribbled surreptitious invitations which were scattered on the winds, and my feline friends would converge from every crack and corner, artfully side-stepping the maid's broom indoors and gracefully slinking toward the banquet outdoors, placed under the old apple tree.

Most of the cats were mere acquaintances. Others I inherited. Several I adopted. But here they were—both cats and dogs embroidering the tapestry of my life with color, drama, and wisdom. (I did not know that their lives would one day fill the inkwell on my desk.)

Now and then someone brought me a pigeon with a broken wing, and in the eloquent silence of the night the bird would speak to me and I would come to know another language. I also learned to communicate with ants, flies, tropical fish, and other of Nature's many children.

My kingdom—peopled by pets and alive with inanimate life—seemed content and complete enough. Then, one day, thunder broke loose in my sky.

I happened to borrow a library book. I read the story of Black Beauty. The horse stumbled and fell into the fold. He lay there under my apple tree.

I came toward him on tiptoe. A horse. I had never straddled a horse in my life and did not know the magic meaning of whip or spur or stirrups. These were words in another language. I longed to learn them all. I yearned to be his friend. I ached to include the horse in my enchanted animal world.

Then and there I determined to own a horse to whom I would be kind. But how could a mere child acquire a magnificent mountain? My Pied Piper magnetism might draw the wandering dog or cat but all my powers of attraction failed me when I tried to lift the shaft of a flower wagon and free the sorry skeleton in harness.

Besides, how could I ever propel a horse—two thousand pounds of neigh, hoof, and flesh—into a self-starting elevator and succeed in concealing the animal in an overcrowded apartment to which we had moved from the country?

However, one night I broached the subject to my parents. I informed them I had seventy six dollars and ten cents in my bank account and would like to buy a horse. That brought my father to his feet. I was sent off to bed without supper.

But it also decided me. I would not only have a horse of my own but in time I would muster two or three of these noble beasts, maybe even a dashing cavalcade of glossy black and brown flashing across the landscape.

And so, with a child's gift of imagination, I started collecting horses. I gathered them, in my mind, under that stunted old apple tree who was my closest friend.

I captured the Enchanted Steed from *The Arabian Nights. Aesop's Fables* were full of prancing equines. I combed the classics and rode the rough seas to harness them from the far shores of Lord Mottistone and Leo Tolstoi and Johan Bojer and MacGregor Jenkins.

Then I bought a thousand-acre ranch in Arizona, and here I built a lavish stable to which I brought the powerful Percheron, the golden Palomino, the wild mustang and the tame work horse. Of course, the ranch was only a figment of my mind. But here I led them all.

Here a small girl bound to the city could ride like the wind to her heart's content, even if it was only in the world of fiction—a world that grew wider as the years went on and she kept letting down the pasture bars.

Here I made room for all the horses I could find—till the grazing fields were crowded with the animals invited out of history and geography and fantasy to fill my great arena. Now and then I wrote a horse story of my own to give me pleasure and expand my mind's horizon.

It needed expanding.

There was so much the horse could teach me. I had no idea how much the horse had contributed to the world in which I lived.

All through the centuries, the dog had been regarded as man's most useful friend as well as loyal companion. The cat had earned her keep and sat in second place upon the human heart. The horse had come in third—and somehow lost the race.

Yet without the horse, civilization might still be a dream. The great brown waste lands might never have turned green. Continents might never have been conquered.

The gray mists of antiquity shroud his early history. It is said that he lived on earth forty million years ago—long before mankind came to people the hemispheres. Back in the beginning of time he was called the dawn horse. He was then no bigger than a small dog and roamed over mountain and plain in great herds that made their way from America to Europe.

Man finally caught this wind on four feet and shaped it to his purpose. Persia trained him for work. Greece sent him to war. Rome reared him for the pleasure of the great chariot races.

The arena of those days of old gave way to new exploits.

The horse was now recruited to play a part in the discovery of lands and seas. Both mare and stallion were aboard his ships when Christopher Columbus set sail for America.

As time moved on, the horse moved with it, filling a thousand roles upon the stage of civilization.

He fought in battles between nations, wearing heavy armor, pulling massive guns, wagons, men, and ammunition. The gallop of hoofs echoed upon peaceful pursuits as well, carrying miners, peddlers, trappers, traders, and settlers through forest and over mountain, across desert and plain. He drew the covered wagon, the stagecoach, and the famous Pony Express.

Cities waited to be built. The horse contributed his brawn in their building. He broke ground for the road, the railroad, the church, the school, the bridge.

Then the dawn of the machine age came rolling toward the horse, threatening to destroy him forever. But the horse met the challenge as centuries had taught him to meet crisis. He looked up from the pasture where he was peacefully grazing and let the giant machine roll up, along the road, and out of sight.

The horse will always have a place upon the earth. He will always play his role of worker on the farm, companion to the mounted police, partner to the cowboy of the plain, and performer in the circus ring.

The horse will never wear out his welcome at the house of his friends.

Polo, hunting, horse show, the race track, the rodeo will always flash with horse flesh. The horse has won too many laurels to bury him beside the ancient dinosaur. He has a nobility of spirit which is found in no other animal on earth.

Here—in these favorite horse stories which I have rounded up— you will find that nobility. You will find adventure and escape, just as I did. You will leap into a saddle, just as I did, and ride through the night into day.

You will meet, just as I did, the Arabian horse of magic and the lowly milkman's horse that retires to a dog hotel. And perhaps you, too, just as I did, will build a stable in the green pasture of your mind and invite these story horses for a stay.

My mother said I could not bring a horse into the house. She never said I could not bring a horse into my heart. And there I have kept them till I made a book. This is where they belong—between covers—where they can never die.

And, when they do, please believe with me—for my apple tree told me so—that *All Horses Go to Heaven!*

Beth Brown

Contents

ALL HORSES GO TO HEAVEN

All Horses Go to Heaven

BETH BROWN

HE REACHED the pasture bars at last.

In a moment he would be going in. He would be going on. He would be riding into the Elysian fields which lay beyond.

But for some strange reason the way was barred. The gate was locked. There was no one here—not even the kindly old keeper who always tended it.

Copper whinnied. Nobody came. He neighed. Only his echo answered. He switched his tail. The bell on his junk cart sounded in the night, and then all was silent again.

The fog rolled toward him in billows. He grew uneasy. Where was the old gatekeeper who had opened the gate before for his flying mane and his thundering hoofs and the burst of joy in his heart?

Then he remembered the promise.

Johnny had promised to be along, and Copper had promised to wait. But time was running out like a river. Only three minutes were left, three short minutes of life. These were given to both human and animal—three minutes of grace here at the boundary between the two worlds to look back upon the past before going on, or going back again.

If only Johnny would hurry.

Copper drew a deep breath. The swift regression began. His body dropped the solidity of its heavy old coat and its weary old bones. He stepped from the shafts of the junk cart. Once more he was young again.

Now impression followed impression as his memory gave up its storehouse. He saw his life from beginning to end—and the reason he was waiting for Johnny. Time swung him in a giant arc to a day on the ranch with its abounding freedom.

I

There it was again, just as he had seen it when he had first come into being—that great sweep of cerulean blue canopy high above the shimmering green pasture lands.

It all came back in a swift flood of images—the color of the great wide world into which he had been tossed, a small, brown, helpless heap. He heard his feeble whinny. He felt his mother nosing him softly. He tried to stand. His awkward forelegs crumpled under him. He lay with the earth beside him and then fought free of its embrace. Life called him to rise, to run, to revel.

Now there was a new sound. Human voices came to him.

"Should I give him a hand?"

"No. Leave him alone."

"Just look at him, will you? He's fighting to win."

"Yeah. And he's making it this time."

The newborn stood there, wobbling uncertainly. But he stood there just the same, regarding the two men who were surveying the odd picture he made. His brown skin lay in folds like those of an old man whose flesh was gone. His legs were long and ungainly. His bulging joints were gnarled like the knobs of an ancient oak tree. His feet were small, much too small for his frame.

One of the men was saying: "He'll fill out. You won't know him. After all, he's only twenty minutes old—"

"Look! Two teeth!"

The tall man seemed the expert. "Ten hands," he reported. "Thirty-two inches heart girth—" The voice droned on and on.

These men seemed strange to him and would always be strangers. But off in the distance he heard a cry. The sound of that voice stirred the sharp fires of memory. He knew that voice. It had called to him long before this sunny morning between the clear blue sky and the sweet green fragrance.

"He's here, isn't he?"

"Yes, Johnny. He's here!"

"Hurry up!"

"I'm coming as fast as I can—"

But it wasn't very fast. That much the horse could see as he watched the twisted approach of the small, crooked body. He heard the uncertain step made by the hobble of a flagging foot. Then he felt the touch of a hand, soft, cool, strong. The glowing face was coming closer. Now Copper was looking into a pair of eyes like pieces of vivid, unexpected blue sky. The eyes were regarding him with boyish wonder and warmth.

"I knew he'd be here! All the way in from town I told myself he'd be waiting for me!"

"How do you like him, Johnny?"

"Isn't he the most beautiful golden copper you ever saw?"

"Copper," echoed Johnny softly. "He was black before—a midnight black—"

"What are you talking about?"

"Black—with a white blaze between his eyes—"

"Crazy kid, that son of mine. That's what comes of having been born with a caul."

Johnny was saying: "He was a mustang then and I was the son of an Indian chief. We used to ride the hills together, didn't we?"

And then the horse remembered it, too. He knew he had belonged to the boy a hundred years ago. And hundreds of years before that, they had shared the adventure of chase. A boy of dark skin was in the saddle then, his dark hair crowned by a white turban. They were riding to the wars on hoofs that were swift as lightning. It was said the Creator had taken a handful of South Wind and given each newborn Arabian the power of flight without wings. In those days of great horses and great horsemen, the Mongol, the Hun, and the Turk had conquered China, India, and Europe. Genghis Khan became master of the world, but then Genghis Khan had a master, too. His horse of fire and thunder was his exalted ruler.

Copper sighed. The past vanished. The picture faded. For a fleeting instant, he felt the aching weight of the junk cart like a nudge reminding him of the chains that still bound him to life. Then he was free again, his memory floating out from him. He was back on the ranch again in those days of joyous comradeship with Johnny.

The boy fed him. He groomed him. He rode him. They shared the sky and the sun and the spring wind and the soft earth. The high hills invited them. The secret valleys received them. The gray caves sheltered them. The silver pool refreshed them. They rode till the stars pricked the sky to say it was time for supper and the sleepy sound of Johnny's voice whispered home without either whip or spur.

Between them there were silences and between them there were words.

"I can hear you plain as day," Johnny would say.

"Know why?"

"No. Why?"

"You hear because you listen."

And Copper taught Johnny to listen to the rest of the world as well—to all the voices of the wind and on the earth and in the trees, each with its own tone, no two alike and all rich in wisdom.

There was wisdom in Copper, too, who knew how to take Johnny's body and cradle it with care as they rode together, faster and faster with the passing of days.

The horse grew taller and the boy grew taller. The horse grew stronger and the boy grew stronger. Now and then, without warning, Copper would charge into the wind with a burst of rage in an effort to drop the weight of that haunting hobble like a bridle lost on the path.

It was only when Johnny walked that Copper was aware of that hobble. When they rode, it was no longer there. They were one, and Johnny was as straight of limb as a soaring pine tree reaching for the sky.

Even now, Copper could see the sky as he saw it the day Johnny brought the news. He was looking out beyond the great double doors at the far horizon of gray hills. Then Johnny stood in the doorway, shutting out the light.

"Oh, Copper!" He stumbled toward Copper and flung both arms around his neck. "Oh, Copper!"

"What's happened?"

"Oh, Copper!"

"What is it?"

"The ranch. We've lost the ranch."

"Don't cry. Crying hurts. Tell me, Johnny. What is it?"

"I told you. We've lost the ranch."

"Everything?"

"Yes."

"Even me?"

"Yes, Copper. Even you. They're taking you away."

"How far away?"

"I don't know."

"Stop crying."

But Johnny could not stop crying. It wasn't easy to comfort himself or to reassure Copper. "No matter where you go, I'll find you," he declared. "I'll be along. Just you wait. Promise me you'll wait."

"I'll wait," said Copper. "I promise."

And he held to that promise.

He waited.

A new life now began for Copper. A new world now revolved around him. He saw a new creature standing before him, and as he stirred up the magic of past memories, he reached into his consciousness and lifted out another image of himself.

Copper was a race horse.

He recalled all of it so clearly. He could see his stall with the brass plate upon which his name and pedigree had been engraved. He could smell the hay piled sweet and dusty. A barn swallow twittered by an open window in the loft.

People came and went. His hours were full of people dancing attendance upon him, of schooling, of grooming until his coat shone like an old coin and his mane swept the wind like a comet.

The food was good. His bed was soft. His sleep was sweet. He was the crown jewel of a kingdom crowded with grooms and exercise boys, betting men, dealers, owners and jockeys—each with a jargon of his own, a goal of his own, a scheme of his own—with Copper being moved like a pawn on a chessboard.

At first, Copper was confused. There were days his jockey would not let him win. There were days he was forced to win. There were times he was spurred, almost beyond his strength, to sweep under the wire a clean length in the lead.

Time raced beside him.

He was sent abroad. He came home with honors. He was sold to a syndicate of betting men. He had a dozen owners now, and thousands cheered him on to victory in the greatest race of the year and the greatest hours of his life.

They hung a huge horseshoe of vivid roses around his neck. There was a whir and click of countless cameras. He was the center of a surging sea of faces. These were the faces of strangers. Johnny was not in their midst.

Then the faces drifted off and the clamor died away. Except for the two men and their secret, Copper was alone with his pain. He had felt the stab as he crossed the finish line. And now he heard the verdict.

"Well, sir, he did it. Just as I thought he would. But he's through—"

"What do you mean? What kind of talk is that?"

"That leg is gone. It was going before he was halfway home—"

"How do you know?"

"I saw it go. It happened on the curve. He twisted it real bad. If you ask me, he made it on the last of his nerve."

"Will he ever ride again?"

"No, sir. He's finished."

"I'm sorry. Take him away."

"Doesn't seem to want to go—"

"Maybe he's waiting for someone. Look! He keeps looking for someone, that's sure."

"Too bad he'll never ride again—"

Copper wheeled about slowly. It was over. The hour of his dream had come and gone—without Johnny.

But he did ride.

He rode inside a paddock—round and round on a treadmill of monotony. He was one of the many saddle horses stabled at the Circle C Ranch.

Again he saw his past unfolding, sequence by sequence, each one linked to the last and all of them linked to Johnny.

The memory of his days at the ranch were sharp in contrast to those that had gone before. The stable was old. The food was poor. The flies were thick and troublesome. All sorts of people clambered up on his back. Some of them knew how to ride. Most of them came here to learn.

He had to learn, too. He had to be patient, gentle, obedient. He flavored the dull taste of his days with the secret spice of listening for the sounds that came up through the earth of his drafty stall, sorting out the approaching footsteps in the hope of hearing a familiar hobble.

Sometimes, in his dreams, he heard its music and awakened with a start, only to find he had lost the sound again. The only footsteps were his own. His leg troubled him, particularly during the long, cold winter weather. He was limping badly.

And then, on a Sunday—their busy day—he fell and threw his rider.

"We were going down the hill," the riding master reported, "when he struck a stone or something—"

"Good thing Mr. Christopher didn't get killed!"

"Yeah. Only the horse got hurt."

"You should have seen the landslide. Dust a mile high—"

"A funny thing happened. When he got to the bottom, he lay there like a goner. Then he lifted his head and looked up. He wouldn't get up. He just lay there, waiting for something or someone—"

"Well, we got a buyer waiting for him!"

And the day before Christmas, Copper was sold. He knew it was Christmas. As they carted him away, he saw the lights go on in the giant tree at the door.

After that, there came a succession of days and of buyers, of new scenes and old stables.

The job at the junk yard was the last stop on the line. His coat was dull. His bones were tired. His eyes were full of years.

At times, the junk man failed to groom him. Sometimes he failed to feed him. It did not matter. He lived in dreams. And one cold day a deep sleep drew him to its bosom and he was warm again and full of oats and hay.

When he awoke, he found the familiar road. He climbed the familiar hill. Now here he was—full of life—waiting outside the pasture gate.

The fog was still rolling toward him in thick, gray, puffy billows. Off in the distance he heard a clock striking the hour of midnight. Now in the gloom he saw a light. The single eye of a lantern came closer and closer. He heard the sound of a key in the lock. The gate swung open slowly—and there was the familiar, kindly old keeper.

The old man was smiling. He swung the lantern high over his

head and blinked in surprise at the sight of the early comer. A beam of light found Copper and held him.

"Why, hello, Copper!"

"Hello, Peter!"

"You're just on time this time. Come on in!"

"Do you mind if I wait?"

"Anybody special?"

"Yes. A boy named Johnny."

The old man chuckled. "Yes, boys are special. I don't blame you for waiting. I know just how you feel—"

"The feeling is mutual, Peter."

"Been waiting a long time?"

"All my life."

"I hope for your sake he comes."

"I wish I knew where to find him."

"Well, the world is smaller than you think. After all, it's not a very big planet!"

"I know—"

"I'd hate to get lost on the North Star!"

"Just the same, it's a wonder to me how they find this place. I'll never forget that last parade. I never saw such a turn-out!"

"We expect double the number this time, Copper." He reflected. "Who would dream there were so many horses down in the world below!" He went on. "Well, they'll have a good, long, refreshing sleep and they'll rest until they're strong again. Then they'll go back to live all over again and give themselves to men. Quite a cycle, don't you think?"

"Yes," said Copper.

The old man set down the lantern thoughtfully. "I'd love to stand here and talk to you for the rest of my life but I've got to open up shop, you know, and be ready for those that are coming. Mind if I get back to work?"

"Don't let me stop you."

"Sure you don't want to come in and be going along with the others? You can't wait forever for your Johnny—"

"I promised I'd wait. I won't go without him."

"You mean you love him so much you'd even give up your chances of getting into heaven?"

"Yes."

"Well, I'm happy to hear it, Copper. Not every horse feels that way about the human race. Seems like every life is a lesson forward. Guess you merit your reward."

"Okay! Let's have that lump of sugar!"

Instead, the old man did an odd thing. He came through the gate, held up the lantern and swung it three times, back and forth, like a signal into the night.

"Well, time's running out." He pushed the gate back—all the way back. "Better stand to one side, Copper. It's three minutes past midnight. They'll be coming through in a second. They'll be here. They'll be—"

The rest of his words were lost. A surge of sound swelled in the distance, shattering the silence of the night. Then they came.

A ghostly rider on a white charger was the first to appear, plume blowing, mane flying, hoofs flashing fire. The rider waved to Peter and called aloud a greeting in a strange tongue.

Now on filed the others in a thundering cavalcade. Farm horses. Race horses. Trotters. Show horses. Red and white and black flashed before Copper's eyes, passing before him in a cloud of golden dust. Now a woman held the reins. Now a farm boy came into view, jogging on the broad, inviting back of a work horse. Now a stage-coach lumbered through the gate. Now the measured hoofbeat of an approaching cavalry brought a young smile to the old face of the keeper. A snow-white filly raced through the gate, the remains of a rawhide rope trailing beside her.

Then suddenly the procession ended. The last echo died away. The dust began to settle. The fog began to thicken. The glow of the old man's lantern reached out to Copper with a dying eye.

"Still there, are you?"

"Yes, Peter."

"Wonderful, wasn't it?"

"Yes," said Copper. Just yes. He was watching the old man reach for his keys. The gate was beginning to move. Soon it would be over. The gate to heaven would be closed.

"I wonder why he's late," said the old keeper. "I sent word you were waiting for him—"

Copper was speechless. "You mean to say he may come—that Johnny may come after all?" Copper was transported with joy. "Oh, Peter—" his voice broke. "And you did this for me?"

"All I did was flash my light for a minute or two. How long did you say you have loved him?"

Then the sound of a hobble broke out in the night. And the voice of a boy began calling.

"Copper! Copper! Where are you?"

"Here, Johnny! Here!"

"Hurry," said the old keeper. "I'm locking up."

And now Copper was yelling: "You'll have to run for it, Johnny! Run for it!"

Johnny ran. He leaped. He was safe on Copper's back, clinging fast to his mane.

"How about me?" shouted Copper. "Don't I even have time to get out of this rig?"

"No," said Peter with a laugh. "Come just as you are!"

But as the horse and the boy came through the gate, the old man gave the cart a kick and it rattled down the hill and out of sight.

"Where are we going?" said Johnny.

The old man chortled. "What a question to ask!" Then his grin glowed with even a brighter light than his lantern. "Where else but heaven, Johnny, my boy!" He barred the gate. "Didn't you know all horses go to heaven?"

My Kingdom for Jones

WILBUR SCHRAMM

THE first day Jones played third base for Brooklyn was like the day Galileo turned his telescope on the planets or Columbus sailed back to Spain. First, people said it couldn't be true; then they said things will never be the same.

Timothy McGuire, of the Brooklyn *Eagle,* told me how he felt the first time he saw Jones. He said that if a bird had stepped out of a cuckoo clock that day and asked him what time it was, he wouldn't have been surprised enough to blink an Irish eye. And still he knew that the whole future of baseball hung that day by a cotton thread.

Don't ask Judge Kenesaw Mountain Landis about this. He has never yet admitted publicly that Jones ever played for Brooklyn. He has good reason not to. But ask an old-time sports writer. Ask Tim McGuire.

It happened so long ago it was even before Mr. Roosevelt became President. It was a lazy Georgia-spring afternoon, the first time McGuire and I saw Jones. There was a light-footed little breeze and just enough haze to keep the sun from burning. The air was full of fresh-cut grass and wisteria and fruit blossoms and the ping of baseballs on well-oiled mitts. Everyone in Georgia knows that the only sensible thing to do on an afternoon like that is sleep. If you can't do that, if you are a baseball writer down from New York to cover Brooklyn's spring-training camp, you can stretch out on the grass and raise yourself every hour or so on one elbow to steal a glance at fielding practice. That was what we were doing—meanwhile amusing ourselves halfheartedly with a game involving small cubes and numbers—when we first saw Jones.

The *Times* wasn't there. Even in those days they were keeping their sports staff at home to study for Information Please. But four of us were down from the New York papers—the *World,* the *Herald,* Tim and I. I can even remember what we were talking about.

I was asking the *World,* "How do they look to you?"

"Pitchers and no punch," the *World* said. "No big bats. No great fielders. No Honus Wagner. No Hal Chase. No Ty Cobb."

"No Tinker to Evers to Chance," said the *Herald.* "Seven come to Susy," he added soothingly, blowing on his hands.

"What's your angle today?" the *World* asked Tim.

Tim doesn't remember exactly how he answered that. To the best of my knowledge, he merely said, "Ulk." It occurred to me that the Brooklyn *Eagle* was usually more eloquent than that, but the Southern weather must have slowed up my reaction.

The *World* said, "What?"

"There's a sorsh," Tim said in a weak, strangled sort of voice—"a horse . . . on third . . . base."

"Why don't they chase it off?" said the *Herald* impatiently. "Your dice."

"They don't . . . want to," Tim said in that funny voice.

I glanced up at Tim then. Now Tim, as you probably remember, was built from the same blueprints as a truck, with a magnificent red nose for a headlight. But when I looked at him, all the color was draining out of that nose slowly, from top to bottom, like turning off a gas mantle. I should estimate Tim was, at the moment, the whitest McGuire in four generations.

Then I looked over my shoulder to see where Tim was staring. He was the only one of us facing the ball diamond. I looked for some time. Then I tapped the *World* on the back.

"Pardon me," I asked politely, "do you notice anything unusual?"

"If you refer to my luck," said the *World,* "it's the same pitiful kind I've had since Christmas."

"Look at the infield," I suggested.

"Hey," said the *Herald,* "if you don't want the dice, give them to me."

"I know this can't be true," mused the *World,* "but I could swear I see a horse on third base."

The *Herald* climbed to his feet with some effort. He was built in the days when there was no shortage of materials.

"If the only way to get you guys to put your minds on this game is to chase that horse off the field," he said testily, "I'll do it myself."

He started toward the infield, rubbed his eyes and fainted dead away.

"I had the queerest dream," he said, when we revived him. "I dreamed there was a horse playing third base. My God!" he shouted, glancing toward the diamond. "I'm still asleep!"

That is, word for word, what happened the first day Jones played third base for Brooklyn. Ask McGuire.

When we felt able, we hunted up the Brooklyn manager, who was a chunky, red-haired individual with a whisper like a foghorn. A foghorn with a Brooklyn accent. His name was Pop O'Donnell.

"I see you've noticed," Pop boomed defensively.

"What do you mean," the *Herald* said severely, "by not notifying us you had a horse playing third base?"

"I didn't guess you'd believe it," Pop said.

Pop was still a little bewildered himself. He said the horse had wandered on the field that morning during practice. Someone tried to chase it off by hitting a baseball toward it. The horse calmly opened its mouth and caught the ball. Nothing could be neater.

While they were still marveling over that, the horse galloped thirty yards and took a ball almost out of the hands of an outfielder who was poised for the catch. They said Willie Keeler couldn't have done it better. So they spent an hour hitting fungo flies—or, as some wit called them, horse flies—to the horse. Short ones, long ones, high ones, grass cutters, line drives—it made no difference; the animal covered Dixie like the dew.

They tried the horse at second and short, but he was a little slow on the pivot when compared with men like Napoleon Lajoie. Then they tried him at third base, and knew that was the right, the inevitable place. He was a great wall of China. He was a flash of brown lightning. In fact, he covered half the shortstop's territory and two thirds of left field, and even came behind the plate to help the catcher with foul tips. The catcher got pretty sore about it. He said that anybody who was going to steal his easy put-outs would have to wear an umpire's uniform like the other thieves.

"Can he hit?" asked the *World*.

"See for yourself," Pop O'Donnell invited.

The Superbas—they hadn't begun calling them the Dodgers yet —were just starting batting practice. Nap Rucker was tossing them in with that beautiful smooth motion of his, and the horse was at bat. He met the first ball on the nose and smashed it into left field. He laid down a bunt that waddled like a turtle along the base line. He sizzled a liner over second like a clothesline.

"What a story!" said the *World*.

"I wonder," said the *Herald*—"I wonder how good it is."

We stared at him.

"I wouldn't say it is quite as good as the sinking of the Maine, if you mean that," said Tim.

"I wonder how many people are going to believe it," said the *Herald*.

"I'll race you to the phone," Tim said.

Tim won. He admits he had a long start. Twenty minutes later he came back, walking slowly.

"I wish to announce," he said, "that I have been insulted by my editor and am no longer connected with the Brooklyn *Eagle*. If I can prove that I am sober tomorrow, they may hire me back," he added.

"You see what I mean," said the *Herald*.

We all filed telegraph stories about the horse. We swore that every word was true. We said it was a turning point in baseball. Two of us mentioned Columbus; and one, Galileo. In return, we got advice.

These Troubled Times, Newspapers no Space for Fiction, Expense Account no Provision Drunken Levity, the *Herald's* wire read. The *World* read, Accuracy, Accuracy, Accuracy, followed by three exclamation points, and signed "Joseph Pulitzer." Charging Your Telegram re Brooklyn Horse to Your Salary, my wire said. That's a Horse on You!

Have you ever thought what you would do with a purple cow if you had one? I know. You would paint it over. We had a horse that could play third base, and all we could do was sit in the middle of Georgia and cuss our editors. I blame the editors. It is their fault that for the last thirty years you have had to go to smoking rooms or Pullman cars to hear about Jones.

But I don't entirely blame them either. My first question would have been: How on earth can a horse possibly bat and throw? That's what the editors wondered. It's hard to explain. It's something you have to see to believe—like dogfish and political conventions.

And I've got to admit that the next morning we sat around and asked one another whether we really had seen a horse playing third base. Pop O'Donnell confessed that when he woke up he said to himself, *It must be shrimp that makes me dream about horses.* Then all of us went down to the park, not really knowing whether we would see a horse there or not.

We asked Pop was he going to use the horse in games.

"I don't know," he thundered musingly. "I wonder. There are many angles. I don't know," he said, pulling at his chin.

That afternoon the Cubs, the world champs, came for an exhibition game. A chap from Pennsylvania—I forget his name—played third base for Brooklyn, and the horse grazed quietly beside the dugout. Going into the eighth, the Cubs were ahead, 2–0, and Three-Finger Brown was tying Brooklyn in knots. A curve would come over, then a fast one inside, and then the drop, and the Superbas would beat the air or hit puny little rollers to the infield which Tinker or Evers would grab up and toss like a beanbag to Frank Chance. It was sickening. But in the eighth, Maloney got on base on an error, and Jordan walked. Then Lumley went down swinging, and Lewis watched three perfect ones sail past him. The horse still was grazing over by the Brooklyn dugout.

"Put in the horse!" Frank Chance yelled. The Cubs laughed themselves sick.

Pop O'Donnell looked at Chance, and then at the horse, and back at Chance, as though he had made up his mind about something. "Go in there, son, and get a hit," he said. "Watch out for the curve." "Coive," Pop said.

The horse picked up a bat and cantered out to the plate.

"Pinch-hitting for Batch," announced the umpire dreamily, "this horse." A second later he shook himself violently. "What am I saying?" he shouted.

On the Cubs' bench, every jaw had dropped somewhere around the owner's waist. Chance jumped to his feet, his face muscles worked like a coffee grinder, but nothing came out. It was the only time in baseball history, so far as I can find out, that Frank Chance was ever without words.

When he finally pulled himself together he argued, with a good deal of punctuation, that there was no rule saying you could play a horse in the big leagues. Pop roared quietly that there was no rule saying you couldn't, either. They stood there nose to nose, Pop firing methodically like a cannon, and Chance crackling like a machine gun. Chance gave up too easily. He was probably a little stunned. He said that he was used to seeing queer things in Brooklyn, anyway. Pop O'Donnell just smiled grimly.

Well, that was Jones' first game for Brooklyn. It could have been a reel out of a movie. There was that great infield—Steinfeldt, Tinker, Evers and Chance—so precise, so much a machine, that any ball hit on the ground was like an apple into a sorter. The infield was so famous that not many people remember Sheckard and Slagle and Schulte in the outfield, but the teams of that day knew them. Behind the plate was Johnny Kling, who could rifle a ball to second like an 88-mm. cannon. And on the mound stood Three-Finger Brown, whose drop faded away as though someone were pulling it back with a string.

Brown took a long time getting ready. His hand shook a little, and the first one he threw was ten feet over Kling's head into the grand-stand. Maloney and Jordan advanced to second and third. Brown threw the next one in the dirt. Then he calmed down, grooved one, and whistled a curve in around the withers.

"The glue works for you, Dobbin!" yelled Chance, feeling more like himself. Pop O'Donnell was mopping his forehead.

The next pitch came in fast, over the outside corner. The horse was waiting. He leaned into it. The ball whined all the way to the fence. Ted Williams was the only player I ever saw hit one like it. When Slagle finally got to the ball, the two runners had scored and the horse was on third. Brown's next pitch got away from Kling a few yards, and the horse stole home in a cloud of dust, all four feet flying. He got up, dusted himself off, looked at Chance and gave a horselaugh.

If this sounds queer, remember that queerer things happen in Brooklyn every day.

"How do we write this one up?" asked the *Herald*. "We can't put just 'a horse' in the box score."

That was when the horse got his name. We named him Jones, after Jones, the caretaker who had left the gate open so he could wander onto the field. We wrote about "Horse" Jones.

Next day we all chuckled at a banner headline in one of the metropolitan papers. It read: JONES PUTS NEW KICK IN BROOKLYN.

Look in the old box scores. Jones got two hits off Rube Waddell, of Philadelphia, and three off Cy Young, of Boston. He pounded Eddie Plank and Iron Man McGinnity and Wild Bill Donovan. He robbed Honus Wagner of a hit that would have been a double against any other third baseman in the league. On the base paths he was a bullet.

Our papers began to wire us. WHERE DOES JONES COME FROM? SEND BACKGROUND, HUMAN INTEREST, INTERVIEW. That was a harder assignment than New York knew. We decided by a gentlemen's agreement that Jones must have come from Kentucky and got his first experience in a Blue Grass league. That sounded reasonable enough. We said he was long-faced, long-legged, dark, a vegetarian and a nonsmoker. That was true. We said he was a horse for work, and ate like a horse. That was self-evident. Interviewing was a little harder.

Poor Pop O'Donnell for ten years had wanted a third baseman who could hit hard enough to dent a cream puff. Now that he had one he wasn't quite sure what to do with it. Purple-cow trouble. "Poiple," Pop would have said.

One of his first worries was paying for Jones. A strapping big farmer appeared at the clubhouse, saying he wanted either his horse or fifty thousand dollars.

Pop excused himself, checked the team's bank balance, then came back.

"What color is your horse?" he asked.

The farmer thought a minute. "Dapple gray," he said.

"Good afternoon, my man," Pop boomed unctuously, holding open the door. "That's a horse of another color." Jones was brown.

There were some audience incidents too. Jonathan Daniels, of Raleigh, North Carolina, told me that as a small boy that season he saw a whole row of elderly ladies bustle into their box seats, take one look toward third base, look questioningly at one another, twitter about the sun being hot, and walk out. Georgia police records show that at least five citizens, cold sober, came to the ball park and were afraid to drive their own cars home. The American medical journals of that year discovered a new psychoneurosis which they said was doubtless caused by a feeling of insecurity resulting from the replacement of the horse by the horseless carriage. It usually took the form of hallucination—the sensation of seeing a horse sitting on a baseball players' bench. Perhaps that was the reason a famous pitcher, who shall here go nameless, came to town with his team, took one incredulous look at Brooklyn fielding practice, and went to his manager, offering to pay a fine.

But the real trouble was over whether horses should be allowed to play baseball. After the first shock, teams were generally amused at the idea of playing against a horse. But after Jones had batted their star pitchers out of the box, they said the Humane Society ought to protect the poor Brooklyn horse.

The storm that brewed in the South that spring was like nothing except the storm that gathered in 1860. Every hotel that housed baseball players housed a potential civil war. The better orators argued that the right to play baseball should not be separated from the right to vote or the responsibility of fighting for one's country. The more practical ones said a few more horses like Jones and they wouldn't have any jobs left. Still others said that this was probably just another bureaucratic trick on the part of the Administration.

Even the Brooklyn players protested. A committee of them came to see old Pop O'Donnell. They said wasn't baseball a game for human beings? Pop said he had always had doubts as to whether some major-league players were human or not. They said touché, and this is all right so long as it is a one-horse business, so to speak. But if it goes on, before long won't a man have to grow two more legs and a tail before he can get in? They asked Pop how he would like to manage the Brooklyn Percherons, instead of the Brooklyn Superbas? They said, what would happen to baseball if it became a game for animals— say giraffes on one team, trained seals on a second and monkeys on a third? They pointed out that monkeys had already got a foot in the door by being used to dodge baseballs in carnivals. How would Pop like to manage a team of monkeys called the Brooklyn Dodgers, they asked.

Pop said heaven help anyone who has to manage a team called the Brooklyn Dodgers. Then he pointed out that Brooklyn hadn't lost an exhibition game, and that the horse was leading the league in batting with a solid .516. He asked whether they would rather have a world series or a two-legged third baseman. They went on muttering.

But his chief worry was Jones himself.

"That horse hasn't got his mind on the game," he told us one night on the hotel veranda.

"Ah, Pop, it's just horseplay," said the *World,* winking.

"Nope, he hasn't got his heart in it," said Pop, his voice echoing lightly off the distant mountains. "He comes just in time for practice and runs the minute it's over. There's something on that horse's mind."

We laughed, but had to admit that Jones was about the saddest horse we had ever seen. His eyes were great brown pools of liquid sorrow. His ears drooped. And still he hit well over .500 and covered third base like a rug.

One day he missed the game entirely. It was the day the Giants were in town, and fifteen thousand people were there to watch Jones bat against the great Matty. Brooklyn lost the game, and Pop O'Donnell almost lost his hair at the hands of the disappointed crowd.

"Who would have thought," Pop mused, in the clubhouse after the game, "that that (here some words are omitted) horse would turn out to be a prima donna? It's all right for a major-league ball player to act like a horse, but that horse is trying to act like a major-league ball player."

It was almost by accident that Tim and I found out what was really bothering Jones. We followed him one day when he left the ball park. We followed him nearly two miles to a race track.

Jones stood beside the fence a long time, turning his head to watch the Thoroughbreds gallop by on exercise runs and time trials. Then a little stable boy opened the gate for him.

"Po' ol' hoss," the boy said. "Yo' wants a little runnin'?"

"Happens every day," a groom explained to us. "This horse wanders up here from God knows where, and acts like he wants to run, and some boy rides him a while, bareback, pretending he's a race horse."

Jones was like a different horse out there on the track; not drooping any more—ears up, eyes bright, tail like a plume. It was pitiful how much he wanted to look like a race horse.

"That horse," Tim asked the groom, "is he any good for racing?"

"Not here, anyway," the groom said. "Might win a county-fair race or two."

He asked us whether we had any idea who owned the horse.

"Sir," said Tim, like Edwin M. Stanton, "that horse belongs to the ages."

"Well, mister," said the groom, "the ages had better get some different shoes on that horse. Why, you could hold a baseball in those shoes he has there."

"It's very clear," I said as we walked back, "what we have here is a badly frustrated horse."

"It's clear as beer," Tim said sadly.

That afternoon Jones hit a home run and absent-mindedly trotted around the bases. As soon as the game was over, he disappeared in the direction of the race track. Tim looked at me and shook his head. Pop O'Donnell held his chin in his hands.

"I'll be boiled in oil," he said. "Berled in erl," he said.

Nothing cheered up poor Pop until someone came in with a story about the absentee owner of a big-league baseball club who had inherited the club along with the family fortune. This individual had just fired the manager of his baseball farm system, because the farms had not turned out horses like Jones. "What are farms for if they don't raise horses?" the absentee owner had asked indignantly.

Jones was becoming a national problem second only to the Panama Canal and considerably more important than whether Mr. Taft got to be President.

There were rumors that the Highlanders—people were just beginning to call them the Yankees—would withdraw and form a new league if Jones was allowed to play. It was reported that a team of kangaroos from Australia was on its way to play a series of exhibition games in America, and Pres. Ban Johnson, of the American League, was quoted as saying that he would never have kangaroos in the American League because they were too likely to jump their contracts. There was talk of a constitutional amendment concerning horses in baseball.

The thing that impressed me, down there in the South, was that all this was putting the cart before the horse, so to speak. Jones simply didn't want to play baseball. He wanted to be a race horse. I don't know why life is that way.

Jones made an unassisted triple play, and Ty Cobb accused Brooklyn of furnishing fire ladders to its infielders. He said that no third baseman could have caught the drive that started the play. At the end of the training season, Jones was batting .538, and fielding .997, had stolen twenty bases and hit seven home runs. He was the greatest third baseman in the history of baseball, and didn't want to be!

Joseph Pulitzer, William Randolph Hearst, Arthur Brisbane and the rest of the big shots got together and decided that if anyone didn't know by this time that Jones was a horse, the newspapers wouldn't tell him. He could find it out.

Folks seemed to find it out. People began gathering from all parts of the country to see Brooklyn open against the Giants—Matty against Jones. Even a tribe of Sioux Indians camped beside the Gowanus and had war dances on Flatbush Avenue, waiting for the park to open. And Pop O'Donnell kept his squad in the South as long as he could, laying plans to arrive in Brooklyn only on the morning of the opening game.

The wire said that night that 200,000 people had come to Brooklyn for the game, and 190,000 of them were in an ugly mood over the report that the league might not let Jones play. The governor of New York sent two regiments of the national guard. The Giants were said to be caucusing to decide whether they would play against Jones.

By game time, people were packed for six blocks, fighting to get into the park. The Sioux sent a young buck after their tomahawks, just in case. Telephone poles a quarter of a mile from the field were selling for a hundred dollars. Every baseball writer in the country was in the Brooklyn press box; the other teams played before cub reporters and society editors. Just before game time I managed to push into Pop O'Donnell's little office with the presidents of the two major leagues, the mayor of New York, a half dozen other reporters, and a delegation from the Giants.

"There's just one thing we want to know," the spokesman for the Giants was asking Pop. "Are you going to play Jones?"

"Gentlemen," said Pop in that soft-spoken, firm way of his that rattled the window blinds, "our duty is to give the public what it wants. And the public wants Jones."

Like an echo, a chant began to rise from the bleachers, "We want Jones!"

"There is one other little thing," said Pop. "Jones has disap-peared."

There were about ten seconds of the awful silence that comes when your nerves are paralyzed, but your mind keeps on thrashing.

"He got out of his boxcar somewhere between Georgia and Brooklyn," Pop said. "We don't know where. We're looking."

A Western Union boy dashed in. "Hold on!" said Pop. "This may be news!"

He tore the envelope with a shaky hand. The message was from Norfolk, Virginia. HAVE FOUND ELEPHANT THAT CAN BALANCE MEDICINE BALL ON TRUNK, it read. WILL HE DO? If Pop had said what he said then into a telephone, it would have burned out all the insulators in New York.

Down at the field, the President of the United States himself was poised to throw out the first ball. "Is this Jones?" he asked. He was a little nearsighted.

"This is the mayor of New York," Pop said patiently. "Jones is gone. Run away."

The President's biographers disagree as to whether he said at that moment, "Oh, well, who would stay in Brooklyn if he could run?" or "I sympathize with you for having to change horses in midstream."

That was the saddest game ever covered by the entire press corps of the nation. Brooklyn was all thumbs in the field, all windmills at bat. There was no Jones to whistle hits into the outfield and make sensational stops at third. By the sixth inning, when they had to call the game with the score 18–1, the field was ankle-deep in pop bottles and the Sioux were waving their tomahawks and singing the scalp song.

You know the rest of the story. Brooklyn didn't win a game until the third week of the season, and no team ever tried a horse again, except a few dark horses every season. Pittsburgh, I believe, tried trained seals in the outfield. They were deadly at catching the ball, but couldn't cover enough ground. San Francisco has an entire team of Seals, but I have never seen them play. Boston tried an octopus at second base, but had to give him up. What happened to two rookies who disappeared trying to steal second base against Boston that spring is another subject baseball doesn't talk about.

There has been considerable speculation as to what happened to Jones. Most of us believed the report that the Brooklyn players had unfastened the latch on the door of his boxcar, until Pop O'Don-nell's Confidential Memoirs came out, admitting that he himself had taken the hinges off the door because he couldn't face the blame for making baseball a game for horses. But I have been a little confused since Tim McGuire came to me once and said he might as well confess. He couldn't stand to think of that horse standing wistfully beside the track, waiting for some one to let him pretend he was a race horse. That haunted Tim. When he went down to the boxcar he found the door unlatched and the hinges off, so he gave the door a little push outward. He judged it was the will of the majority.

And that is why baseball is played by men today instead of by horses. But don't think that the shadow of Jones doesn't still lie heavy on the game. Have you ever noticed how retiring and silent and hangdog major-league ball players are, how they cringe before the umpire? They never know when another Jones may break away from a beer wagon or a circus or a plow, wander through an unlocked gate, and begin batting .538 to their .290. The worry is terrible. You can see it in the crowds too. That is why Brooklyn fans are so aloof and disinterested, why they never raise their voices above a whisper at Ebbets Field. They know perfectly well that this is only minor-league ball they are seeing, that horses could play it twice as well if they had a chance.

That is the secret we sports writers have kept all these years; that is why we have never written about Jones. And the Brooklyn fans still try to keep it secret, but every once in a while the sorrow eats like lye into one of them until he can hold it back no longer, and then he sobs quietly and says, "Dem bums, if dey only had a little horse sense!"

Throw Your Heart Over

STUART CLOETE

HELEN heard her father say, "She's—she's not going to die, is she?"
She was the she, her. *It's me they're talking about,* she thought.

"No, John," Smitty said. Doctor Smith was his real name, but nobody called him that. "There's even a bit of improvement."

"How long will it take her?" daddy said.

"I don't know, Johnnie. You see, we don't even know just what
she's got. It's not polio—at least not an ordinary polio. It's something different—something new. If only this were America. They
know more there. In ten years——"

"Ten years," her dad said. "In ten years she'll be twenty-one and
I'll be forty-two. . . . Marriage, children. What's there for her?
What'll her life be?"

"She's not going to die, Johnnie. There's some improvement. Let's
leave the rest to God. There is a God, you know—that's something
we doctors find out."

"Expecting a miracle, Smitty?" her dad said.

"There are miracles too. Wonderful things still happen. Things
that cannot be explained."

"Like her being struck down with this thing—an innocent child."

That's me, Helen thought. *I'm an innocent child.* The idea
pleased her. Then she thought about God. She thought He must be
something like her grandfather. Bigger, of course, with a bigger
white beard, but resembling him in many ways. It was interesting
to lie here and hear every word they said in the adjoining bedroom.
Of course they didn't know about it. How could they, since she
didn't talk to herself?

Then Smitty said, "The kid's bored. She's an outdoor girl. What
about a pony? Ever think of a pony, Johnnie?"

Helen pulled herself up in bed and clasped her hands together.

25

"A pony?" her father said. "You think she could ride?"

"One of the boys could hold her on. Old Herman, for instance. She could get around and see the veld again. The thorns are in bloom now. Yellow," the doctor said. "Yellow and perfumed." In her mind Helen saw the little fluffy yellow balls of the thorn flowers and smelled them. "I'm going to ask her," Smitty said.

"I can't buy a pony," her father said. "I can't even pay you."

The door banged and Smitty was in the room.

"Do you want a pony, Helen?" he said.

"No, I don't want a pony, doc."

"It would do you good. You could get out. Get around again. Old Herman could hold you on."

Helen gripped the sides of her bed again and leaned forward. The round white enameled bars were hard and cold in her hand. Something big was happening. She was on the edge of an event. Like a precipice, a vast space loomed ahead and below her. This was her opportunity. She had always wanted a pony. But not now.

"Ponies are for kids, doc," she said. "I want a horse—a real horse. I'm a girl now. I'm not a kid any more."

In her mind she saw the horse—a milk-white Arab with a flowing mane and tail. She stared into his liquid eyes. She felt his hot breath in her face. Tears came into her eyes. She brushed her hair back from her face and stared at Smitty and her dad. They looked very big standing there looking down at her in her bed.

"All right, a horse. Do you want one? Do you want to get out?"

Smitty was close to her now. She could smell him. She smelled tobacco, whisky, tweed, dog and the hair stuff he used. His eyes, behind the thick lenses of his glasses, were enormous. She stared into them. She drowned herself in them. *I'll marry him,* she thought. *If he'll wait till I'm grown up and well, I'll marry him.* The tears ran down her cheeks. They were salt in her mouth. She could not speak. There was so much she wanted to say, and all she could do was to cry like a baby, like a kid.

Smitty had her wrist in his hand. She could feel his strength pouring into her. She pulled herself together.

"Yes," she said, "oh, yes. A horse. I want to get out." In her mind she saw it all again: the veld, the thorns, the rocks, the cattle, the tall golden grass bent before the wind; the weaver birds' nests hanging like grass balls from the swaying branches of the willows by the spring. She was sobbing now and he held her. Smitty was holding her. Everything was going to come right. There were Smitty and God and a horse.

Then her mother came in. She held her, too, and her father patted her hand. *I'm too small,* she thought. *If I was bigger everyone could hold me.* She wanted everyone to hold her.

She knew why her mother hadn't been with them. Helen knew she had been afraid of what Smitty might say after he had examined her. Her mother was beautiful. Fair skin with big blue-gray eyes. She smelled of lavender. Dad smelled of gas and grease and oil. Once he had smelled of the farm—of cows and milk and manure and hay all mixed up with tobacco and sweat. He worked for Mr. de Wet of the Central Garage now and mother ran the farm. It was the only way they could make ends meet, they said, since the drought had hit them. Three years of drought and only one spring—the one where the willows with the weaver nests were still strung. Helen often wondered what meeting ends were. What happened when ends did meet? When they didn't the cattle died and dad went to work for Mr. de Wet. Before that he'd been on the farm. But she had been too small to really notice what went on. *I was just small and happy then,* she thought. *Just a baby.*

Vaguely, half asleep, she saw Smitty open the door for her mother and pat her shoulder. "You're a good girl, Grace," he said. It was funny to hear him calling mother a girl. But daddy did, too, sometimes. Grownups were really very funny. There was no way of understanding them—except Smitty. There was something about him with his big owl's eyes. Of course it was the glasses that made them look so big. *But I'd like to marry him,* she thought. The horse, the milk-white horse, was all due to him. The dream that was going to come true. When she'd been well she hadn't wanted a horse or pony. Why should she have, when she could run about so fast on her own two legs? But since she had been ill she'd thought about horses so much. Looked at pictures of horses galloping. How wonderful that must be, to be on the back of a galloping horse.

The last things she remembered were her dad standing at the door looking back at her and the click of her mother's heels on the staircase. Smitty must be waiting for dad.

In the old car on his way back to the garage Johnnie Blackett went over what Smitty had said. No worse . . . getting better . . . trust in God . . . a horse. . . . A horse. What was the old story? For lack of a nail a shoe was lost, for lack of a shoe a horse was lost, for lack of a horse a battle was lost. . . . "A horse, a horse, my kingdom for a horse." That was Shakespeare—or at least he thought it was. *For lack of a horse my daughter may be lost.*

He'd never forget the look in her eyes, big as saucers—she had Grace's eyes—with tears balanced like drops of dew in the corners, and her remark: "Ponies are for kids. I'm a girl now." A girl, and in just a few years she'd be ripe for life, for love. Horses seemed to mean a lot to her. She had never mentioned it before. Perhaps because she was ill. Perhaps because as long as it wasn't mentioned it could not be refused. She was an old-fashioned kid with plenty of courage and a mind and will of her own. That frail little fairylike creature made of ivory and gold had a will of steel. And Smitty had seen it and thought of an answer. If she set her mind on anything, she'd do it, or die in the attempt. He remembered what his own father had told him when he began to jump his first pony: "Throw your heart over first, Johnnie, and you'll follow it, Johnnie boy." After that he'd never been afraid. She was like that. But a horse—— Horses cost money. There weren't even any horses around to look at and maybe borrow any more. Ten years ago a dozen men would have lent him a horse. Ten years ago he could have bought a dozen horses.

He looked out at the veld as he drove along the red dirt road. How beautiful it was. Rolling country dotted with clumps of bush and isolated thorns, all splashed with the gold of spring. Soon it would be summer, and they might get good rains this year.

When Johnnie got to the garage he was surprised to find it unchanged. It looked exactly as it had looked yesterday. But yesterday was so long ago. So much had happened since then. How afraid he had been when he drove home to talk to Smitty. Helen was going to live. She was better. She might get well. *If only I could get her a horse,* he thought. Such a simple thing, really—or it used to be. But now even in Africa a horse was a rare animal, apart from valuable show horses and so on. The ordinary farm riding horses had all disappeared.

Hendrik de Wet came out of the front office to greet him. "Everything O.K., Johnnie?" he said. He meant about Helen, of course. By this time everyone in Boomspruit would know that Smitty had made a new and detailed examination after the specimens came back from the laboratory in Johannesburg.

"O.K. At least she's no worse, and he holds out hope. Slow, of course. But hope."

"Slow but sure," de Wet said. "That's the ticket." He was an Afrikaner and given to such phrases. He became businesslike. "The tractors have come, Johnnie. They're on the siding. Get them down and line 'em up—like soldiers," he said. "Like a lot of bloody

Rooisbadgies—redcoats." He laughed, a big booming laugh that shook the belly that hung out in a great shaking ellipse below his belt. "Nice and straight," he said. "All six of them so that the farmers can't miss them. Spring," he said. "The plowing season. We'll borrow some plows from the store—three furrow plows and disks—and hook them up. Give 'em the idea." He became confidential and took Johnnie's arm. "Farmers," he said. "Got to show 'em. You've got to put two and two together for 'em. See the tractors and they'll never think of plows. See the plows and they'll never think of tractors." He seemed to have forgotten that Johnnie was a farmer.

Two hours later the bright red tractors were aligned with not a six-inch difference between them and each had a plow or a disk hooked on behind it. "All done," he said to de Wet. "Come, Kyk—look at 'em. Pretty as a picture."

They stood together in the sunlight looking at the scarlet tractors glistening in their clean uniforms of paint.

"Pretty," de Wet said. "Beautiful!" He stroked the hood of the one nearest to him.

"See the horses, Johnnie?" he said.

"What horses?"

"In the sale yard. Stock sale tomorrow, you know. Wednesday. The old and the new," de Wet said. "Tractors coming in and the farm horses going out. This lot must be about the last around here. That's why I got the tractors down. I heard a lot of farmers were selling horses to a dealer and jumped in. Took a risk, of course. But a calculated risk. That's business, Johnnie boy. That's what I like."

"Mind if I go up and look at them?" Johnnie said.

"Look at what?"

"The horses."

"No. Sure, go ahead. If you see any of the sellers, bring 'em back to see these beauties." He spoke as if the tractors were chorus girls. "No deposit. Easy terms. Go ahead, my boy." He patted him on the back. Hendrik de Wet was a great patter. Men on the shoulder; children on the head; and women—well, he patted them, too, wherever he could.

The horses, all oldish farm animals, most of them much the worse for wear, work and a long truck ride, stood with lowered heads in the stock kraal. Grays, blacks, bays; there wasn't much to choose between them.

As Johnnie went up and leaned his arms on the rails, one horse, a roan mare that he had not seen before, looked up and came toward him. When she was about a yard away she stopped and extended her nose toward his hands. Her nostrils were wide open. She blew through them softly. Her eyes, one of them a walleye, looked into his. *A horse, my kingdom for a horse. . . . For want of a horse my daughter was lost.* "Remember there's still a God," Smitty had said.

While he and the roan were looking at each other a tall, thin, sunburned man came up to him. "Dog meat," he said. "That's what they are. More's the pity. And to think I've come down to this. There's no good or bad horses no more. Just fat and thin. That's all, mister. Imagine judging men that way, for their worth—fat or thin."

"Yours?" Johnnie said.

"Mine. I was a horse dealer once—real horses, I mean. Saddle horses, cart horses, mares for breeding, studs, even a blood horse now and again. Do you think I like it?" He turned on Johnnie savagely. "Man," he said, "I love horses. Take her, for instance"— he jerked his head at the mare; "that's a good 'un. A good mare. I've never seen a bad roan yet. And I like a walleye. No, she's not blind in it." He caught her head collar—she was close to them now —and flashed his hand over her blue eye. "See her wink," he said.

God, Johnnie thought, *God sent Smitty. God sent the roan. God sent the dealer. God told Hendrik to tell me.* "Will you sell her?"

"Sell? Of course I'll sell her, and much sooner to you than to the knacker."

"How much?"

"Do you know how they sell horses today, mister?"

"How do they?"

"By the pound. Like butter or cheese or old iron. A bad horse is worth as much as a sound one. Meat, that's what they are. Not horses any more. Just dog meat. Meat for pets." He spat in the dust with disgust. "Old horses, yes, old worn-out horses. That's one thing. But her—she's not even aged. Nine years old she is. With nine years of work left in her and nine good foals if you want to breed her. She's bred before. Roomy," he said. "If you put her to a blood horse you'd get something. But nobody'll wait no more. Nearly a year's gestation. Three more years for the foal to come to hand. But what's four years when you think of the pleasure of it?"

"How much?" Johnnie asked again.

"Thirty pounds, mister, and that's what she cost me, more or less, but I'll make enough on the others."

"Will you hold her for me while I get the money?" Hendrik would advance it to him. "Will you wait?"

"I'll wait. I got to hang around anyway till the sale tomorrow.

You'll find me at the hotel. Ask for Frank Sparrow. Sparrow the horse dealer."

As Johnnie turned to go Sparrow said, "Listen, mister, this is a deal you can't lose on. You take her. You'll feed her up a bit naturally, and if you don't like her I'll buy her back any day and give you a profit. Can't lose, man," he said to Johnnie's back, "and there's not many deals like that in the world today."

Hendrik de Wet began to laugh when Johnnie told him what he wanted the thirty pounds for.

"Man," he said, "this is 1959. What do you want a horse for?"

"She's a good mare," Johnnie said, "a roan with a walleye on the near side, and only nine years old—too good for dog meat."

"Man, you're so bust you've got to borrow to buy her. What is it? You going soft or something?"

"I'm not soft, de Wet," Johnnie said. "No, I'm as hard as hell. So hard that I'll chance everything on this gamble."

"You're not going to race her?"

"I am, Hendrik."

"When? How?"

"I'm going to race her with death, and the stakes are high."

"You're mad, Johnnie."

"I'm not. It's Smitty."

"The doctor?"

"Yes. He thinks if I can get Helen on a horse she has a chance."

De Wet pulled out his pocketbook and counted out six fivers. "Here you are, Johnnie, and it's not a loan. You've done more than your job here."

"I'll pay you back, Hendrik."

"In your own time when you are on your feet again."

Johnnie took his hand. They turned away from each other, embarrassed by their unaccustomed emotion. Each had seen something in the other that he had not known existed, for neither had thought the other had a heart.

Mr. Sparrow was in the bar of the Jacaranda Hotel fondling the ears of a crossbred ridgeback with one hand and holding a glass of beer in the other.

Johnnie sat down beside him and put the money on the table. "Here's the thirty quid."

Sparrow put down the glass and stuffed the money into the breast pocket of his coat. "I'm glad," he said. "She was too good for it. It's not her time yet. You know, Mr.——"

"John Blackett," Johnnie said.

"Mr. Blackett," Sparrow went on, "we all come to it—man and horse and dog. One day we'll all come to the end of our tether. But it should be the end, not in the middle, like"—he paused—"nor the beginning."

"Beginning?"

"I lost a boy in the war," he said. "Nineteen he was. And he had the making of a good 'un, though I says it myself."

"That's why," Johnnie said.

"Why what, Mr. Blackett?"

"I want her."

"Go on, tell me."

"It's for my girl. She's paralyzed and the doctor thinks riding might help her. I only wonder if she can hang on. It's her legs, you know."

Mr. Sparrow put a brown veiny hand on his knee. "She's alive, Mr. Blackett. That's something. That's a lot."

Johnnie got up. They shook hands. He seemed to be shaking hands with everybody today. "I'm going to say something funny," Johnnie said, "and if you laugh I'll knock you down." His eyes blazed. "I think God sent you and I don't believe in God. At least I didn't."

Then he turned and went out of the bar. The big ridgeback wagged its tail slowly from side to side and looked up at Mr. Sparrow.

Now it was a matter of getting the mare home. It was only five miles and Johnnie arranged with Franz, the boy who did odd jobs around the garage, to take her.

"I'll tell you when," he said, "and take you up to get her."

"*Ja, baas.*" Five bob he was getting. That was a whole day's wage and the *baas* was driving him back in his car. It was like Christmas. Man, if this happened every day, what a life he would lead!

At five o'clock Johnnie took Franz up to the kraal and they caught the mare. It was not difficult. She seemed to recognize him when he called her, and came up to him on her own.

She led easily. It would take Franz only an hour or so to get her back to the farm. Johnnie drove fast and went straight to Helen's room, and with her wrapped in a blanket on his knees waited on the stoep with his eyes fixed on the farm road till he saw them coming. The black man walked easily, tirelessly. Five miles was nothing to him. The mare followed like a dog, the riem he was holding hanging slack in a loop.

Helen saw them almost as soon as he did. "There's a boy coming, with a horse, daddy," she cried, "a boy with a horse, and they're coming this way. We'll see them. Oh, daddy, we'll see them." To see anything had become an event for Helen.

The man and the horse got bigger.

"It's Franz," Helen said, "with a roan."

"Certainly looks like it," Johnnie said. "I wonder what he wants."

"It's late," Helen said. "Perhaps they could stay the night. Perhaps you could put me up on the horse for a minute, daddy, and we could play pretend."

"Pretend what, darling?"

How stupid could grownups be? "That he's ours," she said, "our very own horse."

"We'll see, darling."

Franz pulled up at the stoep. He tied the riem to the rails. "Here you are, *baas*."

"What's he mean, daddy?"

"What he says."

"He said 'Here you are.'" Helen was wriggling like an eel in her father's arms.

"Well, here she is, Helen," Johnnie said. "Your horse."

"Oh . . . oh, she's really ours!"

"She's yours, darling. With compliments of Dr. Smith and Mr. Hendrik de Wet."

"Put me up, daddy. Put me up."

"She's filthy."

"Never mind. Mother can wash me again. Oh, please, please." She clasped her hands together as if she were praying.

Her mother came onto the stoep. "What is it, Johnnie?" she said.

"I bought a mare, Grace, and Helen wants me to put her on her back, but she's too dirty."

"Put her up, Johnnie. The child will wash and so will her pajamas."

"Put me up, daddy. Mother says I can. Mother says——"

Johnnie lifted her onto the mare's back and held her there.

The horse turned her head and nuzzled the child's knee.

"Oh," Helen said, "she's got blue eyes. Just like mother."

"Only one eye," Johnnie said.

"One of each," Helen said. "One like mother's and one like yours. How wonderful!"

Johnnie laughed. It was wonderful to see her so happy. Then he took her down. "Bed now," he said, "and another bath. Tomorrow we'll wash her. I've got to drive Franz back to the dorp now." He kissed his daughter and put her into her mother's arms.

Helen spent all the next day in the Kraal sitting on a box beside the mare, listening to her munching hay and crunching mealies. Old Herman sat watching them both, smoking his pipe.

Everything the mare did was wonderful. The way she ate. The way she drank from the bucket Herman brought her. The way she rolled, kicking her legs in the air. When she'd done all this the horse came and stood beside the girl with her soft gray nose almost in her lap, while Helen stroked her face and pulled her ears.

Her father found them like that. He had come home early to wash the horse. It took five washings with soap and water to get her clean enough to satisfy Helen. Then she was dried with a whisk of hay and rubbed down with a bit of sacking. Her tail, mane and forelock were combed with a metal comb Johnnie had picked up in the dorp, and the long hairs on her heels were trimmed off with Grace's dressmaking scissors. She looked a very different animal now.

"She's lovely," Helen said, "ever so lovely."

"Wait till tomorrow. When she's really dry we'll brush her." Johnnie threw an old blanket over the horse and fastened it in place with a surcingle. "Bedtime, Helen," he said. "Bedtime for you both."

Old Herman led the mare off to a shed that had been bedded down with veld grass, and Johnnie carried his daughter into the house.

Before he went to work Johnnie went to look at the mare. She raised her head and neighed when she saw him. He went up to her; she rubbed her head against his chest. He gave her some crusts of bread he had brought from breakfast.

This was not the same horse, not the same horse at all. He wished Mr. Sparrow could see her now.

Life on the farm now changed its pattern. Where Helen had been the center, the axle around which the wheel of their lives revolved, it was now the mare, because it was around the mare—that Helen had named, for some reason, Old Lucy—that Helen herself revolved. Old Lucy and old Herman, who took care of both her and Helen.

There was a regular routine. In the morning Lucy was saddled. The saddle consisted of a pillow fastened with a surcingle. Lucy also wore a head collar with a riem that Herman held with one hand while he balanced Helen with the other. In this fashion they covered the whole farm and even went beyond it. In the afternoon Helen rested and Old Lucy grazed near the homestead. In the evening Helen rode again.

Every day the mare put on condition. Every day she became more tame, more human. "More like a dog than a horse," Grace said.

"Perhaps more horses would be like dogs if they were treated like dogs," Johnnie said.

Helen didn't need Herman to hold her on any more now. She managed very well with her fingers twisted around the mare's mane. Sometimes she even managed a slow canter with Herman running in front of the horse. But they were always out of sight of the house when she tried something new. She was getting better—stronger— she could feel it.

I'm going to surprise them all one day, she thought. And happy. She'd never been so happy before. But perhaps you had to be unhappy before you could be happy.

Sometimes the Metz children came over to play with her and ride Old Lucy. Charmian was twelve, a year older than Helen, and Charlie was ten. They were nice children. They always brought an apple or sugar for Old Lucy. Their daddy brought them over in the afternoon and Helen's daddy drove them home when he got back from work. Helen always sat on the front seat beside him.

One day, after they had been coming for about a month, Charmian said, "Can we try to jump her, Helen?"

It seemed a great idea and the children rolled out two empty five-gallon dip drums leaving them on their sides, and set a blue-gum lath across them. Charlie led Lucy up to the jump and told her about it.

"Jump it, Charm," he said to his sister. "You show her how."

Charmian jumped. Then she said, "Let's see if she'll follow." She led Lucy back a few yards and ran to the jump with the mare cantering behind her. She never hesitated, and the two came over side by side.

Helen clapped her hands. "Again," she said, "do it again!"

"Give her an apple," Charlie said.

They gave Lucy half an apple and went over the jump again.

"She likes it," Charmian said. "I'm going to try riding her over." She climbed onto Lucy's back with Charlie's help. The horse seemed to like this even better.

"I'll stand them up," Charlie said. "What about that?"

"O.K.," his sister said. "We'll try it." She patted the horse's neck. The boy stood the drums up on end.

Lucy cocked her ears and popped over.

Helen, sitting on the grass with Herman behind her, was entranced. It was wonderful. It was beautiful the way Old Lucy came up to the jumps and took them clean. Like a buck, flying like a bird through the air. Her coat of alternate chestnut and white hairs shone like shot satin. Her mane and long tail flowed. Her forelock divided itself into two plaits, one each side of the white star on her forehead. Beautiful, that's what it was, with the blue, cloudless sky above and the chickens scratching in the veld behind the sheds and kraals where they had set up the jumps.

After this they jumped almost every day with an audience of Grace and old Herman, Mr. Metz and Johnnie in the evening. Mrs. Metz came over, too, sometimes, to watch. The jumps were regular jumps now—three feet high—the gum laths resting on pegs set into poles Herman had sunk into the ground.

There was no doubt about Helen's improvement, Smitty said. It was not so much her legs. There was very little difference there. But in her general health, the brightness of her eyes, in her happiness. She was, as he had said before Old Lucy came, an outdoor girl who was pining away in the white cage of her bedroom.

That was how the conversation started. Then it came out.

"I've arranged for her to go into hospital for some tests in Johannesburg," Smitty said. "There's a man there now, an American specialist, who's interested in her case."

"Soon?" Johnnie said. "How long is he going to stay?"

"Now," Smitty said. "He's got to get back, so I'll drive her in tomorrow."

"How much will it cost?" Grace asked.

"Not too much. They're friends of mine at the nursing home."

"We'll manage," Johnnie said.

Grace turned to her husband. "I'll go with her and stay with Muriel. You can manage for a bit, can't you, Johnnie?"

"I'll manage." He knew he could manage, and the farm did not need much attention now. They couldn't plow till it rained, and the few cattle they had left could take care of themselves. All they needed was a dipping once a week—and he'd do that on Sunday.

Lucy was the only thing that worried Helen. This was adventure. It was change. She had never been in a big town. She said, "Lucy? She'll miss me. You'll look after her, daddy?" Her voice was anxious.

"I'll look after her, darling."

"Talk to her, daddy. She likes to be talked to, especially while she's eating."

What a wonderful kid she was. No thoughts about herself at all. Just her horse. But the horse had become almost a part of her—a symbol of activity.

"I'll talk to her," he said, "and the Metz kids will be over every day, I expect."

"Bed now," Grace said, and that was the way the evening ended, with Smitty smoking his pipe in silence and Johnnie thinking how lonely he would be.

And Johnnie was lonely. There were letters from Grace almost every day, but there was no Grace to come home to, and he picked the letters up at the post office in the dorp. No little girl to be carried in his arms. No talk of Old Lucy and how wonderful she was.

It was to have been a month, but it was longer and the bills were coming in. Not big bills. Smitty had been right. They were cutting things to the bone, but they were bills and they had to be met.

The cattle went. The two last boys were paid off. Only old Herman stayed on.

Johnnie was standing by the spring looking at the weaver birds' nests, just thinking about things, watching the beautiful black-and-yellow birds flying about, watching the green grass balls of their nests sway.

Yes, a lot of things had gone, including Old Lucy. She'd been the last thing. That was his only justification. He'd sold everything else first: his gold cuff links, his father's watch, the silver tray. And he'd not told Helen. No good worrying her. He looked over the empty veld. Empty to him because not a head of stock on the place was his any more. He'd rented the grazing to a butcher.

It was amazing how he missed the mare. She'd been a link with them, with Helen and her mother—with the girls. Every night she'd been waiting for him when he went to see her before he went to bed. Sometimes he'd taken a walk under the stars with her following like a dog, and now she was gone. Metz had sent a boy over for her this afternoon and everything seemed empty, and more lonely than ever.

What a difference the horse had made in his life and Helen's. That was the thing that worried him. How was he going to explain it? The mare had saved Helen. He saw that, saw that now that it was too late. It was Lucy that had given her the lift, made life worth while again. In every letter she asked about Old Lucy. She'd even posted a handkerchief to give to Lucy to smell. *I had it in bed all night, daddy.* He'd done it. He'd given it to Lucy and she had looked into his face and whinnied, and now he'd sold her. For Helen, of course; and his own things had gone first, everything practically, but how was he to explain it? If only he'd told Grace about the things he'd sold. He hadn't wanted to upset her, but she'd find out when she came back. That was what always happened. One thing led to another. One lie led to the next.

He had his supper and went to bed. The frogs were croaking. There would be rain soon. He would be able to plow if he could get the time off to do it. He had not sold the tractor, thank God. But perhaps he should have; not that it would fetch much—still—— It took him a long time to fall asleep. He woke suddenly. He had been dreaming of Old Lucy—dreaming he heard her.

But he was awake now, and he did hear her. Neigh after neigh. Without bothering to put on a jacket or shoes, he went out. She was there. Lucy was there, standing by the fly-netted door of the stoep.

He went out and she almost tried to climb into his arms, as if she were a dog, as if she were saying, "I'm home again. There has been some awful mistake, but I'm home." She forced her head between his arm and his body. He pulled up her head and kissed her nose. *I've never kissed a horse before,* he thought. *But Helen has kissed her a thousand times, has felt that soft mousy nose with a few prickly hairs against her own lips.* In a way it was almost like kissing Helen. He took the mare for a walk. He needed a walk. Then he watered her, put her in the kraal with some hay.

Sleep came easier now. He was exhausted, but Old Lucy was home. It could not last, of course. She had been sold and paid for. The fifty pounds Metz had given him was in the post on its way to the nursing home. Still, for the moment God was in His heaven and Old Lucy was home.

Frank Metz's shouts woke him. It was hardly light. "Johnnie," he shouted, "she's here, I see."

Rubbing the sleep from his eyes, Johnnie got up. "She's in the kraal," he said.

"I saw her."

"What happened, Frank? I was asleep when she came. She woke me."

"I expect I woke you too."

"You did."

"Well, I had to come at once. The kids are crazy with worry."

"What happened?"

"Happened? We put her into the kraal with mealies and hay, and she seemed to be nicely settled. Then in the night the kids climbed out of their windows to look at her and found her gone. They rushed in to us yelling blue murder. Charlie was crying."

"Did you leave the gate open, Frank?"

"Of course not. She jumped the poles—five there are, imagine it— and came straight here—straight as a crow flies."

"There are six fences between us," Johnnie said. "Barbed wire."

"I know. Imagine it. Barbed wire in the dark."

"I never heard of a horse jumping wire," Johnnie said.

"Nor have I, except in Australia. Some horses do it there. But they train them to. Hang a coat or a bag over it at first and then make it smaller and smaller."

"Can't make a mistake with wire," Johnnie said. "Catch a foot in it and it twists. I've seen kudu caught that way."

"I know. Well, that's that. I'll leave the boy I've got with me and he can bring her back. I'll stable her tonight."

Frank Metz got into his car and gave the boy his instructions. "Give him breakfast, Johnnie," he said. "I must get back to the kids. Pity you had your phone taken out."

That was just another of the things. *I could have phoned Grace,* he thought, *if we still had the phone.* But that would have cost money too. He looked at Frank Metz's shiny new car disappearing down the farm road and wished he was a checkbook farmer too. Still, Metz was a good guy. Very decent. If he hadn't been so decent it would never have happened.

He'd said, "Why don't you let me have the mare, Johnnie? I'll give her a good home. Helen can see her and ride her whenever she wants." He had lit a cigarette and said, "I'll give you fifty quid for her."

That was what had done it. Just the exact figure. Just the number. He couldn't have done it with forty quid or even sixty, though it was ten pounds more. Fifty was the nursing-home account that had just come in the mail. Fifty was the bull's-eye, the target.

"All right," he'd said, and never had anything been less right. It was worse now. Old Lucy hung back in the riem and the boy leading her swung around and hit her with the loose end he had in his hand.

Johnnie was beside him in a flash. Lucy was looking at him. "Don't let him take me," she seemed to be saying. *Nonsense,* he said to himself, *a horse can't talk,* but he knew she was saying it.

He gripped the boy's arm. "Do that again and I'll take the hide off you, and I'll call the *baas* when I get to town and ask him to see if there is a mark on her." He patted Lucy's quarters. She gave him another look and followed the boy slowly with her nose almost on the ground.

Nothing went right that day for Johnnie. Two tractor sales fell through. He got a flat coming home, and old Herman met him with a long face and asked him what he should say to the little missis when she came home. "She loved that horse, *baas.* They used to talk together. *Ja,* horses," he said, "talk like people. The little missis would talk and horse would go 'What . . . what.'" He blew air through his nose as if he were a horse. "*Ja,*" he said, "they talked. They talked like people."

That night Johnnie hardly slept at all. He was listening for Lucy. He knew she couldn't come, that she was stabled. But she came. He heard her galloping, faintly at first, then louder and louder till the hoofbeats pulled up with a scuffing, sliding sound below his window and she neighed. Not as she had last night but wildly, giving almost a scream, the way a horse does if it's caught in a fire. There is only one worse sound and it is the scream of a woman. Johnnie's hair stood on end. He thought, *The wire. She's hurt herself.*

She was standing by the screen door still neighing when he got down. He did not even pat her, but rushed to her hind legs and ran his hands over them, from hocks to pasterns. No blood. Not a cut. *Thank God,* he thought, *thank God.* She had turned to him. Her nose was in his belly. His pajama coat was open and he felt her warm breath. She was blowing hard. It sounded almost as if she were sobbing. Her neck was wet with sweat. So were her ears as he fondled them. He thought, *Suppose she'd made a mistake and put a foot wrong.* There was a bit of a moon. But suppose it had been darker. "Why didn't you come by the road?" he muttered. She whinnied softly as if she were saying, "It's too far by road. I was in a hurry. She might be waiting for me."

I'm mad, Johnnie thought. *I'm mad, thinking she said that,* but he answered her all the same. He said, "I know, Lucy. It's ten miles by road and five as a crow flies." *As a crow flies or a horse jumps.*

That night he didn't go to bed again, but sat outside with Lucy beside him. Just before dawn she lay down as near to him as she could get. *Well, this is it,* he thought. *Now everything is clear.* He'd raise another mortgage on the farm and buy her back. *I'll give Frank a hundred pounds for her and there'll be plenty over to pay for Helen too. More than enough.* He wondered why he hadn't thought of it before. He had thought of it and then he'd stopped thinking because the interest on one bond was almost more than he could pay. But God was in this somehow—or Providence—something that was supernatural, which he felt he must not buck.

This time Frank drove up with the children. They were out before the car had stopped and rushed up to Lucy's legs. "She's not hurt, is she? She's not hurt?" they shouted.

"She's all right, Charlie," Johnnie said. "She's O.K."

The children were patting Lucy and kissing her. Charlie climbed onto her back.

"She wins," Metz said.

"I'll buy her back, Frank," Johnnie said.

"She wins, Johnnie. It's something you have to see to believe. She can stay here."

"I'll give you a hundred pounds for her," Johnnie said.

"No. No. But let's put that value on her. I gave you fifty and so she's half mine and lives here and my kids can ride her whenever they want." He held out his hand.

And that was the way that Lucy came home.

At least the lies were over now, and Johnnie could really write to Helen about Old Lucy instead of having to invent as he had yesterday. That had been a hard letter to write with Lucy just gone. *Lucy's fine. I put her to bed and went to see her before I went to sleep after dinner.* What a tissue of lies. And what could he have said tomorrow if she had not come home? or if she had been hurt? How could he have gone on writing?

Johnnie now began to understand the relationship his daughter had had with the old mare. Not that Lucy was old or looked old now. Helen had given her the name before she'd had her bath and beauty treatment. She had certainly looked old when he'd bought her. But she was still in her prime really. A horse was at its best at five and stayed like that till ten or more if it was looked after.

The worst was over now—even the loneliness—because he had Old Lucy to talk to. Old Herman talked to her too. Of course they didn't really talk to the horse. They just talked and Old Lucy cocked her ears to listen and blew out of her nostrils. She liked the sound of a human voice. But he certainly hoped it didn't get around that he was bats and talking to a horse.

A fortnight later Johnnie was holding a letter from Grace with an enclosure from Helen when Smitty came into the house with a bang that loosened the screen door on its hinges. He was smiling all over his face.

"Good news, Johnnie, very good news."

"Will she walk?"

"No, no, not yet—but she will. There's no real deterioration. They've finished all the tests. They had to wait for the reports to come back from America."

"Then?"

"Now it's just a mental block. You know the way muscles work. The nerve centers send them a message, a sort of telegram, only there's no telegraph boy for Helen. But he'll come, Johnnie—he'll come!"

Smitty was looking around the room. A lot of things had gone. Johnnie's two guns—the Purdy twelve bore, and the Manlicher. So had the big silver tray that had belonged to his father. Queen Anne it was supposed to be. If he hadn't been rooked he should have got a good price for it.

"She can come back, Johnnie. She's coming. I'm driving in to fetch them tomorrow."

He saw tears come into Johnnie's eyes. "I've missed them," he said. "Like the sun," he said. "Like days without any sun and nights without any stars. No sun, no moon, no stars. No time even. Just emptiness and silence."

"They're good girls," Smitty said. "You're a lucky man, Johnnie. One day you'll look back on all this and see what I mean. With Helen well again and Grace happy. Then you'll know the stuff that good women are made of. The guts, my boy. Helen never folded up, never gave up. Grace never complained. Not about the drought that took everything, nor Helen's illness."

"Once she got out she began to improve, Smitty. The horse was a wonderful idea."

"I'm glad you got her back."

"So you knew?"

"Everyone knew."

"It's going to be hard to tell her, Smitty."

"She'll understand. After all, you gave up everything else first."

"So you knew that too?"

"I've got eyes; and besides, do you think you can send all the stuff you have away by post without there being talk? I tell you, Johnnie, your stock's up in the dorp. You'll be mayor someday if you're not careful, Johnnie."

"Then I'll be careful." Johnnie was laughing now. "This time tomorrow they'll be home," he said. "I must go and tell Lucy."

Smitty gave him a queer look. But he didn't care. "I talk to her," he said. "She likes it."

Smitty was laughing now. "That's what they say in the dorp. 'Johnnie's talking to that horse of his now that his wife and kid are away.'"

"Everyone talks to Lucy," Johnnie said. "The Metz kids when they come to jump her, old Herman——"

"Everyone, Johnnie? And who's everyone? Some children and a pensioned-off old Kaffir that's a bit touched in the head, and you. I'll tell you something. It's a good thing to be a bit crazy like that and talk to animals. It shows a capacity for love, and that's something we're short of in the world today. You can't love a car or a tractor," he said. "You can keep them in good order. You can polish 'em and wash 'em, but you can't love 'em. People you can love if they're lovable, and animals. But love is a thing most people don't want. Though they talk about it all the time." He puffed on his pipe. "They want to be admired, to be envied, but not to be loved. To love and be loved is a responsibility.

"I'll go now," he said. He got up. "See you tomorrow when I bring them." He patted Johnnie's shoulder. "You're a good boy."

"Good boy be damned—we're the same age."

"Perhaps I'm a good boy, too, Johnnie. Who knows?"

Everything was ready for the return. The table was laid, the kettle was full of water to make them a cup of tea. He'd bought cakes in the dorp, and cans of peaches that Helen liked. He'd stocked up with

staples—salt, pepper, catchup, flour, sugar, tea, coffee, bacon, potatoes, butter. There was an unopened bottle of sherry on the sideboard beside the glasses. He'd put on his blue suit. Old Herman
had on the clean khaki pants and shirt he'd given him. Lucy, whose
riem he held, shone in the evening light.

Yes, he'd done everything that could be done. Even Grace's stoep
plants had had their leaves washed. But he was still worried at the
reception his news would get. *I'll have to tell her. She'd find out
anyway from the Metz kids or old Herman or someone.* But how did
one do a thing like this? How did one begin?

"They come, *baas*," old Herman shouted. "They come."

Johnnie was furious. *I should have seen them first,* he thought.
He'd been watching the road for an hour and the minute he looked
away they came, and old Herman had seen them first.

After that things were a bit blurred for everyone—a bit choky
and hard to talk. They could only kiss and hug one another. To hug
Helen, Johnnie had to hug Smitty, who was carrying her, and he
almost kissed him in his excitement. Lucy had come into the act and
was nuzzling Helen in Smitty's arms. Old Herman had hold of
Helen's foot. He could not reach her hand and was shaking it and
kissing it. "The little missis," he kept saying, "the little missis."

Grace was a good girl. If she saw anything was missing in the house,
she didn't say so. As a matter of fact, she saw that the silver tray had
gone the minute she came in. *My tray,* she thought, and opened her
mouth to speak. Then she saw the empty gun rack and she knew.
She'd wondered all the time about money. Johnnie had never mentioned it. The visit had cost her nothing. She'd stayed with her sister
Muriel and even used her car to go to the hospital, so she had never
mentioned money in her letters.

She went into the kitchen to make tea and saw that Johnnie had
left everything ready for her. Tears came into her eyes.

Smitty stayed on, of course. Helen sat on her father's lap. Old
Herman hovered in the background and ate a piece of cake. Lucy,
waiting outside, had a piece of cake. Then they all had sherry and
Smitty drove off.

Now's the time, Johnny thought. *I'll get it over with.*

"Helen," he said, "did you know I sold Lucy?"

She looked at him with big sad eyes. "She's back," she said.

"I had to tell you, honey. I sold everything else first. My guns, your
mother's silver tray, the cattle——"

"I must have cost a lot," Helen said.

"It was worth it. You're better."

"I'm better, daddy. They say I'll get well. And Lucy's back."

"I had to tell you," Johnnie said.

"I knew, daddy. Charmian wrote and told me that they had Lucy now and they loved her and would take good care of her."

"And you never wrote to me about it?"

"I think I knew why you'd done it, and then Charmian wrote again to say they didn't have her any more, that she wouldn't stay, and how they worried about her jumping those barbed-wire fences, but that they came over and rode her here nearly every day and that now she was half theirs."

She was quiet for a moment, then she said, "We must buy her back, daddy. I suppose they'll let us buy her back? She's mine, daddy— ours. How can we have half a horse, and which half, which end, is ours?"

It was scarcely light next morning when Helen called her father.

"Get me out, daddy. Show me everything. Get me onto Old Lucy and lead me around."

On the veld beyond the almost empty milking kraals Helen saw the big jumps the Metz kids had put up. "Big jumps for Old Lucy," she said. "Fancy her being able to jump like that."

Johnnie said, "They love it, and she loves it. You've forgiven me?" he asked. "I sold everything else first."

"I know," she said. She could feel his big hand on her thigh. *I could not feel it once,* she thought. Then she said, "And now, is she theirs or ours?"

"She's half ours, darling, and half theirs. So they have riding rights too."

"They don't hurt her, do they?" Her voice was anxious. "Her mouth, I mean. Or use a whip? They never used to, of course, but the jumps are so much bigger."

"They love her," her father said.

"But she's mine, she's mine, isn't she? One day we'll pay them off and she'll be all mine again." In her mind there was a plan forming. *If Lucy can jump I'll jump her,* she thought. *I'll enter the show and win money. I'll tell her and she'll understand.*

They went all around the farm and then it was time for breakfast and the job.

For a month everything went on much as it had before Helen had gone to hospital. There was no doubt about her being better. She was beginning to use her thigh muscles. She rode farther and farther every day and for longer hours. But she had an object in mind, a secret project, and one morning when her father had gone to work Helen got Herman to carry her to the kraal where the mare was munching a mixture of chaffed hay, bran and mealies.

"Put me down," she said.

Herman set her in the soft powdered manure that covered the kraal three feet deep.

"Now," she began a conversation with the mare Lucy, "you've got to jump me. We'll jump in the show and make money and buy you back."

The mare took her head out of the manger and nibbled at her hair, spilling a mixture of chaff and mealies in it.

Herman said, "They say you can't talk to a horse, missis." He felt the time had come to stop this.

"*Ja*, I can, and do. Put her saddle on and lift me up."

"She hasn't finished her scoff yet, missis."

"By the time you've got it on she will have." Helen reached out a hand and held the mare's foreleg below the knee. Lucy moved nearer to her.

"Pas op," Herman shouted. "She'll step on you."

Helen laughed. "You couldn't make her," she said, and holding the leg pulled herself under Lucy's barrel belly. "Put the saddle on, and no bridle, just the head collar."

When the bag and surcingle were on, Helen said, "Now lift me up."

Herman lifted her.

"Now lead her to the jumps."

"No!" Herman said. "What will the *baas* say?"

"The *baas* won't know."

"And if the missis falls and breaks her neck?"

"I won't. I promise."

"*Ja*, you promise, but what about Herman? *Ja*, what about old Herman if the young missis breaks her neck?"

"Put me up," she said.

Herman lifted her up.

"Now to the jumps."

He led her there.

"Take off all the bars except the bottom one. I've got to learn, you know."

Herman took off the top three poles that the Metz children had used.

"Now, Lucy," Helen said, "take it steady."

The mare turned her ears back to listen. Helen stroked her neck and pulled herself forward.

"Now," she said again, and tapped Lucy's flank with her hand.

Lucy started off at a gentle canter. When she reached the jump she went over it without hesitation, drifting over it as lightly as a leaf. She went on for twenty yards or so and came to a stop.

Helen stroked her neck and pulled her ears gently. "Good girl," she said. "Good girl." To Herman she said, "Put up the next bar."

She pulled Lucy round by her ear and the performance was repeated. They jumped for almost an hour. Then Helen said, "Get me down now. We'll try again this evening."

When Johnnie came home he couldn't believe his eyes. Helen was jumping Old Lucy, taking her over three-foot jumps without even a bridle. And what a seat! His heart almost stopped beating and then leaped like a bird into his throat.

The mare cantered up to the jump and popped over like a buck, like a kudu. With Helen up beyond her withers, her face almost hidden in the mare's mane, her arms around her throat. Her thighs were around Lucy's neck and her legs, out of control, wobbled like those of a sawdust doll. After clearing the jump Old Lucy slowed up and stopped. Helen turned her by pulling on her ear. She spoke to her and they jumped again. Then Helen saw her father.

"Hullo, daddy," she said. "We're jumping."

"So I see. But it's pretty high, and are you sure it's safe?"

"Safe?" she said. "I was safe in bed when I couldn't move. Do you want me back there?"

"No, but I still think it's high."

"We're going higher, aren't we, Lucy?" She leaned over the mare's neck.

Lucy raised her head and neighed.

"Magtig," Herman said, *"baas,* this is going on all day. She and the little missis talk together. *Ja,"* he said, "the horse is *tagati,* bewitched, and talks like a man. *Baas,"* he said, "I wish to give my notice. The devil is here."

"Devil," Johnnie said. "Perhaps it is God."

"If the *baas* says so, I will stay."

Johnnie put his arms around his daughter and carried her into the house. Old Herman and his devils! He talked to the horse himself. Herman's notice was just a trick to try to stop all this business in case Helen got hurt and he was blamed.

There were new problems now for Johnnie and Grace. Helen had the bit in her teeth. Nothing would stop her jumping, and the mare was a natural jumper. If Helen showed her a jump, she would clear it on her own. She'd jumped 6'6" clean as a whistle that way and come back to Helen to be petted.

"She's got something in her mind, Grace. She's not the same girl since she came back," Johnnie said. "She's got some secret."

"And have we ever got a secret out of her?" Grace asked.

"It's not natural for a kid to be like that," Johnnie said.

"Well, she is like that and I'm glad in a way," Grace said. "That's what'll cure her. Her will. Her iron will."

"The kid with the iron will," Johnnie said, laughing. He was proud and upset at the same time.

Next time Smitty came over they talked to him about it.

"What'll we do, Smitty?"

"Let her go, Johnnie."

"Suppose she falls?"

"Suppose anyone falls," Smitty said. He put his hand on Johnnie's knee. "There's something in this that's beyond us. Call it what you like. I prefer God myself. But don't interfere. She might come right any day. Just like that. And I believe she will."

But she didn't, and she just went on jumping, with her extraordinary seat, fluttering like a bird above the cushion she still rode on.

Then it came. One evening Helen announced that she was going to compete in the high jump at the Boomspruit stock show.

"No," Johnnie said. "I won't have it."

Helen played her trump. "Then I'll go back to bed. I won't get up." They knew she had them and she knew too.

It was a sensation, that show. Helen Blackett's jumping was all anyone talked about. The cattle were forgotten, the harness horses, hacks, and blood horses that did their stuff in the ring were hardly looked at. Everyone was watching for the paralyzed kid—they called it paralyzed. It was good enough. Crippled, anyway.

It began with the first round. The high jump was set at 4' and three horses failed to clear it clean before Helen and Old Lucy came on. A sort of gasp, a prolonged "Aaah" went up from the crowd when they saw the little girl with long hair on the roan mare. A kid and not even a proper saddle. No stirrups. No bridle. Only a headstall with a riem fastened under the chin. Her parents must be mad. The committee must be mad. It was a disgrace.

But the mare seemed to know what she was doing. The kid leaned forward and spoke to her. Her hands holding the riem were twisted into the mare's mane.

The horse cantered up to the jump and took off. The girl's long golden hair was flying out behind her as she left the horse's back. Her arms were around the mare's throat, her crippled legs dangling. But they were over . . . and safe. For an instant there was dead silence. Then there was a roar of approval and clapping.

It went on like that. Horse after horse was knocked out. At 5′6″ only one other horse, a chestnut gelding, a winner at some of the bigger shows, was left in the competition. He was a big, hot-tempered beast with rolling eyes and touched the bar, knocking it off its pegs at 5′7″.

Smitty and her father were standing beside Helen while she watched.

"You all right?" Smitty said. He knew she was all right—more all right than she'd ever been. She liked the excitement and applause.

"We can do it," was all she said. And they did. As if she knew and wanted to show off, Lucy cleared the bar with inches to spare.

Lucy got her ribbon. Helen got a cup and ten guineas prize money. Everyone congratulated her. But all she said to her father was, "That's the beginning, daddy."

"The beginning of what, darling?"

She didn't answer. She just patted Lucy and began to cry.

That was when Mr. Lonstein came up to them. He was a fat little man who'd made a fortune with diamonds in West Africa.

"You her father?" he said to Johnnie.

"That's right," Johnnie said.

"Magnificent," Mr. Lonstein said. "Wonderful! Wonderful! She ought to jump in Johannesburg."

Helen pulled herself together. "I want to," she said. "Lucy could jump a house."

"It can't be done," her father said.

"Why not?" Mr. Lonstein asked.

"Money," her father said, "entrance fees, expenses; it just can't be done."

"I'll do it," Mr. Lonstein said. "Let me. I'll send the horse up to the city in a trailer, drive you and your daughter up in my car. A pleasure," he said. "What a day it would be. What a thrill."

"It's very kind of you," her father said, "but——"

"We'll go," Helen said. "And thank you very much."

The show was not till the fall; *and a lot can happen between now and then,* Johnnie thought. But nothing happened except that the rains were good and his 100 acres of mealies looked wonderful, and Mr. Lonstein came down every month to see Helen and Lucy.

At first he stayed at the Jacaranda Hotel, but after a while he stayed in the house.

They learned a lot about him. That he was rich they knew. That he was eccentric was obvious. That he was generous, lovable and very funny they soon found out.

"I know what worries you, Mr. Blackett," he said. "Why should a fat little Jewish financier do this? And you're right. There must always be a motive. Well, here it is. Like I told you the first day when I met you, there's the thrill of it, the fun of it. Next there is the fact that the world should see how well Lucy jumps and Helen rides and, finally, the courage." He patted Helen's head. "Brains I've got, but no courage."

After that they took him to their hearts and loved him.

At last the great day came.

Helen and old Herman who carried her piggyback were entranced by the crowds and the livestock at the fair. Many of the beef cattle, dairy cattle, sheep, goats, horses, poultry and rabbits were new to them. Never had they seen oxen so fat or dairy cows with such udders.

There were the usual events: a musical ride by the mounted police, the cattle parades, the hacks, the hunters, the ponies, the ladies' hacks, Thoroughbred stallions, a bayonet-fighting display by the Transvaal Scottish. The jumping—five-bar, stone wall, water jump, in and out and the rest of them. On the third day came the high jumps with forty entries. Of them all—even the old-timers—Helen remained calmest, and Lucy, as long as someone of the family was with her, was undisturbed by the noise or the crowd outside the ring.

As their numbers were called the riders went in.

A black gelding cleared the jump. A brown mare with a dark girl tipped the bar. A gray cleared it. A bay Thoroughbred came next, cleared it, and almost ran away when he landed.

Helen was next. Mr. Lonstein led her out and let go. Once again there was a hush. *Fancy a kid like that competing with adults . . . the horse looks all right, but——*

That was when Lucy started for the jump. No saddle, no proper bridle . . . a crippled girl. How could they—— But there she was, going at it.

Old Lucy cocked her ears and slowed her canter. Helen pulled herself forward by her mane, climbing the mare's mane like a monkey on a stick, as Lucy dug her heels into the ground and shot forward.

"She's off!" someone shouted. But they were wrong. And the mare was over.

Helen jumped twice more that day and each time it was the same. She was watched with a sort of horrified silence that was followed by a roar of approval.

That night the *Star* had headlines:

CRIPPLED GIRL JUMPS

Miss Helen Blackett, of Boomspruit, has no strength in her legs which are crippled, and has developed a style of jumping that brings the hearts of all who watch her into their mouths but gets her over.

Mr. Lonstein was jubilant. "Oh, the fun of it," he said, and took them all out to dinner. Helen was a heroine, but she took it calmly. There was only one thing in her mind: the prize money, a hundred guineas this time; and nothing was going to stop her.

"Then you'll be mine," she whispered to Lucy, "all mine, not the front half or the back half, but all of you . . . all . . . all . . . every bit."

Her mother looked at her and wondered about her. The child wasn't smiling. She wasn't proud. She just seemed preoccupied. Her mouth was a thin, hard line, her little chin stuck out. Her eyes were cold. She was polite to everyone, but no more.

Her dear lovable little Helen had gone. This was a determined girl. What was it she wanted? Kudos? Praise? Adulation? She didn't seem to. Her mother knew she meant to win.

What she did not know was how frightened Helen was. Only Mr. Lonstein knew, because he was so easily made afraid himself. He'd known the first time he saw her in Boomspruit. That was what he had admired so much. This was real courage. Any fool with no brains could be brave, but she was smart enough to be afraid and strong enough to overcome her fear, a kid like that. But he did not know that what she said to herself each time she came up to a jump was, *Throw your heart over, Helen,* and that in her mind she threw it up over the jump like a ball as Old Lucy took off.

In the finals there were only three entries left: a young Englishman riding a gray Irish hunter, a Johannesburg girl riding a bay mare called Kitty, and Helen. The Irish hunter failed at 5'10". He cleared it but, being a chaser, was careless and hit the pole with his near hind hoof. That put him out. Both the girl on the bay and Helen cleared it.

The girl said, "Funny us both being girls and riding mares."

Helen said, "Yes," but didn't think it funny.

The girl was slim and beautiful and could ride. The bay mare was beautiful. The girl's saddlery and gear were beautiful. The girl's jacket and breeches were beautiful. Her boots were beautiful. Her long slim thighs that gripped the beautiful saddle on the beautiful bay mare were beautiful. Helen hated her.

There was only this girl between her and the half of Lucy she did not own. She thought she could have killed her; at least she understood now why people were killed: they were too beautiful. All those actresses that were murdered in the Sunday papers.

She patted Lucy's neck.

Five feet eleven inches. It was the girl again.

Her name was listed as Georgina Haslett, but she was just *the girl* to Helen. The girl cleared it. Helen cleared it. Two men put up the pegs another notch—6′.

"You take it," the girl said. "My girth needs fixing."

Someone shouted to the judge. He shouted back. A man ran up to explain. He put his mouth to the mike.

"Her name is Miss Helen Blackett" came over the air as if God had shouted it.

The girl, Helen thought. *She's afraid. There's nothing wrong with her girth. And I am afraid.* Six feet was so high. As high as daddy. Much, much more than an inch higher than 5′11″. She tried to remember the world's record jump: 6′6″, she thought. Only 6″ more.

Lucy was cantering slowly toward the two black-and-white posts that supported the bar. The closer they got, the higher it seemed to Helen. Then her courage came back.

"It's for you, Lucy," she said.

The mare laid one ear back to listen. Then she cocked it forward and switched her tail. She seemed to think this was fun. This was real jumping. She slowed up a little as she felt Helen climbing up her neck.

"N-n-now," Helen shouted. "Now, Lucy!" and they were off. One—two great bounds that were almost leaps and they were air-borne.

Helen came right up higher than Lucy's head. She could look down on her forehead and the star. She noticed the way her forelock, divided into two as usual, was blowing back. She saw the white faces of the people in the grandstand and then she slid back. They had done it. She patted Lucy and the crowd roared.

Now let her try, Helen thought. *Let that girl and her damn bay mare do it.* She was surprised at herself. She had never said "damn" before.

But the girl did not do it. She was afraid and the mare knew it. The bay never even came up, but struck the bar with her chest.

Everyone was around them now: daddy and mother and Smitty

and old Herman and Mr. Lonstein. They all went up with her, like a deputation, to get her cup, the check in an envelope, and a blue ribbon for Lucy.

She'd done it. It was over.

"You're famous," someone said.

"Fancy a kid winning the Rand Show high jump!"

But Helen hardly heard them. What she did hear was Smitty, who said, "I've got crutches for you, Helen. I'm sure you can use them now," and he slipped them under her arms as he helped her down from the horse. He held her till she got her balance and she found she could use them. Her left leg would support her if someone held her belt.

They stayed two more days. Her left leg could support her. The right was still weak, but she could get about on her own and had seen most of the show again. Everyone knew her and liked her. Most of them had seen her jump Old Lucy.

She was eating an ice-cream cone when a stableboy ran up to her. She knew him well by sight, a boy called Franz. He looked after two other jumpers.

"Missis! Missis!" he shouted. "Come quick. The man," he said. "*Ja,* the *baas,* he's trying to jump her and she won't. Then he hit her with his sjambok."

Helen looked at him wide-eyed, wiping the ice cream from her mouth.

"Jumping? Jumping who?"

"*Die missis se perd,*" he said. "Your horse, Old Lucy. Man he struck her, and your boy is killed."

Before he had finished Helen was off, hopping toward the practice jumps like a wounded rabbit. A man trying to jump Old Lucy. Herman was dead. He had tried to stop it. The man had hit him. He'd hit Lucy.

The blood boiled in her veins. Suddenly she knew that she had never been angry in life before. Not like this. *I said damn,* she thought. She said it again. *Damn him! Damn him!* A murderer! Beating Old Lucy, and old Herman dead!

He—— She increased her pace. Coming around the side of the stables she saw him—a big redheaded young man on Old Lucy's back, trying to force her over a jump that she had refused. Her mouth was bleeding from the heavy bit he had put into her mouth, and she had a curd of froth and foam on her chest.

"I'll teach you," he said. "*Ja,* you damn lazy *skelm.*" He raised his whip and brought it down on Old Lucy's quarters. She laid her ears back and showed the whites of her eyes, but did not move. The man jumped off, holding the riem in his hands, and began to thrash the mare.

Without knowing how she did it, Helen was running. She had let one crutch fall and charged the man, using the other like a bayonet. She struck the man in the side. As he turned to face her, Old Lucy pulled free and swung around to her mistress' side.

"What the hell!" the man shouted.

"My horse," Helen hissed at him. "You dared to hit my horse. And my boy." Old Herman was not dead. He hobbled toward her.

"I was just teaching her," the man said. "A horse must learn to respect a man—a woman too. *Magtig,* never before has a woman struck me. Never before——"

He did not finish. The crutch point took him in the throat. He went down and Helen beat at him as if he were a snake.

He got up and tried to seize her arm. Old Lucy chopped at him. Then with a flash of teeth and flaring nostrils she took him by the collar of his coat and shook him like a rat.

By now a crowd was around them, white and black, visitors, owners, grooms.

"Like a bloody rat," a man said. "I've heard a horse could lift a man in his teeth, but I've never seen it."

Helen was sobbing, with her arms around Old Lucy's neck. Old Herman was patting her shoulder. "Drunk," he said. "*Ja,* he was drunk. I tried to stop him and he hit me flat."

It was all a nightmare, a dream. It wasn't true. The mare pushed her nose into her chest. Helen pulled her ears and rubbed her poll, kneading it with her fingers. Then she looked down and saw her crutch on the ground. It had been broken in the scuffle.

What'll I do? she thought. *How will I get about, and where is the other one?* Then it dawned on her. She was standing. She had run. She had fought a man. She had won a hundred guineas and could buy Lucy back. *I can walk,* she thought, *and Lucy's mine.* That she had won a great competition was forgotten. The little Helen that her mother loved was back.

Helen was standing crying bitterly, her arms wound around her horse's neck, when Grace and Johnnie found her.

Skobelef

JOHAN BOJER

(Translated by Sigurd B. Hustvedt)

SKOBELEF was a horse.

This was in the days when the church bells of a Sunday morning sent out their summons, not over moribund highways and slumberous farmsteads, but over a parish waiting to be wakened into life by the sustained, solemn calling of those brazen tongues. The bells rang, rang, till the welkin rang again:

> *Come, come,*
> *Old and young,*
> *Old and young,*
> *Rich man, poor man,*
> *Dalesman, fisherman, man from the hills,*
> *The forest, the fields,*
> *The strand, the fells,*
>
> *Mads from Fallin, and Anders from Berg,*
> *And Ola from Rein,*
> *And Mette from Naust,*
> *And Mari and Kari from Densta-lea,*
> *Lea, lea,*
> *Come, come,*
> *Come, come,*
> *Come.*

And so the roads grew black with people on their way to church, some walking and some riding. Old codgers wheezed past, stick in one hand, hat in the other, their coats under their arms, and their gray homespun trousers tucked into boots shiny with grease. The women trundled along carrying shawls and hymnbooks, and scenting the breeze with their perfumed handkerchiefs. Out on the lake, bordered with hills and farms, appeared row-boats driven over the water by sturdy oarsmen; from across the fjord swept the sail-boats; far up in the mountains it seemed as if the cattle even stopped grazing; and the boy who was watching them put the goat-horn to his lips and blew a stout blast down toward the folks at home. In those times Sunday was both holy day and holiday.

Looking back after these many years, I have a vivid impression that all the world was sunshine and green forests on a day like that. The old church, brown with tar, standing amidst the crowns of mighty trees, seemed then to be more than just a building; there was something supernatural about it, as if it knew all there was to be known. Many hundreds of years had passed over it. It had seen the dead when they were still alive, when they went to church like ourselves. The surrounding graveyard was a little village of wooden crosses and stone slabs; and the grass grew wild between the leaning monuments. We knew well enough that the sexton mowed it and fed it to his cows; so that when we got a drink of milk at his house we felt as if we were quaffing the very souls of the departed, a kind of angelic milk from which we drew transcendental virtues with every draft.

We boys used to stand outside the church and do as our elders did—size up the people that arrived after us. We judged by appearances, and they all knew it. The cripple made himself look smaller than ever so as to hide in the crowd; the dandies ran the gauntlet of both friendly and unfriendly eyes, and pretty women looked down and smiled. We youngsters searched the gathering throng for someone to admire, some heroic figure we should like to resemble when we ourselves one day should be grown up. There was the new teacher, for instance, stalking along in his homespun with his coat buttoned tight, with a white necktie, top hat, and umbrella. He was at least one stage above the farmer. Not a doubt about it, we too were going to attend the normal school. So we thought, at any rate, until a butcher came up from the city, wearing a suit of blue duffle, a white waistcoat with a gold watch-chain, cuffs, a dazzling white collar, and a straw hat. He was a perfect revelation. With such an exemplar before us it was easy to decide that we were to become butcher's apprentices as soon as we were old enough.

Many were the magnates that paraded through our daydreams. Still it was with no ordinary emotion that we laid eyes for the first time on a city lawyer. His was a truly royal presence. Even his nose had its appropriate ornament, a pair of gold eye-glasses. Our ambitions soared beyond all bounds. Whatever our hopes of higher education might be, most of us were bent on carrying our studies far enough to impair our vision and so to justify the use of gold-rimmed glasses.

Then came Skobelef. And Skobelef was a horse.

For weeks busy little feet had been bringing the tidings to all corners of the parish. Peter Lo had bought a registered stallion that was not simply a horse but a whole Arabian Nights' entertainment. It took six men to lead him ashore from the steamer. Only one man could have turned the trick alone, and that was Peter Lo himself. For the most part the horse walked on his hind legs. He kept whinnying even in his sleep. He was so fierce that he had already killed a number of men. His name was Skobelef. And what do you suppose they fed him? It was neither hay nor oats nor bran; not much! Skobelef's fodder was nothing less than eggnog, made with whiskey, at that. It was common talk that Peter Lo and the stallion munched this provender together out of the same crib. They required stimulants, the two of them.

To return to that particular Sunday—we were standing at the church keeping an impatient lookout across the parish. Peter Lo was bound for the house of worship, driving none other than Skobelef himself.

The long line of vehicles came rolling in from the valleys. It picked up reinforcements at every crossroad until it was like a regular bridal procession. That day we kept our eyes on the horses and estimated the people in the gigs according to their dumb, driven cattle. A whole fated universe passed in review, animals fat and lean, jaded and fiery, old big-bellied nags with long necks and prominent backbones and heads sagging with each step toward the ground under the burden of unceasing tribulation; prosperous-looking brutes that gave manifest proof of good crops and bank deposits. Look at that brood-mare; she has weaned many a colt and therefore carries her head high and surveys the world with maternal eyes. Here and there you can pick out fjord ponies with ragged haunches, stamping against the grade and sweating with the weight of the heavy gig, some of them so small that they make you think of mice. There comes a big old bay with huge watery eyes and quivering knees, looking about as if to ask why there is no Sabbath for the likes of him. Don't miss the physiognomies of those virtuous, censorious fillies proclaiming the vanity of vanities, and just behind them wild young gallants neighing at the world in general. Have a look at that bay gelding. Why is his belly all spattered with mud? That's easy. He is from a mountain farm; early this morning he had to wade through heath and marsh, across brooks and rivers on the way to the parish below, where his master could borrow a cart. He has another tough time coming before he gets back home. Talk about long processions! But what has become of Peter Lo? Where is Skobelef?

At last, there someone comes driving behind all the others. He is still far away beyond the farmhouses. Never mind, he is gaining ground at a pretty smart pace. Hundreds of eyes are fixed in rapt attention.

The church bells rang out. Most of the horses had been unhitched and were tied to the big ash trees; there they stood with their heads buried in bags of hay, grinding at their dinners and gazing absently about. All of a sudden they jerked their heads up, and even the most raw-boned skates made shift to arch their necks as they stared down the road.

Enter Peter Lo. Enter Skobelef.

He came trotting along before the gig, a broad black hulk, his fetlocks dancing, his mane sweeping in billows down his neck, his eyes shooting fire, two red prize ribbons waving at his ears. He raised his head and snuffed the breeze, monarch of all he surveyed; then he lifted up his voice and split the welkin—believe me, that was a trumpet call that fetched the echoes out of the mountains. In the gig sat Peter Lo, holding the reins relaxed, a very debonair man not over thirty-five, broad of shoulder, vigorous, smiling out of a corner of his mouth above his chin-whiskers. It was certainly too bad that his wife, sitting beside him, was so much older than he; her every feature drooped, her red cheeks drooped, her eyes drooped, the corners of her mouth drooped; she always spoke in whimpering tones. As for Peter Lo himself, he had a weakness for all things pretty, even for such as were not his own. As Skobelef neighed to his affinities, Peter Lo glanced at good friends of his own among the crowd and smiled. Skobelef came to a stop, but got a cut of the whip; he reared and got another stroke; then he bounded up the road toward the parsonage, the crowd in his wake, we boys flying ahead like birds on the wing.

It was a circus to watch Peter Lo maneuver Skobelef out from the shafts of the gig and over toward the stable door. Peter Lo for sure looked swell that day; the horse must have lent him a new dignity, his gray suit was so well brushed and he wore a stiff hat just like the teacher's. But every now and then his polished boots flew up in the air. The crowd stared for all they were worth. Too soon the magic horse disappeared behind the stable door; presently Peter Lo came out again, brushing the horse hairs from his hands. He picked his

way carefully so as not to soil those shiny boots as he walked down
to the church. The crowd trekked after him. Peter Lo mounted the
steps to the hall and walked in. The congregation followed at his
heels. Peter Lo sat down in one of the pews, opened a hymnbook,
and began to sing. The congregation did likewise, and the singing
rose in volume.

But on this particular day we youngsters kept watch and ward
outside the stable door. It was a mighty good thing it was locked;
there was no telling what Skobelef would do if he got loose on his
own account. The cold chills ran down our spines as we heard him
rattling his halter and stamping on the floor. Now and again the
walls shook with his neighing. Talk about thrills! We stood still, put
our heads together, and spoke in whispers.

It was a great day for the horses, too. The mares under the ash
trees lost their appetites and stood all the while arching their necks
and trying to look like two-year-olds. Stallions and geldings had that
day caught sight of a rival whose eyes flashed with arrogance. Do you
suppose they would put up with that sort of thing! They pawed the
ground furiously and shook the air with protests from all sides.

At last the bells rang again. The congregation came out, but the
greater number had no thought of hitching up their own horses. The
yard was jammed with people wanting to see Peter Lo lead Skobelef
out of the stable.

The man himself approached. The eyes of all waiting upon him,
he strolled along talking to the sexton as if he were an ordinary mor-
tal. Yet he had already acquired certain of the gestures that the par-
son was accustomed to make use of in the pulpit.

The people gradually drew back from the road. One circumspect
man dragged his gig away from the middle of the yard. The women
took refuge on the landings of the barns. It was just as well to be on
the safe side, but everybody wanted to see what was going on.

Peter Lo unlocked the stable door and disappeared from view. A
seven-fold thunder of neighing sounded from within, the halter rattled, heavy hoofs drummed against the floor, and the next minute a
black barrel of a body appeared on the threshold. Skobelef flung his
battlecry to the four winds; Peter Lo was hurled aloft, but landed on
his feet some distance out in the yard. Women shrieked. Old men
jumped out of the way, hats flying right and left. Peter Lo and Skobelef started to dance around the yard. Skobelef snorted and foamed
so that his dark body was dappled with froth; he had no mind to be
led toward the gig; he reared, pummeled the air with his hoofs, and
plunged from side to side, while a pair of shining boots kept cutting

strange capers through space. It was an apocalyptic vision, something to dream about. The yard was swept clean of vehicles and people in a trice. It had been changed into a ball-room for Peter Lo and Skobelef. Peter Lo yelled at the stallion, and the stallion screamed at the universe and at Peter Lo. On went the dance. Finally Skobelef seemed bound to enter the parsonage and have a chat with the preacher's wife; but Peter Lo got ahead of him and planted his splendid boots with a resounding thump against the steps, so that Skobelef succeeded only in tearing down the railing. Peter Lo grew red in the face. Skobelef's whole body had become a mass of foam. The women gasped out shivering sighs, "Oh, oh!"

At last the wild beast was forced between the shafts. As the reins were loosened he rose on his hind legs, and the lash fell on his neck; he pranced about on all fours with arched neck and flaring nostrils. Then Peter Lo's wife came up, gathering her shawl around her shoulders, and—believe it or not—stepped calmly into the gig while the earthquake was still going on. Now Peter Lo knew that the victory was his; he put his hand on the dashboard and leaped up beside his wife; the horse reared, his eyes shot fire, the foam flew, the whip cracked, and the next second the whole show dissolved in a cloud of dust rushing along beyond the farmhouses.

We stood rooted to the spot. The other men began bashfully to hitch up their own horses. There was really nothing at all left to look at.

From that day Skobelef was an influential personality throughout the parish. To tell the truth, Peter Lo and Skobelef took on together a sort of higher individuality that drew the popular gaze as they flashed by. It seemed as if they were whipping the whole neighborhood up to a more rapid tempo. The farmers came to be men of honor so far as their horses were concerned, fed them well, and groomed them with the utmost care. They drove at a brisker pace along the roads, their speech acquired an added dash of humor, they laughed in the face of heaven and earth, their thoughts assumed a new boldness. On Sundays, as the congregation stood outside the church admiring Skobelef and Peter Lo, a fresh source of vitality seemed to be manifesting itself; men saw with their own eyes the very embodiment of animal spirits, they sensed something venerable in brute strength, they caught the chanted praise of rippling muscles. It began to dawn on them that life is not a mere medley of sins and sorrows, that life on earth has a glory of its own.

As time passed, Peter Lo gave increasing attention to his clothes. He took to reading books, to wearing a white collar, to using a handkerchief when he blew his nose about the precincts of the church. He imitated the sheriff's mannerisms of speech. He knew quite well that he and Skobelef had become the local cynosures; and this persuasion lent him a feeling of responsibility and a desire to serve as a pattern for the herd. If the truth must be told, it was not only we boys who prayed, "Good Lord, help us to be like Peter Lo when we get big!" By no means! The grownups, too, tried to ape his manner. "You are brushing your shoes just the way Peter Lo does," one man would say to another. "And you are wearing a white collar, just like Peter Lo's," they would say. Skobelef, imported to ennoble the rural breed of horse flesh, had become a spiritual force, an educational institution for the entire countryside.

Peter Lo was not quite so fortunate. He could not be happy except in the society of the stallion. He lost interest in work. He was in his element only when racing down the county roads behind his crony, or when he and Skobelef together conducted revival services beneath the very walls of the church. The rumor spread that he had taken to sleeping in the stable. Gossip would have it that horse and man were coming to resemble each other. Skobelef smiled out of the corner of his mouth when he met with his affinities, and Peter Lo greeted good friends at church with something like a whinny in his voice.

Peter Lo's lot was not altogether enviable. He had a fondness for all things pretty, not excepting those that belonged to his neighbors. And when he got into an unusually bad scrape, he made a most pathetic figure. Then he would go to church and take holy communion. Many a time we saw him come driving, not the wild stallion but an old mare. His sour-visaged wife, wrapped in her shawl, would be sitting in the cart, at one side of which walked the sexton, and at the other side Peter Lo, with bowed head. On such a day he would have his mind made up to listen to the sermon with folded hands and not once to glance in the direction of the women's pews—afterward he would step forward to the altar and partake of the sacrament. These penitential pilgrimages occasioned more than one good laugh. "Peter has had a sorry adventure again," people would say.

A day or two later you would see him tearing down the highway with Skobelef. So he kept on laying up stores of gayety and æsthetic appreciation of the beautiful, until his conduct became more reprehensible than ever. His wife insisted upon Skobelef's deportation from the farm; it was impossible to convert Peter to virtuous ways so long as he maintained a companionship of that sort.

Meanwhile, round about in the parish there grew up a numerous race of black, prancing horses, and the wheels rumbled faster on all the roads. A whinnying joy of life took sovereign possession of the community. Men lifted up their heads and cast jovial eyes on their surroundings, women plucked up courage actually to laugh out loud, and young folks discovered anew the pleasures of the dance.

But Skobelef was not to reach old age. He broke out of the stable one night and ran off in the mountains to find his affinities, who were accustomed to graze there during the summer.

When Peter Lo came along and saw the empty stable, he started shouting clamorous complaints; he evidently suspected at once that misfortune had stamped her mark upon his brow. He had a pretty shrewd idea where his comrade had fled; and witnesses reported that the whole day long they heard Peter Lo tramping over the hills neighing just like Skobelef, calling and coaxing his old chum.

At last he found him. Skobelef was standing up to his neck in a marsh far off in the foothills. He had fought so hard to extricate himself that he had broken one of his forelegs, out of which protruded splinters of bone. The flies had stung his eyes till they bled.

Peter wiped his pal's eyes with a tuft of grass and gave him a raw egg and a shot of whiskey. For a little while he let his own tears roll, but finally there was nothing to do but to draw his knife.

After that day Peter Lo drove more slowly along the roads. His head bent lower and his whiskers turned gray.

Now he is an old man; but he still dresses better than most of his neighbors and affects a city brogue as before. When someone reminds him of Skobelef, his eyes grow dim. "Yes, yes," he replies; "Skobelef was not like other horses. He was a regular high school; he taught us all a thing or two."

Memories

JOHN GALSWORTHY

Some quarter of a century ago there abode in Oxford a small book-maker called James Shrewin—or more usually, Jimmy—a run-about and damped-down little man, who made a precarious living out of the effect of horses on undergraduates. He had a so-called office just off the Corn, where he was always open to the patronage of the young bloods of Bullingdon, and other horse-loving coteries, who bestowed on him sufficient money to enable him to live. It was through the conspicuous smash of one of them—young Gardon Colquhoun—that he became the owner of a horse. He had been far from wanting what was in the nature of a white elephant to one of his underground habits, but had taken it in discharge of betting debts, to which, of course, in the event of bankruptcy, he would have no legal claim. She was a three-year-old chestnut filly, by Lopez out of Calendar, bore the name Calliope, and was trained out on the Downs near Wantage. On a Sunday afternoon, then, in late July, Jimmy got his friend George Pulcher, the publican, to drive him out there in his sort of dogcart.

"Must 'ave a look at the bilkin' mare," he had said; "that young Cocoon tole me she was a corker; but what's third to Referee at Sandown, and never ran as a two-year-old? All I know is, she's eatin' 'er 'ead off!"

Beside the plethoric bulk of Pulcher, clad in a light-colored box-cloth coat with enormous whitish buttons and a full-blown rose in the lapel, Jimmy's little, thin, dark-clothed form, withered by anxiety and gin, was, as it were, invisible; and compared with Pulcher's setting sun, his face, with shaven cheeks sucked in, and smudged-in eyes, was like a ghost's under a gray bowler. He spoke off-handedly about his animal, but he was impressed, in a sense abashed, by his ownership. "What the 'ell?" was his constant thought. Was he going to race her, sell her—what? How, indeed, to get back out of her the sum he had been fool enough to let young Cocoon owe him; to say nothing of her trainer's bill? The notion, too, of having to confront that trainer with his ownership was oppressive to one whose whole life was passed in keeping out of the foreground of the picture. Owner! He had never owned even a white mouse, let alone a white elephant. An an 'orse would ruin him in no time if he didn't look alive about it!

The son of a small London baker, devoted to errandry at the age of fourteen, Jimmy Shrewin owed his profession to a certain smartness at sums, a dislike of baking, and an early habit of hanging about street corners with other boys, who had their daily pennies on an 'orse. He had a narrow, calculating head, which pushed him toward street-corner books before he was eighteen. From that time on he had been a surreptitious nomad, till he had silted up at Oxford, where, owing to vice-chancellors, an expert in underground life had greater scope than elsewhere. When he sat solitary at his narrow table in the back room near the Corn—for he had no clerk or associate—eyeing the door, with his lists in a drawer before him, and his black shiny betting book ready for young bloods, he had a sharp, cold, furtive air, and but for a certain imitated tightness of trouser, and a collar standing up all around, gave no impression of ever having heard of the quadruped called horse. Indeed, for Jimmy "horse" was a newspaper quantity with figures against its various names.

Even when, for a short spell, hanger-on to a firm of Cheap Ring bookmakers, he had seen almost nothing of horse; his race-course hours were spent ferreting among a bawling, perspiring crowd, or hanging round within earshot of tight-lipped nobs, trainers, jockeys, anyone who looked like having information. Nowadays he never went near a race meeting—his business of betting on races giving him no chance—yet his conversation seldom deviated for more than a minute at a time from that physically unknown animal, the horse. The ways of making money out of it, infinite, intricate, variegated, occupied the mind in all his haunts, to the accompaniment of liquid and tobacco. Gin and bitters was Jimmy's drink; for choice he smoked cheroots; and he would cherish in his mouth the cold stump of one long after it had gone out, for the homely feeling it gave him while he talked or listened to talk on horses. He was of that vast number, town bred, who, like crows round a carcass, feed on that which to them is not alive. And now he had a horse!

The dogcart traveled at a clinking pace behind Pulcher's bob-tail. Jimmy's cheroot burned well in the warm July air; the dust powdered his dark clothes and pinched, sallow face. He thought with malicious pleasure of that young spark Cocoon's collapse—high-'anded lot of young fools thinking themselves so knowing; many were the grins, and not few the grittings of his blackened teeth he had to smother at their swagger. "Jimmy, you robber!" "Jimmy, you little blackguard!" Young sparks—gay and languid—well, one of 'em had gone out.

He looked round with his screwed-up eyes at his friend George Pulcher, who, man and licensed victualer, had his bally independence; lived remote from the Quality in his Paradise, the Green Dragon; had not to kowtow to anyone; went to Newbury, Gatwick, Stockbridge, here and there, at will. Ah! George Pulcher had the ideal life—and looked it; crimson, square, full-bodied. Judge of a horse, too, in his own estimation; a leery bird—for whose judgment Jimmy had respect—who got the office of any clever work as quick as most men!

And he said, "What am I going to do with this blinkin' 'orse, George?"

Without moving its head the oracle spoke, in a voice rich and raw: "Let's 'ave a look at her, first, Jimmy! Don't like her name—Calliope; but you can't change what's in the stud-book. This Jenning that trains 'er is a crusty chap."

Jimmy nervously sucked in his lips.

The cart was mounting through the hedgeless fields which fringed the Downs; larks were singing, the wheat was very green, and patches of charlock brightened everything.

It was lonely—few trees, few houses, no people, extreme peace, just a few rooks crossing under a blue sky.

"Wonder if he'll offer us a drink," said Jimmy.

"Not he; but help yourself, my son."

Jimmy helped himself from a large wicker-covered flask.

"Good for you, George—here's how!"

The large man shifted the reins and drank, in turn tilting up a face whose jaw still struggled to assert itself against chins and neck.

"Well, here's your bloomin' horse," he said. "She can't win the Derby now, but she may do us a bit of good yet."

II

The trainer, Jenning, coming from his Sunday afternoon round of the boxes, heard the sound of wheels. He was a thin man, neat in clothes and boots, medium in height, with a slight limp, narrow gray whiskers, thin shaven lips, eyes sharp and gray.

A dogcart stopped at his yard gate and a rum-looking couple of customers.

"Well, gentlemen?"

"Mr. Jenning? My name's Pulcher—George Pulcher. Brought a client of yours over to see his new mare. Mr. James Shrewin, Oxford City."

Jimmy got down and stood before his trainer's uncompromising stare.

"What mare's that?" asked Jenning.

"Cal'liope."

"Calli'ope—Mr. Colquhoun's?"

Jimmy held out a letter.

Dear Jenning: I have sold Calliope to Jimmy Shrewin, the Oxford bookie. He takes her with all engagements and liabilities, including your training bill. I'm frightfully sick at having to part with her, but needs must when the devil drives.

Gardon Colquhoun.

The trainer folded the letter.

"Got proof of registration?"

Jimmy drew out another paper.

The trainer inspected it and called out: "Ben, bring out Calliope. Excuse me a minute," and he walked into his house.

Jimmy stood shifting from leg to leg. Mortification had set in; the dry abruptness of the trainer had injured even a self-esteem starved from youth.

The voice of Pulcher boomed. "Told you he was a crusty devil. And 'im a bit of his own."

The trainer was coming back.

"My bill," he said. "When you've paid it you can have the mare. I train for gentlemen."

"The hell you do!" said Pulcher.

Jimmy said nothing, staring at the bill—seventy-eight pounds three shillings! A buzzing fly settled in the hollow of his cheek, and he did not even brush it off. Seventy-eight pounds!

The sound of hoofs aroused them. Here came his horse, throwing up her head as if inquiring why she was being disturbed a second time on Sunday! In the movement of that small head and satin neck was something free and beyond present company.

"There she is," said the trainer. "That'll do, Ben. Stand, girl!"

Answering to a jerk or two of the halter, the mare stood, kicking slightly with a white hind foot and whisking her tail. Her bright coat shone in the sunlight, and little shivers and wrinklings passed up and down its satin because of the flies. Then, for a moment, she stood still, ears pricked, eyes on the distance.

Jimmy approached her. She had resumed her twitchings, swishings and slight kicking, and at a respectful distance he circled, bending as if looking at crucial points. He knew what her sire and dam had done, and all the horses that had beaten or been beaten by them; could have retailed by the half hour the peculiar hearsay of their careers; and here was their offspring in flesh and blood, and he was dumb! He didn't know a thing about what she ought to look like, and he knew it; but he felt obscurely moved. She seemed to him a picture.

Completing his circle, he approached her head, white-blazed, thrown up again in listening or scenting, and gingerly he laid his hand on her neck, warm and smooth as a woman's shoulder. She paid no attention to his touch, and he took his hand away. Ought he to look at her teeth or feel her legs? No, he was not buying her; she was his already; but he must say something. He looked round. The trainer was watching him with a little smile. For almost the first time in his life the worm turned in Jimmy Shrewin; he spoke no word and walked back to the cart.

"Take her in," said Jenning.

From his seat beside Pulcher, Jimmy watched the mare returning to her box.

"When I've cashed your check," said the trainer, "you can send for her."

And, turning on his heel, he went toward his house. The voice of Pulcher followed him.

"Blast your impudence! Git on, bob-tail, we'll shake the dust off 'ere."

Among the fringing fields the dog cart hurried away. The sun slanted, the heat grew less, the color of young wheat and of the charlock brightened.

"The tyke! Jimmy, I'd 'ave hit him on the mug! But you've got one there. She's a bit o' blood, my boy! And I know the trainer for her, Polman—no blasted airs about 'im."

Jimmy sucked at his cheroot.

"I ain't had your advantages, George, and that's a fact. I got into it too young, and I'm a little chap. But I'll send the—my check to-morrow. I got my pride, I 'ope."

It was the first time that thought had ever come to him.

III

Though not quite the center of the Turf, the Green Dragon had nursed a coup in its day, nor was it without a sense of veneration. The ownership of Calliope invested Jimmy Shrewin with the impor-tance of those out of whom something can be had. It took time for one so long accustomed to beck and call, to molelike procedure and the demeanor of young bloods to realize that he had it. But, slowly, with the marked increase of his unpaid-for cheroots, with the way in which glasses hung suspended when he came in, with the edgings up to him, and a certain tendency to accompany him along the street, it dawned on him that he was not only an out-of-bounds bookie but a man.

So long as he had remained unconscious of his double nature he had been content with laying the odds as best he might, and getting what he could out of every situation, straight or crooked. Now that he was also a man, his complacency was ruffled. He suffered from a growing headiness connected with his horse. She was trained, now, by Polman, further along the Downs, too far for Pulcher's bob-tail; and though her public life was carried on at the Green Dragon, her private life required a train journey overnight. Jimmy took it twice a week—touting his own horse in the August mornings up on the Downs, without drink or talk, or even cheroots. Early morning, larks singing and the sound of galloping hoofs! In a moment of expansion he confided to Pulcher that it was bally 'olesome.

There had been the slight difficulty of being mistaken for a tout by his new trainer, Polman, a stoutish man with the look of one of those large sandy Cornish cats, not precisely furtive because reti-cence and craft are their nature. But, that once over, his per-sonality swelled slowly. This month of August was one of those inter-ludes, in fact, when nothing happens, but which shape the future by secret ripening.

An error to suppose that men conduct finance, high or low, from greed, or love of gambling; they do it out of self-esteem, out of an itch to prove their judgment superior to their neighbor's, out of a longing for importance. George Pulcher did not despise the turning of a penny, but he valued much more the consciousness that men were saying: "Old George, what 'e says goes—knows a thing or two—George Pulcher!"

To pull the strings of Jimmy Shrewin's horse was a rich and subtle opportunity absorbingly improvable. But first one had to study the animal's engagements, and secondly to gauge that unknown quantity, her form. To make anything of her this year they must get about it. That young toff, her previous owner, had, of course, flown high, entering her for classic races, high-class handicaps, neglecting the rich chances of lesser occasions.

Third to Referee in the three-year-old race at Sandown Spring— two heads—was all that was known of her, and now they had given her seven two in the Cambridgeshire. She might have a chance, and again she might not. He sat two long evenings with Jimmy in the private room off the bar deliberating this grave question.

Jimmy inclined to the bold course. He kept saying: "The mare's a flyer, George—she's the 'ell of a flyer!"

"Wait till she's been tried," said the oracle.

Had Polman anything that would give them a line?

Yes, he had The Shirker—named with that irony which appeals to the English—one of the most honest four-year-olds that ever looked through bridle, who had run up against almost every animal of mark —the one horse that Polman never interfered with, for if interrupted in his training he should run all the better; who seldom won, but was almost always placed—the sort of horse that handicappers pivot on.

"But," said Pulcher, "try her with The Shirker, and the first stable money will send her up to tens.

"That 'orse is so darned regular. We've got to throw a bit of dust first, Jimmy. I'll go over and see Polman."

In Jimmy's withered chest a faint resentment rose—it wasn't George's horse—but it sank again beneath his friend's bulk and reputation.

The bit of dust was thrown at the ordinary hour of exercise over the Long Mile on the last day of August—the five-year-old Hangman carrying eight stone seven, the three-year-old Parrot seven stone five; what Calliope was carrying nobody but Polman knew. The forethought of George Pulcher had secured the unofficial presence of the press. The instructions to the boy on Calliope were to be there at the finish if he could, but on no account to win. Jimmy and George Pulcher had come out overnight. They sat together in the dogcart by the clump of bushes which marked the winning post, with Polman on his cob on the far side.

By a fine warm light the three horses were visible to the naked eye in the slight dip down the start. And, through the glasses, invested in now that he had a horse, Jimmy could see every movement of his mare with her blazed face—rather on her toes, like the bright chestnut and bit o' blood she was. He had a pit-patting in his heart, and his lips were tight pressed. Suppose she was no good at all, and that young Cocoon had palmed him off a pup! But mixed in with his financial fear was an anxiety more intimate, as if his own value were at stake.

From George Pulcher came an almost excited gurgle.

"See the tout! See 'im behind that bush. Thinks we don't know 'e's there, wot oh!"

Jimmy bit into his cheroot. "They're running," he said.

Rather wide, the black Hangman on the far side, Calliope in the middle, they came sweeping up the Long Mile. Jimmy held his tobaccoed breath. The mare was going freely—a length or two behind —making up her ground! Now for it!

Ah! She 'ad the 'Angman beat, and ding-dong with this Parrot! It was all he could do to keep from calling out. With a rush and a cludding of hoofs they passed—the blazed nose just behind the Parrot's bay nose—dead heat all but, with the Hangman beaten a good length!

"There 'e goes, Jimmy! See the blank scuttlin' down the 'ill like a blinkin' rabbit. That'll be in tomorrow's paper, that trial will. Ah! but 'ow to read it—that's the point."

The horses had been wheeled and were sidling back; Polman was going forward on his cob.

Jimmy jumped down. Whatever that fellow had to say, he meant to hear. It was his horse! Narrowly avoiding the hoofs of his hot fidgeting mare, he said sharply: "What about it?"

Polman never looked you in the face; his speech came as if not intended to be heard by anyone.

"Tell Mr. Shrewin how she went."

"Had a bit up my sleeve. If I'd hit her a smart one, I could ha' landed by a length or more."

"That so?" said Jimmy with a hiss. "Well, don't you hit her; she don't want hittin'. You remember that."

The boy said sulkily, "All right!"

"Take her home," said Polman. Then, with that reflective averted air of his, he added: "She was carrying eight stone, Mr. Shrewin; you've got a good one there. She's the Hangman at level weights."

Something wild leaped up in Jimmy—the Hangman's form unrolled itself before him in the air—he had a horse—he damn well had a horse!

IV

But how delicate is the process of backing your fancy? The planting of a commission—what tender and efficient work before it will flower! That sixth sense of the racing man, which, like the senses of savages in great forests, seizes telepathically on what is not there, must be dulled, duped, deluded.

George Pulcher had the thing in hand. One might have thought the gross man incapable of such a fairy touch, such power of sowing with one hand and reaping with the other. He intimated rather than asserted that Calliope and the Parrot were one and the same thing. "The Parrot," he said, "couldn't win with seven stone—no use thinkin' of this Calliope."

Local opinion was the rock on which, like a great tactician, he built. So long as local opinion was adverse, he could dribble money on in London; the natural jump-up from every long shot taken was dragged back by the careful radiation of disparagement from the seat of knowledge.

Jimmy was the fly in his ointment of those balmy early weeks while snapping up every penny of long odds, before suspicion could begin to work from the persistence of inquiry. Half a dozen times he found the little cuss within an ace of blowing the gaff on his own blinkin' mare; seemed unable to run his horse down; the little beggar's head was swellin'! Once Jimmy had even got up and gone out, leaving a gin and bitters untasted on the bar. Pulcher improved on his absence in the presence of a London tout.

"Saw the trial meself! Jimmy don't like to think he's got a stiff 'un."

And next morning his London agent snapped up some thirty-threes again.

According to the trial the mare was the Hangman at seven stone two, and really hot stuff—a seven-to-one chance. It was none the less with a sense of outrage that, opening the *Sporting Life* on the last day of September, he found her quoted at a hundred to eight. Whose work was this?

He reviewed the altered situation in disgust. He had invested about half the stable commission of three hundred pounds at an average of thirty to one, but now that she had come in the betting he would hardly average tens with the rest. What fool had put his oar in?

He learned he explanation two days later. The rash, the unknown backer was Jimmy! He had acted, it appeared, from jealousy; a bookmaker—it took one's breath away.

"Backed her on your own, just because that young Cocoon told
you he fancied her!"

Jimmy looked up from the table in his "office," where he was sitting in wait for the scanty custom of the long vacation.

"She's not his horse," he said sullenly. "I wasn't going to have
him get the cream."

"What did you put on?" growled Pulcher.

"Took five hundred to thirty, and fifteen twenties."

"An' see what it's done—knocked the bottom out of the commission. Am I to take that fifty as part of it?"

Jimmy nodded.

"That leaves an 'undred to invest," said Pulcher, somewhat mollified. He stood, with his mind twisting in his thick still body. "It's
no good waitin' now," he said. "I'll work the rest of the money on today. If I can average tens on the balance, we'll 'ave six thousand
three hundred to play with and the stakes. They tell me Jenning
fancies this Diamond Stud of his. He ought to know the form with
Calliope, blast him! We got to watch that."

They had! Diamond Stud, a four-year-old with eight stone two,
was being backed as if the Cambridgeshire were over. From fifteens
he advanced to sevens, thence to favoritism at fives. Pulcher bit on it.
Jenning must know where he stood with Calliope! It meant—it
meant she couldn't win! The tactician wasted no time in vain regret.
Establish Calliope in the betting and lay off. The time had come to
utilize The Shirker.

It was misty on the Downs—fine weather mist of a bright October.
The three horses became spectral on their way to the starting point.
Polman had thrown the Parrot in again, but this time he made
no secret of the weights. The Shirker was carrying eight seven, Calliope eight, the Parrot seven stone.

Once more, in the cart, with his glasses sweeping the bright mist,
Jimmy had that pit-patting in his heart. Here they came! His mare
leading—all riding hard—a genuine finish! They passed—The
Shirker beaten a clear length, with the Parrot at his girth.

Beside him in the cart, George Pulcher mumbled, "She's The
Shirker at eight stone four, Jimmy!"

A silent drive big with thought back to a river inn; a silent breakfast. Over a tankard at the close the Oracle spoke.

"The Shirker, at eight stone four, is a good 'ot chance, but no
cert, Jimmy. We'll let 'em know this trial quite open, weights and
all. That'll bring her in the betting. And we'll watch Diamond
Stud. If he drops back we'll know Jenning thinks he can't beat us

now. If Diamond Stud stands up, we'll know Jenning thinks he's still got our mare safe. Then our line'll be clear: we lay off the lot, pick up a thousand or so, and 'ave the mare in at a nice weight at Liverpool."

Jimmy's smudged-in eyes stared hungrily.

"How's that?" he said. "Suppose she wins!"

"Wins! If we lay off the lot, she won't win."

"Pull her!"

George Pulcher's voice sank half an octave with disgust.

"Pull her! Who talked of pullin'? She'll run a bye, that's all. We shan't ever know whether she could 'a' worn or not."

Jimmy sat silent; the situation was such as his life during sixteen years had waited for. They stood to win both ways with a bit of handling.

"Who's to ride?" he said.

"Polman's got a call on Docker. He can just ride the weight. Either way he's good for us—strong finisher, and a rare judge of distance; knows how to time things to a *t*. Win or not, he's our man."

Jimmy was deep in figures. Laying off at sevens, they would still win four thousand and the stakes.

"I'd like a win," he said.

"Ah!" said Pulcher. "But there'll be twenty in the field, my son; no more uncertain race than that bally Cambridgeshire. We could pick up a thou, as easy as I pick up this pot. Bird in the 'and, Jimmy, and a good 'andicap in the busy. If she wins, she's finished. Well, we'll put this trial about and see 'ow Jenning pops."

Jenning popped amazingly. Diamond Stud receded a point, then reestablished himself at nine to two. Jenning was clearly not dismayed.

George Pulcher shook his head and waited, uncertain still which way to jump. Ironical circumstances decided him.

Term had begun; Jimmy was busy at his seat of custom. By some miracle of guardianly intervention, young Colquhoun had not gone broke. He was up again, eager to retrieve his reputation, and that little brute, Jimmy, would not lay against his horse! He merely sucked in his cheeks and answered, "I'm not layin' my own 'orse." It was felt that he was not the man he had been; assertion had come into his manner, he was better dressed. Someone had seen him at the station looking quite a toff in a blue box-cloth coat standing well out from his wisp of a figure, and with a pair of brown race glasses slung over the shoulder. All together the little brute was getting too big for his boots.

And this strange improvement hardened the feeling that his horse was a real good thing. Patriotism began to burn in Oxford. Here was a snip that belonged to them, as it were, and the money in support of it, finding no outlet, began to ball.

A week before the race—with Calliope at nine to one, and very little doing—young Colquhoun went up to town, taking with him the accumulated support of betting Oxford. That evening she stood at sixes. Next day the public followed on.

George Pulcher took advantage. In this crisis of the proceedings he acted on his own initiative. The mare went back to eights, but the deed was done. He had laid off the whole bally lot, including the stake money. He put it to Jimmy that evening in a nutshell. "We pick up a thousand, and the Liverpool as good as in our pocket. I've done worse."

Jimmy grunted out, "She could 'a' won."

"Not she. Jenning knows—and there's others in the race. This Wasp is goin' to take a lot of catchin', and Deerstalker's not out of it. He's a hell of a horse, even with that weight."

Again Jimmy grunted, slowly sucking down his gin and bitters. Suddenly he said, "Well, I don' want to put money in the pocket of young Cocoon and his crowd. Like his impudence, backin' my horse as if it was his own."

"We'll 'ave to go and see her run, Jimmy."

"Not me," said Jimmy.

"What! First time she runs! It won't look natural."

"No," repeated Jimmy. "I don't want to see 'er beat."

George Pulcher laid his hand on a skinny shoulder.

"Nonsense, Jimmy. You've got to, for the sake of your reputation. You'll enjoy seein' your mare saddled. We'll go up over night. I shall 'ave a few pound on Deerstalker. I believe he can beat this Diamond Stud. And you leave Docker to me; I'll 'ave a word with 'im at Gatwick tomorrow. I've known 'im since 'e was that 'igh; an' 'e ain't much more now."

"All right!" growled Jimmy.

The longer you can bet on a race the greater its fascination. Handicappers can properly enjoy the beauty of their work; clubmen and oracles of the course have due scope for reminiscence and prophecy; bookmakers in lovely leisure can indulge a little their own calculated preference, instead of being hurried to soulless conclusions by a half hour's market on the course; the professional backer has the longer in which to dream of his fortune made at last by some hell of a horse—spotted somewhere as interfered with, left at the post, running green, too fat, not fancied, backward—now bound to win this race. And the general public has the chance to read the horses' names in the betting news for days and days; and what a comfort that is!

Jimmy Shrewin was not one of those philosophers who justify the great and growing game of betting on the ground that it improves the breed of an animal less and less in use. He justified it much more simply—he lived by it. And in the whole of his career of nearly twenty years since he made hole-and-corner books among the boys of London, he had never stood so utterly on velvet as that morning when his horse must win him five hundred pounds by merely losing. He had spent the night in London anticipating a fraction of his gains with George Pulcher at a music hall. And, in a first-class carriage, as became an owner, he traveled down to Newmarket by an early special. An early special key turned in the lock of the carriage door, preserved their numbers at six, all professionals, with blank, rather rolling eyes, mouths shut or slightly fishy, ears to the ground; and the only natural talker a red-faced man, who had been at it thirty years. Intoning the pasts and futures of this hell of a horse or that, even he was silent on the race in hand; and the journey was half over before the beauty of their own judgments loosened tongues thereon. George Pulcher started it.

"I fancy Deerstalker," he said.

"Too much weight," said the red-faced man. "What about this Cal'liope?"

"Ah!" said Pulcher. "D'you fancy your mare, Jimmy?"

With all eyes turned on him, lost in his blue box-cloth coat, brown bowler and cheroot smoke, Jimmy experienced a subtle thrill. Addressing the space between the red-faced man and Pulcher, he said. "If she runs up to 'er looks."

"Ah!" said Pulcher, "she's dark—nice mare, but a bit light and shelly."

"Lopez out o' Calendar," muttered the red-faced man. "Lopez didn't stay, but he was the hell of a horse over seven furlongs. The Shirker ought to 'ave told you a bit."

Jimmy did not answer. It gave him pleasure to see the red-faced man's eye trying to get past, and failing.

"Nice race to pick up. Don't fancy the favorite meself; he'd nothin' to beat at Ascot."

"Jenning knows what he's about," said Pulcher.

Jenning! Before Jimmy's mind passed again that first sight of his horse, and the trainer's smile as if he—Jimmy Shrewin, who owned her—had been dirt. Tike! To have the mare beaten by one of his! A deep, subtle vexation had oppressed him at all times all these last days since George Pulcher had decided in favor of the mare's running a bye. He took too much on himself! Thought he had Jimmy Shrewin in his pocket! He looked at the block of crimson opposite. Aunt Sally! If George Pulcher could tell what was passing in his mind!

But driving up to the course he was not above sharing a sandwich and a flask. In fact, his feelings were unstable and gusty—sometimes resentment, sometimes the old respect for his friend's independent bulk. The dignity of ownership takes long to establish itself in those who have been kicked about.

"All right with Docker," murmured Pulcher, sucking at the wicker flask. "I gave him the office at Gatwick."

"She could 'a' won," muttered Jimmy.

"Not she, my boy; there's two at least can beat 'er."

Like all oracles, George Pulcher could believe what he wanted to.

Arriving, they entered the grandstand inclosure, and over the dividing railings Jimmy gazed at the Cheap Ring, already filling up with its usual customers. Faces and umbrellas—the same old crowd. How often had he been in that Cheap Ring, with hardly room to move, seeing nothing, hearing nothing but "Two to one on the field!" "Two to one on the field!" Threes Swordfish!" "Five Alabaster!" "Two to one on the field!"

Nothing but a sea of men like himself, and a sky overhead. He was not exactly conscious of criticism, only of a dull glad-I'm-shut-of-that-lot feeling.

Leaving George Pulcher deep in conversation with a crony, he lighted a cheroot and slipped out on to the course. He passed the Jockey Club inclosure. Some early toffs were there in twos and threes, exchanging wisdom. He looked at them without envy or malice. He was an owner himself now, almost one of them in a manner of thinking. With a sort of relish he thought of how his past life had circled round those toffs, slippery, shadow-like, kicked about; and now he could get up on the Downs away from toffs, George Pulcher, all that crowd, and smell the grass, and hear the bally larks, and watch his own mare gallop!

They were putting the numbers up for the first race. Queer not to be betting, not to be touting around; queer to be giving it a rest! Utterly familiar with those names on the board, he was utterly unfamiliar with the shapes they stood for.

"I'll go and see 'em come out of the paddock," he thought, and moved on, skimpy in his bell-shaped coat and billycock with flattened brim. The clamor of the Rings rose behind him while he was entering the paddock.

Very green, very peaceful there; not many people yet. Three horses in the second race were being led slowly in a sort of winding ring; and men were clustering round the farther gate where the horses would come out. Jimmy joined them, sucking at his cheroot. They were a picture! Damn it, he didn't know but that 'orses laid over men! Pretty creatures!

One by one they passed out of the gate, a round dozen. Selling platers, but pictures, for all that!

He turned back toward the horses being led about; and the old instinct to listen took him close to little groups. Talk was all of the big race. From a tall toff he caught the word "Calliope."

"Belongs to a bookie, they say."

Bookie! Why not? Wasn't a bookie as good as any other? Ah! And sometimes better than these young snobs with everything to their hand! A bookie—well, what chance had he ever had?

A big brown horse came by.

"That's Deerstalker," he heard the toff say.

Jimmy gazed at George Pulcher's fancy with a sort of hostility. Here came another—Wasp, six stone ten, and Deerstalker nine stone—bottom and top of the race!

"My 'orse'd beat either o' them," he thought stubbornly. "Don't like that Wasp."

The distant roar was hushed. They were running in the first race! He moved back to the gate. The quick clamor rose and dropped, and here they came—back into the paddock, darkened with sweat, flanks heaving a little!

Jimmy followed the winner, saw the jockey weigh in.

"What Jockey's that?" he asked.

"That? Why, Docker!"

Jimmy stared. A short, square, bowlegged figure, with a hardwood face!

Waiting his chance, he went up to him and said, "Docker, you ride my 'orse in the big race."

"Mr. Shrewin?"

"The same," said Jimmy. The jockey's left eyelid drooped a little. Nothing responded in Jimmy's face. "I'll see you before the race," he said.

Again the jockey's eyelid wavered; he nodded and passed on.

Jimmy stared at his own boots; they struck him suddenly as too yellow and not at the right angle. But why, he couldn't say.

More horses now—those of the first race being unsaddled, clothed and led away. More men; three familiar figures—young Cocoon and two others of his Oxford customers.

Jimmy turned sharply from them. Stand their airs? Not he! He had a sudden sickish feeling. With a win he'd have been a made man —on his own! Blast George Pulcher and his caution! To think of being back in Oxford with those young bloods jeering at his beaten horse! He bit deep into the stump of his cheroot, and suddenly came on Jenning standing by a horse with a star on its bay forehead. The trainer gave him no sign of recognition, but signed to the boy to lead the horse into a stall, and followed, shutting the door. It was exactly as if he had said, "Vermin about!"

An evil little smile curled Jimmy's lips. The tike!

The horses for the second race passed out of the paddock gate, and he turned to find his own. His ferreting eyes soon sighted Polman. What the cat-faced fellow knew or was thinking, Jimmy could not tell. Nobody could tell.

"Where's the mare?" he said.

"Just coming round."

No mistaking her; fine as a star, shiny-coated, sinuous, her blazed face held rather high! Who said she was shelly? She was a picture! He walked a few paces close to the boy.

"That's Calliope . . . H'm! . . . Nice filly! . . . Looks fit. . . . Who's this James Shrewin? . . . What's she at? . . . I like her looks."

His horse! Not a prettier filly in the world!

He followed Polman into her stall to see her saddled. In the twilight there he watched her toilet—the rub-over, the exact adjustments, the bottle of water to the mouth, the buckling of the bridle —watched her head high above the boy keeping her steady with gentle pulls of a rein in each hand held out a little wide, and now and then stroking her blazed nose; watched her pretense of nipping at his hand. He watched the beauty of her, exaggerated in this half-lit isolation away from the others, the life and litheness in her satin body, the willful expectancy in her bright soft eyes.

Run a bye! This bit o' blood—this bit o' fire! This horse of his! Deep within that shell of blue cloth against the stall partition a thought declared itself: "I'm damned if she shall! She can beat the lot!"

The door was thrown open, and she was led out. He moved alongside. They were staring at her, following her. No wonder! She was a picture, his horse—his. She had gone to Jimmy's head.

They passed Jenning with Diamond Stud waiting to be mounted. Jimmy shot him a look. Let the—wait!

His mare reached the palings and was halted. Jimmy saw the short square figure of her jockey, in the new magenta cap and jacket —his cap, his jacket! Beautiful they looked, and no mistake!

"A word with you," he said.

The jockey halted, looked quickly round.

"All right, Mr. Shrewin. I know."

Jimmy's eyes smoldered at him. Hardly moving his lips he said intently: "You damn well don't! You'll ride her to win. Never mind him! If you don't, I'll have you off the turf. Understand me! You'll damn well ride 'er to win."

The jockey's jaw dropped.

"All right, Mr. Shrewin."

"See it is!" said Jimmy with a hiss.

"Mount, jockeys!"

He saw magenta swing into the saddle. And suddenly, as if smitten with the plague, he scuttled away.

He scuttled to where he could see them going down—seventeen. No need to search for his colors; they blazed. Like George Pulcher's countenance, or a rhododendron bush in sunlight, above that bright chestnut with the white nose, curvetting a little as she was led past.

Now they came cantering—Deerstalker in the lead.

"He's a hell of a horse, Deerstalker," said someone behind.

Jimmy cast a nervous glance around. No sign of George Pulcher!

One by one they cantered past, and he watched them with a cold feeling in his stomach.

The same voice said, "New colors! Well, you can see 'em; and the mare too. She's a showy one. Calliope? She's goin' back in the bettin' though."

Jimmy moved up through the Ring.

"Four to one on the field!" "Six Deerstalker!" "Sevens Magistrate!" "Ten to one Wasp!" "Ten to one Calliope!" "Four to one Diamond Stud!" "Four to one on the field!"

Steady as a rock, that horse of Jenning's, and his own going back!

"Twelves Calliope!" he heard just as he reached the stand. The telepathic genius of the Ring missed nothing—almost!

A cold shiver went through him. What had he done by his words to Docker? Spoiled the golden egg laid so carefully? But perhaps she couldn't win, even if they let her! He began to mount the stand, his mind in the most acute confusion.

A voice said, "Hullo, Jimmy! Is she going to win?"

One of his young Oxford sparks was jammed against him on the stairway!

He raised his lip in a sort of snarl, and, huddling himself, slipped through and up ahead. He came out and edged in close to the stairs, where he could get play for his glasses. Behind him one of those who improve the shining hour among backers cut off from opportunity was intoning the odds a point shorter than below: "Three to one on the field!" "Fives Deerstalker." "Eight to *one* Wasp."

"What price Calliope?" said Jimmy sharply.

"Hundred to eight."

"Done!" Handing him the eight, he took the ticket. Behind him the man's eyes moved fishily, and he resumed his incantation:

"Three to one on the field. Three to one on the field. Six to one Magistrate."

On the wheeling bunch of colors at the start Jimmy trained his glasses. Something had broken clean away and come half the course—something in yellow.

"Eights Magistrate. Eight to one Magistrate," drifted up.

So they had spotted that! Precious little they didn't spot!

Magistrate was round again, and being ridden back. Jimmy rested his glasses a moment, and looked down. Swarms in the Cheap Ring. Tattersalls, the Stands—a crowd so great you could lose George Pulcher in it. Just below, a little man was making silent signals with his arms across to someone in the Cheap Ring. Jimmy raised his glasses. In line now—magenta third from the rails!

"They're off!"

The hush, you could cut it with a knife! Something in green away on the right—Wasp! What a bat they were going! And a sort of numbness in Jimmy's mind cracked suddenly; his glasses shook; his thin weasly face became suffused, and quivered. Magenta—magenta—two from the rails! He could make no story of the race such as he would read in tomorrow's paper—he could see nothing but magenta.

Out of the dip now, and coming fast—green still leading—something in violet, something in tartan, closing.

"Wasp's beat!" "The favorite—the favorite wins!" "Deerstalker wins!" "What's that in pink on the rails?"

It was in pink on the rails! Behind him a man went suddenly mad.

"Deerstalker—come on with 'im, Stee! Deerstalker'll win—Deer stalker!"

Jimmy sputtered venomously: "Will 'e? Will 'e?"

Deerstalker and his own out from the rest—opposite the Cheap Ring—neck and neck—Docker riding like a demon.

"Deerstalker! Deerstalker!" "Calliope wins! She wins!"

His horse! They flashed past—fifty yards to go, and not a head between 'em.

"Deerstalker! Deerstalker!" "Calliope!"

He saw his mare shoot out—she'd won!

With a little queer sound he squirmed and wriggled on to the stairs. No thoughts while he squeezed, and slid, and hurried—only emotion—out of the Ring, away to the paddock. His horse!

Docker had weighed in when he reached the mare. All right! He passed with a grin. Jimmy turned almost into the body of Polman standing like an image.

"Well, Mr. Shrewin," he said to nobody, "she's won."

"Damn you!" thought Jimmy. "Damn the lot of you!" And he went up to his mare. Quivering, streaked with sweat, impatient of the gathering crowd, she showed the whites of her eyes when he put his hand up to her nose.

"Good girl!" he said, and watched her led away.

"Gawd! I want a drink!" he thought.

Gingerly, keeping a sharp lookout for Pulcher, he returned to the stand to get it, and to draw his hundred. But up there by the stairs the discreet fellow was no more. On the ticket was the name O. H. Jones, and nothing else. Jimmy Shrewin had been welshed! He went down at last in a hot temper. At the bottom of the stairway stood George Pulcher. The big man's face was crimson, his eyes ominous. He blocked Jimmy iinto a corner.

"Ah!" he said. "You little crow! What the 'ell made you speak to Docker?"

Jimmy grinned. Some new body within him stood there defiant. "She's my 'orse," he said.

"You Gawd-forsaken rat! If I 'ad you in a quiet spot I'd shake the life out of you!"

Jimmy stared up, his little spindle legs apart, like a cock sparrow confronting an offended pigeon.

"Go 'ome," he said, "George Pulcher, and get your mother to mend your socks. You don't know 'ow! Thought I wasn't a man, did you? Well, now, you damn well know I am. Keep off my 'orse in future."

Crimson rushed up on crimson in Pulcher's face; he raised his heavy fists. Jimmy stood, unmoving, his little hands in his bellcoat pockets, his withered face upraised. The big man gulped as if swallowing back the tide of blood; his fists edged forward and then—dropped.

"That's better," said Jimmy. "Hit one of your own size."

Emitting a deep growl, George Pulcher walked way.

"Two to one on the field—I'll back the field. Two to one on field."
"Threes Snowdrift—Fours Iron Dock."

Jimmy stood a moment mechanically listening to the music of his life; then, edging out, he took a fly and was driven to the station.

All the way up to town he sat chewing his cheroot with the glow of drink inside him, thinking of that finish, and of how he had stood up to George Pulcher. For a whole day he was lost in London, but Friday saw him once more at his seat of custom in the Corn. Not having laid against his horse, he had had a good race in spite of everything; yet, the following week, uncertain into what further quagmires of quixotry she might lead him, he sold Calliope.

But for years, betting upon horses that he never saw, underground like a rat, yet never again so accessible to the kicks of fortune, or so prone before the shafts of superiority, he would think of the Downs with the blinkin' larks singin', and talk of how once he—had a horse.

The White Horse Mystery

ALICE ALISON LIDE

LIBBA AND KATHY, like lots of other girls of many years ago, wore high-necked dresses, long black stockings, side-button shoes, and hair braided in long plaits with big ribbon bows on the ends. But they really were a rollicking pair! The fun they had wading in the creek or making peep shows with bits of grass and flowers!

In Greendale District, where they lived, there was just one single solitary automobile. But if autos were a rarity, horses were quite plentiful. Daddy Brown, the girls' father, had a stable lot full of horses and mules that plowed the land on his farm. Grandpa Brown, on the next-door farm, had mules and horses, too.

And now, thrilling event, Libba and Kathy were to have a horse of their very own! Daddy had already got them a little buggy to ride in. Grandpa Brown, who was giving them the horse, had bought it from a gypsy—for gypsies were great traders, buying stock in one section and trading it in the next. The two girls had perched perilously on the very top of the high rail fence to enjoy every exciting moment of the horse-buying. Here into Grandpa's side yard had come Gypsy John, a swarthy fellow with gold rings in his ears and a red kerchief knotted about his head. He led a beautiful silvery white horse that limped on a forefoot.

"Heem gooda horse," said the swarthy one, with a grin and a toss of his turbaned head. "I sell heem for just feefty dollar. Heem soon no more limp. Heem gooda horse for the leetla ladies . . ." he jingled his earrings in the direction of the girls. "So gentle, even a babee could ride. But one thing only, never, never, never hit heem with the whip!"

Grandpa Brown, who knew horses and was a good trader, too, looked well at hoofs, teeth, eyes. He stroked the shoulder, felt the leg muscles, and eventually traded forty dollars cash, a goat, a wagon wheel, a pair of hens, and a setting of eggs for the big white horse with the limp.

"He's ours," whispered Libba in ecstasy.

For a whole long month Grandpa Brown kept the new horse in his own pasture. When he was quite sure the limp had gone out of the leg and when he was quite sure, too, that Jehoshaphat, as the girls had named him, had no runaway habits or balky tricks, he turned him over to his owners. They were the proudest pair in the whole State of Alabama.

They had reason to be proud. Their Jehoshaphat was the sleekest, handsomest creature that ever stepped the Greendale roads. His back was so broad that when Libba and Kathy sat astride of him, their legs simply stuck straight out on either side. His coat was silvery white, his flowing mane and tail were all silvery, too. And he had the kindest, gentlest eyes that seemed to say, "You be good friends to me, and I'll be a good friend to you."

By the time autumn came the girls could drive nicely. They could put the harness on their horse, too, or back him between the shafts and harness him to their buggy. Driving themselves the three miles to school was fun. Especially since the buggy was so roomy they could pick up their friends along the way: Jessie and Martha, who would scrooge in nicely on the seat with them; the Beazley twins, who sat on two little stools backed up against the dashboard; and Billy and Ben Wright, who usually stood up on the iron steps at the sides of the buggy and held on tight.

But if going to school in the morning was fun, coming home in the afternoon was even more fun. Billy Wright said that horse was so smart he had learned to stop every time he saw a pretty flower or a thicket of haw apples or even a patch of deer-berries by the road-side. Then his passengers would hop out and entertain themselves with these delights along the way.

The real surprise about Jehoshaphat, though, came the day of the Saturday storm. That day proved there was a real mystery in Jehoshaphat's past.

Of course, nobody dreamed it was going to storm that afternoon. It just looked sort of cloudy, as if a rain were blowing up. Kathy and Libba were sure they'd have plenty of time to carry Martha home before any drops began to fall. So off they set, three girls astride the big white horse, with the lap robe across his middle for a saddle and the red halter round his neck instead of bridle and reins.

By the time they reached One-Mile Creek, though, the clouds

had massed up terribly black. A dreadful rumbling began to vibrate through the air. Then the storm burst—a hailstorm. At first just a scattering of hailstones fell. Some pattered against the girls' heads and shoulders. Then a bunch of big ones struck Jehoshaphat's fat flanks. They hit hard and sharp as whiplashes. (And the Gypsy had said one must never, never, never hit Jehoshaphat with a whip.) At the first lashing blow, Jehoshaphat reared straight up on hind legs, pawed the air with his forefeet. Right then three girls and a lap robe slid from his back to land in a huddle on the ground.

Faster, faster pounded the hailstones. The girls crouched together, pulled their hats down tight, and held the robe over their heads like a canopy. They almost forgot to be scared as they watched a very strange sight. Jehoshaphat was running, but he wasn't running away. Instead, as the hailstones tapped him, flick, flick, flick, like taps of a whip, he ran round and round, in a fine, high-stepping gallop. Every once in a while he'd leap high in the air, as though clearing some hurdle. Then thunder, like a mighty whip-crack, roared through space. It seemed to signal the big white horse to change to still another stunt. He would stand for a moment, shaking his head from side to side. Then he would begin to dance—yes, really dance! Lifting feet high, crossing them over, all in a stately way as if he were doing it in time to the grand music of horns and drums and trumpets of a circus band.

"Circus horse—a real circus horse!"

The children shouted, as the idea hit them at the same time. Their circus was finished now, however. The patter of hail changed into a downpour of rain. Jehoshaphat stopped in his tracks, then ambled over, his proud neck drooping. He rubbed his nose against the huddled group of children, as if asking forgiveness for having dumped them on the ground.

About that time there came Daddy astride Calico Bet and Grandpa on Big Black and Jim-the-hired-man on Tippy, all loaded with raincoats and umbrellas. The girls didn't really need to be rescued. They'd had the time of their lives, and talked the whole way home of their wonderful horse, their *real circus horse*.

"Circus horse . . . eh . . ." Grandpa Brown scratched an ear. "Now I wonder if that gypsy got him there . . . seems to me I do recollect that the Bergo-Hagen Consolidated shows played in Selma City just the week before I bought this white horse."

Being an honest man and not liking to harbor what might be stolen property, Grandpa Brown went right home and wrote a letter to the manager of the Bergo-Hagen Consolidated Shows. As for Kathy and

Libba, they were heartbroken. Their horse was so smart, they loved him so, and now they might have to give him up!

The days mounted into weeks, into a month, into two months. Not a word did anyone hear from the circus folk. Kathy and Libba began to take heart again. Then one springtime afternoon, the livery-stable hack from the railroad station rolled up to Grandpa's door and a lady stepped down through the door. She was Madam Zantine, she said, and she had come to see about her horse. As she talked, she pulled from her purse the letter Grandpa Brown had written so many weeks before.

Down to the pasture they went, Grandpa and Madam Zantine leading; Mother, Daddy, Jim, and two doleful girls trailing along behind. Kathy'd give a little sob, then Libba'd give a little sob, and finally they both stuffed their handkerchiefs into their mouths, for they didn't want to make too terrible a scene.

"Ah . . . my so beautiful Jo-Jo, it is . . ." cried Madam as they came to the pasture bars. She gave a shrill whistle, then an odd little quavery call. The white horse lifted his head, stood like a beautiful picture. Then he came galloping across the green, right to the gap, and thrust his head over the bars to rub lovingly against Madam's shoulder.

"The darling . . . my own Jo-Jo, the smartest of them all." Without waiting for the bars to be lowered, Madam scrambled nimbly over and stood with her arms around the neck of the big white horse.

And now, as if the pasture hadn't seen enough excitement, something even more amazing began to happen. Madam broke a long, slender willow switch, gave the white horse three taps on the flank. Like the trained circus animal that he was, the horse reared straight up on hind legs, pawed the air, and began to circle round and round in the gallop that looked so fast, but really wasn't. The beautiful Madam Zantine cast off gloves, hat, shoes. One moment she stood on the ground, the next moment, she had leaped lightly on the broad back of the galloping horse!

The circus lady rode standing. Sometimes she rode with a foot on his head, sometimes she rode facing his tail. And then, as she clapped her hands in a sharp, powerful sound, the white horse began to do his own dance—right foot, left foot, swing low. Oh, it was too beautiful!

When everybody had gone back up to the house, Grandpa Brown said, "He is yours, I can see that."

"Yes," said Madam, "at least, he once was mine. But he wasn't stolen from me . . . oh, no, indeed! The gypsy was a friend of mine.

When Jo-Jo the Dancing Horse strained a leg, I knew he couldn't hold out as a trick horse. So I sent for Gypsy John. I asked him to find a good home for my darling, a place where Jo-Jo would have

just light work to do, and where people loved their cats and dogs and cows and horses and treated them nicely. And Gypsy John, who seems to be a good judge of people as well as horses, picked the Brown family."

"You're not going to take him back?" squealed Kathy.

"He's still ours?" cried Libba.

"He certainly is still your horse," said Zantine. "I didn't come to take him away, I just wanted to see for myself that he was happy and that he was making the girls that owned him happy, too."

As Zantine stepped into the hack that was to take her back to the railroad station, she leaned down and gave Libba and Kathy each a kiss. "The broad back of my Jo-Jo, it is enticing," she said. "You will perhaps try the, oh, so fine tricks, but," her eyes twinkled, "my dears, for your necks' sake, learn the trick with the horse standing still. And for the horse's hide's sake, never, no never, ride him standing in the shoes . . . and . . . and," her voice trailed back out of the moving hack, "always, always love my Jo-Jo."

"We will!" Libba and Kathy shrieked after her.

The Ghost Horse

CHIEF BUFFALO CHILD LONG LANCE

With the first touch of spring, we broke up our Indian camp and headed southwest across the big bend of the upper Columbia, toward the plateau between the Rockies and the Cascades. It was on this high plateau that the world's largest herd of wild horses had roamed for more than a hundred and fifty years. Several hundred head of them were still there. It was these horses that we were after, to replace the herd which the storm had driven from our camp.

We struck the herd in the season of the year when it was weakest: early spring, after the horses had got their first good feed of green grass. Since these wild creatures can run to death any horse raised in captivity, it is doubly a hard job to try to ensnare them on foot. But, like wolves, wild horses are very curious animals. They will follow a person for miles out of mere curiosity. And, when chased, they will invariably turn back on their trails to see what it is all about; what their pursuers look like, what they are up to.

The method our warriors used to capture wild horses was first to locate a herd and then follow it for hours, or perhaps days, before making any attempt to round it up. This was to get the horses used to us and to show them that we would not harm them.

We had been trailing fresh tracks for five days before we finally located our first herd away up on the Couteau Plateau of central British Columbia. There, grazing away on the side of a craggy little mountain on top of the plateau, was a herd of about five hundred animals. Their quick, alert movements showed that they would dash off into space like a flock of wild birds at the slightest cause for excitement. A big steel-dust stallion ruled the herd. Our warriors directed all of their attention to him, knowing that the movements of the entire herd depended on what he did.

When we had approached to within about five hundred yards,

our braves began to make little noises, so that the horses could see us in the distance. Then they would not be taken by surprise and frightened into a stampede at seeing us suddenly at closer range.

"Hoh! Hoh!" our braves grunted softly. The steel-dust stallion uttered a low whinny, and all the herd raised their heads high into the air. Standing perfectly still, they looked at us with their big, nervous nostrils wide open. They stood looking at us for moments, without moving a muscle. Then as we came too near, the burly stallion dashed straight at us with a deep, rasping roar.

Others followed him, and on they came like a yelling war party, their heads swinging wildly, their racing legs wide apart, and their long tails lashing the ground. But before they reached us the speeding animals stiffened their legs and came to a sudden halt in a cloud of dust. While they were close they took one more good look at us. Then they turned and scampered away.

But the big steel-dust stallion stood his ground alone for a moment and openly defied us. He dug his front feet into the dirt far out in front of him, and wagged his head furiously. Then he stopped long enough to see what effect his antics were having upon us. He blazed fire at us through the whites of his turbulent, flint-colored eyes. Having displayed his courage and defiance, he turned and pranced off, with heels flying so high and so lightly that one could almost imagine he was treading air.

Our braves laughed and said, "Ah, ponokamita, vain elkdog, you are a brave warrior. But trot along and have patience. We shall yet ride you against the Crows."

For five days we chased this big herd of horses, traveling along leisurely behind them. We knew that they would not wander far, and that they would watch us like wolves as long as we were near.

By the fifth day they had become so used to us that they merely moved along slowly when we approached them, nibbling the grass as they walked. All during this time our braves had been taming them by their subtle method. At first they just grunted, but now they were dancing and shouting at them. This was to let the horses know that, although men could make a lot of noise and act fiercely, he would not harm them.

On the tenth night of our chase our warriors made their final preparations to capture the herd. They had maneuvered the horses into the vicinity of a huge half-natural corral which they had built of logs against the two sides of a rock-bound gulch. From the entrance of this corral they had built two long fences, forming a runway, which gradually widened as it left the gate of the corral. This funnel-shaped entrance fanned out into the plateau for more than half a mile, and was cleverly hidden with evergreens.

The mouth at the outer end of the runway was about one hundred yards wide. From this point on, the runway was further extended and opened up by placing big tree tops, stones, and logs along the ground for several hundred yards. This was to direct the herd slowly into the mouth of the fenced part of the runway. Once wedged inside, the horses would be trapped; and the only thing left for them to do would be to keep on going toward the corral gate.

There was subdued excitement in our hidden camp on this tenth night of our chase, for it was the big night, when we would "blow-in" the great, stubborn herd of wild horses. No one went to bed. Shortly before nightfall more than half of our braves quietly slipped out of our camp and disappeared. According to prearranged directions, they fanned out to the right and left in a northerly route. They crept noiselessly toward the place where the herd had disappeared that afternoon. All during the early night we heard wolves, arctic owls, night hawks, or panthers crying out in the mystic darkness of the rugged plateau. These were the signals of our men, informing one another of their movements.

Then, about midnight, everything became deathly quiet. We knew that our braves had located the herd and surrounded it. They were now lying on the ground, awaiting the first streaks of dawn and the signal to start the drive.

One of our subchiefs, Chief Mountain Elk, went through our camp, quietly giving instructions for all hands to line themselves along the great runway to "beat in" the herd. Every woman, old person, and child in the camp was called to take part in this part of the drive. We children and the women crept to the runway and sprawled along the outside of the fence. The men went beyond the fenced part of the runway and concealed themselves behind the brush and logs, where it was more dangerous.

We crouched on the ground and shivered quietly for an hour or more before we heard a distant "Ho-h! . . . Ho-h!" It was the muffled driving cry of our warriors, the cry which they had been uttering to the horses for ten days. Thus, the horses did not stampede, as they would have done had they not recognized this noise in the darkness of the night.

We youngsters lay breathless in expectancy. We had all picked out our favorite mounts in this beautiful herd of wild animals. We felt like the white boy lying in bed waiting for Santa Claus. Our fathers had all promised us that we should have the ponies that we had picked, and we could hardly wait. My favorite was a calico pony, a beautiful roan with three colors splashed on his shoulders and flanks like a crazy-quilt of exquisite design. He had a red star on his forehead between his eyes. I had already named him Naytukskie-Kukatos, which in Blackfoot means One Star.

Presently we heard the distant rumble of horses' hoofs—a dull booming which shook the ground on which we lay. Then, Yip-yip-yip, he-heeh-h-h," came the night call of the wolf from many different directions. It was our braves signaling to one another to keep the herd on the right path. From out of this medley of odd sounds we could hear the mares going, "Wheeeee-hagh-hagh," calling their colts.

Our hearts began to beat fast when we heard the first loud "Yah! Yah! Yah!" We knew that the herd had now entered the brush portion of the runway and that our warriors were jumping up from their hiding-place. They made fierce noises in order to stampede the horses and send them racing headlong into our trap.

Immediately there was a loud thunder of hoofs. Horses were crying and yelling. Above the din we heard one loud, full, deep-chested roar which we all recognized. It sounded something like the roar of a lion. It was the steel-dust stallion, furious king of the herd. In our imagination we could see his long silver tail thrown over his back, his legs lashing apart, and the whites of those terrible eyes glistening. We wondered what he would do if he should crash through that fence into our midst.

But now he came, leading his raging herd, and we had no more time to think about danger. Our job was to lie still and wait until the lead stallion had passed us. Then we were to jump to the top of the fence and yell and wave fiercely. This was to keep the maddened herd from crashing the fence and to hasten them into our trap.

"Therump, therump, therump." On came the storming herd. As we youngsters peeped through the brush-covered fence, we could see their sleek backs bobbing up and down in the starlit darkness like great billows of raging water. The turbulent stallion was leading them with front feet wide apart and his forehead sweeping the ground like a pendulum. His death-dealing heels were swinging to the right and left with each savage leap of his mighty frame.

Once he stopped and tried to breast the oncoming herd, but it struck and knocked him forward with terrific force. He rose from his knees, and uttered a fearful bellow of defiance. The herd that had watched his very ears for their commands was now running wildly over him.

I believe that, if at that moment there had been a solid iron wall in front of that stallion, he would have dashed his brains out against it. I remember looking back into the darkness for a convenient place to hop, if he should suddenly choose to rush headlong into the noise that was driving him wild with helpless rage. I heard a whistling sound, and as I looked back to the runway I saw the steel-dust king stretching himself past us like a huge greyhound. With each incredible leap, his breath shrieked like a whistle.

No one will ever know why he so suddenly broke away from his herd. But on he went, leaving the other horses behind like a deer leaving a bunch of coyotes. A few seconds later the rest of the herd came booming past. I had never seen so many horses before. We stuck to our posts until it was nearly daylight, and still they came straggling along.

When we climbed down from the fence and went to the corral at daylight, we saw four of our best warriors lying bleeding and unconscious. When our mothers asked what was the matter, someone pointed to the corral, and said, "Ponokomita—akai—mahkahpay!" ("That very bad horse!")

We saw a dozen men trying to put leather on that wild steel-dust stallion. With his heavy moon-colored mane bristling over his bluish head and shoulders, he looked more like a lion than a horse. His teeth were bared like a wolf's. Four men had tried to get down into the corral and throw rawhide around his neck. While the other wild horses had scurried away to the corners of the corral, this ferocious beast of a horse had plunged headlong into them and all but killed them before they could be dragged away.

He had proved to be a rare kind of horse—a killer. A man might live a hundred years among horses without ever seeing one of those hideous freaks of the horse world. He had already killed two of his own herd there in our corral.

Our braves were taking no more chances with him. They were high up on top of the seven-foot corral fence, throwing their rawhide lariats in vain attempt to neck the beast. He would stand and watch the rawhide come twirling through the air. Then, just as it was about to swirl over his head, he would duck his shaggy neck and remain standing defiantly on the spot.

It was finally decided to corner him with firebrands and throw a partition between him and the rest of the herd. Then our braves could get busy cutting out the best of the other animals, before turning the rest loose. This was done, and by nightfall we had captured and hobbled two hundred of the best horses in the Northwest.

The next day our braves began breaking the wild horses to halter. They used the Indian method, which is very simple. While four men held a stout rawhide rope which was noosed around the animal's neck, another man would approach the horse's head gradually, "talking horse."

"Horse talk" is a low grunt which seems to charm a horse and make him stand perfectly still for a moment or so at a time. It ssounds like "Hoh-Hoh," uttered deep down in one's chest. The horse will stop his rough antics and strain motionless on the rope for a few seconds. While he is doing this and looking straight at the approaching figure, the man will wave a blanket at him and hiss, "Shuh! Shuh!" It takes about fifteen minutes of this to show the horse that no motion or sound which the man makes will harm him.

When the man has reached the head of the horse, his hardest job is to give him the first touch of man's hand. Of this the horse seems to have a deathly fear. The man maneuvers for several minutes before he gets a finger on the struggling nose. Then he rubs it and allows the horse to get his smell or scent. When this has been done, the brave loops a long, narrow string of rawhide around the horse's nose. He carries it up behind the ears, brings it down on the other side, and slips it under the other side of the nose loop. This makes something like a loose-knotted halter which will tighten up on the slightest pull from the horse.

This string is no stronger than a shoe-lace. Yet, once the warrior has put it on the horse's head, he tells the other men to let go the strong rawhide thong. From then on he alone handles the horse with the small piece of string held lightly in one hand. Whenever the horse makes a sudden pull on the string, it grips certain nerves around the nose and back of the ears. This either stuns him or hurts him so badly that he doesn't try to pull again.

With the horse held this way, the warrior now stands in front of him and strokes the front of his face and hisses at him at close range. It is the same noise that a person makes to drive away chickens—"shuh, shuh"—and perhaps the last sound an untrained person would venture to use in tamng a wild, ferocious horse. Yet it is the quickest way of gaining a horse's confidence.

When the warrior has run his fingers over every inch of the horse's head and neck, he starts to approach his shoulders and flanks with his fingers. The horse will start to jump about again, but a couple of sharp jerks on the string stop him. As he stands trembling with fear, the warrior slowly runs his hand over his left side. When this is finished he stands back and takes a blanket and strikes all of the portions of his body that he has touched. With each stroke of the blanket, he shouts, "Shuh!"

When he has repeated this on the other side of the horse, he starts to do his legs. Each leg, beginning with his left front leg, must be gone over by the warrior's hand, with not an inch of its surface escaping his touch. This is the most ticklish part of the work; for the horse's feet are his deadly weapons. But two more jerks on the string quiet the horse's resentment. Within another fifteen minutes every inch of the horse's body has been touched and rubbed.

Now, there is just one other thing to do, and that is to accustom the horse to a man hopping on his back and riding him. This is done in about five minutes.

The warrior takes the blanket and strikes the horse's back a number of blows. Then he lays the blanket gently on his back. The horse will at first start to buck it off, but another jerk on the string, and he is quieted. The warrior picks the blanket up and lays it across his back again. The horse will jump out from under it, perhaps twice, before he will stand still. When he has been brought to this point, the man throws the blanket down and walks slowly to the side of the horse and places both hands on his back and presses down lightly. He keeps pressing a little harder and harder, until finally he places his elbows across the horse's back and draws his body an inch off the ground. A horse may jump a little, but he will stand still the next time.

After the warrior has hung on his back by his elbows for several periods of about thirty seconds each, he will gradually pull himself up, up, up. Finally he is ready to throw his right foot over to the other side. It is a strange fact that few horses broken in this manner ever try to buck. Usually the horse will stand perfectly still. The man will sit there and stroke him for a moment and then gently urge him to go. Then the horse will awkwardly trot off in a mild, aimless amble, first this way and that. He appears so bewildered and uncertain in his gait that one would think it was the first time he had ever tried to walk on his own feet.

Four months after we had captured the horses we were again back on our beloved plains in upper Montana. Our horses were the envy of every tribe who saw us that summer. They all wanted to know where we got them. Our chief told the story of this wild-horse hunt so many times that it became a legend among the Indians.

But at the end of the story our venerable leader would always look downcast. In sadly measured words, he would tell of the steel-dust stallion with the flowing moon-colored mane and tail, which he had picked out for himself. He would spend many minutes describing this superb horse, yet he would never finish the story, unless someone asked him what became of the animal.

Then he would slowly tell how our band had worked all day trying to rope this beast, and how that night they had left him in the little fenced-off part of the corral. But the next morning when they visited the corral, he had vanished. The horse had climbed over more than seven feet of fence which separated him from the main corral. There, with room for a running start, he attacked the heavy log fence and rammed his body clear through it. Nothing was left to tell the tale but a few patches of blood and hair and a wrecked fence.

That should have ended the story of the steel-dust beast, but it did not. The horse became famous throughout the Northwest as a lone traveler of the night. He went down on the plains of Montana and Alberta, and in the darkest hours of the night he would turn up at the most unexpected points in the wilderness of the prairies. He had lost his mighty bellow. And no person heard a sound from him again. He haunted the plains by night, and was never seen by day.

This silent, lone traveler of the night was often seen silhouetted against the moon on a butte, with his head erect, his tail thrown over his back. The steel-blue color of his body melted completely into the inky blueness of the night. His tail and mane stood out in the moonlight like shimmering threads of lighted silver, giving him a halo which had a ghostly aspect. He became known throughout the Northwest as the Shunkatonka-Wakan—The Ghost Horse.

Pool of Sand

CHARLOTTE EDWARDS

WHEN Dan Mangren left Bend Hollow one early sunny morning in 1873, he was two months short of his nineteenth birthday. His dream was three months over six years old.

A small crowd collected to watch his leave-taking. They made no special noise about it. They were still sleepy. It was easier to lean against a near post with their shoulder blades than to stand up straight. It was simpler just to look than to do any vocal funning.

Anyhow, only three of them really got up for the occasion. The rest were there by accident, not caring much, if at all. The three cared, though.

Dan's mother, fixing the heavy breakfast, helping him stow the extra food and water on Bonnie's already overloaded back, showed her concern with butterfly sighs, gone as she was beyond arguing any more.

Old Man Pike, never one to give up easily, fussed and chattered. "Fool thing to do, boy like you. Give up all you know. Reach out for whatever." The tobacco juice arched a dark-golden rainbow in the morning light and hit against the dust before the stable with a hiss. "Stubborn crazy young 'un. You'll kill the pony—half kill yourself, and all the time there's that spread you could buy down by the river——"

Dan went about his readying. He tried not to hear the words, so many times slammed into his ears, nor the sighs. In his mind a phrase repeated itself, insulation against them all. *Don't touch my dream. Don't touch my dream.*

It worked fine until Bonnie was saddled, the tarpaulin was pulled tight and cinched over the extra saddle on her rump. Dan was ready to lift himself up—to begin. To plod on the pony out of the town of Bend Hollow, down the familiar paths, beyond them toward the mountains to the north, and over them. Then he looked at Nora.

The amount of Nora's caring was written sharp and clear in her blue eyes. It was told in the special way she had combed her dark straight hair and piled it high, and the fact that her best yellow dress was on her, ribboned and belted and fresh, a reminder of the picnic by the river.

Dan touched his hard stomach where the money was tied close and hidden, enough to buy the spread by the river. He stared down at Nora, and his chest lumped his breath. He put out his hand. "Be happy," he said. It was as if you told a hurt child to stop crying pronto.

Nora put her hand into his. It was cold despite the sun. It did not touch heavily or cling at all. But Dan somehow knew that the feel of it would stay with him across the desert, over the mountains and right into California. Then Nora was gone, slipped from his fingers.

His mother's sighs thickened to sobs. She rushed at him. Her good solid arms were around him, wanting to hang on forever.

"Ma," he begged. "Ma. Please."

She grabbed a long breath, kissed him quickly and backed away.

Dan mounted Bonnie. "Well," he managed, "so long, all."

Old Man Pike kept his eyes on the ground. "Fool boy," he muttered. "Fool kid. Good luck."

Dan pulled sharp on Bonnie. They turned their backs to Bend Hollow, to ma, Nora, Old Man Pike, the stables, the spread, the greenness. Over Bonnie's steady hoofbeats there was the sound of a mild hurrah, the sleepy ones coming for a moment to life, to cheer young Dan Mangren on his way.

On my way. On my way.

It was the rhythm of his first thoughts, there alone with his pony, heading out of town. It became the rhythm of Bonnie's trot, as they passed the bank, the saloon, the church, the scattering of houses on the outskirts. It stayed for a pair of hours. It left no room for other thinking.

At the end of that time the excitement began. It tickled in his stomach at first, almost like being hungry, although Dan knew he had stashed away enough of ma's food to last him the day. Then it ran into his chest and began to blow up, until every breath was filtered with joy and like no breathing he had done before. He looked around him. The view had a strangeness, although he had ridden this far before. He'd been as much as a day's journey away from Bend Hol-

low many times. The strangeness was in his own looking—that was it.
He was seeing it free. It was country passed through to reach the
new, not just to ride, camp and go back to Bend Hollow.

It seemed to him that he was standing still. The trees on either
side of the wagon road moved past him. Bend Hollow retreated,
back and back away from him and Bonnie and the canvas-covered
extra saddle. Old Man Pike and ma and Nora got smaller and smaller
there behind him. The mountains, vaguely seen and looming gray
across the desert flats, stayed small and retreated too. Dan Mangren
and Bonnie held still between the moving two of them, large, more
than life-size. Dream-size and free.

He rode all day, staring and tranced. Occasionally he patted Bonnie's neck, saying nothing, not whistling or singing, just riding steadily, in no hurry now it had begun, tiring neither himself nor the pony.
By dusk he had gone farther than he had ever been before.

He dismounted and pulled the heavy tarpaulin bulk from Bonnie's rump, setting it carefully beneath a tree. He yanked her own
worn saddle off, smoothed her down, led her with him to the sound
of a stream. They drank, the two of them, friends for years, with relish
which was mutual and understood.

Very neatly and carefully then he tied Bonnie to the tree, laid out
his slicker and bedroll and built a small fire. He fed himself and
gave Bonnie one of ma's carrots. Then he lay down, warm in the roll,
and fell instantly asleep before he could watch for the stars as he had
meant to.

The second morning was the real beginning. To cook and eat and
saddle up in an unknown place, to take off from there for another unknown place, blotted Bend Hollow from his mind. The three who
waved good-by to him were three in a book, unreal and imagined.

The land began to change. The greenness shifted to tan. The trees
grew sparse and altered their shapes, turned bare and clutched, blown
to odd, deformed shapes by many winds. Under Bonnie's hoofs the
trail stayed wide, sand packed hard by unnumbered hoofs, by wagon
trains, express, coaches, all of the travel into Bend Hollow which
Dan had watched the full years of his growing, back there ever since
his father died, working in Old Man Pike's stables.

There had been the wheels to fix and tired horses to feed and
curry. There had been the strong hard-bitten men to serve and listen
to. There had been the families and canvas to fasten tight on covered
wagons. All of Old Man Pike's business, all work in the stable, was
preparation for this trail, the last long hard haul toward the mountains, over them, the drop down into the golden land of California.

From the South and the East they came into Bend Hollow. To the North and the West they went out of Bend Hollow. They stopped only long enough to drink—too much, some of them. Pray in the little church, others of them. Eat of ma's cooking at the Holly House. Flirt with Nora at the stables. Make fun of Dan at his tooling. And go on and ahead and find the gold or the easy rich earth.

A couple of them didn't make fun of him, though. Couple of them, seeing what he was working at and how it was turning out, offered him money for the saddle. Dan wouldn't discuss it. He clutched his dream tight, went about his business and they didn't get an answer, nor a rise.

One of them tried, a big fat guy with jollity on his cheeks and meanness in his eyes. He said, "This your pony, boy?" He yanked Bonnie's scanty mane.

Dan stood up fast. "Leave her alone."

"Glad to, glad to." The man walked over to the saddle in the far corner where Dan had set up the low flat table, two pieces of wood nailed onto a pair of cut logs. He ran his hand over the rich carved leather. He laughed sharply.

"Thousand-dollar saddle on a twenty-buck horse," he snorted.

Dan looked quickly at Bonnie. She was smart. Sometimes he thought she understood talking better than most people. Better than this fat one, for instance. "Leave that alone too," he commanded.

The man squinted his eyes. "I'll give you two hundred cash for it. More money than you'll ever see, bub."

Dan shook his head. The fat man didn't know anything, except a good saddle when he saw it.

He didn't know about Bend Hollow, for one thing. The way Dan figured it, every town that size had to have somebody to make fun of. Ma was proud of him; Nora was fierce in his defense; Old Man Pike gave him a place in the stables and was gentle with him.

But most everybody else, watching him talk more to horses than to humans, seeing him brush them as lovingly as you'd brush a baby's hair, or looking at him back there in the far corner of the stable working on his saddle, got in the habit of laughing about him.

Dan didn't mind. He didn't even hear it much, tangled as he was in his dreaming. So long as Old Man Pike paid him regularly and he could give ma what was right to help out, so long as there was some left to save in the bank, safe, with a slip to prove it, he didn't mind what anybody said. You get patient with a dream.

From the far edge of the stable Dan could get the most light. Each day when everything Old Man Pike asked of him and the horses needed of him was finished, he went to the corner and pulled the tarpaulin off the saddle.

There was a way the sun walked itself proud from the high window to wash the leather with a shimmer that never failed to set his heart going. It was as if the sun spooned gold into every runnel, every fine curl, every minute lift and swirl of his tooling. The whole saddle seemed to glisten, molten and rippling.

Dan didn't have the words for it. He was a quiet boy turned to silent man. But he had the feel of it. It kept him going, late each afternoon and all day after church on Sunday.

Old Man Pike didn't care. "On your own time, lad," he said when Dan first asked the favor. "You do as you like so long as it isn't carousing. I don't take to carousing, especially with Nora around."

Dan had answered him shortly. "I got no money for that sort of thing, and no taste." It satisfied them both.

And Bend Hollow and Old Man Pike and all of them knew about the saddle. But nobody, nobody but Bonnie, knew about the dream. Until the moment of its coming true. Which was now.

His thoughts had taken him to the high of the sun. It burned down on his shoulders. Bonnie moved with a slight unsteadiness, as if she, too, felt the weight of the great gleaming ball above them, pushing on her loaded back.

Dan slipped to the ground. The sand slid loose under his boots. He took out the canteen and drank from it with care. He moistened Bonnie's mouth, then poured some of the water into the canvas bucket and held it close to her muzzle. She drank daintily and carefully.

He looked around him. The trees had turned, as if by magic, into stumps and bushes. They spread, punctuated by an occasional Joshua, as far as he could see. Beyond them the mountains, during the morning of his thinking, had opened themselves out like a full accordion, rimming the horizon, floating, shifting a little from the heat rising off the desert, fluid and graceful.

The trail marched straight ahead of him, discernible in its brighter tan. Dan scanned it. As far as he could see there was no movement, no small approaching dot of horseman or wagon or coach.

In the place where the tickle of excitement had attacked him, another sensation began to grow—loose, sagging, empty as the spot it tried to fill. Dan couldn't put a name to it, but he didn't feel larger than life-size any more, nor did Bonnie seem that way. He felt squeezed down to littleness, and alone and lonely, with nobody ahead of him on the trail.

He labeled it hunger, having no better word. He and Bonnie rested beside one of the larger bushes with its thin layer of dusty shade. He ate of ma's prepared bundle of food. It was cold fried chicken, heated to grease and warmness from the sun, but good enough. For a moment ma's twisted face and butterfly sighs rippled through his mind. Then he was up again and they were on their way. Thing to do in the desert, the hard-bitten men and the covered-wagon families always said, was to keep moving: "Slow, steady but moving. One day, today. Another day, tomorrow. Third day, by nightfall, to the foothills on this trail. Shortest, surest, safest, quickest, boy. You can't miss the pass."

The hours of the afternoon rode steadily toward the mountains. It would do to think of Nora now, maybe. She was far enough back there, her yellow dress blended with the harsh tan of the desert, her blue eyes lost in this place where there was no blue water. It was time, maybe, to think about the picnic.

The hamper was big and hand-woven. Nora had filled it with things which proved what a good wife she could be. The minute she set out the high-piled fluted pie, Dan knew what she was about. He held the knowledge tenderly, but he backed it with stubbornness, like a wall set firm before a rose garden. All the same it was a good day.

The grass was soft as a wool blanket for their sitting. The river down the slant of the pasture spoke words they both understood. Nora's hand was in his. After a time her head was on his shoulder. After another time, as natural as breath, their close faces turned to meet. Her lips were like roses, all right. Soft and cool and fragrant.

The weakness went all through him, and the wall of his dream cracked a little to let her in. He began to talk.

Suddenly then, with the greatest of ease and no strangeness, he was a boy again. There was once more the scratch of the sprawled tree limbs outside of his bedroom window, the feeling against his lids of a pale sun struggling its way through thick dark-green leaves.

Beside his bunk bed, put there by his father, lugging it on shoulders as broad as a good fireplace log, was the new saddle. The leather smell was all through the small room, seeping into his sleep, turning his lips up to a smile and setting the dream for the first time, and deeply, into his mind.

"Someday, lad," his father said on that twelfth birthday, "someday we'll trick the saddle up, carve it worth its leather. We'll buy you a horse, a strong big Arabian from the land of California——"

A white horse. An Arabian. Flying. With a mane like silk in the wind. Proud and white. A saddle on his back. A carved lifetime saddle on his proud back. And Dan up there high, higher than he had ever sat Bonnie, faster than he had ever ridden. A new Dan Mangren. Worth his saddle. Worth his horse. Worth his father.

It was where his father came from, California. *Did he go back there somehow,* Dan used to wonder when he set the first swirls of design into the leather, *to ride a white horse forever after he was dead?*

"So," he finished, not looking at Nora, run-down and spent from revealing the dream, "the saddle is finished. There's no more room for tooling. I have enough money, with what Bonnie will bring in California."

He stood up and walked slowly toward the river. He felt shy and naked with the dream bared to the daylight, no longer his alone.

After a while he felt her there beside him. "And when you have the Arabian? When the saddle is on the white horse and all of your savings are gone, Dan, what will you do then?"

He shook his head and was impatient with the woman of it. How could you look beyond a dream?

Nora said, "I know what it will be. You'll have the saddle and the horse to match it. Next, you'll want a girl to match, in a satin dress from a big house. You will be at it all of your life, Dan." She sounded as if she had tears in her throat.

Dan still didn't look at her. *Don't touch my dream,* he thought; *don't touch it.* But regret ate at him that he had spoken the words.

She went away from him and packed the leftovers in the hamper. She stood for a long time after he joined her, quiet and different, as if their lips had never touched. She looked over the spread and listened to the river. Then she ran her hand up and down Bonnie's muzzle. "Poor girl," she said to Bonnie, as if they were both human and women.

When Dan was back in the stable he went directly to the saddle. He uncovered it. But it was late in the day, and no sun came to the back of the place to set gold in its leather. For a moment it looked dull and without life. He put the canvas back quickly and went early to bed.

Three days later, and two days ago, Nora's hand slipped from his, and Bend Hollow slipped from him. It seemed as if a hundred years had slipped by too.

A thing was happening, he noticed, brought back to himself and Bonnie by her slight nicker. Over the desert, as far as he could see, little puffs of dust lifted and whirled like tumbleweed. He felt no wind direct upon him, but the loose sand knew the breeze and frisked with it.

Each puff, wherever he looked, had the purple cast of early evening. The trail ahead of him seemed strangely narrower, as if it tightened itself to make a more rugged way into the foothills, ready to curl through the mountains.

Bonnie made the slight noise again, a whimper like a sigh. Then, crashing down upon them both, integrating the dust puffs, aligning them into waves of sand swirling in all directions, came the sudden wind.

Dan was immediately blinded by it. He pulled down his hat and lowered his head as Bonnie's was lowered before him. The steady stream of wind and sand pushed against them both, savagely plastering his clothes to his skin and whipping them like pennants behind his back.

What should have been a long slow desert twilight was brown midnight. What should have been a sight of mountains was fuzzed out into sheets of sand. What should have been a trail was quickly, shockingly, covered over, thick-piled as blown snow on an open town street.

Bonnie struggled and made no progress. Dan pulled out a bandanna and tied it over the lower part of his face. He reached his hand to touch the harsh hair on the pony's head. He talked to her, the words refusing to strain themselves through the bandanna. But Bonnie heard him. He felt the twitch of her wind-flattened ears.

There were no trees. If there were bushes for shelter Dan could not see them. There was nothing to do but try to move blindly forward, hoping the wind would die with the same suddenness with which it had been born.

The night was endless, black and wailing. Toward what must have been the end of it, Bonnie squealed, tripped, sprawled. Pony, saddles, gear and man were tossed on the sharp, moving sand.

Dan didn't know how long he lay there, but at last he earned strength enough to reach toward the pony. He loosened the ropes that held the tooled saddle, fingering for them from memory. He scurried his hands around in the sand, trying to pull toward him the unseen circle of the canteen which was to be tomorrow's water.

With the lightening of the load, Bonnie struggled to her feet. She stood patient and still, hunched against the wind and the stinging sand. Dan, on hands and knees now, no dream in him, only fear and a great loneliness, scratched at an ever-widening crescent, tearing his hands on hidden bits of rock, in his search for the canteen.

When it came against his fingers relief was so sweet in him that he curled—a twelve-year-old boy again—around the canteen on the sand. He fell instantly asleep in the wind and the noise, as if there were sheets above him and below.

He woke to stillness, twice as loud as yesterday. Bonnie stood over him, making shade against the midmorning sun. The first thing Dan noticed, eyes opening stickily and painfully, was the gash and the bruise on her right knee. The second thing he knew with full consciousness was that the canteen had dribbled in his arms, its cap loosened, leaving only a precious damp spot on his shirt.

Once on his feet, not allowing himself to feel anything, swallowing down all emotion, he pulled on aching muscles to make himself tall and a man again. He saw that the trail was gone, covered over in hummocks and drifts. The mountains were there, though—pink, pale purple, unbelievably high and mocking.

He dug frantically around the place of their fall. He came upon the saddle and put his arms around it for an unmeasured length of time. A little more digging turned up the wind-blown tarpaulin. He scraped clear the place, which revealed the bedroll and the slicker with its hoard of food. He pushed sand from the biscuits, gave one to Bonnie and together they munched, swallowing harshly, trying to muster saliva.

The pony nickered dryly in her throat. Dan ran his hand gently over the bruise and the gash. He took his extra shirt from the roll, shredded it and wrapped it around Bonnie's knee. With great effort he lifted the carved saddle to her rump and fastened it once agan. He added the bedroll and the slicker. Then he picked up the reins and began to lead her. The weight of the extra saddle behind the shabby cinched one was all the sore knee and the caked breath of the animal could bear. Bonnie could not hold the weight of a man.

As the sun went higher and the mountains drew no nearer and the trail was gone, the dust was on them like dried salt water. Dan would have drunk salt water in great killing gulps if there had been any. But there was none. None at all. Nor had there been any water since the tinny warmed drink from his canteen sometime the afternoon before.

He put one foot before the other, pulling gently on the reins. The pony limped forward with him. Minutes had no value, hours had no life. Only the mountains were alive, there ahead of them, aloof and untouchable.

Dan began to talk to Bonnie in broken phrases. "Just a little way now, girl," he whispered. "Soon there will be that Arabian.

White. Flying. A mane like silk in the wind. Cool wind. Proud and white. You, girl, out to pasture. Broad green pasture. Green and peace after the years and years of desert behind us."

The dream had no consolation and would not come real. For the first time since he was twelve, it gave him no hope. What was behind them limped beside them. It also pushed, like yesterday's wind, forcing them on over an unseen trail in a total blaze.

Then it began to pull, gentle as Dan's hands on the pony's reins. "Take my hand," the breeze seemed to say. "There now. Easy, easy. One foot, two feet. You can make it."

He followed the unheard voice and touched the unreal hand. Strange; first it was Nora's hand. Then ma's arms. Then Old Man Pike's voice. Then the silver river at the foot of the spread. It was all pain as flickering, and weariness as vague, as the weird colors which stirred around him before he fell.

Some time later he found himself riding again on Bonnie's back, his face against the stubble of her head. He heard himself say, a far tone carried in echoes through the miles of the empty place, "I'm sorry, girl. I can't walk any more. Forgive me."

Funny, funny, to speak so to a pony. It was black then and quiet, and there was a new dream. It was a dream of cool greenness and a small brown house at the top of the spread. Nora in a yellow dress came out of a door with an extravagant spilling pail of water in her hands.

Dan woke to the sound of water. The word refused to come through the split, caked crevices of his lips. It refused, even in his dried mind, to be acknowledged. He swung his head, vision blurred. Bonnie's mane scratched against his chin. Her muzzle was slanted down in front of him.

The sound he heard was the great gulping slosh of her drinking. Dan slid from her back and fell forward beside her. The water was chilled from shade and clear. He cupped a little of it and drank it slowly. He rested and drank his fill.

They were in a shelter. Scrubby trees, dried and brown, but trees, made a semicircle around them. The water hole was deep. The hills rode steep beside them, no longer far away and remote. Beyond stretched the mountains, seeming to reach the sky itself.

Dan pulled his eyes down from them and examined Bonnie's knee. Filth caked the wound, and the bruise stood out like a grapefruit beside it. Very gently, murmuring to her, he bathed it in the water and rinsed out the ripped shirt and bandaged the leg again.

The grass was sparse, but Bonnie ate of it. She lifted her head from time to time to watch Dan as he shook out the bedroll, pulled what food was left from the slicker and built a small fire, cramped by stones so that it wouldn't overrun onto the dry brush.

When it was done he tied Bonnie to a tree. Strong and young again, he walked down the thin path that led from the water hole. It didn't take him long. The mountain trail was there, untouched by dust storms, secreted and protected by the brush which grew more strongly away from the rioting sun of the desert.

He looked up the trail. It was clear-cut and not too steep, broad enough for the stage coach or the wagon or four horsemen abreast.

When Bonnie's knee was healed in a day or two, they could go on —up there toward the sky. When they reached the peak of the pass they could look down to the green below them, a stream maybe, a cool place where he could lie, tree-blanketed, and sleep until the dryness replaced itself with fluid, and his blood began to move ripely inside of his shrunken veins.

He could find the city his father had told him about, the ranch where they raised Arabians famous around the world. He could untie the money belt and count it out and reach up to place the saddle on the broad beautiful white back. He could mount, matched, complete, a thousand-dollar saddle on a thousand-dollar horse, with a man, full-grown and new, astride.

"And when you have the Arabian?" Nora seemed to ask again, "When the saddle is on the white horse and all of your savings are gone, Dan, what will you do then?"

He moved slowly away from the trail, back toward Bonnie and the small fire. The pony waited patiently, jerking her stubby muzzle in welcome. Her scrawny mane flipped awkwardly with the movement. Three of her legs took the brunt of her weight and tried to protect the injured knee.

Dan went over to her. He stroked her. The loneliness was out there, behind him and up there, ahead of him. There was nobody to break the loneliness, except Bonnie. No strange Arabian. Bonnie.

"Forgive me," he said again and this time he knew why. "How did you find the way, girl?" he asked her. "All last night and this long morning? How many times did you stumble with the weight of the extra saddle and me, heavy on your back?"

Bonnie nuzzled against him at the sound of his voice.

There were no carrots to repay her. They were back in the sand somewhere, the sand which must have bitten deeply against her sore leg as she plodded in search of water, saving them both, the pair of them, friends for the long good growing years.

Dan rubbed hard and firm against her head. He put her old blanket on her and untied the tarpaulin from the saddle. He lifted it, heavy, odorous, shining in the sunlight and sparked by the small fire, to Bonnie's back. He cinched it tight and stood away to look.

It fitted her. It suited her fine. She was suddenly hands higher, longer-limbed, flaring of nostril and flying of mane. She lifted her head in a full proud gesture and neighed out, clear and loud.

The excitement tickled against Dan's stomach and came out in a roar to match Bonnie. He knew how it would be. He would watch and wait. There would be the coach or the rider or the wagon coming down the trail. It might take a day or so, because more people went through Bend Hollow toward California than ever came from the Golden Land heading east. But one or more were bound to come.

When they did, there would be supplies he could borrow and company for him on the way back home. There would be somebody to talk to as he rode the tooled saddle on the back of the pony who had earned it.

It wouldn't matter about the old dream, left lonely in the desert.

Not at all. Now there was another dream, woven in the black and the quiet and the fear. It was a cool green dream of a small brown house on a wide spread of earth, and Nora in a yellow dress. The biggest excitement of all was in him, separating the boy from the man. He felt suddenly full to the lips with words, saved and added for years back.

"I'm going back home to buy a spread," he would tell the rider or the people in the wagons or the stage driver. "I'm going to have me a spread free and clear and a pony named Bonnie, and a wife named Nora. And, oh, yes, I got me a tooled saddle."

He wasn't even surprised when he heard the sound of hoofs and wheels from the trail up above them. How else would it work out when at last you had a dream you could share?

That Colt Pericles

HENRY H. KNIBBS

For more than two years he ran the Arizona uplands with as wild a
bunch of broom tails as ever pawed snow to winter feed. He was free.
He expected always to be free. His mother, a strawberry roan with a
wide eye and a black stripe down her back, taught him how to keep
alive, chiefly by instructing him what not to do. At first young Pericles thought that his feet were simply to stand on, and his nose
merely a guide to a warm meal. But not very long after he was born
he discovered that his nose was his best friend, and that his heels
would be next best when he could kick hard enough; also that he had
a voice.

One day, straying beyond sight of his mother, he suddenly discovered that he was alone. On the edge of the timber encircling the
mesa a long gray shadow caught his eyes. He didn't know what it
was, but tribal instinct told him it was an enemy. He quivered with
fright. The gray shadow squatted and grew shorter. Pericles' shrill
cry for help was quick with terror. Over a low, rounded ridge appeared the head of his mother. Her ears flat, she came swiftly. As
Pericles started toward her, the gray shadow rose in the air.

Pericles heard a thud behind him. The mare whirled and kicked,
the mountain lion dodging and leaping at her. Once he leaped
clear over her, missing her neck by a few inches.

The colt Pericles stood in one spot and kicked at nothing, like an
old-fashioned pump handle gone crazy. Out of the timber surged
another shadow, flashing silver in the sunlight—the gray stallion
that Pericles had been warned to keep away from. Eyes furious, teeth
bared and head twisted sideways, the stallion charged into the fight.
Rearing, he struck with his forefeet. The gray shadow rolled over
and over, screamed, and was up and bounding down the meadow, the
stallion following like a thunderbolt.

Young Pericles wabbled up to his mother. He was frightened and expected sympathy. But she merely nosed him all over, and, finding he was uninjured, paid no more attention to him. To make it worse, the gray stallion was coming back. Foam-breasted, magnificent, he plunged to stop and whistled. Pericles got behind his mother, remembering that she had told him the stallion didn't like colts. Pericles felt that his mother should have been grateful. The stallion had undoubtedly saved them from a terrible fate. But when he offered to touch noses with her, she promptly kicked him in the ribs. However, he didn't seem specially offended. He simply shook his head and walked off in a stately manner. Pericles was puzzled. But that wasn't all of it. When Pericles pressed against his mother's shoulder for the comfort of her nearness, she gave him a nip on the rump that told him to trot along back to the spot where he had left her. Didn't he see what might have happened if it hadn't been for his father?

When two years old, Pericles considered himself not only grown up but a mighty fine specimen. Already he had whipped two young stallions of his age and had managed to keep out of reach of the big gray who led the band. Long since, his mother had ceased to act at all maternal. One stretch of country in particular interested him—the lowlands on the north side of the high mesas where he had been born. For some reason the wild horses had always shunned this country, although the grass stood thick and green, and the climate was much warmer than that of the high country. But Pericles was inquisitive.

Toward the end of June, on a bright morning with a tang of melting snow still in the air, young Pericles stood on a ridge looking down upon the rolling green reaches below. He was alone. Neck arched like a drawn bow, ears sharply forward and his nostrils wide as he drank the breeze, the young roan stallion seemed a part of the bronze-hued rock on which he stood. In his dark eye was mirrored the figure of a tiny horse, grazing placidly along that queer line of little posts his mother had told him to keep away from. Quivering with suppressed excitement, his young life hot in him, he trumpeted a shrill call. The horse below raised its head, then went calmly to grazing again. Pericles whistled, snorted, reared and pawed the air in sheer exuberance. But the tiny figure below paid no further attention.

The water-soaked earth spraying from his hoofs, young Pericles took a long slant down the slope, and fetched up opposite the stranger on the other side of the range fence. He was grayish around the eyes and muzzle, this old horse, and had some big white spots on his back. His knees were swollen and stiff. And that queer scar on his shoulder? Pericles looked at the scar curiously, with a sharp tingle. Not of fear, he told himself. But that scar meant something he not only did not understand but for which he felt a blood distrust. The old cow horse watched him with benevolent amusement.

Pericles' nostrils worked. Who was he? What was he? And what was he doing on the other side of those funny posts? The old horse turned his head and gazed down the drift fence. Another horse came plodding along in a leisurely fashion. Pericles stared. It was a horse, yet it looked queer—had something on its back. Pericles' eyes grew big.

So that was a man! It stepped off its mount to inspect a sag in the drift fence then, and young Pericles was amazed. Something was wrong with it. It walked on its hind legs. And it wasn't half as big as a horse!

A look came into the old cow pony's eyes which seemed to say, "Keep wild as long as you can, young fellow. Stick to the high mesas. And if you happen to see a cow-puncher riding your country, high-tail it for the pinnacles. You're too young and handsome to take any chances. There isn't a cowboy on the Moonstone that wouldn't give a month's wages to get a rope on you."

Even then Pericles was loath to take the hint and go. The idea that that strange animal walking around like a horse on its hind legs could catch him seemed humorous. But presently when a drift of wind brought the smell of man, the young roan thrilled with the old primordial fear. He struck up the slope on a run. Halfway to the ridge, he turned and looked down. The old cow horse was grazing placidly. But the man was standing staring up at the wild stallion. "What a mount!" said the man.

Trumpeting shrill defiance, young Pericles curled his tail and struck on up the slope, chunks of water-soaked earth rocketing from his heels.

The man was Peter Annersley, owner of the great Moonstone ranch, a solid comfortable-looking man, neither young nor old. Peter had never outgrown his fondness for a good saddle horse. He was riding a splendid mount. And he had several other top horses in his personal string. But never had he seen so handsome a piece of horse-flesh as the wild roan stallion.

"I'd admire to get my twine on that broom tail," he said as young Pericles disappeared over a ridge.

But the roan didn't hear that. His only idea was to get back into the high country and find his wild kindred again. From now on he would keep that fence between himself and horses that worked for a living.

In the uplands the leaves of the quaking asp were changing color. Mornings were nippy with the tang of fall. Pericles grazed, grew bigger and stronger, and began to take on a heavier coat. One day, overtaken by one of those inexplicable terrors that suddenly beset horses, the band started on a wild run through the timber and swept down to the lower country. Pericles again saw the old cow horse, Piecrust. The band quieted down and began to graze south of the drift fence. Pericles lagged behind, signifying his willingness to visit.

The horse that worked for a living drifted up to his own side of the fence. Pericles arched a proud neck. He hadn't been caught yet! The old cow horse looked wise. Bleak Saunders—foreman of the Moonstone—and Buck Connor had ridden over his way recently. After the fall round-up, Bleak said, he was going to establish a relay clear across the high country to the desert, keep the bunch away from water till he tired 'em out; then trap 'em in Blue Canyon. There was a young roan stallion running with the wild horses that the Old Man wanted. The old cow pony knew only too well that when Peter Annersley set out to get something, he usually got it. Pericles felt that he was being warned of some danger. He was grateful for this friendliness. He touched noses with Piecrust, wished that he ran with the wild horses of the high mesas. At times Pericles was lonesome.

The mares and colts had strung out and were climbing the hill, the big gray stallion nipping the laggards. Swinging wide of the band, young Pericles took his own trail up the slope. Halfway he turned and nickered a farewell to the old cow horse. Piecrust answered in a tremulous, horse whinny. The old cow horse watched him enviously. Pericles was the stoutest pony he had seen for many a day. But that wouldn't help him much if Peter Annersley sent Bleak Saunders after him.

Streaming across the tops of the pines, the morning sunlight flooded the mountain meadow, which shimmered like a lake of pale gold. In the middle of the meadow was an emerald hollow where a tiny stream ran, spreading to a shallow pool edged with wild iris—a spot known to Moonstone cowboys as "the place where the ponies come to drink." Young Pericles never understood why the old gray stallion would not allow the band to graze that meadow for any length of time.

Twice this morning the old stallion had started toward the timber on the edge of the meadow, and twice he had sheered back, snorting as if he had smelled a rattlesnake. The mares and colts paid little attention, nipping the dry grass as they drifted slowly across the open.

Pericles hung toward the rear of the band, carrying on a mild flirtation with a young mare. That the old stallion permitted this was evidence of his intense preoccupation.

The old gray stallion had good reason to be nervous. Without warning, two horsemen appeared on the southern edge of the clearing. The band crowded together. The gray stallion whistled, shot across the meadow and plunged into the timber along its northern edge. Heads and tails up, the colts bobbing awkwardly beside them, the mares followed.

"There he is!" cried one of the horsemen as they spurred out onto the meadow. "That red roan with the blaze face and one white foot."

Instead of following the band, Pericles swung south through the timber. A half mile farther south he stopped and looked back. There were no riders in sight. But the wind told him they were following. Again he headed south, going at a steady lope. Striking through a belt of timber, he swung out into another meadow. He could hear no sound of pursuit, but again the wind told him he was followed. It was not the band the horsemen followed. They were after him!

West of this meadow the timber ran up to the barren ridges of Barlow Peak. For an hour Pericles traveled toward the peak, slowing from a lope to a trot, and finally, as the wind brought him no scent of his pursuers, to a walk. But the nerves in his spine, his neck, his shoulders—every nerve in his body—told him they were still following him. As he climbed higher his wind grew short. Pausing on an open ridge, his flanks heaving, he looked back. Far below, the two horsemen were crossing the second meadow, riding easily. Young Pericles would have enjoyed the hot excitement of a chase. But this slow, dogged tracking worried him.

In an hour he reached timber line. Scant grass, fed by the melting snows of summer, showed among the rocks and boulders. A hundred yards ahead stood a square something made of tree trunks. Pericles was puzzled. Never having seen a building, he could not know it was the summer lookout for the fire patrol. Whatever it was, it was wrong. He went cautiously, nosing the wind. As he passed the ranger station he smelled horses, commingled with an alien smell that sent him bounding on up among the rocks and pinnacles.

From in back of the station two horsemen swung out. Young Pericles had crossed the peak and, the loose shale and broken rock slithering beneath his feet, was going down the steep western slope on the run. Far below, the timber swallowed up the figure of Pericles. Wade and Bill Varney took up his tracks. At the foot of the mountain the stallion had turned south down Barlow Valley. Two more riders were out after him; but unaware that still farther south each known water hole was watched by Moonstone hands, young Pericles kept on down the valley. The sweat was drying on him and he was beginning to get thirsty.

Two hours later he came in sight of open country again. Occasionally he stopped to view the back track, his eye white-rimmed, his nostrils wide. A few miles below was water. Excitement had made him sweat fully as much as exercise. With no pursuers he could have made twice the distance without feeling thirsty. Pericles approached the water hole warily. Being chased was one thing, but having men bob up in front of you was quite another matter. Within a hundred yards of the water hole he stopped. His mane bristled. His forefeet drummed the hard earth. Near the water hole stood two horses. Their riders were sitting on the ground, playing seven-up.

Tonto Charley and Shorty White dropped their cards and rose. "Reckon there's our meat," said Shorty.

"When we get it," said Tonto, "That son of a gun's playing a lone hand."

The young roan whirled and started back up the valley, Shorty and Tonto Charley after him. Presently the wind brought him more bad news. Men were also riding down the valley. He plunged up the western slope and struck across the ridge. He now wished that he had stayed with the band. Not until nightfall did he get a chance to rest. And then he sought a high, barren ridge, dozing only occasionally. Never once that night was he off his feet. With the first ray of dawn he was on his way south again. He walked, and grazed a nip at a time. His coat was stiff with dried sweat, and dust had caked on his back and sides where he had rolled.

It was red-earth country, dotted with piñons and junipers. There was little grass and the ground was spotted with outcroppings of red rock. Horse tracks there were none. Toward noon thirst bothered him so much that he crossed the low ridge into Barlow Valley again. On the flat far below, strung out and going at a slow trot, were the wild horses, the old gray stallion in the lead.

Young Pericles whinnied. Out from the water hole came two horsemen. Instantly the gray stallion swung away from the water hole and struck up Barlow Valley, the mares following. This time the horsemen's ropes were up and circling. Young Pericles dashed down the slope and among the mares and colts. He was with his own again. The two horsemen drew nearer. Halfway up the valley they crowded the band so close that it split, one bunch going into the timber of the eastern slope; the old gray's bunch, Pericles among them, taking to the western.

All that day the old stallion led the remnant of his band, craftily circling each relay camp. And all that night the band drifted from meadow to timberland, restlessly searching for water.

The morning of the third day, with the mares pinchflanked and weary and the colts all but used up, the band followed the old gray stallion back toward their own country. Past Turkey Springs, rimmed with lush green in the heart of the timberlands, sped the jaded horses. Bill Varney, Wade, Bleak and Buck Connor followed at a judicious pace, so as not to stampede and scatter them. Across a stretch of slick rim rock, Varney, a reckless, hard rider, roweled his tired horse. A piece of loose tufa turned under the horse's forefeet. The leg-weary animal pitched forward, struck on his head and, turned completely over, crashed down on Varney. Varney lay on his face, his head twisted far to one side.

"Varney's quit," said Buck.

"Stay with him, Wade," said Bleak.

Bleak and Buck Connor rode on after the horses. And they rode fast. Thundering along the rim rock, the mares and colts followed the gray stallion. As the band approached the narrow cliff trail leading down into Blue Canyon, the gray stallion swerved. The band shot past him, stringing down the steep trail on the run. Young Pericles would have followed, but the gray stallion reared and struck at him. Pericles swung his head and seized the old stallion's neck. Squealing, the old stallion whirled and broke loose. He kicked as he whirled. A hoof crashed on Pericles' jaw. Mad with fury of battle, Pericles rushed at his foe.

But the old gray saw that which young Pericles in his rage did not see—Bleak Saunders, his loop wide and singing, coming at a short lope. Dodging Pericles' mad rush, the old gray took off down the canyon trail after the mares. Too late, Pericles swung round. He reared to strike down Bleak's horse, his hoofs raw gold as he hammered the sky. Bleak's loop circled. A vicious, whining whisper, and the young horse felt an invisible snakelike something bind his forelegs, burn and bite, and he went down. As Pericles' hind feet flashed in a wild struggle to rise, Buck Connor swung a short loop and heeled him. Blind mad, Pericles kicked and struggled, battering his head on the rim rock. Again and again his enemies stretched him, but each time he managed to fight up to his feet, battling so close to the canyon rim that both men were put to it to keep from being dragged over.

Pericles staggered up again, full of fight. But that invisible something jerked his front legs from under him and he crashed down. This time he lay still. He wanted to get up, wanted to destroy the horses and men that had trapped and were fighting him. But his young strength was going. For nearly three days he had been without water and had had little chance to graze.

Pericles heard the dull plodding of hoofs on the rim rock as Tonto Charley rode up. The cowboy said nothing; simply sat his horse gazing at the fallen stallion. Slowly the Tonto man took down his rope. He whistled. Pericles head went up. Again that vicious, whining whisper, and young Pericles felt something grip and bite into his neck. As Tonto took his dally, Pericles, half blind and raging, struggled to his feet. He never knew just what happened, only that the sky grew black, and he fell, and all feeling went out of him.

Bleak and his men gazed down upon their captive. "He's a wonder!" said Tonto Charley.

"A fightin' fool," murmured Buck.

"What I mean"—Tonto's experienced eye traveled over the magnificent young stallion from muzzle to hoofs—"he's the best-made hoss I ever laid my twine on."

"And he's cost the Old Man plenty."

"You mean Varney?"

No one answered. The weathered faces of the Moonstone punchers grew grave. Bill Varney had gone out—not in the hot excitement of the chase, but crossing a smooth little stretch of rock at a lope. But their eyes never left the young stallion stretched on the gray rim rock. That was the job in hand.

Pericles became conscious of the sound of voices. He didn't know, at first, where he was. The voices were low and mild. He did not understand. Had he not battled with them? Would he not have killed them had he been able? Now they had him down and unable to move. Why didn't they go ahead and kill him?

"We'll just haze him over to the old log corral," he heard the lean foreman say.

Sullen and savage by turns, young Pericles fought every foot of the way. It was a bitter thing to him that his own kind were so keen to help their riders conquer him. When, after a sullen spell, Pericles launched into a savage break for freedom, Buck's wise old pony, Rowdy, would set back on the rope and stop him. If Pericles persisted in fighting, Bleak's mount would whirl and start off at right angles, jerk Pericles off his feet and, facing him, squat almost on his haunches to keep the rope taut.

At the edge of a broad meadow stood the old log corral with its scarred and weathered snubbing post. Near the corral was the chuck wagon. A team of paint ponies, gaunt-flanked and their bellies plastered with mud, stood hitched to a buckboard. Bed rolls lay on the ground around a heap of ashes. All this flashed across Pericles' vision. But rage had dulled his curiosity. He felt that these strange things were his enemies.

Boomer, the cook, left the wagon and let the corral bars down. The smell of water came to Pericles. Mad with thirst, he made a final, desperate struggle to get free. But again the ropes flickered out and he was thrown. The round, log-sided inclosure awakened a new fear. It was a trap. He lunged to his feet and tried to break back. Behind him three riders yelled and beat their chaps with their quirts. The rope on his neck drew down. Frenzied, he dashed into the corral, stopped and gazed wildly about. There was Bleak on his pony, Walking John. With ears back, Pericles charged. Walking John side-stepped cleverly, the rope was flipped off Pericles' neck, and Walking John and his rider shot out through the gateway, leaving him there. Pericles made for the opening. He crashed against heavy bars that somehow a few seconds ago were not there. All lust for fighting was consumed in the burning desire to get back into the open again.

Gaunt, weary and weak from hunger and fatigue, he hadn't the strength to put up much of a fight when, in the morning, he was again roped and hazed out of the corral. Already he had begun to fear a rope. From morning till noon he went sullenly. When the outfit reached the Moonstone fence and he was turned loose in the horse pasture, he thought he was free again. Twice he charged into the heavy barbed wire. His breast lacerated and bleeding, he gave up trying to break through the fence, and took to following it, searching for a way out. Finally he began to graze a few minutes at a time, moving along the fence, always looking for a way back to the high country.

That afternoon he met the old cow horse, who didn't seem at all surprised to see him. Pericles snorted. They had caught him, but they wouldn't keep him. Some day he would get away! As they grazed together, Pericles wondered what they would do to him. The old cow horse gazed at the wire cuts on Pericles' breast. The young stallion had been fighting the fence. Well, any wild horse would do that, any horse worth his feed would—at first. But it never did any good to fight a fence or a rope or a man.

The old cow horse knew what it was like. Pericles didn't question that. But he didn't believe that any little two-legged animal could best him. Before Piecrust went over to a cedar to take a little nap, Pericles learned that there were certain things worth remembering. Don't strike with your forefeet. Don't bite. And above all things, don't go against a spade bit. The old cow horse lolled his tongue. Across it ran a deep scar. Pericles' eyes widened. The very thought of having his tongue cut or lacerated chilled him.

The old cow horse dozed in the shade of the cedar, one hind leg hunched and his head low. A sudden homesickness beset young Pericles. He yearned for his kindred, for the freedom of the high mesas, fenceless, rugged and wild. It amazed him that the old cow horse had shown no special dislike for men, nor for the work he had been obliged to do.

Grazing near the south fence of the horse pasture that afternoon, Pericles became aware of movement far up on the edge of the timber. No bigger at that distance than mice, six or seven horses had come out of the timber and were traveling slowly toward the west. They were his kindred. Charging up to the fence, he lifted his head and trumpeted. But the wild horses kept on, moving in single file along one of their narrow trails. Pericles started running west along the inside of the fence. Somewhere he would find a way out and rejoin the band. He came upon the gateway through which he had entered. He battered the heavy gate with his forefeet; fought it as if it had been a living thing.

All that day he ranged the horse pasture looking for a way out. Why had the Moonstone riders captured him? The old cow horse had said something about his being a handsome fellow. Handsome? Perhaps. But lonely. Again and again he came back to the drift fence and gazed up at the far, timbered hills, yearning for his kind.

Early the following day, along with five or six cow ponies, Pericles was hazed into the home corral. When the dust had settled the other horses were gone.

He moved about restlessly. He could smell horses and men. And his ear was sharpened toward every sound. Peter Annersley, his wife and the hands were joking and laughing, but underneath their talk ran a current of seriousness. Between the bars he saw Tonto Charley shake out a rope and re-coil it. The rope! That was something he couldn't fight. It would shoot out and take hold before you could strike or dodge it. Facing the entrance, Pericles stood stiff-legged, watching. He didn't know what was going to happen, but he knew it was something concerning himself. He could feel it in the air. Worst of all, he was alone. With the other horses he would have felt no fear. He was afraid, not of the men but of the rope and the unknown.

Wade crawled through the bars and shook out a loop. Pericles snorted and circled. Tonto Charley rode into the corral, and Buck on his mount, Rowdy. Wade made a backhand cast. The loop spread. He dodged as the young stallion made for him. The loop jumped from the ground and drew tight round Pericles' forelegs. He reared and fought. Something whistled close to his head. Too late, he dodged. Tonto Charley had him roped round the neck.

Behind him Buck was swinging a short noose. Pericles lashed out with his heels. "Got him!" cried Buck.

Rearing, Pericles tried to strike with his forefeet. He was blind mad with fear and rage. His legs were jerked from under him and he landed on his side. Still he fought to get free. Slowly his head was drawn short up to the snubbing post. The noose round his neck slackened a little. He lay still, his flanks heaving. He felt the cinch slip under him, felt the saddle clamp down.

Something was slipped over his head—another kind of rope that didn't choke him—but the feel of the hackamore round his nose drove him frantic. Buck was standing astride him. The rope on Pericles' neck grew slack. He lunged up. As he felt the clinging weight on his back all his pent-up fury was let loose. Buck was in the saddle, his spurs in Pericles' shoulders. Pericles went into the air like a catamount. There was no shouting, no comment. This was no ordinary bronc taking his first lesson in manners. This was a stick of dynamite spinning in a cyclone.

Twice Pericles jolted his rider loose and almost threw him. A spur shot across his ribs like a string of hornets. He went up, his back bent like a bow. When he hit the ground the cinch snapped. Again he went up. Flying ends of the broken cinch and Buck, the saddle gripped between his knees, flew skyward. Clearing the top of the corral, man and saddle lit in a heap outside, and directly under the noses of Mrs. Annersley's team of paint ponies.

Snorting, the team broke away from Shorty, who was standing on the seat looking into the corral, and hightailed it for home.

"Never mind the team," Ma Annersley's voice was placid. "We need a new buckboard anyway . . . Are you hurt, Buck?"

He sat on his wrecked saddle, looking about in a dazed manner.

"No, ma'am," he said. "But I'd sure like to know which way is north."

Pericles circled the corral, the hackamore still on his head. So that was what was meant by riding him? Well, he had got rid of that rider! But here was Tonto Charley again, a coil of rope in his hand. Pericles dashed across the corral and battered at the heavy timbers. He couldn't dodge the rope, but he could run away from it.

Bleak Saunders rode in on Walking John. Pericles stopped, whistled and laid back his ears. He had three men to watch now— three men and three ropes. Tonto moved forward. Pericles reared and started away. From somewhere that all-but-invisible rope shot out and he felt the loop tighten on his forelegs. Again he was snubbed up to the post and saddled. Before Bleak could get his foot in the stirrup, Pericles was on his feet and in the air. But the fore- man kicked his foot home as Pericles came down.

Furious, Pericles pitched and pin-wheeled, but he could not get rid of that clinging weight that gave to every jolt with a swing and a re- covery that were maddening. The cinch biting into him, the rowels scoring him, he did a hump and a twist in the air that became known later as his specialty—the double corkscrew. Bleak was an old-time, straight-up rider. This double corkscrew was a new one to him. He went out of the saddle and he went high. As he turned over in the air, Pericles lashed out with his heels. Bleak hit the ground, rolled to one side and tried to rise. His right leg was broken between the knee and ankle. Shorty ran in and dragged Bleak to safety, while Tonto and Wade fought Pericles down.

Ma Annersley made Bleak as comfortable as she could while Vine- garoon went for the buckboard. Peter Annersley, who had been watching the riding, began to buckle on his own chaps.

"Peter Annersley, what are you doing?" cried Ma Annersley.

"Buckling my chaps."

"You keep off that horse!"

"Yes, Madam." Peter went on adjusting his chaps.

"You're old enough to know better."

"Yes, Ma'am. But I kind of like that little horse."

"Peter!"

But Peter had crawled through the bars.

Snubbed close to the post, Pericles stood watching out of a white- rimmed eye. Another one! A big man, solid without being over- heavy. And calm and easy-going as sunshine. Pericles remembered. It was the man he had seen the first day he had met the old cow pony

and wondered about the scar. Now he wondered no longer. That scar was a brand. They put it on all the horses that worked for a living.

The young roan stallion felt a hand on his neck. "Why, you ain't bad!" The voice was deep and friendly. "You're just a mite scared. So am I. But don't let on to the boys." Peter stroked Pericles' shoulder. Pericles sidled and kicked, but the big man wasn't there.

"Now, I wouldn't do that," said Peter. " 'Cause why? Why, I'm goin' to ride you, little horse. Depends on you whether we get along comfortable or not."

Pericles felt differently toward this man. Not that he wouldn't pitch and unload him if he could. But toward Peter Annersley, Pericles held no definite enmity—only the natural fear of a wild creature captured and bound. Peter was not a better rider than either Bleak Saunders or Buck. Yet man for man and horse for horse, he could outride them.

"The Old Man puts something on 'em," the superstitious Vinegaroon used to say.

No spell, no magic accounted for Peter Annersley's success with broncos. However, he did put something on them. Peter weighed close to a hundred and eighty—heavier than either Buck or Bleak Saunders by some twenty or thirty pounds. Heavier, but not a whit less active. Though Peter was called the Old Man, he was younger than Bleak, and considerably more painstaking in educating a bronco. Instead of using the short hackamore rope, Peter tied his own rope to the jaws of the hackamore, took the coil in his hand and slipped into the saddle like a hand slipping into an old glove.

Pericles knew that he now had something different to contend with—a rider who, although knowing that he would, did not urge him to pitch. Pericles arched his back, bunched his feet as he came down. Peter took the jolt with bent knees, and told Pericles to try again. Never once did he use the spur. Try as Pericles would, he could not shake the solid weight from his back. Jumping forward, he began to pitch from side to side.

"Drop the bars!" cried Peter.

Pericles made for the opening. With the loose coil Peter whipped the stallion's flanks from side to side. Rocketing into the open in long, plunging pitches, Pericles lit out across the pasture on the run. Mrs. Annersley and the boys watched the young stallion bore into the distance like the speeding end of an express train. Horse and rider grew smaller and smaller. Ma Annersley smiled. Vinegaroon pulled to the corral with the runaway team and an apparently undamaged buckboard. Bleak was loaded in and Ma Annersley climbed to the seat. "Tell pa I've got a name for that colt, when he gets back."

Far down the pasture Pericles and his rider were having an understanding. Pericles was sweating from ear to hoofs, and he was breathing hard. The saddle was empty. He hadn't pitched Peter Annersley, however. Peter, afoot, the sweat dripping from his face, had the coil of the rope in his hand. About fifteen feet of the rope was taut between Peter and Pericles' head. Peter began to work up the rope toward the stallion. Pericles quivered. Peter set back. The hackamore pinched down. Pericles reared as it shut off his wind. When he came down he could breathe. It didn't take him long to realize that if he came to the rope he could go on breathing.

Peter grinned. "Remember, young fellow, I'm just as scared as you are—but don't you let on to the boys!"

Again he began to work up the rope. This time Pericles allowed him to get within a few feet before he reared. When Pericles came down, Peter was still there, his body hot, but his brain cool. Pericles' body and brain were both hot. Peter was giving the stallion a chance to cool his brain. Then he could be reasoned with.

The roan stallion couldn't understand it. The man at the other end of the rope didn't seem to want to fight, and he wouldn't let go. The constant repetition wore on the young stallion, numbed his will. Only occasionally the man spoke, and then in a low, easy tone without startling or maddening him. Pericles never knew exactly when he gave in to that solid figure, that quiet, easy tone. Finally Peter's hand was on Pericles' hot neck. Pericles quivered, but stood still. If he had known what he wanted to do, he might have tried to break away. But his will to do anything was submerged in the will of the man.

Telling Pericles he was a good little horse, Peter reached slowly for the stirrup and eased himself into the saddle. Pericles started off at a sullen trot. He went in a big circle. At the pull of the hackamore he made the second round in a smaller space. At last he was moving in so narrow a circle that Peter stopped him. A touch of the spurs and Pericles jumped forward. This time he was headed toward the home corral.

Buck and Tonto and Shorty shaded their eyes against the morning sun. The young stallion was coming back at a lope, Peter sitting him easily, the hackamore rope slack. On either side of Pericles, Tonto and Shorty hazed him quietly into the corral. Peter snubbed him, worked the saddle off and turned him loose. Again Pericles found himself alone. He snuffed at the bars and, walking over to some loose earth, lay down and rolled.

"Did Ma get Bleak over to the house all right?" Peter asked.

"Yep. And say, chief, she said to tell you she's got a name for that colt."

"Uh-huh?"

"Ma said his name was Pericles."

Peter scratched his head. "Did ma say that?"

"She done did!"

Peter put on his hat aslant. "Pericles, eh?" He tried it out to himself: "That colt Pericles. Huh! Ma's been readin' in that dictionary again. I knew she'd get even with me some way."

Free of the saddle and hackamore, away from the sound of voices, Pericles began to recover himself. The man called Peter had made him do things, then he had gone away. Would he come back and make him do things again? Pericles gazed out toward the southern country, the distant, high mesas edged with timber. He couldn't go back there—not yet. He put all his distraction, all his loneliness, into a shrill neigh of protest.

Shorty, riding beside Peter Annersley on their way to the house, turned and looked back. "By gosh! Sounds like he ain't through yet. Now, I thought when he lay down and rolled—"

Though Pericles had been ridden to a standstill once, there wasn't a hand on the Moonstone who was foolish enough to imagine the young stallion wouldn't pitch again. Both Tonto Charley and Buck were willing to make the experiment. But the Old Man declared he thought his saddle fitted Pericles just a mite better than Buck's, and that as Bleak's leg had just been set, it might be as well to let Nature take its course.

"What did he mean—Nature takin' its course?" said Buck.

Bleak, propped up in his bunk reading his old stand-by, *Robinson Crusoe*, frowned. "I reckon he was referrin' to dismountin' with your saddle between your knees. It's kind of a new style round these parts."

"Like busted legs, Eh?"

"You kin go plumb to hell. But wait just a minute afore you start. The Old Man's tooken a fancy to that—" Bleak paused. "Is ma around anywhere?"

Buck shook his head.

"And such bein' the case," continued Bleak, "he don't want to have to fly over the top of the corral every time he gits off that—Where is ma, anyhow?"

"Over in the kitchen. The name of that hoss is Pericles."

"Thanks. He's a one-man hoss, and allowin' you bronc stompers all the glory you might git if you was able to stick on him, the Old

Man is the one. No use bowin' your neck and pawin', Pete's got us all beat when it comes to ridin' lunatics."

"Or dismountin'" added Buck, gazing pointedly at Bleak's un-bending leg.

Each morning for a straight week Peter Annersley had ridden Pericles, and ridden him hard. Then, to the surprise of the hands, he turned the young stallion loose. The boys argued that the Old Man would have it all to do over again. But Peter Annersley didn't think so. Pericles had begun to go sour. The young stallion had learned saddle, cinch, spurs, bit and hackamore. He was even be-ginning to understand a few words—his name for one. "Here, you!" or "That'll do, now!" or "Quit your nonsense!" all meant about the same thing, only in a different degree. He soon found out that when, like a proper cow horse, he gave to the pull of the hackamore, noth-ing else happened. If he fought, something always happened. It wasn't so much the reprimand or the rowels as having to do it all over again.

Intuition told him that Peter Annersley was giving him a square deal. Yet the pride of the wild was still in his blood. Once more away from corral, saddle and Peter's voice, Pericles ranged the south pasture, his tail arched, his neck like the bend of a breaking wave, the reach of his stride as free as when he ran with his kindred of the high mesas.

Straight for the fence he thundered. He slid to a stop and snorted, his breast almost against the wire. Whirling, he rocketed out into the pasture again, kicking as he ran. This was the life! . . . What? A bunch of cow ponies grazing over there? Whoosh! Pericles bore down the pasture. The cow ponies raised their heads. He veered off as he came near them, expecting them to run with him. But they went on grazing again. He swung back and, kicking right and left, scattered them like wind-blown leaves. On he went, the wind singing past his sharpened ears. Somewhere, sometime, he would find a way out. Then the high mesas again—miles and miles of unfenced country, clear down to the Tonto Basin.

The old gray cow pony stood near the water hole, apparently deep in thought. Pericles dashed up. Piecrust stretched a stiff hind leg. Curiosity was in his eye. Now that the young stallion had been rid-den, how did he like it?

Pericles didn't. But, it surprised him to reflect, the Old Man was different. One felt that he expected you to behave. With the others, Pericles felt that they expected him to throw a whingding. And maybe he didn't. The old cow horse nodded. He would always be a one-man horse, that magnificent roan. And he was lucky. The other rawhides would keep off him, now that the Old Man had taken a fancy to him. The veteran sighed and rubbed his nose on his foreleg. "I was the Old Man's top horse once," he mused. "I was lucky too."

When Piecrust had become so old and stiff and short-sighted he couldn't do his work, one of the hands said it was about time to shoot him. That riled the Old Man. He said Piecrust had earned the right to take it easy the rest of his life. Pensioned, they called it.

Piecrust had been lucky—and lonesome until he and the young stallion became friends. But it's hard to keep a friend when you grow old. Something always happens.

"I suppose," thought the old cow horse mournfully, "that some day he'll find a break in the fence and high-tail it for the mesas again."

Pericles dropped his head to graze, but the far-away look in his eye said plainly: "That's exactly what I intend to do!"

When spring came and the snow-softened earth let some of the fence posts sag until in two or three sections the wire was down, Pericles found the chance he had been looking for. Peter Annersley, riding him along the drift fence, saw the down wire and dismounted.

Pericles, who had been taught to stand to rein, waited until Peter's back was turned. Now was his chance! With reins dragging sideways, he dashed through and started for the high country. He heard Peter call him. But no! Up there were his kindred, grazing the open reaches and running—running. Pericles stepped on one of the reins. The spade bit cut his mouth. He stopped. All the weeks of his training bore in on him. And now the Old Man was coming toward him, coming slowly, talking quietly, telling him to stop his nonsense.

Quivering, Pericles faced him. Step by step Peter approached. One more step and Pericles would turn and run. The Old Man saw it in his eyes. He stopped.

"Perry," he said, "don't be a fool. You ain't wild any more. You only think you're wild." Peter chuckled just as though he didn't care much whether Pericles stayed or not.

It all hung on Peter now. If he had made one wrong move, raised his hand or changed the tone of his voice, Pericles would have left on the instant. But the owner of the Moonstone simply came forward as if he expected the roan stallion to stand, raised his hand so slowly that Pericles hardly knew it, took up the reins and, reaching for the stirrup, mounted leisurely.

"Let's go back and look at that fence once more," he said as Pericles moved forward like a creature in a dream.

They returned to the damaged fence. Pericles was still quivering inside. Not another hand on the Moonstone would have chanced it. But as casually as if his mount were an old trained cow pony, Peter stepped off him and again let the reins fall. Pericles rolled his eye toward the high country. He fidgeted, breathing deep of the warm spring air. But he did not move from where Peter had left him.

For a half hour the Old Man worked at propping up the fallen posts. With a stone for a hammer, he restapled the wire. Then he came back to the waiting Pericles and took up the reins. "That was the best thing you ever did, little horse," he said as he mounted and rode on down the fence.

Pericles wondered.

Chiltipiquin

WILLIAM BRANDON

A *Chiltipiquin* is a little red pepper. There is a poem in Spanish about small women being best, small jewels being best, small horses being best, and small peppers being hottest. A *chiltipiquin* is so hot it is customary to use one *chiltipiquin* to roast another *chiltipiquin*, if you are making cold camp, or so they say. Being small and hot and red altogether, it gave its name to the colt as a matter of course.

Chiltipiquin, the colt, was foaled in the *manada* of one Luis María Rodríguez, who was not exactly a bandit and cow thief, and not exactly an honest man either, and who dwelt sometimes on one side of the border and sometimes on the other, in consequence. It was at the time of an unexpected move across the Rio Grande that his mares were hastily gathered and he found the little red roan among the new yearling colts, but it was not until Don Luis went to stamp the branding iron on his hide that the colt earned his name.

The colt fought the rope and Don Luis and the iron, and he fought the rawhide *peales* brought to tie him quiet, and he fought on until there were four men around him, and until a twitch was finally twisted on his lip to subdue him.

"*Diablo,* but he is a little pet," one of the *vaqueros* said, more or less, calling him Sancho, and another added, "No bigger than a piñon nut. It should seem a man could hold him in his hands."

The others stood by and spoke in uncomplimentary terms of his mother while the colt shivered his stiffened legs at the smell of his burning hair, and then Don Luis stepped back with the iron, wiping sweat from his eyes.

"He will be called Chiltipiquin," he said, sounding pleased. "He is coal red and fire hot, and he is small. He will be quick. You will be able to tail down a gopher from his back. I like him. He has mixed blood in him. It is my will that he be left a horse. He will be the first possession of my old age," and the old man puffed with pleasure, watching the colt kick and fight the dust when he was released.

They went ahead with their labor in the hot summer sun; it was an odd time for the work and the stock was at an odd age, but these things were sometimes necessary in Don Luis' way of life; and that night the Rodríguez household moved to cross the almost dry bed of the river.

Here befell the first calamity. The Chiltipiquin colt, vastly excited by the excitement around him, occasioned by the hopeful yells and occasional shots of the *rurales,* who had suddenly appeared, raced along in the darkness after his mother. She, in turn, was trying, with the rest of the mares, to follow the big red stud who captained the *manada.* They were halfway across the river bed. The stallion smelled danger and suddenly wheeled, screaming an order to his women and plunging in amongst them, lashing out with his heels in furious kicks that sounded in great thuds against the mares' barrels, doing his utmost to turn them. Don Luis' *vaqueros* drove into the flank of the melee and the *rurales* fired twice down into the river flats.

A few of the mares, Chiltipiquin's dam among them, swept on, wild with panic, and thundered into the quicksand the stallion had been trying to avoid.

Chiltipiquin bolted along after them. Don Luis himself saw the red colt flash past him in the moonlight and, for no sensible reason, he pulled away from his men, trying to work the remaining mares, and built a loop in his rope and dropped it over the head of the colt, who by this time was floundering deep in the bog. Dallying his rope expertly, Don Luis spurred his horse back and pulled the colt free. The mares in the quicksand, struggling frantically, grotesque humping shadows in the darkness, were already down to their shoulders, and lost. And Don Luis, standing in his stirrups, saw that the *manada* had broken through the opening he had left and had streamed back to the Mexican side, where the *rurales* waited. It was a bitter loss.

Still, he had his three hundred head of cattle, which should by now be well across the river; and just as he was thinking that even at nine dollars around for wet stock, they would bring enough to set him up in business again—after a decent interval to let the weather clear—shouts from his men told him that a body of the police had treacherously crossed the river and not only cut off and surrounded his bunch of cows but his *vaqueros* as well. It was against international law, sporting practice and professional ethics, but it had been done, and

Don Luis, enraged, had no choice but to ride fast down the river alone to escape capture himself. He took the Chiltipiquin colt with him.

"I was a *rico*," Don Luis said aloud at his breakfast of half-cooked jack rabbit the next morning, "and now I am reduced to the place of a miserable *charro*. I was a man of good family and fortune, grown old with prosperity and fat with contentment, which enabled me to forget that I was childless and alone. Now I am a nothing." He looked at the colt out of sleepy, red-rimmed eyes and hurled a bone at him. Chiltipiquin jumped away and stopped, facing him again with legs braced.

"Go!" Don Luis said, waving his arms. The colt quivered. "You are the cause of everything! I stopped to save your execrable life, and so I lost my mares and I lost my cattle and I lost my men! Go! Out of my sight!" In a fury, Don Luis rose from his fire and ran awkwardly at the colt and threw a stone at him. Chiltipiquin gave a frightened sidewise bound or two and then trotted away, looking over his shoulder. "Go!" Don Luis roared. "Before I waste a bullet on you!"

The colt trotted on and stopped half in the cover of some high chaparral.

Don Luis smoothed his ruffled gray mustaches. "He is a devil," he said. "All red horses are devils. He brought this calamity on me."

Then he sat down again near his dead fire, feeling lonely and out of breath, and his depression grew on him as the sun came up. He was too old for such a defeat. There was nothing for him now but to die. Before, Don Luis had lived with the day and lived with the world, and he had devoted his life to the cultivation of a happy philosophy. That at least would always be there to fall back on when everything else was gone. But now it, too, had disappeared, like sunlight blinking out in the evening, and Don Luis was bewildered without it.

Something wet touched the back of his neck and he yelled and shot to his feet and spun around, and saw the Chiltipiquin colt galloping away to hide in a near-by mesquite thicket. Don Luis yelled curses after him and shook his fists.

"It is not enough," he shouted hoarsely, tears of rage in his eyes, "that you ruin me, but you must come back to kiss my neck! Devil pigdog, go! Go back to your brothers, the *rurales!*" He stuffed the rest of the rabbit in his pocket and kicked the cold fire apart and caught up his hobbled gelding and rode on.

The colt was indeed a devil, stealing up to nuzzle him. What

range-bred colt will walk up to a man? Don Luis put his horse at a long Spanish trot while the sun was not yet hot, and left the camp of Chiltipiquin far behind. He looked back often to see if the colt was following, but saw nothing of him.

He would feel better now, he told himself. His thoughts would not have been so cold this morning if the colt had not been there to parade like a symbol of what he had lost. He had brought him along last night on his escape without thinking. What did an old man on the dodge want with a yearling colt? It was better to be rid of him. Much better. A little red devil with misfortune bred in his flat bones.

Nevertheless, he did not feel better. When he found shade to lay over for nooning, he was more irritable than before. He thought he would sleep, but found it difficult. He kept starting up, knocking his sombrero off his eyes, thinking he heard things, and finally he crawled up on the rock shoulder at his back to have a look over the country.

He found Chiltipiquin under his nose. The colt had followed him without being seen and, while Don Luis rested, had stood hidden behind the jut of rock. Chiltipiquin saw him at the same moment. His appearance had been weary and disconsolate, but now his head went up and he sidled away a few feet, looking both guilty and wary. There were burs in his scrubby tail and the gloss was leaving his coat.

Don Luis, in the act of reaching automatically for another rock, stopped his hand. It was bereavement that showed itself in every line of the colt. His mother had died last night. For that reason the colt had followed him and nuzzled him. With Don Luis was the last vestige of the home smell.

Don Luis sighed and called himself a rough name. "I," he said—"I have lost wealth. You, Sancho Chiltipiquin, have lost more than life itself. I have the stupidity to feel sorry for myself. I am an old burro, Chiltipiquin. My foot is sure, but my brains have gone to ears."

The colt flickered his ears forward at the old man's tone.

"You will stay with me," Don Luis said. "You will be the first possession of my old age."

Chiltipiquin took a hesitant step toward him. Don Luis smiled behind his mustaches and closed his eyes, feeling peaceful in the sun. He opened his eyes again and saw the colt still watching him. He cursed him fondly, and Chiltipiquin stretched his neck curiously and, presently, nickered softly in reply.

From this time on, Don Luis felt better. His soul returned to live once more with him. What, he thought, if the sun did go out in the evening? There was always the afterglow that followed, and to a man of thoughtful philosophy that was the best part of the day.

Through some involved process of reasoning, the old man, now that his first burst of anger and distress was over, thought all the more of the colt because he had saved its life at the expense of all his belongings. He gave some consideration to this and decided it was only human to regard most warmly that which you have helped and to hate most warmly those who have helped you and to whom you are in debt. That the colt did not therefore hate him Don Luis filed away as final proof, after all, that horses are not human.

Together they traveled to the rough foothills of the Diablos, where Don Luis' cousin, Estevanico, beat a living from a small outfit. Before reaching Estevanico's *rancheria*, Don Luis killed a prime beef he happened upon and dressed it out and took the quarters to his cousin and his family as a gift. It is never good, Don Luis knew, to visit relatives empty-handed. For Estevanico's daughter, the lovely Rosita, he parted with the valued silver chain from his watch and offered it to her with elaborate casualness as a trinket that might do for a poor bracelet, to jingle on her wrist at the *baile*.

Thus Estevanico and his family were glad to see him, even though they learned later, when they found the hide under a rock, that the steer he had butchered for them had been one of theirs; and Estevanico urged him to stay forever.

"I will stay no more than a lifetime," Don Luis said, chuckling until his cheeks squinted his old, shrewd eyes almost shut, while he took in all the evidence about him of the degree to which Estevanico had prospered since he had last seen him. Beef was going up, and Estevanico, in his slow, plodding fashion, was going up with it. "I am an honest man now," Don Luis said. "That little red colt has made me honest. He is a devil and he does away with all my gains that are too quick, and so I am forced to be honest to live." Here he burst into a roar of laughter, and they all laughed with him.

The months passed smoothly with this august beginning. Don Luis helped Estevanico hunt cows in the fall, and in the winter plaited rawhide, and he broke the roan colt to lead and stand tied.

The next summer Don Luis broke him to ride. It was as he had expected. Chiltipiquin was clever enough to turn on a peg, faster than a ball of fire, willing and full of heart.

So the time passed and Don Luis was content. At Estevanico's he had all the comfort he could want and in his business he was doing well. He had, early in his stay at his cousins, formed a quiet working arrangement with Estevanico's lone hand, a youth named Pedro, and together they drifted out on neighboring ranges frequently and cut out a few head—who would miss them?—and blotched the brands and held them in a hidden corral until occasion offered to run them across the border for a quick sale.

Surely and not so slowly, Don Luis was building up again to his former eminence. The boy Pedro was foolish; he worked for a near nothing; his conscience troubled him and he seemed to feel that the less he made the less guilty he was. He was, Don Luis learned, hopeful of someday marrying Rosita. It was this dream that had tempted him to listen to Don Luis' arguments and finally to join him in his venture. Don Luis found it touching. As for Pedro's lack of business sense, Don Luis was doing his best to cure him of that before his marriage by letting him do most of the work and get least of the money in their partnership. That was experience for the boy, and was not experience the best teacher? Pedro hoped to make money quickly, so he could be married, for example, and that was admirable, but it illustrated his lack of experience. He would find, after his marriage, that he would need to make money quicker than ever. And, too, Rosita would not stand for such an easy, pleasant way of making money as this, if she knew of it; and Don Luis had an idea Rosita, as a wife, would know of it. She would make a good wife, and good wives always know everything. *Es verdad.*

Amusing himself in this way, giving much thought to what did not concern him, which is the most comfortable kind of thought, Don Luis enjoyed the summer and fall, growing always richer, and he could now take honest pride in his cousin Estevanico's prosperous gather in the beef roundup.

Here befell the second calamity. Don Luis was away when it happened—in town with the wagon, restocking supplies. He returned late in the evening, too late to see the smoke, but he could smell it, and when he swung at a rocking gallop around the cottonwoods to come within sight of the rancho, he saw the outbuildings still smoldering. The main house had not been touched.

They came like the blue norther, Rafael, one of Estevanico's black-thatched younger kids, told him excitedly. They took all the cattle—all—out of the corrals and pens, and they fired the buildings, and they took the *remuda,* and they went away with everything Estevanico owned.

"The colt!" Don Luis cried in a voice of pain. "Chiltipiquin, my red colt!"

They took him, the boy said, beginning to sob. Fighting all the way, but they took him. He had been standing by the house when they had come up, and when one had gone for the house, Rosita had screamed and the Chiltipiquin colt had kicked the one's horse and broken his leg, and the one had run away from the house, and even now the horse with the broken leg lay dead behind the house.

Don Luis unhooked the near horse of his team and swung aboard him bareback and rode out, while Rafael still talked. He knew what had happened. He had thought, a month ago, that he had been seen at work on a neighbor's stock. And then he had decided that the rider who had come suddenly into view and whirled as suddenly away again had not been near enough to recognize him. But his horse had been recognized. Chiltipiquin. Everyone knew the red colt. He had been crazy to use him at mavericking. But it was done now.

The neighboring ranchers had done nothing at once. They had known the red colt belonged at Estevanico's, and while they doubt-less knew Estevanico well enough to know that he himself had not been robbing their herds, still they would hold him responsible. Did not the thief, his old cousin, live under his roof?

So they had waited until he had gathered his own stock, and then they had come and taken it away in payment for theirs which Don Luis had stolen. And with it the Chiltipiquin colt.

"They will not take you far," Don Luis said aloud. "I swear it to you, Sancho Chiltipiquin. Not while I live."

He rode on at a lope, following the well-marked trail. He found the colt in a stretch of broken, timbered country near the little hut that was Estevanico's only line camp. Chiltipiquin lay on his side, his flanks heaving, his nostrils dilated, and turned up his head to poke his nose at Don Luis' fumbling hand in the dusk.

The colt's right foreleg was broken. Whether it had happened ac-cidentally or been done deliberately, in payment for the dead horse back at the *rancheria,* did not matter. Don Luis knelt for a long time at the colt's side, his head bowed. When he stood up, finally, Chiltipi-quin pawed to rise with him, and Don Luis shouted, "No, stay down!" The colt looked up at him questioningly and Don Luis rode away quickly. He heard the colt call to him once, a soft begging whinny, and nothing more.

At the *rancheria,* Estevanico was not troublesome, not after Don Luis had given him in cash enough to buy his choused-off stock twice over. Rosita was worse. Pedro, like the fool he was, had confessed to her his part in stealing their neighbors' cattle. But even Rosita was mollified after Don Luis gave her the considerable sum of his wealth he had held out from Pedro for himself, and, in a voice of muttering thunder, advised Pedro on living in the future the honest life he was made for. The money, Don Luis said sternly, was a wedding gift.

They were all impressed by the solemnity of his manner. They wondered what he had found out about the colt, but they were afraid to ask him. It was without understanding that they gave him what he wanted, and when Estevanico hesitantly suggested riding with him when he was ready to leave in the wagon, Don Luis refused in a fashion that brooked no further interference.

So he returned to Chiltipiquin with the wagon bed cluttered with equipment and with a latern for light. He worked through the night making the sling and attaching it to tree limbs overhead and arranging it so it would lift the colt and bear his weight, and when it was ready, he drew the ropes to the wagon, and with the colt's own help brought him up standing, and then drew him yet a little higher, so the colt could not get leverage to kick and harm himself. Now he strapped splints on the broken leg, and here, when Chiltipiquin struggled against the pain, he had a test of the tarp-and-rope sling. It held. When the leg was set, he spent hours again adjusting the sling to the exact position he wanted, where it would allow no possible weight on the colt's off foreleg, but would not squeeze his belly. Chiltipiquin would be living in the sling for a long time.

In the false light of predawn, Don Luis bedded down between the colt and the wagon and slept. In midmorning he awoke and brought feed from the wagon and water from the stream behind the camp. Then he worked again at the rigging of the sling, and he was engrossed in it when Estevanico spoke soberly behind him. "No horse with a broken leg will ever be right again, never."

"This will." Don Luis gave him an ugly look over his shoulder. "And it will please me if you will stay away. He would be excited."

"I came," Estevanico said, "to tell you we are leaving. We have the money to go someplace else and start better than here. And it would be better for you—"

"I stay with this beast," Don Luis said shortly.

"There is one Villagrá," Estevanico insisted, sounding troubled, "who claims he did not get back a tenth part last night of what he has lost. A friend has told me this morning. It was this one, Villagrá, who tried to take away your Chiltipiquin colt last night. The colt is valuable, he says, and would bring him more money to help make up his loss. I know this one, and he will not give up. He will be looking for you and for the horse."

Don Luis remained silent, working on the sling. The Chiltipiquin colt butted him and knocked off his sombrero and slobbered on his gray hair.

"You cannot live here, old one," Estevanico said. "There is no food."

Don Luis spat. "I will eat grass."

Estevanico went away. He returned later in the day with a load of provisions and Don Luis' belongings, and left them at the shack, but the old man did not see him. He was asleep again near the colt.

Estevanico looked back, as he left, at the colt, awkward and comical in the sling. *Ciertamente,* it was a sorrow. One did not save a horse with a broken leg, no matter how fine the horse.

Don Luis thought differently. There was life in his hand, life that would pass into the colt's leg and make it new again.

But the first thing: patience.

"You make me patient, Sancho Chiltipiquin," Don Luis said, "after you have made me honest, for a patient man is honest. What I steal, you cause to be taken from me. When I would hurry, you hold me back. You are one possession for my old age, in truth."

He came on tracks once, sign of a ridden horse, at the edge of the woods, almost within sight of the line camp, and for a few days he woke up at odd hours and walked out quietly to listen, out he saw no one. The time passed and he forgot to worry. He worked too much with the Chiltipiquin colt to have time left for worry.

There came the day that the sling was gently moved again and the colt stood square on all four legs. Square—Don Luis walked around him time and again, his heart in his throat—square as a box. He was anxious, the red colt, to try his leg now. He was restless and thin. He bit at the sling and stomped his feet, the off forefoot gingerly at first and then with abandon, pleased at the way it worked.

But it took time. At first he walked, led, until the last trace of shortness was gone from the leg, and then cautiously trotted, still to the rope, with Don Luis running beside him, blowing and fat and clumsy.

Winter came near and a snow sprinkled the trees and melted in an hour. Chiltipiquin ran, with Don Luis on his back. He pivoted and turned, he skidded to a stop when Don Luis dabbed a loop on a stump. He ran figure eights among the trees and threw up clods of dirt to explode among their branches. The leg was well.

"So," Don Luis said, chuckling, "who wins, my Chiltipiquin? So how do you keep me honest, when you can now outrun the *rurales?*"

The colt raised his head and snorted.

"We will see," Don Luis said. "We are both hungry. We will see. You have given me a lesson in patience. Soon now we will go on with our life, and we will see."

Here befell the third calamity. Don Luis' food was low and he went out on foot after a bird or a rabbit. He had set snares, and he inspected these, and it took a good while. When he returned, the colt was gone. As before, there was sign of a struggle, but it had ended with Chiltipiquin leading quietly away. Probably they had blindfolded him.

In his madness, Don Luis did not trail them. He was afoot; they would outdistance him anyway. Instead, he walked the eleven miles to the Villagrá spread. He reached it after dark and found it deserted.

The next day he appeared in town, haggard and exhausted. He sold his silver-mounted saddle and bridle and his guns, and rode out in a wagon with the purchaser to the line camp to get them. He could have knocked the man in the head and left with the wagon team. Instead he took his money and went back to town. After another twenty-four hours he had learned what he wanted to know.

"Patience," he said to himself, "patience, old man. Patience, old one," and he looked at his trembling hands and cursed them softly, his eyes smiling in their pouches of fat. He was old.

He hired to work with a freighter hauling north, going up empty for another load of goods. It would be a fast trip.

Winter had settled down in Kansas, but at the sale barn there were still auctions every Saturday, and they would continue as long as the late trail stuff was consigned to them.

The owner of the barn liked the stallion so well that he had thoughts of keeping him for himself. Maybe he would bid him in if his price didn't get high enough. Strange that a trail bunch would be carrying this stud with them. Mexican outfit, man named Villagrá. Horse might be stolen. Road brand on his left shoulder; an old curlicued Mexican monogram brand under it. Well, somebody came up with a horse to trade for beef. Throw him in with the cavy, the trail boss said, and then it turns out he's a stud. And what a stud.

Hot, though. Vicious-tempered brute. No one in the barn could handle him except that old Mexican he'd hired a couple of days ago. Damfool horse treated him like an old friend.

Mexican horse, through and through, that was it. You'd have to talk to him in cowpen Spanish.

"Hey, there, you *viejo*! Get away from that red son of a dog for a minute and muck out this floor! There's a sale tomorrow!"

"*Si señor*," Don Luis muttered hastily.

Chiltipiquin poked his nose and nudged him as he scrambled away, and knocked off his ragged hat.

"It is the last thing I will steal," Don Luis said, chuckling. "I swear it to you."

It was almost morning. The sale barn was eighty miles behind them. The snow was not deep and the day would be clear. Soon the snow would be less, and then it would be gone, and the southern country would come over the horizon to meet them.

"Three misfortunes, Sancho Chiltipiquin," Don Luis said. He shivered in his threadbare clothes and felt his age in his bones, but his voice smiled. "Three misfortunes make a life. That is an antique proverb. Now we walk with God."

"Walk with God," Chiltipiquin said.

Perhaps the old man only imagined the words in the hiss of the morning wind over the snow and the rattle of bit rings as the colt tossed his head, or perhaps the red colt said them. Perhaps.

Quién sabe?

The Runner

JANE AND PAUL ANNIXTER

THAT afternoon, when Shadow took the binoculars to the ridge for his daily check, he saw five strange horsemen in the valley below. There was only one explanation; they were after the wild band.

Shadow sped downgrade at a rocking run. He didn't know what he could do, but he must try to get to The Runner. He paused at intervals, panting, to watch the progress below. With a muffled thunder that filled the lap of the hills, the roan stallion and his band broke for the valley's narrow throat, the first rider pounding close behind. But only for seconds, for the wild ones left the horseman as if he were roped to a tree. When the second man in the cordon broke out of cover with fearsome yips designed to scatter them, the eleven broke about him, passing like a cataract to either side. And so with the third. But the fourth man, breaking cover from the opposite side of the valley, produced a panic in the band which the fifth man was able to utilize as he lanced in with swinging lariat.

The rope snaked through the air and curled about the forelegs of the roan stallion himself. As it went taut the roper and his mount were flung to the ground. But the stallion had fallen, too, and the other four riders were closing in before he could rise. The Runner and the mares fled on. In a matter of moments the stallion was trussed and helpless.

Shadow was running downward again, shouting unheard. Inevitably he fell, pitching forward on chest and hands. He rose, breathless and groggy, and plunged on. For now the five men were slowly closing in about the valley head where The Runner and the mares were cornered. Of course it was The Runner they wanted now. Without a leader the mares could easily be caught later.

As he broke out into the open, gasping for breath, Shadow saw that four of the riders were converging through the trees, bent on cutting off The Runner. The fifth man sat his mount in the open with a rifle resting across the pommel of his saddle.

Shadow knew what this meant. They would try the cruel crease shot, most dangerous of all methods for capturing wild horses. The rifleman would try to graze the base of The Runner's neck where it met the spine, stunning him just long enough for capture. At least a hundred horses were killed by the crease shot for every animal captured.

A great cry burst from Shadow as he ran, but no one heard. With the mares wheeling and screaming at the edge of the woods, he saw The Runner chivvied into the open. In the moment that he paused in consternation the rifleman aimed and fired. The Runner's legs buckled under him and he pitched forward on his nose, then onto his side, to lie motionless and apparently lifeless. Three riders spurred forward.

Shadow's legs had gone out from under him, too. He crouched, sobbing, on the ground. He could not watch now, yet he had to. He saw ropes in the hands of two of the riders. Right in the midst of this the miracle occurred. The luck of the hundredth horse was with The Runner. He had been stunned, but came to with a sudden heave and gained his feet. Blood was running down his neck and shoulder. He reared, screamed, and charged. The mounted rifleman in front of him went down, horse and rider knocked to the ground beneath The Runner's slashing forehoofs. Then The Runner was through the cordon and thundering down the valley toward the dense pines, like a wild duck in flight.

Only two riders gave chase. The other two stayed behind, bent over the stricken man and his mount. Still helpless in the legs, with a hollow cave in his chest, Shadow remained where he was. No one, it seemed, had seen him. After a time he dragged himself over to the shade of some berry bushes and waited, trembling, listening, agonized over the struggle of the roan stallion against his bonds that went on and on to the point of exhaustion, when he simply lay there inert.

A long time passed while the two men who had stayed behind worked over the fallen one. Shadow heard groans and the pained cough of the man's downed horse, which had not risen. Evidently a leg had been broken. When the man on the ground had received first aid, one of the other men knelt by the fallen horse, a hand on its nose, and stroked its neck. When the revolver was slowly drawn from its holster Shadow turned away.

Dusk was close when the other two men emerged from the woods. They had failed to capture The Runner. Shadow could only hope they had not killed him.

He crouched where he was while they close-hobbled the roan stallion and hazed him to his feet. Then the invaders left the valley, a mounted man on either side of the stallion, one of the other horses carrying double.

When all was quiet again Shadow emerged from the thickets and went limping down the valley. They would be expecting him at home, but he could not go until he had found The Runner, no matter how long it took. Probably the men who had caught the stallion would be back tomorrow. Shadow did not know what he could do except find The Runner and stay by him if he were still alive.

He located the coil of rope and the small hand axe he had hidden with it two weeks before, then he entered the woods, following the tracks of The Runner and the two riders who had gone after him. The tracks led in and out through a maze of thickets cut by a swampy, spring-fed creek that later joined the larger stream in the valley bottom. From time to time Shadow's eyes picked out the slim-hoofed tracks of The Runner from among the deep marks of the heavier horses, but darkness was already falling and he could not follow much longer.

He sought higher ground and a spot to spend the night. On a slope he found a dry hide-out beneath the low-sweeping boughs of a spruce. It was not until he sank down on the mat of dry needles that he was aware of how exhausted he was. His weariness was far more than the body's fatigue and the pain of his bad leg; the strength had been wrung from his very heart.

Even if The Runner had escaped vital injury, all his work was undone, for the young stallion would have lost his faith in man. Under the best conditions it would take a long time to win him back. But in this valley conditions would never be right again. That Shadow knew. All this revolved in his mind in addition to a full sense of the pain and consternation his absence would cause at home.

After he had lain there for a time in silence there came a soft, nervous nickering of a mare from the darkness far ahead, answered by another. The familiar sounds soothed Shadow to a sense of companionship and he slept. He was awake many times, uncomfortable and cold. Once he heard coyotes making a rabbit kill in the valley below. A horned owl alighted in the spruce a dozen feet above him and went through its horrid gamut of shrieks and gibbers and booming hoots, as if bent on scaring him into a rout. He pulled his hat down over his face, but it did no good. Finally he just lay awake waiting for the first light.

Hunger drove Shadow along the dawn-lit slopes searching for nuts or berries to eat. His breakfast was a handful of hazel nuts, eatable though not yet ripe, and a few beech nuts. He limped down to the creek for water, then took up the trail again. The way still led along the soggy creek bed. The going grew wetter; water oozed up in his tracks.

Shadow found the place where the two riders had turned back the night before. Their mounts had evidently sunk too deep in the muck to keep on. Farther along the little stream spread out in a boggy swamp overgrown with tough, reed-like grass and moss. Shadow heard the nickering of mares again. Guarding each step for silence, he pressed on until a sort of blasting snort and the sound of struggle came from a thickety place ahead.

Through parted bushes Shadow saw where the young roan was fettered belly-deep in the clutch of black, viscous mud. The Runner's wound and the panic of pursuit had evidently robbed him of the inherent judgment of the wild, and he had taken one chance too many. All night he must have struggled against the mud, only to mire himself deeper. Now he was white-eyed with renewed frenzy.

Cautiously and slowly, stepping on the grass tussocks and fallen branches wherever he could, Shadow moved into the open, talking as he had always talked to The Runner, holding out his empty hand. When the roan struggled again, Shadow hummed until he quited him. Finally he was crouched down close to The Runner's shoulder, running his hand along the straining neck to soothe him.

There was a foam of fever and thirst on the black lips. Not far away Shadow found a pool on the bog's surface. He dipped up a hatful of water and returned. At first The Runner was too terrified to drink, but his great need and the cool smell of water overcame that. Afterward Shadow made six more trips with his dripping hat. Then he set to work to do what he could.

Without this mud, he thought gratefully, he might never have gotten near The Runner again. He tore the bottom of his shirt, soaked it in water, and he cleansed the bullet wound on the roan's crest. It was not deep and had long since ceased to bleed. Shadow unraveled some strands of his rope and tied the cloth over the wound to keep off the gnats and flies. The Runner loosed his pain and fear in blast upon snorting blast through distended red nostrils, but gradually white panic left his liquid eyes. Shadow never stopped talking or humming and he made all his movements slow and rhythmic.

Later he went to higher ground and gathered a big armful of grass. He found a wide, flat slab of bark to lay it upon, within easy reach of The Runner's nose. He knew the roan would be loathe to eat pulled grass with the man-smell upon it, but sooner or later he would be driven to it. Shadow slipped away to forage again for himself. He found some wild blackberries and some more beech nuts. Then he carried several slabs of bark back to the bog and laid them about The Runner for his own footing. Meanwhile he had felt out all the most solid tussocks of grass and moss between the horse and the pool and the horse and the firm bank beyond, for some spots that looked like tussocks were mere traps of mud.

Finally he set to work close to The Runner's mired forelegs, digging with a slab of bark. The wet mud slithered back into the hole almost as fast as he could scoop it out, but flinging it far aside he gradually gained depth. It was slow, killing work. Gnats and mosquitoes whined about him and he had to stop often to get his breath. The Runner ruckled and tossed his head and whipped his muddied tail.

It was mid-afternoon before Shadow had dug down to the horse's knees. He was trembling and sick with exhaustion, but he was beginning to hope. He ranged through the woods with his short-axe, cutting a score of thin saplings to lay in the hole he had dug. Over these he laid many more flat slabs of pine bark.

By this time The Runner sensed he was being helped and whinnied greeting as Shadow returned through the trees, making the exhausted youth so happy he forgot his fatigue and struggled on until dusk. By that time he had cleared enough space for The Runner to move sideways a little and saw, to his great relief, that the horse had sunk as far he was going to.

Before it was dark he brought water again, several hatfuls, and gathered another armful of grass. Now he had to think about his own sleeping place. The night would be chill and the evening full of mosquitoes. He should, he knew, sleep on higher, drier ground. With this in mind he gathered a pile of pine knots and cones and left them on the bank beyond the pool. With his hand axe he cut a large pile of dry branches, knowing he would need a good fire before morning. But The Runner was still whinnying wildly from time to time and he decided to stay as close as possible through the night.

He cut more pine boughs and gathered still more bark and cones and made a platform bed on the soggy ground almost within touch of the young roan's reaching muzzle. Beside this he lit a smudge of bark and leaves—no fire because that would have startled the horse—to help both of them through the worst of the mosquito time. Then he lay down and gazed up at the brilliant high-country stars. Now that it was dark and still, Shadow could feel how glad the young roan was not to be alone. He was glad, too. How much better it was for both of them than last night. In their day-long struggle and strange night-sharing a new bond was growing between them that he hoped nothing would ever break!

Shadow roused with a jerk. The smudge had gone out and the chill, spare wind of midnight was flowing down from the heights. The Runner's frightened snorting told him they were not alone. He sat up and the back of his neck tingled, for in the darkness he made out the slow turning of The Runner's head, the rolling eyes fixed upon the circle of the spruces. His own eyes tried to follow, but could make out nothing. Yet something was happening out there in the blackness, something that only The Runner could interpret. In that moment cold fear seeped through Shadow's blood.

From the glowing, phosphorescent terror in the young stallion's eye he knew it was one of the ancient enemies of horse out there. That meant cougar or bear. If it was cougar the danger was slight, for the big cats were too cowardly to attack a man. But a grizzly, for instance, would be a different matter.

Shadow crept over to a place directly in front of The Runner, stepping on the bark slabs he had laid across the mud. He crouched down, facing the bank and the spruces beyond, holding the light axe in his hand. He knew, of course, that the great paw of a grizzly could strike him down before he could ever use his inadequate weapon. But he sat on, talking quietly to The Runner, waiting for what would come. He could light a fire, but there was the wild horse to think of, with his natural terror of flame. Fear-filled as the roan was, and with many hours of trapped torment behind him, the added shock might break his spirit for all time.

Moments dragged by, blind and black. A sharp sound, the snapping of a sizable branch in the thicket, brought Shadow to his knees, wire-taut. No cat-thing would have been clumsy enough to make that sound. It had been made by a ponderous creature of great weight and with little or no concern for any foe. Hard upon that sound came a vast windy breath from the darkness. The Runner's nostrils ruckled in sheer terror, and he heaved and struggled in new frenzy. No doubt in Shadow's mind now but that it was a grizzly watching and circling there in the blackness. The bear must have sensed the plight of the horse. Only man's presence here had held him from immediate attack, and probably he was nerving himself to it.

An aroused grizzly, Shadow knew, feared nothing at all, not even a magazine rifle, but so far there had been nothing to rouse this one but his own hunger. Fire might hold him at bay without touching off his fury. Shadow would have to light a fire.

Some of the leaves and pine cones he had brought for the smudge had not been used, and there were the bark slabs and pine boughs of his bed. Even so, it seemed an interminable time before flame was started and the needles set ablaze. Shadow feverishly chipped bits of bark to strengthen the flame. At last, in its light, a great boulder-like form took shape from the deeper blackness of the trees less than twenty yards away. It was a grizzly. Even in that flickering light Shadow saw the small, wrathful eyes burning with a red violence, but the bear was as motionless as a museum piece. Moments passed. Shadow could scarcely tear his eyes from the creature to put another branch on the fire. In the renewed light he looked again. Still no movement, just an unbreathing pause with only the little red eyes alive in the great head.

The Runner, too, was silent in the grip of that prolonged, primeval spell of terror. His was the stillness of the conscious victim awaiting the lethal rush. Shadow, a frail human thing frozen in this ancient tableau between predator and prey, knew the awful truth—that the bear was thinking, figuring every instant.

Shadow could stand it no longer. He snatched a burning bough and plunged forward a dozen feet, screaming, then flung his brand. That broke it. The grizzly moved slightly aside, head swinging, but only to advance a moment later, the mud sucking beneath the great feet. In the same instant Shadow was back at the fire, building it up again. The Runner, roused from his fearful trance, was heaving and struggling.

The grizzly advanced to within ten yards, then reared up on his hind legs as if the better to size up the situation, looking vaster than anything Shadow had ever seen. A low, coughing roar came from the open mouth as the fire blazed high with a resinous crackle. Shadow shouted again, an involuntary war cry as old as man. The grizzly moved farther to one side, keeping to the tussocks of grass on the boggy surface.

With two long pieces of bark Shadow forked a flaming branch in that direction and started a new fire, piling on more bark. The grizzly watched. The swirling smoke was not the least of Shadow's defenses. The enemy showed no fear but was obviously nonplussed.

He maneuvered again to the opposite side. Shadow moved to face him, a burning branch in his hand.

The bear stood stolidly, all four great feet ludicrously bunched on a tussock. A spark of inspiration flashed across Shadow's mind. He shouted again and hurled his fiery branch. Momentarily confused, the grizzly floundered aside, to bring up belly-deep in a sucking, viscous hollow. When he roared again it was a bawl of sheer consternation as he fought with giant swimming strokes toward another grass hummock. For a space his struggles only drove him deeper. Shadow seized the moment to spring from grass bunch to tussock toward the bank, as he had done so many times the day before, and return with more of the dry fuel he had gathered there. He heaped it on his fire and was free to go again, the bear still struggling in the mire.

Systematically now, adding to the growing demoralization of the
enemy, Shadow flung his burning brands. One, a flaring pine knot, lit
directly on the broad, undulating back, sizzling a minute in the
coarse brown hair before burning through to the hide. A bellow of

torment sounded. Shadow continued his barrage of shouts and fire.

When he had once reared out of the mire, the grizzly waited a short time, obviously trying to figure out a fresh attack. Tentatively he moved to the right, then to the left. Abruptly he pivoted on his hind quarters, sloshed to higher ground, and, without once turning, lumbered away into the woods as if it were all a matter of his own decision.

Dawn was not far away. In delayed reaction from the stress of those dark hours Shadow trembled and sobbed a little. He crouched now close to The Runner, sharing the horse's warmth in the pre-dawn chill. The soft nose lifted at times to nudge his neck or shoulder. Together the two had met and bested the most terrible foe the mountain wilderness concealed. The Runner seemed to know this, but Shadow still could not believe. It took the full golden dawn of the September morning to reasure him that the bear was gone.

Even then he could not be sure that the grizzly was not lurking close. Ravenous as he was, he forewent searching the thickets for nuts or berries and set to work immediately clearing the mud away from beneath The Runner's forelegs and belly. The mud was even softer here and progress was very slow. Hours passed before he was able to scrape the mud away. Then he floored the hole he had made with more bark and pine boughs, and was ready for the telling trial.

One of the Runner's forelegs was now quite free, resting upon the floor of bark and branches at the bottom of the excavation. Shadow tied his rope about the stallion's neck in a slipless knot and backed up to solid ground. Then he yipped out an order and pulled on the rope. With a prodigious effort The Runner flung himself upward and forward, gaining a full foot. The inexorable mud still held, but he had practically freed the other foreleg. Two more heaving struggles and both forehoofs rested on the improvised ramp. Half his belly was free.

Shadow let him rest awhile. He talked soothingly, stroking the sweat-damp neck and shoulders, praying in his heart that deliverance was near. Finally he pulled from the bank once more, putting a lilt of encouragement into his yell. With snorting, whistling breath, The Runner put forth all that was in him. Two or three times the forehoofs slipped on the ramp. Bark and saplings bent and snapped beneath him, yet offered enough solid purchase to raise his weight. With a final, sucking sigh the quag released its prisoner. The stallion scrambled wildly up the solid bank and there rescuer and rescued stood together, the young roan's chestnut mane falling in a cloud about Shadow's shoulders.

A grizzly will attack as readily in daylight as in darkness, and even now the bear might be lurking anywhere about. When they started moving out of the woods, Shadow kept The Runner to the open places. Also at any moment the wild blood of the roan might reassert itself. For the Runner's own sake Shadow could not chance that now. The young stallion might elude the bear, but if the horse wranglers returned he was doomed. So Shadow rode The Runner out of the swamp woods, keeping to the stream bed until they came to the meadows where the wild band had fed. Some of the mares were in sight there, feeding by the stream. They answered The Runner's whinny and circled closer. The stallion reared and trembled, on the verge of bolting, but Shadow knew that he was riding an exhausted horse. Down by the stream he dismounted while The Runner drank, then led the horse into the water and washed the caked mud from his legs and belly. Later, while The Runner grazed, he fashioned a loose hackamore from a piece of his rope. There was the inevitable near frenzy as he slipped it on, but the trust of the long night prevailed and he fastened it loosely into place, allowing for further grazing if The Runner would.

All this time Shadow was mulling over what lay ahead. It was blacker than anything he had ever faced before. For two days and nights without explanation he had been away from home and job. Considering his uncle's wrath at other times, when he had been away but a few hours, this might end things. Also, Aunt Martha would have worried herself sick and that, too, would be held against him.

The bitless bridle was a final conquest, but Shadow was too hungry, weak, and tired for so much as a quiver of pride as he guided The Runner up out of the wild-horse valley. Thinner than ever, shirtless, mud-caked, slumped above The Runner's wounded crest, he was more a picture of trail's end than victor as they climbed the last steep slope.

It was nearing dusk when he halted The Runner at the gate of his uncle's cow lot. There were no cows there now but the fence was solid and high. Trembling only slightly, The Runner let himself be ridden into the railed enclosure. Talking softly, promising swift return, Shadow barred the gate and limped down toward the house.

Uncle Nathan was sitting in the lamp-lit kitchen with his pipe and a copy of the *Horseman's Journal,* when Shadow quietly opened the door. Nathan gave a start and took the pipe from his mouth, but said no word. He simply sat and stared.

Shadow stood just inside the door as a diffident stranger might, feeling the grateful warmth of the room, smelling the good food smells, but suffering the owner's scrutiny.

"So you came back at last!" Nathan said.

"Yes, sir. But if I can just get something to eat and change my clothes I'll be going again. I guess that's what you want, isn't it?"

"Now then, I don't take it kindly at all, your saying that! Look here, Clem, I want to know what you've been doing all this time. Where have you been?"

Abruptly then Aunt Martha was with them and had him in her arms, dirt and all. "Clem—Clem—"

"The boy's done in, Martha," Nathan said. "Best let him go wash. We'll get the story later. Go on, Clem, Martha will fix you some supper—"

After his timeless ordeal, his neat room with its pictures and books, all his own things around, seemed an unbelievable haven. He had never known before how comforting it was here or how privileged he had been. Sitting on the edge of the bed he almost slipped into oblivion. He had to keep shaking his head to stave off unconsciousness, but he managed to peel off his caked clothes and wash.

He was trembling with weakness when he sat down to the hot soup and warmed biscuits his aunt had ready. Uncle Nathan still sat in his chair, pipe and *Journal* forgotten. He did not speak until the soup bowl had been emptied three times and the whole plateful of biscuits eaten.

"You've been through a lot, Clem," Nathan said then. "No need to go into it all, it's plain to be seen. I've a good idea where you've been; I know, of course, what happened in the valley two days ago."

Aunt Martha, who had been hovering in the background seeing that Shadow got enough to eat, gave a quick, searching look at Nathan's face and said, "Don't talk too long, you two. I'm going upstairs."

"You were down there and saw the whole of it, I daresay," Nathan went on. "That horse wrangler was pretty bad hurt, they say. Heard they creased your horse, too." Nathan paused to let that sink in. "Did he die, Clem?"

Shadow's head had come up with an amazed jerk.

"You needn't worry," Uncle Nathan said. "I've known your secret

for some time. I'm not quite a fool, you know! More than once I
went up on the ridge yonder to see what drew you over the mountain so often. When I caught sight of that young stallion, I knew all
right! I watched your tactics with him through the glass. Tell you
the truth, I never gave you the ghost of a chance to get near him, but
you did. Last time I looked you'd practically tamed him. That
took time and endurance, Clem; courage too. It's a thing I'd like
to have done myself at your age, but I'd never have had the
patience."

Shadow sat in a trance, regarding the older man with a deep,
questioning look. There were sides to his uncle he had never
understood. The fact that he should admit that he could never
have done it—a horseman like Nathan—that was a revelation. Still,
he wasn't sure of anything right now.

"You didn't answer me, Clem. Did your horse die?"

"No, Uncle."

In Nathan's aging face there was a tinge of softness that had never
been there before, or if it had Shadow had never seen it.

"Where is he now, Clem?"

"I left him up in the cow lot."

Nathan started up from his chair, pipe and magazine slithering
to the floor, his whole face a ruddy gleam. "You don't mean to say
you brought that red rascal in! How? You couldn't get a hackamore
on him!"

"I couldn't have except for what happened. He got into the bog
up beyond Bullhide, after they creased him. That's what I've been
doing the last two days—digging him out. He's really mine now!"

Nathan sank back in his chair. "I guess nobody's likely to con-
fute that!" he muttered.

"But I don't know what's going to happen to him," Shadow added
miserably.

Nathan shot him a covert glance. "Since you're going away, you
mean. No, that's not exactly the horse I'd pick for a young man to
ride out into the world on." Uncle Nathan was looking at the wall
with the faintest ghost of a grin on his lantern jaw.

Shadow had no answer.

"Of course, you're free to do as you like, but there's one or two
things I'd like to get straight first. Whether you go or stay this place
will be yours some day. It's to go to you after I'm gone. That's
the way we want it, your Aunt Martha and I. Of course I had hopes
that by degrees you'd shoulder part of the work and worry in my

time, and after a while let me slack off a bit. I'm getting on, you know. But all that's up to you." Nathan paused to pick up his pipe, and methodically reloaded it.

Shadow watched him, swallowing repeatedly but saying nothing.

"From the first your aunt and I wanted to make a son of you. It may sound queer to you but we've wanted that more than anything, ever since your parents died. But—I might as well say right now—I never liked your father. I was sorry when my sister married him. And I was afraid you might take after him—city-bred, soft, spendthrift—and I had to find out about that. Well, I have. I've watched you close. I came up hard myself and always figured it best for a boy. So I didn't make it too easy for you, but you took it right. I waited a long time, Clem, to make sure. Yes, you're a stronger, bigger man than if you'd never been sick."

For Shadow, inside the harsh old image, had appeared the real person, and he sensed need and loneliness there, something like his own. There were a lot of things in all this that he would have to think about for a long time to come. But this much he knew: all his life he would be grateful for this home-coming night.

Uncle Nathan held another match to his pipe. "How you ever brought in that wild animal I don't know, but all that aside, I'm proud of you, Clem." He added shrewdly, "Too bad I had to wait till you're leaving to tell you this—"

Shadow burst out, "I don't really want to go, Uncle! I just thought maybe you'd rather."

Nathan hawked loudly. "Haven't I just been saying how we want you here? As for that horse, of course he's yours, to do with as you please."

Dark Child

EDWARD NORTH ROBINSON

AFTER Dark Child left the paddock, I followed and went across to the infield to get away from the crowd. I didn't want to think about the race at all, but I couldn't help thinking about it all the same. Like always, Dark Child started slow and was well back at the turn. In the back-stretch he began to move up; coming slowly, like it was awful hard. In the turn he was still far back, and it didn't seem possible for him to overtake the front line. But you could see he was running for all he was worth. Coming for home, he was still driving forward hard. And when I saw him trying so hard, a lump came into my throat.

Then it happened. Even though I knew it was going to happen, I couldn't look. I closed my eyes and everything got strange. I felt something inside me turn over.

This happened the year they built the wonderful new tracks in New England, and Yanks, who, they said, had hardly ever seen a horse, had gone mad about racing. All the time that year men kept coming around buying horses, until my father, who runs a feed store in Thomasville, began to say, joking, he was going to move up North, too, because pretty soon there wouldn't be any horses left in Kentucky any more.

But he didn't joke much. He was worried. I wasn't sure why; only I knew it came over him when we heard that my brother Lefty had quit working for Mr. Van Horn and started training horses for a man called Kapnick. I asked my father what part of Kentucky Mr. Kapnick came from, because I'd never heard of anybody talk about his farm. "He don't come from Kentucky; he don't come from nowhere," my father said, walking away.

When I tried to find out about Mr. Kapnick from Anselm, who is an old Negro that has forgot more about horses than any white man ever knew and who knows about anybody on the tracks, all he would say was that Kapnick was a low-down no-account.

Well, when I heard that, I felt awful bad, because my brother Lefty was about the swellest guy anybody ever had for a brother. It was him who taught me to ride Dark Child when he was the most promising two-year-old in Kentucky.

Maybe exercising a horse like Dark Child don't mean nothing to you. Well, that's probably because you're a Yank, and don't know nothing much about horses, and can't understand why it is I feel the way I do. I know Yanks who talk, talk, talk about how they was positive sure such and such a horse was going to win, and say they were going to bet as much as one hundred dollars on him, without even going around to the stables to see what that horse looked like. More than that, I've heard about Yanks who bet on horses with bookies by telephone, without even going to see the race. I've heard them talk, and they don't care nothing about the horse they bet on, they don't care who owns him, where he's from, or what color he is, or how he steps. They don't care about a thing except that he wins the race.

So, if you're a Yank, then there's some things I got to tell you about horses, so you will be able to understand why exercising a horse like Dark Child meant so much to me. Sometimes, though, the way I feel about a horse worries me, because the way I feel is the way some Negroes like Anselm feel, and it makes me wonder if I wasn't supposed to be born a Negro.

Right off, I want to say there is only one way to learn about horses. I don't care how many races you've seen or how much money you've bet, unless you've really lived with horses, then you can't understand about them. Like I have with Dark Child. I don't mean you've got to be like that with every horse to know about him, but if you haven't lived with some, then you can't understand about any at all.

Ever since I was old enough to walk out to the farms from town, where our house is, I began going to see the horses exercised in the morning. I don't think there is anything finer than watching horses running. Especially early in the morning, when the turf is black with dampness and the air is sharp and clear and the sun feels good, shining on your back as you sit on the top rail watching the horses working on the track and listen to the nigger swipes talking and laughing. And there isn't anything finer than this in the whole world, unless you're lucky enough, like me, to be small, so you can get up on a horse yourself and take him out on the track and go slop-jogging around to unflex his muscles. And then, after a lap or so breezing, you climb up on his neck, cluck to him, and it is wonderful to feel him cut loose, to feel the power of his running, the fresh morning air sharp in your face and the horse going like hell-fire for the pure love of running.

That's the way it was when I rode Dark Child. I don't know what it was that happened inside me, but something did. When I'd stretch out along his neck and let him go, and then feel all the power and drive of him under me, the way he would respond, trying to go faster and faster, I just was sure he was going to be a winner. Maybe even the greatest horse who ever ran. It used to make me ache to ride him, because he would run so hard when I wanted him to run. He was the most obliging horse I ever knew. He would react perfect to the slightest pull on the reins, and if I wanted him to run, I would just cluck at him and he would give all he had.

Maybe he tried so hard to please partly because he was a gelding, and partly because he was not a pretty horse and never got a lot of attention from people, like some of the pretty colts did. He had awful big feet and big bones all the way through, and when he walked, he carried his head down between his knees and shambled like a sleepy milk horse. He wasn't proud at all but meek and gentle.

Dark Child was one of those horses who think more of you than just that you bring them oats. I know, because after I would feed him and finish doing chores and start away, he would stop eating and stick his head out of the stable and whinny at me. He always wanted to be petted. If I was walking around in his stall, he would keep turning around, rubbing his head against me, as affectionate as a kitten. I got to think an awful lot of him, and when they sent for him up North, that was how I came to go North too.

It was during the summer, when we were hearing all sorts of talk about how insane the Yanks had gone over racing and how wonderful the new tracks at Pomfret Park and Salt Meadows were, that Mr. Van Horn himself came down to the farm to look the horses over to get some to take up North. One of those he took was Dark Child.

Anselm and I were both glad when Mr. Van Horn selected him, even though he did nothing as a two-year-old. All along, Anselm had said he was going places as a three-year-old. Anselm said he was too rangy to untrack fast enough to win in two-year-old sprints, and that was why he had done poor last year. But Anselm said that when he started running a mile and a mile and a quarter, then he was going to town. Anselm is so smart that he can most often tell what a foal is going to look like even before he is born. I never knew a white man what could do that.

After Mr. Van Horn took Dark Child and the other horses away, there was only the yearlings left. The farm seemed deserted, and I began to feel an all-powerful urge to go North too. I knew it wasn't any use asking my father if I could go, because he'd say I was

too young. That's the way my father is. There isn't anything in the world he likes better than horses, and it nearly broke his heart when he had to stop training, going from track to track, on account of his asthma, and settle down. I can remember him talking to Lefty and me about all the horses he had trained and about all the tracks they had run at—about Tropical Park and Bowie and Churchill Downs and Saratoga, and in Cuba too. But then he'd say what an awful life it was, and after Lefty had gone he used to talk about me being a lawyer or a doctor, and he'd try to make me eat lots of food, so I'd be too heavy to ride, which I wanted to do more than anything in the world.

One day I saw that Dark Child was entered at Niantic and I could hardly wait for the next day to come to find out how he would do. Only all the time I was sure he would win, and I told Anselm so. Anselm said he would win all right, so long as he didn't get boxed up in the stretch turn, which is bad at Niantic, it is so sharp. Although I was positive sure that he would win, when I read in the paper that he did win by two lengths and driving hard, something funny happened to me. All the words blurred together like the white posts do when you're riding fast close to the rail. I couldn't see the words at all, only a vision of a big black horse flashing by the judges' stand in the bright sunlight while thousands of people were looking and cheering. Right then it was that I knew I had to go North. I just had to see Dark Child win.

The only person I told about running away was Anselm. Because you can trust a nigger not to tell on you. It wasn't hard. I just kept my ears open to hear when somebody was going to ship some horses, and when I heard that Colonel Saunderson had a carload going, why, I just went too.

It was in the middle of the morning when I got off the horse car at the track. There were rows and rows of barns. Even though I knew there were over two thousand horses there, I didn't think it would be so big. Although it was at a quiet time, there was an awful lot of people and niggers around—more, even, than in the whole town of Thomasville. I was hungry, so I found out from some boys pitching nickels where the restaurant was, and went there and had a piece of Catawba melon, a stack of wheat cakes with maple sirup and sausages, coffee, two pieces of pie and a bottle of milk. I felt better then and went out to look at the track.

It was beautiful. Clean and well kept, like a park. The infield was all grass, smooth as a lawn except for the tanbark strip where the horses crossed to the paddock. On the opposite side was the big grandstand, with rows of flags on top, flying in the breeze. In front was the judges' stand, all glassed in, and across the track the tote board. Even so far away the grandstand looked awful big, and I wondered where all the people came from to fill all the seats.

I didn't look around any more because I wanted to see Dark Child. It wasn't hard finding Mr. Van Horn's string. His colors ran the whole length of a barn, and right away I recognized old King Knute looking out of his stall. It seemed mighty good to see the horses again. There was Jim Dandy, with his Flying Don, short-hitched to keep him from pacing; a couple of new fillies I didn't know; Black Devil, who was out of the same dam as Dark Child; and His Royal

Highness, who never once ran first, yet lots of times second or third. But Dark Child wasn't there.

I walked the length of the barn again, but he wasn't there. Then I met Monty, one of Mr. Van Horn's niggers. He wanted to know how come I was there. I told him, to see Dark Child run, and Monty agreed he was doing some powerful running. When I asked him where he was, he wanted to know where I'd been all my life if I didn't know my own brother was training him for Mr. Kapnick and that he was supposed to run that afternoon; only he probably was scratched, because he pulled up lame last time out.

I had to do some tall hunting and ask two niggers before I found where Kapnick's horses was. It made me worried when I heard that Dark Child was lame, not because I wouldn't see him run that afternoon, but that he might have to go back to the farm, because when a horse with weak pasterns like him goes lame, it's bad news.

Finally, I found him standing in his stall with his head down and different looking—not sleek any longer. Then I saw he was standing with one leg in a tub of ice water, and all at once I knew they were trying to get him ready to run, and it made me ache to see him standing, so quietly and of his own accord, holding his leg in the ice water.

Just then a man came with more ice in a bucket and dumped it in the tub. I asked him where Lefty was, and he asked me what the cripes I wanted. I said that I just wanted to see him, and when would he be back?

"Back?" he said. "He ain't been yet!"

"Where is he?" I asked.

"Up at the Town Inn with a dame," he said, "and if it's anything to you, that's where I'd be, too, if I had this three-legged gold mine."

I felt bad because it sounded like my own brother Lefty was campaigning Dark Child. I didn't believe it and started away. As I was going, a shiny car swung around the other end of the barn, and I saw my brother and another man, both dressed up swell, get out, and in the car I could see two women dolled up like movie actresses. I felt ashamed and went away quick, so they wouldn't see me.

That afternoon I went over into the infield to watch the races. Dark Child was running in the fourth. When I was riding up from Kentucky in the horse car, it seemed like I couldn't get there fast enough to see him run. But now, after finding out his condition, I kept wishing the fourth wouldn't come, and I kept telling myself that when Lefty saw how bad his leg was, he wouldn't let them run him.

It was a mile race, so the start was right in front of the grandstand. From the infield, I could see all the people in the clubhouse and grandstand milling around, and there was more than I thought could be in the whole world almost.

When the horses paraded out, Dark Child looked homely beside the rest. He shambled along with his head down, following the horse in front of him just like he was supposed to do, without any fuss or capers. The marshal in his red coat paraded the horses way up by the clubhouse and then back by the grandstand and down into the stretch. It seemed as if he would never get them to the barrier. I couldn't understand why he walked them so far.

All the while the people were rushing to the betting windows and the announcer was urging them to hurry and not get shut out. Finally the horses were at the barrier. After about three minutes, the starters got them in line and the bell rang and they broke off almost together. Right away, a filly called Cleo went to the lead, followed by a mare from the Baywood Stables, and then four bunched up, and Dark Child trailing with the rest. Most of the horses were new to me and I couldn't make out the silks without any glasses, so I couldn't tell exactly how they went into the far turn. But it was about the same order, with the filly leading and Dark Child well back. That was because he wasn't able to untrack fast. The minute I saw him come up on the backstretch, I knew he would win. Going into the turn, he was fifth and coming strong. But suddenly he stumbled and his jockey went off, flying. In the grandstand there was a loud noise from the people. The field passed Dark Child. As they did, he started after them. Then a funny thing happened. Instead of chasing after them, he turned around and went back to where his jockey was getting up. Himself, he didn't care about winning. He only ran because his jockey wanted him to.

After they led Dark Child across the infield, I followed. When they got to the barn I went right up to him and patted him.

Right off, he knew me, and I could see how glad he was to see me, rubbing his sweaty head against me and whinnying softly. When they took his bandages off and I saw the swelling, I knew he was through running for a good long time.

I didn't care if Lefty would come and send me home any more, because I felt so fond of that horse I would rather be back home with him than up here with all the others.

Lefty didn't come until after all the races were over. He came in the car with one of the same women. They sat in the car for a while and didn't notice me standing by the stall, because they were arguing about something. And then I heard Lefty start swearing at the woman about betting, and the woman swearing back like I never heard a woman talk before.

At first, when he got out of the car, he didn't see me. When he did, he said, "What are you doing here?" I told him I wanted to see Dark Child run. And he said, "Well, you seen the stumbling dog run all right, didn't you?" Then he wanted to know if the old man had got tired feeding me and sent me. I felt awful to hear him talk like this. I told him no. "Well," he said, "now that you're here, you can stay until the meeting is over." I told him that I thought I'd stay a few days and go back maybe with Dark Child. "What the hell do you mean—back with that dog?"

"He's lame," I said.

"Lame," he said, laughing. "Of course, he's lame. He was lame when we got him. But he still can run. Kid," he said, "take the hay-seed out of your hair. You ain't down on the farm no longer."

I didn't know what to say. If I didn't know this was Lefty, then, from his actions, I'd know it wasn't Lefty. I wanted to go some-where away, but I didn't want to leave Dark Child.

The next day Lefty came out with a big man who wore glasses. They looked at Dark Child's legs, and the big man said it was bucked shins and the only thing to do was have him fired. I heard Lefty arguing, saying, "But, doc, I'll have to lay him up for a month." Then the big man, who, I figured, must be a horse doctor, got mad and told Lefty to go to hell and do what he wanted, because if he hadn't earned enough on that horse without hollering about lay-ing him up for a month, he ought to get out of racing.

I was glad he said that. I almost wished he'd put Lefty off the track for a while.

The next morning Lefty and the horse doctor and another man came. I saw the electric firing irons and knew they were going to try to pull the muscles back by firing him. I had never seen a horse fired before, and I didn't want to see them do it to Dark Child. But Lefty made me stand by his head and pat him. The first thing they did was to paint him below the knees with something that smelled like hospitals.

Dark Child didn't seem to care at all what they did, just so long as I kept patting him. He hardly moved, even when they cut open his legs and injected the irons. He just stood quiet and let them do any-thing. All the time I kept saying to myself that it didn't hurt him, because his legs were numb. After it was done, the doctor gave him a smack and said it was a good job and ought to last until next year.

When the meeting closed, Lefty left me there with Dark Child and he went to Pomfret. It was about a month before the next meeting would open up, and that was just about how much longer it would take for the wounds to heal. Almost everybody went away and, as Lefty came down only twice, I would have been awful lonely if it hadn't been for Dark Child.

A few days after the next meeting opened, Lefty ran Dark Child for the first time since he was fired. He wasn't the favorite, but the odds on him were low. Like always, he got away slow and began to make ground in the backstretch. When his jock started driving him in the turn, he came up more. In the stretch he pushed up with the leaders. Toward the finish he was running neck and neck with Chatterfoe. In running so hard, Dark Child looked like he was coming apart. At the last few yards he just seemed to throw himself forward like he would die, even, to win for the boy riding him. And when I saw him trying so hard, I just felt that there wasn't a gamer horse living.

The finish was so close that nobody knew who won until the numbers flashed. It was Dark Child who won. When they led him into the winner's circle, he looked as though he would topple over, he was so all in. Standing there, he didn't seem to have any interest at all in winning. He just stood quiet, to be unsaddled and led away.

Three days later Lefty entered him again. This time the handicapper put seven pounds more weight on him. The race was a mile and seventy yards. When I led him out to go across the infield, I knew he didn't want to go. He wasn't a fighter or a show-off, like some horses who love to race. Mostly you can tell them by the cake walk they do in front of the grandstand. Dark Child hated racing. I could tell. But he came along just the same. He never caused any trouble.

He was the favorite this time. But the track men realized he was carrying a lot of weight, and most of them knew about his bad legs, so they stayed off him. Again he started slow, but he broke clean. And he ran the same way, stretching out and driving all the way in the backstretch, to come up with the leaders. Then, under the constant hammering of his jock, staying right up there around the turn, to give everything he had in the stretch and win by a nose.

Not until I led him away after the race did I realize how tired he was. It wasn't only that he was all lather and sweat and twitching muscles. It wasn't just the exhaustion of one race, but a tiredness from too many races without resting.

I couldn't understand why Lefty kept running him so often. I knew he did it for the money, but what I couldn't figure was why he kept running him continually, instead of resting him and training for a big purse. Because he was only a three-year-old, and if he was built up instead of being run so much, he could become a great horse and maybe win twenty-five thousand dollars in one race, even. I knew he would be a great horse, because he was big and perfect to train, and because he had courage. Why Lefty ran him like he was, I didn't know, and I began to think about it all the time, trying to figure out why.

One day I found out. I had just brushed Dark Child and was putting a stable blanket on him to protect him from the horseflies, which were bothering him bad. As I bent under him to reach the blanket strap, a big horsefly stung his near foot and he kicked, nearly clipping me. Then I saw the same fly light on his other foot, and he didn't move at all. I wouldn't have thought about it, only I remembered how that was the foot that Lefty was always looking at. So I looked at it close and I couldn't see anything the matter with it; only somehow it didn't look healthy. I got thinking about what could make it look like that, and all at once I thought of something that just made me sick. It was the thing, my father said, any man who did it to a horse ought to be shot for. Even though I couldn't believe what I was thinking, I had to know, because I was so crazy over Dark Child.

So I got a horse-blanket pin and unbent it, so it was like a lancet. Then I went into Dark Child's stall. Bending over from where I stood in front of him, I stabbed him in his right shank. The horse-blanket pin went in deep, but he didn't move. It didn't hurt him, because all the nerves had been cut out. And that was why he didn't go lame any more—because no matter how sore he was, he couldn't feel it. Pretty soon his hoof would be dead, and that was why Lefty kept running him all the time—because where the nerves were cut out, his hoof would become more and more brittle, and it was only a question of time when it would break off.

It was all clear then. But suddenly everything became foggy, and I thought of what my father had said to both me and Lefty about any trainer who did such a thing to a horse. I couldn't realize it was my own brother Lefty who had done it. Like a flash, I remembered how quiet and peaceful it was walking between the poplars at the Van Horn farm, and how Anselm was the smartest nigger who ever lived, and how Lefty and I used to listen to him talk about the most glorious sport that there ever was, horse racing, and the sound of the frogs in the marsh by the railroad at night. And it seemed a long time ago. And I remembered the way my father's feed store looked, with my father sitting in the office, and mash feeders and drinking fountains for chickens in the show window, and things were all clear and fine.

But at the same time, ugly and jumbled together, was the crowd of people pushing one another and fighting to get to the ticket windows, the women dolled up fine, but acting like bad women, the white trash hanging around the restaurant, bragging and drinking, the tote board flashing and the people shoving one another around. All this was jumbled up and spinning in my head.

Then Dark Child rubbed against me like he was always doing, and I just threw my arms around his neck and cried.

The next day when Lefty was saddling Dark Child in the paddock and I was there holding his head and the people were crowding around the paddock rail, looking at their programs to see what horse was the one they'd bet on, I saw Lefty look down at Dark Child's right foreleg. He looked up and saw me watching him, and he knew that I knew. Without saying anything, he walked away and left me there with Dark Child.

Like I said, after the horses left the paddock, I went into the infield. And Dark Child started to run hard in the backstretch and the far turn, coming slowly, like it was awful hard. And that was when it happened. And I couldn't look at first.

When I opened my eyes, Dark Child had got up and was hobbling on three legs, with the hoof of his right foreleg flopping. His jockey was up too. And some men were running toward him from the infield, and pretty soon they got to him so he wouldn't try to walk. Then the big man who was the doctor went out, carrying his bag, and when he got there he made the men hold his head down while he jabbed something in his neck. Then they let him go, and he stood there weakly, trying to rub his head against the doctor, balancing on three legs for a while and then toppling over.

The next day they dug a grave out in the infield and had a funeral just before the first race. And before they pushed him into the grave, the announcer read over the loudspeaker, while church music was playing soft, what a fine horse Dark Child was and how much the people liked him, and he told about how much Dark Child liked to race and how he died a death that was fitting for a gallant horse to die, and he said a lot more while the music was playing softly and all the people stood watching to see the men with poles push Dark Child into the grave.

But all the time I knew what the announcer said was all lies, because he didn't like to race, and the only reason he tried so hard was because he wanted to please somebody. He didn't care anything about winning. He only ran because he wanted somebody to pat him. And all of a sudden I began to hate horse racing, and betting on horses, and the people pushing around, and the fat judges sitting in the stands smoking big cigars, and the ritzy people in the clubhouse with their fancy clothes, and the amount of money bet flashing on the tote board alongside the numbers for the horses, and the announcer's voice urging everybody to hurry and get their bet in.

Then, inside me, I felt awful sick, and I knew I would never be a rider at a big track and I didn't want to see any more races. I just wanted to go home.

The Look of Eagles

JOHN TAINTOR FOOTE

I HAD WAITED ten minutes on that corner. At last I ventured out from the curb and peered down the street, hoping for the sight of a red and white sign that read: "This car for the races." Then a road horn bellowed, too close for comfort. I stepped back hastily in favor of the purring giant that bore it, and looked up into the smiling eyes of the master of Thistle Ridge. The big car slid its length and stopped. Its flanks were white with dust. Its little stint that morning had been to sweep away the miles between Lexington and Louisville.

"Early, aren't you?" asked Judge Dillon as I settled back contentedly at his side.

"Thought I'd spend a few hours with our mutual friend," I explained.

I felt an amused glance.

"Diverting and—er—profitable, eh? What does the victim say about it?"

"He never reads them," I confessed; and Judge Dillon chuckled.

"I've come over to see our Derby candidate in particular," he informed me. "I haven't heard from him for a month. Your friend is a poor correspondent."

The gateman at Churchill Downs shouted directions at us a few moments later and the car swung to the left, past a city of stables. As we wheeled through a gap in a line of whitewashed stalls, we heard the raised voice of Blister Jones. He was confronting the hapless Chick and a steaming bucket.

"Fur the brown stud, eh?" we heard. "Let's look at it."

Chick presented the bucket in silence. Blister peered at its contents.

"Soup," he sniffed. "I thought so. Go rub it in your hair."

"You tells me to throw the wet feed into him, didn't you?" Chick inquired defensively.

"Last week—yes," said Blister—"not all summer. Some day a thought'll get in your nut 'n' bust it!" His eye caught the motor and his frown was instantly blotted out.

"Why, how-de-do, Judge!" he said. "I didn't see you."

"Don't mind us," Judge Dillion told him as we alighted. "How's the colt?"

Blister turned and glanced at a shining bay head protruding from an upper door.

"Well, I'll tell you," he said deliberately. "He ain't such a bad sort of a colt in some ways. Fur a while I liked him. But here lately I get to thinkin' he won't do. He's got a lot of step. He shows me a couple o' nice works; but if he makes a stake hoss I'm fooled bad."

"Huh!" grunted Judge Dillion. "What's the matter? Is he sluggish?"

"That wouldn't worry me so much if he was," said Blister. "They don't have to go speed crazy all at once." He hesitated for a moment, looking up into the owner's face. Then, as one breaking terrible news: "Judge," he said, "he ain't got the class."

There followed a silence. In it I became aware that the blue and gold of Thistle Ridge would not flash from the barrier on Derby Day.

"Well, ship him home," said Judge Dillion at last as he sat down rather heavily on a bale of hay. He glanced once at the slim bay head, then turned to us with a smile and said, "Better luck next year."

I was tongue-tied before that smile; but Blister came to the rescue.

"You still like that Fire Fly cross, don't you?" he asked with a challenge in his voice.

"I do," asserted Judge Dillion firmly. "It gives 'em bone like nothing else."

"Yep," agreed Blister—"'n' a lot of it goes to the head. None of that Fire Fly blood fur mine. Nine out of ten of 'em sprawl. They don't gather up like they meant it. Now you take old Torch Bearer—"

I found a chair and became busy with my own thoughts. I wondered if, after all, the breeding of speed horses was not too cruelly disappointing to those whose heart and soul were in it. The moments of triumph were wonderful, of course. The thrill of any other game was feeble in comparison; but oh, the many and bitter disappointments!

At last I became conscious of a little old man approaching down the line of stalls. His clothes were quite shabby; but he walked with crisp erectness, with something of an air. He carried his soft hat in his hand, and his silky hair glistened like silver in the sunshine. As he stopped and addressed a stable boy, a dozen stalls from where we sat, the courteous tilt of his head was vaguely familiar.

"Who's that old man down there?" I asked. "I think I've seen him before."

Blister followed my eyes and sat up in his chair with a jerk. He looked about him as though contemplating flight.

"Oh lord!" he said. "Now I'll get mine!"

"Who is it?" I repeated.

"Ole Man Sanford," answered Blister. "I ain't seen him for a year. I hopped a hoss fur him once. I guess I told you."

I nodded.

"What's he talking about?" asked Judge Dillon.

And I explained how Old Man Sanford, a big breeder in his day, was now in reduced circumstances; how he had, with a small legacy, purchased a horse and placed him in Blister's hands; how Blister had given the horse stimulants before a race, contrary to racing rules; and how Mr. Sanford had discovered it and had torn up his tickets when the horse won.

"Tore up his tickets!" exclaimed Judge Dillon. "How much?"

"Fifteen hundred dollars," I replied. "All he had in the world."

Judge Dillon whistled.

"I've met him," he said. "He won a Derby thirty years ago." He bent forward and examined the straight, white-haired little figure. "Tore up his tickets. eh?" he repeated. Then softly: "Blood will tell!"

"Here he comes," said Blister uneasily. "He'll give me the once over 'n' brush by, I guess."

But Old Man Sanford did nothing of the sort. A radiant smile and two extended hands greeted Blister's awkward advance.

"My deah young friend, how is the world treatin' you these days?"

"Pretty good, Mr. Sanford," answered Blister and hesitated. "I kinda thought you'd be sore at me," he confessed. "While I didn't mean it that way, I give you a raw deal, didn't I?"

A hand rested on Blister's sleeve for an instant.

"When yoh hair," said Old Man Sanford, "has taken its color from the many wintuhs whose stohms have bowed yoh head, you will have learned this: We act accohdin' to our lights. Some are brighter, some are dimmer, than others; but who shall be the judge?"

Whether or not Blister got the finer shadings of this, the sense of it was plain.

"I might have knowed you wouldn't be sore," he said relievedly. "Here's Chick. You remember Chick, Mr. Sanford."

Chick was greeted radiantly. Likewise "Petah."

"And the hawses? How are the hawses? Have you a nice string?" Blister turned and "made us acquainted" with Old Man Sanford.

"Chick," he called, "get a chair fur Mr. Sanford. Pete—you boys start in with the sorrel hoss 'n' bring 'em all out, one at a time!"

"Why, now," said Mr. Sanford, "I mustn't make a nuisance of myself. It would be a great pleasuh, suh, to see yoh hawses; but I do not wish to bothah you. Suppose I just walk from stall to stall?"

He tried to advance toward the stalls, but was confronted by Blister who took him by the arms, smiled down into his face, and gave him a gentle shake.

"Now listen!" said Blister. "As long as we're here, you treat this string like it's yours. They'll come out 'n' stand on their ears if you want to see it. You got me?"

I saw a dull red mount slowly to the wrinkled cheeks. The little figure became straighter, if possible, in its threadbare black suit. I saw an enormous silk handkerchief, embroidered and yellow with age, appear suddenly as Old Man Sanford blew his nose. He started to speak, faltered, and again was obliged to resort to the handkerchief.

"I thank you, suh," he said at last, and found a chair as Judge Dillon's eyes sought mine.

We left him out of our conversation for a time; but as the string was led before him one by one, the horseman in Mr. Sanford triumphed. He passed loving judgment on one and all, his face keen and lighted. Of the colt I had just heard doomed he said:

"Well-made youngsteh, gentlemen; his blood speaks in every line of him. But as I look him oveh I have a feeling—it is, of cohse, no more than that—that he lacks a certain quality essential to a great hawse."

"What quality?" asked Judge Dillon quickly.

"A racin' heart, suh," came the prompt reply.

"Oh, that's it, is it?" asked Judge Dillon and added dryly: "I own him."

Mr. Sanford gave one reproachful glance at Blister.

"I beg yoh pahdon, suh," he said earnestly to Judge Dillon. "A snap judgment in mattehs of this sawt is, of cohse, wo'thless. Do not give my words a thought, suh. They were spoken hastily, without due deliberation, with no real knowledge on which to base them. I sincerely hope I have not pained you, suh."

Judge Dillon's big hand swung over and covered one of the thin knees incased in shiny broadcloth.

"No sportsman," he said, "is hurt by the truth. That's just exactly what's the matter with him. But how did you know it?"

Mr. Sanford hesitated.

"I'm quite likely to be mistaken, suh," he said. "But if it would interest you, I may say that I missed a certain look about his head, and moh pahticularly in his eyes, that is the hallmark—this is merely my opinion, suh—of a really great hawse."

"What kind of a look?" I asked.

Again Mr. Sanford hesitated.

"It is hard to define, suh," he explained. "It is not a matteh of skull structure—of confohmation. It is—" He sought for words. "Well, suh, about the head of a truly great hawse there is an air of freedom unconquerable. The eyes seem to look on heights beyond our gaze. It is the look of a spirit that can soar. It is not confined to hawses; even in his pictures you can see it in the eyes of the Bonaparte. It is the birthright of eagles. They all have it. . . . But I express myself badly." He turned to Judge Dillon.

"Your great mayeh has it, suh, to a marked degree."

"Tres Jolie?" inquired Judge Dillon, and Mr. Sanford nodded.

I had heard of a power—psychic, perhaps—which comes to a few, a very few, who give their lives and their hearts to horses. I looked curiously at the little old man beside me. Did those faded watery eyes see something hidden from the rest of us? I wondered.

Blister interrupted my thoughts.

"Say, Mr. Sanford," he asked suddenly, "what did you ever do with Trampfast?"

"I disposed of him, suh, for nine hundred dollahs."

Blister considered this for a moment.

"Look-a-here!" he said. "You don't like the way I handled that hoss fur you, 'n' I'd like a chance to make good. I know where I can buy a right good plater fur nine hundred dollars. I'll make him pay his way or no charge. What do you say?"

Mr. Sanford shook his head. "As a matteh of fact," he stated, "I have only six hundred dollahs now in hand. Aside from having learned that my racing methods are not those of today, I would not care to see the pu'ple and white on a six-hundred-dollar hawse."

"Why, look-a-here!" urged Blister. "All the big stables race platers. There's good money in it when it's handled right. Let a goat chew dust a few times till you can drop him in soft somewheres, 'n' then put a piece of change on him at nice juicy odds. The boy kicks a win out of him, maybe; 'n' right there he don't owe you nothin'."

Once more I saw a dull red flare up in Mr. Sanford's face; but now he favored Blister with a bristling stare.

"I have difficulty in following you at times, suh," he said. "Am I justified in believing that the word 'goat' is applied to a thoroughbred race hawse?"

"Why, yes, Mr. Sanford," said Blister, "that's what I mean, I expect."

The old gentleman seemed to spend a moment in dismissing his wrath. When he spoke at last, no trace of it was in his voice.

"I am fond of you, my young friend," he said. "Under a cynical exterior I have found you courteous, loyal, tender-hearted; but I deplore in you the shallow flippancy of this age. It is the fashion to sneer at the finer things; and so you call a racin' thoroughbred a goat. He is not of stake quality perhaps." Here the voice became quite gentle: "Are you?"

"I guess not, Mr. Sanford," admitted Blister.

"Never mind, my boy. If man breeds one genius to a decade, it is enough. And so it goes with hawses. Foh thirty years, with love, with reverence, I tried to breed great hawses—hawses that would be a joy, an honoh to my state. In those days ninety colts were foaled each spring at Sanfo'd Hall. I have spent twenty thousand dollahs foh a single matron. How many hawses—truly great hawses—did such brood mayehs as that produce? How many do you think?"

Judge Dillon gave Mr. Sanford the warm look of a brother.

"Not many," he murmured.

"Why, I dunno, Mr. Sanford," said Blister. "You tells me about one—the filly that copped the Derby fur you."

"Yes; she was one. And one moh such. Two in all."

"I never hear you mention but the one," said Blister.

"The other never raced," explained Mr. Sanford. "I'll tell you why."

He lapsed into silence, into a sort of reverie, while we waited. When he spoke, it was totally without emotion. His voice was dull. It sounded somehow as though speech had been given to the dead past.

"It has been a long time," he said, more to himself than to us. "A long time!" he repeated, nodding thoughtfully, and again became silent.

"In those days," he began at last, "it was the custom of their mistress to go to the no'th pastuh with sugah, and call to the weanlin's. In flytime the youngstehs preferred the willow trees by the creek, and there was a qua'tah of a mile of level blue grass from those willows to the pastuh gate. She would stand at the gate and call. As they heard her voice the colts would come oveh the creek bank as though it were a barrier—a fair start and no favohs asked. The rascals like sugah, to be sure; but an excuse to fight it out for a qua'tah was the main point of the game.

"One year a blood bay colt, black to the hocks and knees, was foaled in January. In June he got his sugah fuhst, by two open lengths. In August he made them hang their heads foh shame—five, six, seven lengths he beat them; and their siahs watchin' from the paddocks.

"In the spring of his two-year-old fohm he suffered with an attack of distempah. He had been galloped on the fahm track by then, and we knew just what he was. We nuhsed him through it, and by the following spring he was ready to go out and meet them all foh the honoh of the pu'ple and white.

"Then, one night, I was awakened to be told that a doctah must

be fetched and that each moment was precious. I sent my body sehvant to the bahns with the message that I wished a saddle on the best hawse in the stable. When pahtially dressed, I followed him, and was thrown up by a stable man. . . .

"There was a moon—a gracious moon, I remembah—the white road to Gawgetown, and a great fear at my heart. I did not know what was under me until I gave him his head on that white, straight road. . . . Then I knew. I cannot say in what time we did those four miles; but this I can tell you—the colt ran the last mile as stanchly as the first, and one hour later he could barely walk. His terrific pace oveh that flinty road destroyed his tendons and broke the small bones in his legs. He gave his racin' life for his lady, like the honest gentleman he was. His sacrifice, howeveh, was in vain. . . . Death had the heels of him that night. Death had the heels of him!"

In a tense silence I seemed to hear a bell tolling. "Death had the heels of him!" It boomed over and over again.

Blister's eyes were starting from their sockets, but he did not hear the bell. He wet his parted lips.

"What become of him?" he breathed.

"When the place was sold he went with the rest. You have seen his descendant race on until his name has become a glory. The colt I rode that night was—Torch Bearer."

Blister drew in his breath with a whistling sound.

"Torch Bearer!" he gasped. "Did you own Torch Bearer?"

"I did, suh," came the quiet answer. "I bred him and raised him. His blood flows in the veins of many—er—goats, I believe you call them."

"Man, oh, man!" Blister, and became speechless.

I, too, was silent of necessity. There was something wrong with my throat.

And now Judge Dillon spoke, and it was apparent that he was afflicted like myself. Once more the big hand covered the thin knee.

"Mr. Sanford," I heard, "you can do me a favor if you will."

"My deah suh, name it!"

"Go to Lexington. Look over the colts at Thistle Ridge. If you find one good enough for the purple and white—bring him back here. . . . He's yours!"

I went along. Oh, yes: I went along. I should miss two days of racing; but I would have missed more than that quite willingly. I was to see Old Man Sanford pick out one from a hundred colts—and all "Bred clear to the clouds," as Blister explained to us on the train. I wondered whether any one of them would have that look—"the birthright of eagles"—and I hoped, I almost prayed, that we should find it.

That the colt was to be a purchase, not a gift, had made our journey possible. Five hundred dollars cash and "my note, suh, for a like amount."

Judge Dillon had broken the deadlock by accepting; then offered his car for the trip to Lexington.

"I thank you, suh, foh yoh generosity." apologized Mr. Sanford. "It gives me the deepest pleasuh, the deepest gratification, suh; but, it you will pahdon me, I shall feel moah at home on the train."

We spent the night at the hotel and drove to Thistle Ridge early next morning behind a plodding pair. Even in Kentucky, livery horses are—livery horses.

A letter from Judge Dillon opened the big gates wide and placed us in charge of one Wesley Washington—as I live by bread, that was his name—suspicious by nature and black as a buzzard. I reminded him of my previous visit to Thistle Ridge. He acknowledged it with no sign of enthusiasm.

"What kind a colt you want?" he asked Blister.

"A good one!" answered Blister briefly.

Wesley rolled the whites of his eyes at him and sniffed.

"You ain' said nothin'," he stated. "Dat's all we got."

"You're lucky," Blister told him. "Well, trot 'em out."

Then Wesley waved his wand—it chanced to be a black paw with a pinkish palm—and they were trotted out; or, rather, they came rearing through the doorway of the biggest of the big stables. Bays, browns, blacks, sorrels, chestnuts, roans—they bubbled out at us in an endless stream. Attached precariously to each of them—this was especially true when they reared—was a colored boy. These Wesley addressed in sparkling and figurative speech. His remarks, as a rule, were prefaced by the word "Niggah."

At last Blister shouted through the dust.

"Say," he said, "this ain't gettin' us nowhere. Holy fright! How many you got?"

"Dat ain't half," said Wesley ominously.

"Cut it out!" directed Blister. "You'll have me pop-eyed in a minute. We'll go through the stalls 'n' pick out the live ones. This stuff's too young anyway. We want a two-year-old broke to the barrier. Have you got any?"

I turned to Mr. Sanford. He was standing hat in hand, as was his custom, his face ablaze.

"The grandest spectacle I have witnessed in thirty yeahs, suh!" he informed me.

"Has we got a two-year-old broke to de barrieh?" I heard Wesley. "Hush! Just ambulate ovh disaway."

He led us to a smaller stable. It contained two rows of box stalls with a wide alley down the middle. Through the iron gratings in each stall I could see a snakelike head. The door at the opposite end of the stable looked out on the tawny oval of the farm track, and suddenly something flashed across the doorway so quickly that I only guessed it to be a thoroughbred with a boy crouching along his neck.

Wesley's eye swept up and down the two lines of box stalls. He looked at Blister with a prideful gleam.

"All two-yeah-olds," he said, " 'n' ready to race."

If this statement made any impression, it was concealed. Blister yawned and sauntered to the first stall on the right.

"Well, there might be a plater among 'em," he said. "This all you got?"

"Ain' dat enough?" inquired Wesley with a snort.

"Not if they're the culls," said Blister. "You read that letter, didn't you? We're to see 'em all. Don't forget that."

"Hyar dey is," said Wesley. "Jus' use yoh eyes an' yoh han's."

"All right," said Blister as he opened the stall door—"but don't hold nothin' out on us. Mr. Sanford here is an old friend of the Judge."

Wesley rolled an inspecting eye over Mr. Sanford.

"I ain' neveh seen him roun' hyah," and honors were easy.

The battle was on in earnest a moment later. The colt in the first stall was haltered and led out into the runway. He was jet black with one white star, and wonderful to see.

"Nothin' finah on fo' laigs," said Wesley, and I mentally agreed with him; but Blister walked once round that glorious creature and waved him back into his stall.

"Yep," he said; "he's right good on four legs, but he'll be on three when that curb begins to talk to him."

"Shuh!" said Wesley in deep disgust. "You ain' goin' to call dat little fullness in de tendon a curb, is you? He'll die of ole aige an' neveh know he's got it."

"He dies of old age before I own him," said Blister, and walked to the second stall.

And so it went for an hour. Mr. Sanford was strangely silent. When he ventured an opinion at all, it was to agree with Wesley, and I was disappointed. I had hoped for delightful dissertations, for super-human judgments. I had expected to see a master at work with his

chosen medium. Instead, he seemed a child in the hands of the skillful Wesley; and I felt that Blister was our only hope.

This opinion had become settled when the unexpected happened. After a more than careful inspection of a chestnut colt,
Blister turned to Wesley.

"What's this colt done?" he asked.

"Half in fifty," Wesley stated. "Jus' play foh him."

"Put a boy on him 'n' let's see him move," said Blister.

Then Mr. Sanford spoke.

"It will be unnecessary," he said quietly. "I do not like him."

A puzzled expression spread itself over Blister's face.

"All right," he said with a shade of annoyance in his voice. "You're
the doctor."

And then I noticed Wesley—Wesley, the adroit—and a look of
amazement, almost terror, was in his eyes as he stared at Mr. Sanford.

"Yessuh," he said with a gulp. "Yessuh." Then he pulled himself
together.

"Put him up, black boy," he directed magnificently, and moved to
the next stall.

I stayed behind and displayed a quarter cautiously.

"Do you like this colt?" I asked, looking the boy straight in the face.

For a moment he hesitated. Then:

"No, suh," he whispered.

"Why not?" I inquired.

There was a flicker of contempt in the white eyeballs.

"He's a houn'," I barely heard as the quarter changed owners.

"It was a well-spent quarter; it had purchased knowledge. I knew
now that among our party was a pair of eyes that could look
deep into the heart of things. Old they were and faded, those eyes;
but I felt assured that a glistening flank could not deceive them.

We worked down one side of the stable and up the other. We
had seen twenty colts when we arrived at the last stall. It contained a
long-legged sorrel, and Blister damned him with a grunt when he
was led out.

"If he ever gets tangled up," was his comment, "you don't get his
legs untied that year. This all you got?"

Wesley assured him it was. We seemed to have reached an im-
passe. Then, as Blister frowned absently at the sorrel colt, a voice
began singing just outside the stable. It was a rich treble and it
chanted in a minor key. I saw the absent look wiped slowly from
Blister's face. It was supplanted by a dawning alertness as he listened
intently.

Suddenly he disappeared through the doorway and there came to me a regular scuff-scuff on the gravel outside, in time to the words of the song, which were these:

> *"Bay colt wock in fo'ty-eight,*
> *Goin' to de races—goin' to de races;*
> *Bay colt wock on fo'ty-eight,*
> *Goin' to de races now."*

I felt my jaw begin to drop, for Blister's voice had joined the unknown singer's.

> *"Bay colt wock in fo'ty-eight,"*

sang the voice; and then a bellow from Blister:

> *"Goin' to the races—goin' to de races,"*

the voice repeated:

> *"Bay colt wock in fo'ty-eight,"*

and resigned to Blister's:

> *"Goin' to de races now!"*

I went hastily through that doorway and arrived at the following phenomena:

EXHIBIT A—One chocolate-colored boy, not more than three feet high. His shoes—I mention them first because they constituted one-half of the whole exhibit—were— But words are feeble—prodigious, Gargantuan are only mildly suggestive of those shoes. His stockings—and now I cross my heart and hope to die—were of the variety described commercially as ladies' hose, and they were pink and they were silk. Somewhere beneath their many folds two licorice sticks performed the miracle of moving those unbelievable shoes through an intricate clog dance.

EXHIBIT B—One Blister Jones, patting with feet and hands an accompaniment to the wonders being performed by the marvelous shoes.

Both exhibits were entirely in earnest and completely absorbed. As has been already told, they were joined in song.

As I assured myself that the phenomena were real and not imaginary, the words of the song changed.

> *"Bay colt wock in fo'ty-eight,"*

came steadfastly from the smaller singer; but Blister, instead of "Goin' to the races," sang

> *"Where's he at? Where's he at?"*
> *"Bay colt wock in fo'ty-eight,"*

insisted Exhibit A; and Exhibit B sang:

> *"Where's that bay colt now?"*

They learn early, in Kentucky, that track and farm secrets are sacred. A suspicion of all outsiders, though dulled by the excitement of white folks' appreciation, still flickered somewhere in the kinky dome of Exhibit A. The song was twice repeated without variation, and the "Where's he at?" became tragic in its pleading tone.

At last Exhibit A must have decided that his partner in song was a kindred spirit and worthy of trust. At any rate

> *"Oveh in de coolin' shed—oveh in de coolin' shed,"*

I heard; and Blister brought the duet to a triumphant close with:

> *"Over in the coolin' shed now!"*

He swung round and grinned at Wesley, who was standing stupefied in the doorway.

"Why, Wes!" he said reproachfully, "I'm surprised at you!"

Wesley glowered at Exhibit A.

"You ramble!" he said, and the marvelous shoes bore their owner swiftly from our sight.

So, through song, was the wily Wesley brought to confusion. We found four two-year-olds in the long, squatty cooling shed, and Wesley admitted, under pressure, that they were the pick of their year, kept for special training.

Three of them stood in straw to their knees, confined in three tremendous box stalls. One was being led under blankets up and down the runway. His sides lifted their covering regularly. His clean-cut velvet nostrils widened and contracted as he took his breath. His eyes were blazing jewels. To him went Blister, like iron filings to a magnet.

"Peel him for a minute," he said, and the still dazed and somewhat chastened Wesley nodded his permission.

Then appeared the most perfect living creature I had ever seen. He was a rich bay—now dark mahogany because of a recent bath—and the sheer beauty of him produced in me a feeling of awe, almost of worship. I was moved as though I listened to the Seventh Symphony or viewed the Winged Victory; and this was fit and proper, for my eyes were drinking in a piece by the greatest of all masters.

Blister was cursing softly, reverently, as though he were at prayer.

"If he's only half as good as he looks!" he sighed at last. "How about *him*, Mr. Sanford?"

I had forgotten Old Man Sanford. I now discovered him standing before a stall and gazing raptly at what was within. At Blister's words he turned and surveyed the bay colt.

"The most superb piece of hawse-flesh," he said, "I have eveh had the pleasuh of observing. I could not fault him with a microscope. He is nothing shawt of perfection, suh—nothing shawt of perfection." His eyes lingered for an instant on the wet flanks of the uncovered colt. "He's too wahm to be without his clothing," he suggested, and turned again to the stall before him.

Blister covered the colt with one dextrous swing. He glanced at the name embroidered on the blankets.

"Postman," he read aloud. "He'll be by Messenger, won't he?" The boy at the colt's head nodded. "Worked in forty-eight just now, eh?" said Blister to no one in particular. Again the boy nodded. "Well," decided Blister, "we'll take a chance on him. Train fur Looeyville at four o'clock—ain't they, Wes?"

Wesley gave a moan of anguish.

"My Gawd!" he said.

"What's bitin' you?" demanded Blister. "We're payin' fur him, ain't we?"

"Lemme have dat letter one moh time," said Wesley. He absorbed the letter's contents as though it were poison, and came at last to the fatal "John C. Dillon" at the end. This he read aloud slowly and shook his head. "He's los' his min'," he stated, and glared at Mr. Sanford. "What you payin' fo' dis hyar colt?" he demanded.

Mr. Sanford glanced in our direction. His eyes had a faraway look.

"Were you addressing me?" he asked.

"Yessuh," replied Wesley. "I was inquirin' de price you aim to pay foh dis colt."

"That is a matteh," said Old Man Sanford, "that concerns only yoh mas—employeh and myself. Howeveh, I am not going to pu'chase the colt to which you refeh." He glanced dreamily into the stall before which he seemed rooted. "I have taken a fancy to my little friend in hyar. . . . Could you oblige me with a piece of sugah?"

As one man, Blister and I made a rush for that stall. We peered through the bars for a moment and our amazed eyes met. In Blister's an angry despair was dawning. He turned savagely on Mr. Sanford.

"You going to buy that shrimp?" he demanded.

"Yes, suh," said Old Man Sanford mildly. "I expect to pu'chase him. . . . Ah, here's the sugah!" He took some lumps of sugar from the now beaming Wesley and opened the stall door.

Blister stepped inside the stall and devoted some moments to vain pleadings. Mr. Sanford was unmoved by them.

Then the storm broke. Blister became a madman who raved. He cursed not only the small black two-year-old, standing knee-deep in golden straw, but the small, white-haired old gentleman who was placidly feeding him sugar. The storm raged on, but Mr. Sanford gave no sign.

At last I saw a hand that was extended to the colt's muzzle begin to tremble, and I took Blister by the arm and drew him forcefully away.

"Stop!" I said in an undertone. "You're doing no good and he's an old man."

Blister tore his arm from mine.

"He's an old fool!" he cried. "He's chuckin' away the chance of a lifetime." Then his eyes fell on the bay colt and his voice became a wail. "Ain't it hell," he inquired of high heaven. "Ain't it just hell."

At this point Wesley saw fit to emit a loud guffaw. Blister advanced on him like a tiger.

"Laugh, you black boob!" he shot out, and Wesley's joyous expression vanished.

I saw that I was doing no good and joined Mr. Sanford in the stall.

"Rather small, isn't he?" I suggested.

"He could be a little larger," Mr. Sanford admitted. "He could stand half a han' and fifty pounds moh at his aige; but then, he'll grow. He'll make a hawse some day."

And now came Blister, rather sheepish, and stood beside us.

"I got sore, Mr. Sanford," he said. "I oughta be kicked!"

Old Man Sanford proffered a lump of sugar to the slim black muzzle. It was knocked from the extended hand. Mr. Sanford pointed a reproving finger at the colt.

"Not quite so fast, young man!" he exclaimed. Then he turned to Blister with a gentle smile. "Youth is hasty," he said, "and sometimes —mistaken."

I returned to Cincinnati and work that night, filled with speculations about a small black colt and his new owner. The latter, I felt, had reached a stubborn dotage. Two months rolled by. Those were full days but I found time somehow for a daily glance at the racing news. One morning I read the following:

"Postman, a bay colt, bred and owned by John C. Dillon, cap-

tured the two-year-old event without apparent effort. It was the
winner's first appearance under colors. He is a big, rangy youngster,
as handsome as a picture. He appears to be a very high-class colt and
should be heard from."

"Poor Blister!" I thought; and later, as I read again and again of
smashing victories by a great and still greater Postman, I became
quite venomous when I thought of Old Man Sanford. I referred to
him mentally as "That old fool!" and imagined Blister in horrid
depths of despair.

Then the bugle called for the last time that year at Lexington,
and the thoroughbreds came to my very door to listen for it.

For days thereafter, as luck would have it, I was forced to pound
my typewriter viciously, everlastingly, and was too tired when night
came to do more than stagger to bed. At last there came a lull,
and I fled incontinently to Latonia and the world of horse.

I approached Blister's stalls as one draws near a sepulcher. I felt
that my voice, when I addressed him, should be pitched as though in
the presence of a casket. I was shocked, therefore, at his lightness of
mein.

"Hello, Four Eyes!" he said cheerfully. "How's the ole scout?"

I assured him that my scouting days were not yet over. And then:

"I've been reading about Postman," I said.

Some colt!" said Blister. "He's bowed 'em home five times now.
They've made him favorite fur the Hammond against all them
Eastern babies."

There was genuine enthusiasm in his voice and I was filled with
admiration for a spirit that could take a blow so jauntily. His attitude was undoubtedly the correct one, but I could not accomplish it.
I thought of the five thousand dollars that went, with the floral
horseshoe, to the winner of the Hammond stake. I thought of a gentle, fine, threadbare old man who needed that five thousand—oh, so
desperately—and I was filled with bitter regrets, with malice and
bad words.

"Of course he'll win it?" I burst out spitefully.

"Why, I dunno," drawled Blister, and added: "I thought Judge
Dillon was a friend of yours."

"Oh damn!" I said.

"Why, Four Eyes!" said Blister. " 'n' Chick listenin' to you too!"

Chick grinned appreciatively.

"Don't let him kid ya," he advised. "He wasn't so gay hisself
till—"

"Take a shot of grape juice," interrupted Blister, " 'n' hire a hall."

Chick's voice trailed off into unintelligible mutterings as he turned away.

"How about Mr. Sanford's colt?" I asked. "Have you still got him?"

To my astonishment Blister broke into one of his rare fits of laughter. He all but doubled up with unaccountable mirth.

"Say, Chick," he called when he could control his voice, "he wants to know if we still got the Sanford colt!"

Chick had turned a rather glum face our way; but at the words his expression became instantly joyous.

"Oh, say!" he said.

Then began a series of hilarious exchanges, entirely without meaning to me.

"He's hangin' round somewhere, ain't he, Chick?"

"Why, maybe he is," said Chick.

"You still throw a little rough feed into him occasionally, don't you, Chick?"

"When I got time," said Chick: and the two imbeciles roared wth laughter.

At last Blister began beating me between the shoulder blades.

"We got him, Four Eyes," he told me between thumps. "Yep—we got him."

"Stop! I shouted. "What the devil's the matter with you?"

Blister became serious.

"Come here!" He threw back the upper door and a shaft of sunlight streamed into the stall's interior, bathing a slim black head and neck until they glistened like a vein of coal.

"Know him?" asked Blister.

"Yes," I said. "He's bigger, though."

"Look at him good!" ordered Blister.

I peered at the relaxed inmate of the stall, who blinked sleepily at me through the shaft of sunlight. Blister pulled me back, closed the stall door, and tightened his grip on my arm.

"Now listen!" he said. "You just looked at the best two-year-old God ever put breath in!"

I took in this incredible information slowly. I exulted in it for a moment, and then came doubts.

"How do you know?" I demanded.

"How do I know!" exclaimed Blister. "It'ud take me a week to tell you. Man, he can fly! He makes his first start tomorrow—in the Hammond. Old Man Sanford'll get in tonight. Come out 'n' see a real colt run."

My brain was whirling.

"In the Hammond?" I gasped. "Does Mr. Sanford know all this?"
Blister gave me a slow, a thoughtful look.

"It sounds nutty," he said; "but I can't figger it no other way. As
sure as you 'n' me are standin' here—he knowed it from the very
first."

Until I closed my eyes that night I wondered whether Blister's
words were true. If so, what sort of judgment, instinct, intuition had
been used that day at Thistle Ridge? I gave it up at last and slept, to
dream of a colt that suddenly grew raven wings and soared over the
grandstand while I nodded wisely and said, "Of course—the birthright of eagles!"

I got to Blister's stalls at one o'clock next day, and found Mr. Sanford clothed in a new dignity hard to describe. Perhaps he had
donned it with the remarkable flowered waistcoat he wore—or was it
due to his flowing double-breasted coat, a sprightly blue in color and
suggesting inevitably a leather trunk, dusty, attic-bound, which had
yawned and spat it forth?

"Welcome, suh; thrice welcome!" he said to me. "I take the liberty
of presuming that the pu'ple and white is honored with yoh best
wishes today."

I assured him that from the bottom of my heart this was so. He
wrung my hand again and took out a gold watch the size of a bun.

"Three hours moh," he said, "before our hopes are realized or shattered."

"You think the colt will win?" I inquired.

Mr. Sanford turned to the southwest. I followed his eyes and saw
a bank of evil-looking clouds creeping slowly up the sky.

"I like our chances, suh," he told me; "but it will depend on those
clouds yondeh. We want a fast track foh the little chap. He is a
swallow. Mud would break his heart."

"She's fast enough now," said Blister, who had joined us, and Mr.
Sanford nodded.

So for three hours I watched the sky prayerfully and saw it become
more and more ominous. When the bugle called for the Hammond
at last, Latonia was shut off from the rest of the world by an inverted
inky cup, its sides shot now and then with lightning flashes. We
seemed to be in a great vacuum. I found my lungs snatching for
each breath, while my racing card grew limp as I clutched it spas-
modically in a sweating hand.

I had seen fit to take a vital interest in the next few moments; but
I glanced at the faces all about me in the grandstand and found

them strained and unnatural. Perhaps in the gloom they seemed whiter than they really were; perhaps my own nerves pricked my imagination until this packed humanity became one beating heart.

I do not think that this was so. The dramatic moment goes straight to the soul of a crowd, and this crowd was to see the Hammond staged in a breathless dark, with the lightning's flicker for an uncertain spotlight.

No rain would spoil our chances that day, for now, across the center field at the half-mile post, a mass of colors boiled at the barrier. The purple and white was somewhere in the shifting, surging line, borne by a swallow, so I had been told. Well, even so, the blue and gold was there likewise—and carried by what? Perhaps an eagle!

Suddenly a sigh—not the customary roar, but a deep intaking of the grandstand's breath—told me they were on the wing. I strained my eyes at the blurred mass of them, which seemed to move slowly in the distance as it reached the far turn of the back stretch. Then a flash of lightning came and my heart skipped a beat and sank.

They were divided into two unequal parts. One was a crowded, indistinguishable mass. The other, far ahead in unassailable isolation, was a single spot of bay with a splash of color clinging above.

A roar of "Postman!" shattered the quiet like a bombshell, for that splash of color was blue and gold. The favorite was making a runaway race of it. He was coming home to twenty thousand joyful backers, who screamed and screamed his name.

Until that moment I had been the victim of a dream. I had come to believe that the little old man, standing silent at my side, possessed an insight more than human. Now I had wakened. He was an old fool in a preposterous coat and waistcoat, and I looked at him and laughed a mirthless laugh. He was squinting slightly as he peered with his washed-out eyes into the distance. His face was placid; and as I noticed this I told myself that he was positively witless. Then he spoke.

"The bay colt is better than I thought," he said.

"True," I agreed bitterly, and noted, as the lightning flashed again, that the blue and gold was an amazing distance ahead of those struggling mediocre others.

"A pretty race," muttered Old Man Sanford; and now I thought him more than doddering—he was insane.

Some seconds passed in darkness while the grandstand gave off a contented murmur. Then suddenly the murmur rose to a new note. It held fear and consternation in it. My eyes leaped up the track.

The bay colt had rounded the curve into the stretch. He was coming down the straight like a bullet; but—miracle of miracles!—it was plain that he was not alone. . . .

In a flash it came to me: stride for stride, on the far side of him, one other had maintained a flight equal to his own. And then I went mad; for this other, unsuspected in the darkness until now, commenced to creep slowly, surely, into the lead. Above his stretching neck his colors nestled proudly. He was bringing the purple and white safe home to gold and glory.

Nearer and nearer he came, this small demon whose coat matched the heavens, and so shot past us, with the great Postman—under the whip—two lengths behind him!

I remember executing a sort of bear dance, with Mr. Sanford enfolded in my embrace. I desisted when a smothered voice informed me that my conduct was "unseemly, suh—most unseemly!"

A rush to the track followed, where we found Blister, quite pale, waiting with a blanket. Suddenly the grandstand, which had groaned once and become silent, broke into a roar that grew and grew.

"What is it?" I asked.

Blister whirled and stared at the figures on the timing board. I saw a look of awe come into his face.

"What is it?" I repeated. "Why are they cheering? Is it the time?"

"Oh, no!" said Blister with scornful sarcasm and a look of pity at my ignorance. "It ain't the time!" He nodded at the figures. "That's only the world's record fur the age 'n' distance."

And now there came mincing back to us on slender, nervous legs, something wet and black and wonderful. It pawed and danced wildly in a growing ring of curious eyes.

Then, just above the grandstand, the inky cup of the sky was broken and there appeared the light of an unseen sun. It turned the piled white clouds in the break to marvels of rose and gold. They seemed like the ramparts of heaven, set there to guard from earthly eyes the abode of the immortals.

"Whoa, man! Whoa, hon!" said Blister, and covered the heaving sides.

As he heard Blister's voice and felt the touch of the blanket, the colt grew quiet. His eyes became less fiery wild. He raised his head, with its dilated blood-red nostrils, and stared—not at the mortals standing reverently about him, but far beyond our gaze—through the lurid gap in the sky, straight into Valhalla.

I felt a hand on my arm.

"The look of eagles, suh!" said Old Man Sanford.

The Enchanted Horse

From The Arabian Nights

Retold by BETH BROWN

In the faraway land of Persia, the most popular holiday of the year is New Year's Day. It is on this day that the entire kingdom turns out to pay homage to the King and his court. The day is spent in feasting and merriment, in singing and in sports. It begins at dawn and ends at the setting of the sun.

Many, many years ago, just such a celebration was going on when the Captain of the Guards arrived at the throne with the breathless news that an Indian traveler was at the gates, knocking for admission and asking to see the King on a matter of the greatest importance.

The King agreed to receive him, and the stranger entered the throne room. He was an Indian of low caste, dressed in shabby old robes. But the horse he was leading wore the richest of trappings, and jewels were braided into his flowing mane. He had hoofs of gold and huge white wings that folded to his side. No blood flowed through his veins, yet his coat was silky and warm. His eyes were big and bright. He appeared to be a horse, yet was not a horse in the ordinary sense of the word.

"Who are you?" demanded the King. "And what sort of steed is this?"

"I am a traveler," answered the Indian. "I have come a long way to bring you one of the seven wonders of the world. Behold an enchanted horse!"

"I see nothing unusual," replied the King. "True, the mane is a handsome one. Yes, he is twice the size of the horses we keep here in the stables. His form is handsome. His eyes are bright—"

"That is not all," interrupted the traveler. "You have only to climb on his back and wish yourself anywhere in the world—and, no matter how far the distance, in a flash of time too short to count you will find yourself there. It is this, Your Highness, that makes my horse so wonderful."

The King shook his head. The ministers shook their heads. All doubted such a claim.

"How can such a thing be true?"

"Yes, prove it!" declared the King.

"Well, you need only mount him, your Highness, and call out some far-off continent to find yourself there. It is this, Your Highness, that makes my horse so wonderful!"

"How can such a thing be true?" murmured the doubting ministers.

"Yes! Prove it!" declared the King.

"Mount on his back, Your Highness! Call out some far-off continent! See for yourself, Your Highness! My enchanted horse is eager to obey you."

This made the King more anxious than ever not only to test the Indian's claim but to own the animal as well. He pointed to a mountain far off in the distance. "At the foot of that mountain," he told the Indian, "is a grove of palm trees. Go there and bring me back a palm leaf within the hour."

The King had scarcely finished these words than the Indian leaped into the saddle, turned a small peg in the horse's neck and was off. Both steed and rider went high into the sky and out of sight.

They had not been gone more than half an hour before the King and his court saw them returning, flying swiftly toward the earth. Soon the Indian leaped down from the saddle, bearing the palm leaf in his hand. This he laid before the King.

The King was astounded. The court was speechless. Even the murmuring ministers ceased any longer to murmur. All crowded around the horse, admiring the magic animal. The King patted the wooden neck. He stroked the silken mane. He admitted that the enchanted horse was truly enchanted and confessed that he wished to have him for his very own.

"Name your price," he told the Indian traveler.

The Indian bowed to the ground. "I am happy you admit that my horse has power such as no other animal on earth possesses. I am flattered that you desire to own him, Your Highness. Indeed, he can be yours. But on one condition only—"

"And what is that?"

"This horse may not be sold for money. All the money in the world could never buy him. He may only be taken in exchange for something of equal value."

The King smiled broadly. "I have many cities in my kingdom. You can choose the one you wish and become the ruler over many people."

"I do not wish a city," answered the Indian. "Nor will I take even two cities in exchange for the enchanted horse."

"What will you take?"

"Your daughter," replied the Indian calmly. "I will exchange my horse for the hand of your daughter in marriage."

At this demand, a great murmur arose from the vast assembly gathered about the throne. The ministers objected strongly. The Queen burst into tears. The Princess fainted on the spot. The Prince leaped to his feet. He waved his sword high in the air.

"You cannot do such a thing!" he declared to his father. "You cannot make such a bargain. The blood of our ancestors is pure and uncontaminated. You cannot give my sister to a stranger of unknown ancestry."

"True," replied the King. "But if I refuse to give the hand of your sister in exchange for this remarkable animal, our Indian friend will go elsewhere in search of some other monarch with a suitable daughter to marry and we will not have this seventh wonder of the world here in our own stables. However, I have not said that I have accepted his offer. It is quite likely that I shall do so. But first, I wish you, my son, to look the horse over very carefully and try him for yourself. In other words, my Indian friend, my own son must take your horse for a trial ride into the sky."

"I am willing to agree to your wishes, oh Monarch. Here!" and he called to the young prince to mount the steed. "See this peg?" He pointed to the wooden peg in the neck of the animal and showed the Prince how to use it in order to guide himself in his travels.

The Prince turned the peg three times to the left and then three times to the right. Soon both horse and rider left the earth and vanished into the sky. Everyone waited for their return. An hour passed. Two hours went by. The North Star lighted the heavens but there was still no sign of the Prince or the enchanted horse.

The Indian became alarmed. He flung himself at the feet of the King. "Your Honor," he declared, "I fear for the safety of your son. You see, in his haste to take off, he did not permit me to show him how to turn the peg in order to return to earth."

"A fine state of affairs," fumed the King. "What if he dashes into a mountain, loses his way on the desert, or sinks down into the sea?"

"Do not fear," replied the Indian. "My magic horse can travel with

safety wherever he is sent. But unless the peg is turned from left to right and from right to left, and the second peg turned from right to left and from left to right, I cannot answer for your son."

"In that case," shouted the King, "your own life will answer for you. If my son does not return to me safely before the month is up, then you shall be beheaded. Take him away!" he ordered the soldiers of the kingdom. "Clap him into prison!"

Meanwhile, the Prince had been sailing gaily in the air, higher and higher and still higher until he no longer saw the tops of the mountain peaks, and now even the clouds were left far below. He had never before enjoyed himself half as much. The horse's back was like a gentle cradle rocking him through the air. For hours upon hours they rode this way and that, over mountain and sea, into clouds and out of clouds. Finally the Prince grew hungry. It was time, he decided, they return home to earth. He remembered the peg. But when he tried to turn it around, he found himself traveling higher and faster. Now what should he do? He realized that he was in danger. But being a prince, he did not lose his head. Instead, he set about to examine the horse more closely and at last he found the second peg behind the horse's ear. This he turned in all directions until he had come upon the right combinations. He then began dropping down to earth, down, down, down through the starry night until far below he saw the gleaming lights of a beautiful white city.

He touched the rein and called out his orders. The horse glided slowly to a stop. The Prince found himself alighting on a roof of a great marble palace. A marble stairway led below. He followed this stairway till he found himself in a splendid throne room. At one end, guarding the far door, were a hundred servants, all sleeping soundly. The Prince made his way softly past them and came to a door that was thickly curtained. Drawing back the curtains, he saw another door, and upon opening this door, he stepped into a room beautiful beyond words. Here lay a hundred female slaves, all fast asleep in a circle on the floor. A gilded couch stood in the center and upon it reposed the most beautiful princess he had ever seen.

The Prince drew his breath. He came closer on tiptoe in order to look again upon such beauty and make sure that this was not a dream. He knelt at her side and touched her hand. The Princess sighed, opened her eyes, and was about to cry out in terror when the Prince whispered that he had not come to harm her. She had only to hear him out to be sure of his intentions.

"I am a Prince of Persia," he told her, "come on an adventure so strange that it is hard of believing. Only yesterday, I was in my father's kingdom celebrating the yearly feast-day. And now, today, I am here at your side in danger of my life."

At this the Princess assured him that no harm would come to him. "You are in the kingdom of Bengal," she told him, "and we are hospitable here. No doubt you are faint for want of food and rest. You shall have both here at my palace."

"I thank you, my Princess," answered the Prince.

"Rest and refresh yourself first," suggested the Princess, "then you may tell me all your adventures." And with that, she ordered her servants to bring the finest foods and to attend to the wants of the handsome Prince.

Indeed, she had never seen so handsome a prince nor had he seen so lovely a princess. She had dressed herself in her most beautiful robes and placed the biggest and most brilliant jewels upon her hair, throat, wrists, and fingers. When she entered the throne room, the Prince gasped at the sight of so much beauty. He fell in love on the spot. It was hard to relate his adventures with his mind on the love in his heart. As for the Princess, she, too, had fallen in love. She listened sadly, for she knew that before the day was over, he would be leaving her to return home to his own kingdom.

The Prince, however, soon declared himself. "I owe you my life," he told her. "By the law of nations, I am already your slave, and I offer you my heart which was yours the moment I laid eyes upon you. I know that I must leave you to return home to my people but I shall surely return to claim you as my bride."

At this the Princess blushed and smiled. She held out both her hands, which he took into his own. "I have one request," she told him. "You have been here so brief a time. Truly, I cannot part with you so soon. You must stay for a while and let me entertain you before you go home."

This was agreeable to the Prince, who could not bear the thought of leaving her side either. So he accepted her invitation and stayed on for a visit. The days that followed were full of joy. There were feasts and hunting parties and royal dinners and plays. Time passed swiftly. Every now and then he thought of his kingdom at home and of his father and mother who no doubt grieved for him.

Finally one night he told the Princess that he must return to his kingdom. "Why don't you come with me?" he invited. "Ride with me upon the enchanted horse. Once we are in Persia, our marriage can take place and we can return here to your father and your kingdom for a visit."

The Princess agreed to this, and so together they mounted the magic horse. The Princess held tightly to the Prince. The Prince turned the proper peg and up they flew over sea and land, up, up over the tall mountains and down into the familiar valley. Now the Prince turned the second peg and they began to descend into the city below. Here the Prince led the horse to the gates of the Palace and here he asked the Princess to wait for him while he went to the throne room and broke the news to the court.

The Prince found the city in mourning. Every man, woman, and child was dressed in deepest brown. The bells of the churches were tolling mournfully.

"What has happened?" inquired the Prince. "Why are you so sad?"

"We have lost our Prince," a blind man informed him.

But his wife, who could see, called out to all who walked the roads: "The Prince! The Prince! The Prince is here! The Prince has returned to us."

Soon the news spread throughout the kingdom. The bells stopped tolling and rang out joyously instead. The King came running to meet the Prince and to embrace him warmly. The Prince related his many adventures. He concluded by telling the King about the Princess who even now was waiting outside the palace gates.

At this, the King was overjoyed. "Have her brought in without further delay," he ordered. "Make the marriage feast ready!"

He also gave orders that the Indian be freed from prison and permitted to depart with his enchanted horse.

But the Indian had vowed to avenge himself. So instead of departing immediately from the kingdom, he decided first to punish all who had harmed him. He would kidnap the Bengal Princess, he decided, and carry her off with him. The wicked plan took shape as he mounted his horse and went to her quarters. There he told her slaves that he had been ordered to return her to her father's kingdom in order to fetch her father for the wedding.

The Princess was overjoyed to hear this. She dressed for the journey with great care and mounted the horse behind the Indian. But as soon as he had turned the first peg, she realized that he had no intention of returning to her father's kingdom. In fact, he himself meant to marry her. When the Princess heard this news, she burst into tears.

Meanwhile, the Prince had discovered his loss. He was beside himself with grief. He vowed he would find his Princess if it meant traveling to the ends of the earth. So he said farewell to his parents, dressed himself in the garments of a dervish, and began his long journey out into the world.

By this time, the enchanted horse and his riders was thousands of miles away. At the end of the day, the Indian grew hungry and decided to return to earth to obtain some food for himself and the Princess. He found a little woods and here he left the Princess while he went into town to purchase meat and fruit. He soon returned to the woods and shared what he bought with the Princess. Once she had eaten, she grew strong again. This time, when the Indian ordered her to leap behind him on the horse's back, she did not obey. Instead, she fought him off. Her cries for help were heard by men on horseback who happened to be riding through the woods. The head of the party was none other than the Sultan himself. He heard her story, ordered his soldiers to kill the Indian, and took the Princess back to his own palace.

True, the Indian had caused her great grief. But the Sultan proved even more troublesome. He had made up his mind to marry her, and even though she insisted that she was already in love with a prince, he proceeded with the wedding plans and fixed the day for the wedding. In vain the Princess pleaded. In vain she begged to be sent home to the Prince. The Sultan merely smiled and stroked his long black beard at the prospect of having so beautiful a queen beside him upon the throne.

Finally the Princess thought of a plan by which she might be free of him. She pretended to have a fit. She frothed at the mouth. She spoke in gibberish. She broke the furniture, the cups and the saucers, and so frightened her serving maids that the doctors came on the run. But they could prescribe no medicine for her, and the mere sight of a doctor brought on an even more violent fit. No doctor could so much as take her pulse. She allowed no one to come near her, for she knew that if they discovered her secret, all would be lost.

Now the Sultan who had fallen in love with her began to fear for her life. He called in the court doctors to consult with the city doctors, and the city doctors to consult with the country doctors. He sent messengers to doctors of neighboring states, offering handsome rewards for any doctor who might be able to cure the beautiful Princess. However, since she did not permit any doctor to approach her, no doctor could prescribe and be of any help to the helpless Princess.

Meanwhile, the Prince, wandering hopelessly from kingdom to kingdom, eventually heard of the mad princess who refused to marry the richest Sultan in the world. He knew at once that this was his own promised bride and he made a plan to rescue her.

First he bought the robe of a doctor and then he let his beard grow long. When he was ready, he sought out an audience with the Sultan. The captain of the guards listened to his claim that he had a secret drug which never failed to heal the ill. The captain assured him that not only would he receive a warm welcome at the hands of the Sultan but, if he proved his claim, a huge reward would be awarded to him.

And so the Prince was brought to the throne room. The Sultan received him most graciously. He warned the Prince that the Princess might not be so gracious. In fact, the sight of a doctor never failed to throw her into a violent fit. At this, the Prince requested that he see the Princess without being observed by her. He was led to a small room under the eaves which had a tiny opening through which he could see the Princess without being seen.

Yes, he could see the Princess. There she was, lying on a couch, tears in her eyes, singing a soft little song about her lost love. The Prince now knew that she still loved him and he at once returned to the Sultan and demanded to enter her room alone, else, he added, the cure would fail.

The Sultan agreed to this. The Prince entered the room, and the Princess was about to go into one of her fancied fits when she heard a familiar voice saying: "It is I, my fair Princess, come to rescue you."

Her joy was indeed great. She flung her arms around him and wept tears of welcome.

"We must plan to escape at once," the Prince told her.

"But how?"

"Where is the enchanted horse?" he wanted to know.

"I have not the answer to that," she replied. "No doubt the Sultan had hidden the horse away in some safe place."

"That being the case, you will need to learn where he is stabled," answered the Prince. Then he told her the plan to follow. She was to dress in her finest costume and brightest jewels and dine with the Sultan that evening. She was to be most charming and feminine. She was to lead the Sultan to think that she was cured of her malady and ready to marry him. She was to learn the hiding place of the enchanted horse and to help the Prince in his role of doctor.

That night, the Princess dined with the Sultan. Of course, the Prince was present at the feast, disguised in his robe of doctor.

"I have discovered the cause of her illness," he informed the Sultan. "It is due to an enchantment brought about by the enchanted horse. Though she seems to be cured, that cure is not permanent until the enchantment is broken."

"And how may that be done?" inquired the Sultan.

"Bring the horse into the public square at sharp noon tomorrow.

Place the Princess upon its back. I will meanwhile prepare some magic perfumes of which I alone know the secret. Once she is seated in the saddle, I will do the rest. She will be cured forever, I promise you!"

"No sooner said than done!" declared the Sultan.

And so, on the following day, the enchanted steed was brought out into the public square where the entire kingdom had assembled. The doctor had promised a permanent cure. The Princess was ready. She came forth dressed in the finest of robes and decked out in the brightest of jewels. The Sultan cheered as she appeared. Now she mounted the horse.

Meanwhile the Prince ordered four braziers full of burning coal placed east, west, north, and south of the enchanted horse. Now he threw handfuls of perfume into the fire. Thick clouds of perfumed smoke filled the air, hiding both the Princess and the horse.

The Prince now leaped into the saddle, turned the wooden peg, and up they went into the air. They circled over the Sultan's head. The Prince shouted down: "Oh, Sultan! Next time you want to marry a Princess who has pleaded with you for protection, be sure you get her consent first!"

And in this manner, the Prince carried off the Princess to his kingdom for the second time. The enchanted horse moved swiftly till it came to the kingdom, and here the wedding was celebrated with feasting which lasted a year and a day.

But you will ask, what has become of the enchanted horse?

That is a question which no one can answer, not even the wisest of men.

Palomino

BUD MURPHY

AMONG the bands of wild horses that roamed Arizona's plains and prairies, sheltered by her mountains and fed by her fertile valleys, was a distinct strain of Palomino blood. Through a natural instinct to keep the strain pure, many fine horses ran with the scrubby little broom-tailed mustangs. On this occasion a wealthy Easterner had come to Arizona to taste the life in the open. He bought a big ranch (about sixty-two sections of grazing land) with three thousand head of cattle, built a nice home with all modern conveniences, and hired about twenty or so cowpunchers to help him run the outfit. I happened to be one of the well-paid but unfortunate cowboys. He loaded us down with newfangled contraptions and thingamabobs till our poor cayuses could barely walk. Then losing interest in cattle, he ordered us all out on a wild-goose chase for the last of this line of purebred Palomino wild ones.

Now, I've been in this country for nearly twenty-nine years December, and so have many other reputed riders and longer, but in all my life I've never seen the likes of this wonder horse. I've met many a horse wrangler that has thrilled at the sight of him, but never one who could come close enough to even chance a shot at him. For there was a bounty on his head, placed by horse traders from the Rockies to the Rio Grande. They would see his tracks the next morning after several prize mares had deserted the remuda, but his speed and cunning were more than a match for the best of them. He would visit their herd about the middle of the night, steal up to the corral and nicker, then like a phantom would melt into the darkness. A few hours later a long shrill neigh would break the silence and the foreman of the outfit would sit up and say, "There go some more blooded fillies, or I'm a yearlin'." And sure enough, a dozen or more oval imprints outside the hewn log corral would meet the gaze of the first one up.

These remarkable tales are the only things that kept us faithful to the job we were handed. My eyes yearned for a sight of this magnificent animal, and my bowed legs itched to fork his powerful back. Emory Hudson, the owner of the spread, decided to remain at home because of a lack of stamina and horse sense. Consequently, after we had covered several miles, the foreman, much to our relief, cached all our "newfangles" in a big cave, and we made better time up into the hills.

The long, sweeping plains were covered with tall, green grass that would ripple when the range breezes blew, like waves on an emerald lake. The green expanse rolled far off to the low foothills that swelled up to the purple mountains in the hazy distance. Deep shadows revealed rocky gorges, and high bluffs reared their lofty heads to the azure skies overhead. Great fleecy clouds drifted past the breasts of jagged peaks and slowly changed their shapes as they divided or molded themselves into one. The creaking of saddle leather and jangling of spur rowels added to the range music. A calf bawled in the distance, while a crow flapped over a nearby pasture, cawing at the small clusters of baldfaced cattle that dotted the surrounding country. Little dust devils danced, whirling merrily, on the trail ahead, and a cottontail scurried to the safety of a mesquite bush.

Scrub oaks and sweet cedar trees grew more plentiful as we advanced into horse country. The trails were less visible and strewn with cat-claw and boulders, while the main trail narrowed as it wound up and around, zigzagging along the side of the gorge. After several hours' climbing we emerged from the thickly wooded forest of swaying pines into an open glade that looked out upon the vast chasm from whose bottom we had just ascended. One, two, three—nearly four thousand feet down—a sheer drop-off. We were skirting the rim of one of the largest box canyons in Arizona. The sun was just setting, leaving the sky full of clouds, etched with gold, crimson, and blue. A soft glow of delicate pink fell over the rocks of the canyon as twilight passed into the enveloping robes of night.

The foreman called a halt, and we made camp in the little glen. A mountain spring, clear as crystal and sparkling as it gushed from beneath a rocky precipice, ran swiftly down the slope till it reached the edge of the gorge, then tumbled madly down its side, splashing on protruding boulders, whirling in deep, quiet pools, gurgling through little ravines, and at last emptying in the Arivipa far below. Making camp was a simple problem, but kept us at work till nightfall. The cowboys were tired from the day's ride and after a cup or two of black coffee with some stew and frijoles, they hit their "soogans." Life was quiet and serene, and the wind murmured softly, gently through the boughs of the pines above. Hoary with moss, the great branches swayed and bent with the night breeze, and I pulled the blankets closer around me. The star-sprinkled sky overhead was splotched here and there with great fleecy clouds, framed in soft moonlight.

All the cowboys had gone to sleep except the night watch, who tended the fire and kept a pot of coffee boiling. The slow, ominous crackle of the flames and sputter of the red coals soon caused even him to nod. The horses were staked off from camp about three hundred yards, and an occasional clink of hobble chains or a nicker would tell us they were all right. A mountain lion screamed the unearthly shriek of a terrified woman, causing the watch to look up suddenly and glance about uneasily. Soon the entire camp was asleep, the fire having died down to a gray heap of ashes.

When I woke up, I was sitting upright in bed. Everything was in a turmoil, and the waddies were crawling out of their beds. I was soon to know the cause of the clamor. A distant rumbling like the roll of thunder could be heard far up the canyon, increasing in volume until the entire earth shook with the vibration. Now it seemed right beneath us, and so deafening that shouted orders of the foreman were completely drowned out. Every hand in camp rushed to the lip of the chasm to see what was causing the noise. There in the light of a full moon was the most breath-taking scene I have ever beheld. The floor of the canyon was literally covered with horses—thousands of them—the largest band of living mustangs I have ever seen, manes and tails whipping about quivering flanks, heels kicking, and hoofs pounding. Then as quickly as they appeared they sank from view in their mad rush down the basin, rounding a sharp bend and fording the Arivipa a half mile or so beyond. A long, shrill cry drew our attention to the leader. No one spoke. Every mouth hung agape as seconds of silence passed after the bunch had disappeared.

I had often dreamed of a horse like that leader but had awakened only to see his image—a living horse that seemed to have stepped from the portals of my imagination. He raced majestically far ahead of the others, his silvery mane flowing in the wind, his showy white tail trailing parallel with the ground reflecting like a beam of starlight on four creamy-colored ankles. Pounding hooves bore his graceful body over the rocky paths. As sure of step and bearing as a mountain goat, he leaped over slippery rocks and treacherous gulleys with

the precision of a panther. Deep shadows revealed tense muscles beneath his light bay hide. All this was seen in a glimpse of the mighty stallion. No one slept the remainder of the night. Such exclamations as "I teel ya, Red, he's the most likely lookin' piece of hoss flesh that ever saw daylight." The baldheaded cook's loud bellow of, "Come an' git it or I'll throw it out," came none too soon for me.

After finishing our hardtack and coffee, the boss called us all around the fire and told us his plans of capture. I don't believe there's any waddie west of the Mississippi that knows horses any better than Red Saunders, our foreman. He wrangled horses from the time he was old enough to sit a saddle till now when his legs are so bent out of shape he can't make time across a corral on foot. Well, old Red, though his hair is streaked with gray and the red is bleaching out from years in the sun, motioned us to cluster around the bog log on which he was seated. Then with a piece of match he outlined the canyon and surrounding country.

In the middle of the gorge rose a towering plateau about a quarter mile long and five hundred wide. The Arivipa flowed on one side between the wall of the canyon and the wall of the butte. On the other side a rock pass narrowed to a small opening about forty feet across. It was through this pass that the horses ran every night; then they would come out into the river basin again and race along one side until they came to another ford. Red planned to close up the narrow end of the pass with a huge gate and camouflage another gate at the opening of the pass. He sent some of us out to get poles and some to stretch wire, while others cut white rag strips from old sheets. We rode in pairs, so I singled out Tim and we started up the trail to get logs. I rode a big Morgan and Tim's mount was a little bay mustang, both a wiry breed of horses suited to hauling logs or sitting back on a rope. We brought two poles apiece and laid them on a rapidly rising pile.

Charlie and Red were just leaving for another load when we pulled into camp. Everything was stirring and being done at once. Hank was palavering with the cook about his poles which that gentleman was about to chop into firewood, and Tim was tightening up his double cinch which had come loose during the last haul.

By night, we had about thirty poles apiece piled near the camp in little groups. Wild-horse trapping was nothing new to most of us, but this was different. We were after a beautiful prize as evasive as a criminal genius. All were pretty tired and consequently went to bed early. We slept by watches, each pair being given two hours' watch. Tim and I were given the first watch just before midnight. Charlie and Red took the graveyard watch, with all the other waddies being given the less important watches, because it was just before midnight that we saw the band the first time. Not one cowboy on the outfit would miss seeing that horse again.

I lay in bed looking up at the stars and wishing that I owned that horse. Over in another bunk, the steady breathing of Tim told me he had dozed off, and different sounds indicated that certain punchers were snoring louder than others. Charlie's wheeze and gasp rang out above all the rest, while Hank did his best to keep up with him. As time wore on and nothing exciting happened, I dropped off to sleep, the hard day's work acting as a lullaby.

Then it came, the slow, ever-increasing rumble far off up the canyon. I had settled in my "soogans" after my watch with Tim when the sound roused me from a half-asleep stage. Tim was already at the canyon edge looking up the basin with Charlie and Red. No one else had heard it yet, so Red bawled lustily for all hands to get up. This was hardly necessary, though, as the thundering hooves had increased to such volume that all were either crawling from beneath blankets or running over to join the others. Here and there glimpses of Palomino could be caught through parted branches of trees or between boulders. "Thar he is," someone would shout. "See—see— right thar roundin' thet leetle bend!" Similar calls came from about the camp. When it was all over, little groups formed about the campfire to talk about the second appearance of the mighty horse. Some thought it risky to camp so near the pass, but as Red said, "They make sich a fuss a'comin' down through that, we'uns 'er hyar so high they'd never notice us."

The next day's work consisted of getting the logs down into the pass where it was more barren, building the gates, and stringing cable. Red used wire about the size of your little finger. The wire was smooth and strong, with rags tied every fifteen feet that would flutter in the breeze. Then when the band rushed up against the gate, they would shy at the bright cloths and fewer would hit the wire. Some horses were bound to be killed, no matter what method was used, but this was the most practical and killed fewer horses. Building the barrier took several days of hard work, but when it was finished it might easily have "held a freight train," as Charlie put it. When the trap was completed, the gate was swung wide and covered with branches and carefully laid with rocks. The horses would come down the ravine, enter the pass, and hit the barrier at the other end. Then they would mill around, start back up the other way, and meet with the gate at that end, which would be swung shut and bolstered with hewn-log poles. It was a good plan, and Red was proud of it.

In the afternoon the work was completed and all rested, to be fresh for the night's encounter. About eleven o'clock each one slipped quietly to the place either at gates or bolster beams or supports, used to withstand the shock of the horses' bodies against the gates.

Then for the third time the sensation of quivering earth told us the herd was coming down the canyon. As they drew near, the shaking ground began to rumble, and like peals of thunder the sound echoed down the gorge. Every nerve was tense, every heart pounding as though it would spring from its bosom. My cheeks tingled, and something seemed to prick me in my chest. I peeped between the two rails of the fence and saw the mad stampede of horses coming down upon us. I tightened my grip on the support I was holding and clenched my teeth till I thought I should grind them to bits.

The band surged forward like the wave on a stormy sea, dust rising like a great cloud to the rim of the canyon. The leaders hit the gate and bounced back ten or fifteen yards, bowling some over and slowing down the entire herd to a milling trot. Some of the leaders lay sprawled on the rocks with broken necks or twisted legs, tongues lolling from bleeding mouths, and foam trickling down their quivering flanks. All was a turmoil of craning necks, rearing breasts, bulging blood-rimmed eyes, pawing hoofs, and wide nostrils streaked with sticky froth. At last the squirming, writhing mass of horses turned in the general direction from which they had come and stampeded back up the pass. I climbed to the top of the barrier and could see huge bolts being slipped into place on the closed gate at the entrance of the trap. Soon the braces were all secured, and the band, except for a few stragglers, was captured.

All eyes searched vainly for Palomino, but had he been beneath our very noses, we could not have seen him for the dust and the flying, kicking hooves. The din was terrific and the stomping started little rockslides on the sides of the canyon. Sweat rolled down our faces and dripped from our backs, trickling in crooked lines through the dirt on our tired limbs. We finally went back to camp, a grimy, dusty group of men, panting from the fray. It was morning when we at last lay on our bunks, and we decided to wait till noon to look over our catch.

Red estimated that we must have at least three thousand head of blood mares, a thousand or so mustangs, and several hundred good colts. Except for a few high-spirited Hambletonians, the bunch had quieted down in general. The gates had baffled them, and, save for a bare wire here and there, they felt as though they were boxed in a natural trap.

No trace of Palomino could be found. He seemed to have vanished like a ghost. Had he been one of the leaders to hit the wire and be killed? Why was he not in the herd? Had some uncanny power urged him to remain behind? Perhaps he had seen the wisp of smoke from our campfire that curled and twisted up above the tree tops or had chanced upon the niche where we cached our supplies when we built the trap. A strange feeling told us that he had not run with his famous band that night. Most of the horses were branded and new to the band. Thus, they were not as wild as the mustangs and were considerably easier to separate. Mustangs were worthless stock anyway, so we shed our remuda of them first, turning them out and hieing them up the canyon. The colts went with their mammies and the bunch was soon ready to work on. We left the corral that night and camped a little way off instead of going back up the canyon to our other camp on the rim.

Night fell before we had finished our supper, and the clear red light of the fire shone on fifteen haggard faces. Disappointment reigned in camp as well as a good share of bewilderment. Old Red just couldn't figure it out. The great animal seemed to know every move we made. When all the waddies had crawled in bed for the night, a lone figure sat solemnly at the fire, gazing intently at the glowing coals and occasionally poking the dying embers with a crooked stick. He seldom voiced his emotions by facial expression, but everyone knew Red was stumped.

Suddenly, like the scream of some unearthly phantom, high and shrill as the wild cry of an eagle, a weird blasting wail shattered the stillness of the night, echoing and re-echoing down the canyon till it was a mere fading whine. Some of the cowboys raised their heads, sure of one answer. It was Palomino calling to his band.

As more punchers woke up and gaped around, someone looked up and whispered, "Where's Red? He was a'sitting thar when I went to sleep. Hey, fellers! Red's gone! Wake up!" Soon the whole camp was buzzing, and people were moving about. Then when someone suggested that a searching party be organized to find the absent puncher, old Charlie rose from his bunk and prepared to make a speech. He clambered up on a stump, and there in the light of the moon in his red flannels the comical old-timer turned sober. A serious look passed over the faces of the cowboys as they gathered around the stump. His appearance was ridiculous, but no one laughed. Something about the manner in which the old cowboy presented what he had to say kept everyone's attention. He started in a slow Texas drawl, deep and threatening as the snarl of a wolf.

"Red is gone. You all know that. I know why. You young uns don't. Ever since I met Red some thirty-four years ago, I've learned more about him—his ways, his habits, and so on. Only once have I seen him act like this before. That was when his wife died. He has a strange habit of semiconsciousness. I don't understand it. He doesn't either. But don't you go out to look for him. You could never find him. If you did it would only make him sad. He likes to be alone when he thinks so hard. Now get back to your 'soogans'—all of ye!" Then he dismounted the stump and plodded off to bed. A silence as great and powerful as death hung over camp.

I was worried and decided to take a little stroll. I crept stealthily by Charlie's bunk and entered the grove of trees at the right of camp. In the light of small moonbeams that filtered through the branches of overhanging firs, I made my way down the rocky path. Soft nickers and stomping hooves told me that I was nearing the corral. As I drew closer, the wild ones stampeded to the opposite end of the trap. I started in a wide semicircle about the nearest side barrier and advanced to the far gate. Then, before I realized it, I was in the open again, looking in upon the basin, with the gate about a hundred feet away.

A stirring sound a little ways up the canyon drew my attention from the remuda. I walked cautiously up the boulder-covered basin, trying to keep my balance on the slimy rocks as I neared the river. As I rounded the bend in the ravine I came upon a strange sight. There was Palomino, tied and shackled. On top of him sat Red calmly smoking a battered corncob. Both were wet and bedraggled, while water covered the rocks from the shore to the two figures. What happened came as clear as a picture to my mind. I have seen it done by expert ropers twice, but had never been able to perform the feat successfully myself. Red had snared Palomino while the mighty horse was swimming the river, that he might join his band. Using a pine stump as a snubbing post and managing to rope both front and back ankles, Red caught Palomino and also kept him from killing himself in an attempt to get away.

He seemed to be waiting for something. I didn't want to startle Red or the horse, so I sauntered up casually and spoke softly to Red. He didn't answer me for a full two minutes. He just sat there and puffed thoughtfully at his pipe. He seemed to be struggling within himself. Then he looked straight into my eyes. I caught the old-timer's meaning perfectly. He didn't have to say anything. His eyes expressed his feelings. I nodded that I had the same idea. Then he rose and drew a knife from his sheath, cutting the bonds that bound the most magnificent animal in horse kingdom. He loosened the shackles and slipped off the lariat loop. "Take a last look, Bill," he said slowly. "He deserves everything he was born into." Palomino lay quiet still for a few fleeting seconds, then stirred. Finding himself free, he rose with a mighty bound. He kicked up his heels a few times, bucking hard, and bowing his neck, then raced regally off up the canyon. His thundering hooves rocked the ground, and with head held high, mane flapping around his shining neck, and nostrils quivering, he sped over the rocky bottom. Again his long neigh rent the silence with a long note of triumph. Together we watched him until the tip of his silvery tail disappeared around a bend in the canyon.

Skipper

SEWELL FORD

AT THE age of six Skipper went on the force. Clean of limb and sound of wind he was, with not a blemish from the tip of his black tail to the end of his crinkly forelock. He had been broken to saddle by a Green Mountain boy who knew more of horse nature than of the trashy things writ in books. He gave Skipper kind words and an occasional friendly pat on the flank. So Skipper's disposition was sweet and his nature a trusting one.

This was why Skipper learned so soon the ways of the city. The first time he saw one of those little wheeled houses, all windows and full of people, come rushing down the street with a fearful whirr and clank of bell, he wanted to bolt. But the man on his back spoke in an easy, calm voice, saying, "So-o-o! There, me b'y. Aisy wid ye. So-o-o!" which was excellent advice, for the queer contrivance whizzed by and did him no harm. In a week he could watch one without even pricking up his ears.

It was strange work Skipper had been brought to the city to do. As a colt he had seen horses dragging ploughs, pulling big loads of hay, and hitched to many kinds of vehicles. He himself had drawn a light buggy and thought it good fun, though you did have to keep your heels down and trot instead of canter. He had liked best to lope off with the boy on his back, down to the Corners, where the store was.

But here there were no ploughs, nor hay-carts, nor mowing-machines. There were many heavy wagons, it was true, but these were all drawn by stock Percherons and big Western grays or stout Canada blacks who seemed fully equal to the task.

Also there were carriages—my, what shiny carriages! And what

213

smart, sleek-looking horses drew them! And how high they did hold their heads and how they did throw their feet about—just as if they were dancing on eggs.

"Proud, stuck-up things," thought Skipper.

It was clear that none of this work was for him. Early on the first morning of his service, men in brass-buttoned blue coats came to the stable to feed and rub down the horses. Skipper's man had two names. One was Officer Martin; at least that was the one to which he answered when the man with the cap called the roll before they rode out for duty. The other name was "Reddy." That was what the rest of the men in blue coats called him. Skipper noticed that he had red hair and concluded that "Reddy" must be his real name.

As for Skipper's name, it was written on the tag tied to the halter which he wore when he came to the city. Skipper heard him read it. The boy on the farm had done that, and Skipper was glad, for he liked the name.

There was much to learn in those first few weeks, and Skipper learned it quickly. He came to know that at inspection, which began the day, you must stand with your nose just on a line with that of the horse on either side. If you didn't, you felt the bit or the spurs. He mastered the meaning of "right dress," "left dress," "forward," "fours right," and a lot of other things. Some of them were very strange.

Now on the farm they had said, "Whoa, boy," and "Gid a-aap." Here they said "Halt!" and "Forward!" But "Reddy" used none of these terms. He pressed with his knees on your withers, loosened the reins, and made a queer little chirrup when he wanted you to gallop. He let you know when he wanted you to stop, by the lightest pressure on the bit.

It was lazy work, though. Sometimes when Skipper was just aching for a brisk canter he had to pace soberly through the park driveways —for Skipper, I don't believe I mentioned it before, was part and parcel of the mounted police force. But there, you could know that by the coat of arms in yellow brass on his saddle blanket.

For half an hour at a time he would stand, just on the edge of the roadway and at an exact right angle with it, motionless as the horse ridden by the bronze soldier up near the Mall. "Reddy" would sit as still in the saddle, too. It was hard for Skipper to stand there and see those mincing cobs go by, their pad-housings all a-glitter, crests on their blinders, jingling their pole-chains and switching their absurd little stubs of tails. But it was still more tantalizing to watch the saddle horses canter past on the soft bridle path on the other side of the roadway. But then, when you are on the force you must do your duty.

One afternoon as Skipper was standing post like this he caught a new note that rose above the hum of the park traffic. It was the quick, nervous beat of hoofs which rang sharply on the hard macadam. There were screams, too. It was a runaway. Skipper knew this even before he saw the bell-like nostrils, the straining eyes, and the foam-flecked lips of the horse, or the scared man in the carriage behind. It was a case of broken rein.

How the sight made Skipper's blood tingle! Wouldn't he just like to show that crazy roan what real running was! But what was Reddy going to do? He felt him gather up the reins. He felt his knees tighten. What! Yes, it must be so. Reddy was actually going to try a brush with the runaway. What fun!

Skipper pranced out into the roadway and gathered himself for the sport. Before he could get into full swing, however, the roan had shot past with a snort of challenge which could not be misunderstood.

"Oho! You will, eh?" thought Skipper. "Well now, we'll see about that."

Ah, a free rein! That is—almost free. And a touch of the spurs! No need for that, Reddy. How the carriages scatter! Skipper caught hasty glimpses of smart hackneys drawn up trembling by the roadside, of women who tumbled from bicycles into the bushes, and of men who ran and shouted and waved their hats.

"Just as though that little roan wasn't scared enough already," thought Skipper.

But she did run well; Skipper had to admit that. And had a lead of fifty yards before he could strike his best gait. Then for a few moments he could not seem to gain an inch. But the mare was blowing herself and Skipper was taking it coolly. He was putting the pent-up energy of weeks into his strides. Once he saw he was overhauling her he steadied to the work.

Just as Skipper was about to forge ahead, Reddy did a queer thing. With his right hand he grabbed the roan with a nose-pinch grip, and with the left he pulled in on the reins. It was a great disappointment to Skipper, for he had counted on showing the roan his heels. Skipper knew, after two or three experiences of this kind, that this was the usual thing.

Those were glorious runs, though. Skipper wished they would come more often. Sometimes there would be two and even three in a day. Then a fortnight or so would pass without a single runaway on Skipper's beat. But duty is duty.

During the early morning hours, when there were few people in the park, Skipper's education progressed. He learned to pace around in a circle, lifting each forefoot with a sway of the body and a pawing movement which was quite rhythmical. He learned to box with his nose. He learned to walk sedately behind Reddy and to pick up a glove dropped apparently by accident. There was always a sugar-plum or a sweet cracker when Reddy stopped and Skipper, poking his nose over his shoulder, let the glove fall into his hands.

As he became more accomplished, he noticed that Reddy took more pains with his toilet. Every morning Skipper's coat was brushed until it shone almost as if it had been varnished. His fetlocks were carefully trimmed, a ribbon braided into his forelock, and his hoofs polished as brightly as Reddy's boots. Then there were apples and carrots and other delicacies which Reddy brought him.

So it happened that one morning Skipper heard the Sergeant tell Reddy that he had been detailed for the Horse Show squad. Reddy had saluted and said nothing at the time, but when they were once out on post he told Skipper all about it.

"Sure an' it's app'arin' before all the swells in town you'll be, me b'y. Phat do ye think of that, eh? And mebbe ye'll be gettin' a blue ribbon, Skipper, me lad; an' mebbe Mr. Patrick Martin will have a roundsman's berth and chevrons on his sleeves afore the year's out."

The Horse Show was all that Reddy had promised, and more. The light almost dazzled Skipper. The sounds and the smells confused him. But he felt Reddy on his back, heard him chirrup softly, and soon felt at ease on the tanbark.

Then there was a great crash of noise and Skipper, with some fifty of his friends on the force, began to move around the circle. First it was fours abreast, then by twos, and then a rush to troop front, when, in a long line, they swept around as if they had been harnessed to a beam by traces of equal length.

After some more evolutions, a half-dozen were picked out and put through their paces. Skipper was one of these. Then three of the six were sent to join the rest of the squad. Only Skipper and two others remained in the center of the ring. Men in queer clothes, wearing tall black hats, showing much white shirt-front and carrying long whips, came and looked them over carefully.

Skipper showed these men how he could waltz in time to the music, and the people who banked the circle as far up as Skipper could see shouted and clapped their hands until it seemed as if a thunderstorm had broken loose. At last one of the men in tall hats tied a blue ribbon on Skipper's bridle.

When Reddy got him into the stable, he fed him four big red apples one after the other. Next day Skipper knew that he was a famous horse. Reddy showed him their pictures in the paper.

For a whole year Skipper was the pride of the force. He was shown to visitors at the stables. He was patted on the nose by the Mayor. The Chief, who was a bigger man than the Mayor, came up especially to look at him. In the park Skipper did his tricks every day for ladies in fine dress who exclaimed, "How perfectly wonderful!" as well as for pretty nursemaids who giggled and said, "Now did you ever see the likes o' that, Norah?"

And then came the spavin. Ah, but that was the beginning of the end! Were you ever spavined? If so, you know all about it. If you weren't, there's no use of my trying to tell you. Rheumatism? Well, that may be bad; but spavin is worse. For three weeks Reddy rubbed the hump on the back with stuff from a brown bottle, and hid it from the inspector. Then, one black morning it was discovered. That day Skipper did not go out on post. Reddy came into the stall, put his arm around his neck and said "Good-by" in a voice that Skipper had never heard him use before. Something had made it thick and husky. Very sadly Skipper saw him saddle one of the newcomers and go out for duty.

Before Reddy came back, Skipper was led away. He was taken to a big building where there were horses of every kind—except the right kind. Each one had his own peculiar "out," although you couldn't always tell what it was at a first glance.

But Skipper did not stay here long. He was led out before a lot of men in a big ring. A man on a box shouted out a number and began to talk very fast. Skipper gathered that he was talking about him. Skipper learned that he was still only six years old, and that he had been owned as a saddle horse by a lady who was about to sail for Europe and was closing out her stable. This was news to Skipper. He wished Reddy could hear it.

The man talked very nicely about Skipper. He said he was kind, gentle, sound in wind and limb, and was not only trained to the saddle but would work either single or double. The man wanted to know how much the gentlemen were willing to pay for a bay gelding of this description.

Someone on the outer edge of the crowd said "Ten dollars."

At this the man on the box grew quite indignant. He asked if the other man wouldn't like a silver-mounted harness and a lap robe thrown in.

"Fifteen," said another man.

Somebody else said "Twenty." Then there was a hitch. The man on the box began to talk very fast indeed.

"Thutty-thutty-thutty-thutty—do I hear five? Thutty-thutty-thutty-thutty—will you make it five?"

"Thirty-five," said a red-faced man who had pushed his way to the front and was looking Skipper over sharply.

The man on the box said "Thutty-five" a good many times and asked if he "heard forty." Evidently he did not, for he stopped and said very slowly and distinctly, looking expectantly around, "Are you all done? Thirty-five—once. Thirty-five—twice. Third and last call—sold, for thirty-five dollars!"

When Skipper heard this he hung his head. When you have been a $250 blue-ribboner and the pride of the force it is sad to be "knocked down" for thirty-five.

The next year of Skipper's life was a dark one. We will not linger over it. The red-faced man who led him away was a grocer. He put Skipper in the shafts of a heavy wagon very early every morning and drove him a long way through the city to a big downtown market where men in long frocks shouted and handled boxes and barrels. When the wagon was heavily loaded, the red-faced man drove him back to the store. Then a tow-haired boy, who jerked viciously on the lines and was fond of using the whip, drove him recklessly about the streets and avenues.

But one day the tow-haired boy pulled the near rein too hard while rounding a corner and a wheel was smashed against a lamp-post. The tow-haired boy was sent head first into an ash-barrel, and Skipper, rather startled at the occurrence, took a little run down the avenue, strewing the pavement with eggs, sugar, canned corn, celery and other assorted groceries.

Perhaps this was why the grocer sold him. Skipper pulled a cart through the flat-house district for a while after that. On the seat of the cart sat a leather-lunged man who roared, "A-a-a-a-puls! Nice a-a-a-a-puls! A who-o-o-ole lot fer a quarter!"

Skipper felt this disgrace keenly. Even the cab-horses, on whom he used to look with disdain, eyed him scornfully. Skipper stood it as long as possible and then one day, while the apple fakir was standing on the back step of the cart shouting things at a woman who was leaning halfway out of a fourth-story window, he bolted. He distributed that load of apples over four blocks, much to the profit of the street children, and he wrecked the wagon on a hydrant. For this the fakir beat him with a piece of the wreckage until a blue-coated officer threatened to arrest him. Next day Skipper was sold again.

Skipper looked over his new owner without joy. The man was evil of face. His long whiskers and hair were unkempt and sun-bleached like the tip end of a pastured cow's tail. His clothes were greasy. His voice was like the grunt of a pig. Skipper wondered to what use this man would put him. He feared the worst.

Far up through the city the man took him and out on a broad avenue where there were many open spaces, most of them fenced in by huge billboards. Behind one of these sign-plastered barriers Skipper found his new home. The bottom of the lot was more than twenty feet below the street level. In the center of a waste of rocks, ash heaps, and dead weeds tottered a group of shanties, strangely made of odds and ends. The walls were partly of mud-chinked rocks and partly of wood. The roofs were patched with strips of rusty tin held in place by stones.

Into one of these shanties just tall enough for Skipper to enter and no more, the horse that had been the pride of the mounted park police was driven with a kick as a greeting. Skipper noted first that there was no feed-box and no hay-rick. Then he saw, or rather felt— for the only light came through cracks in the walls—that there was no floor. His nostrils told him that the drainage was bad. Skipper sighed as he thought of the clean, sweet straw which Reddy used to change in his stall every night.

But when you have a lump on your leg—a lump that throbs, throbs with pain, whether you stand still or lie down—you do not think much on other things.

Supper was late in coming to Skipper that night. He was almost starved when it was served. And such a supper! What do you think? Hay? Yes, but marsh hay; the dry, tasteless stuff they use for bedding in cheap stables. A ton of it wouldn't make a pound of good flesh. Oats? Not a sign of an oat! But with the hay there were a few potato peelings. Skipper nosed them out and nibbled the marsh hay. The rest he pawed back under him, for the whole had been thrown at his feet. Then he dropped on the ill-smelling ground and went to sleep to dream that he had been turned into a forty-acre field of clover, while a dozen brass bands played a waltz and multitudes of people looked on and cheered.

In the morning more salt hay was thrown to him and water was brought in a dirty pail. Then, without a stroke of brush or curry-comb, he was led out. When he saw the wagon to which he was to be hitched, Skipper hung his head. He had reached the bottom. It was unpainted and rickety as to body and frame, the wheels were un-mated and dished, while the shafts were spliced and wound with wire.

But worse of all was the string of bells suspended from two up-
rights above the seat. When Skipper saw these he knew he had fallen
low indeed. He had become the horse of a wandering junkman. The
next step in his career, as he well knew, would be the glue factory
and the boneyard. Now when a horse has lived for twenty years or so,
it is sad enough to face these things. But at eight years to see the glue
factory close at hand is enough to make a horse wish he had never
been foaled.

For many weary months Skipper pulled that crazy cart, with its
hateful jangle of bells, about the city streets and suburban roads
while the man with the faded hair roared through his matted beard,
"Buy o-o-o-o—olt ra-a-a-a-a-ags! Buy o-o-o-o-olt ra-a-a-a-a-ags! Olt bod-
dles! Olt iron! Vaste baber!"

The lump on Skipper's hock kept growing bigger and bigger. It
seemed as if the darts of pain shot from hoof to flank with every step.
Big hollows came over his eyes. You could see his ribs as plainly as the
hoops on a pork-barrel. Yet six days in the week he went on long
trips and brought back heavy loads of junk. On Sunday he hauled
the junkman and his family about the city.

Once the junkman tried to drive Skipper into one of the park
entrances. Then for the first time in his life Skipper balked. The
junkman pounded and used such language as you might expect
from a junkman, but all to no use. Skipper took the beating with
lowered head, but go through the gate he would not. So the junkman gave it up, although he seemed very anxious to join the line of
gay carriages which were rolling in.

Soon after this there came a break in the daily routine. One morning Skipper was not led out as usual. In fact, no one came near him,
and he could hear no voices in the near-by shanty. Skipper decided
that he would take a day off himself. By backing against the door he
readily pushed it open, for the staple was insecure.

Once at liberty, he climbed the roadway that led out of the lot. It
was late in the fall but there was still short, sweet winter grass to be
found along the gutters. For a while he nibbled at this hungrily.
Then a queer idea came to Skipper. Perhaps the padding of a smartly
groomed saddle horse was responsible.

At any rate, Skipper left off nibbling grass. He hobbled out to the
edge of the road, turned so as to face the opposite side, and held up
his head. There he stood just as he used to stand when he was the
pride of the mounted squad. He was on post once more.

Few people were passing and none of them seemed to notice him.
Yet he was an odd figure. His coat was shaggy and weather-stained. It
looked patched and faded. The spavined hock caused one hind

quarter to sag somewhat, but aside from that his post was strictly according to the regulations.

Skipper had been playing at standing post for a half-hour, when a trotting dandy who sported ankle-boots and toe-weights pulled up before him. He was drawing a light, bicycle-wheeled road-wagon in which were two men.

"Queer?" one of the men was saying. "Can't say I see anything queer about it, Captain. Some old plug that's got away from a squatter; that's all I see in it."

"Well, let's have a look," said the other. He stared hard at Skipper for a moment and then, in a loud sharp tone, said:

" 'Ten-shun! Right dress!"

Skipper pricked up his ears, raise his head and side-stepped stiffly. The trotting dandy turned and looked curiously at him.

"Forward!" said the man in the wagon. Skipper hobbled out into the road.

"Right wheel! Halt. I thought so," said the man as Skipper obeyed the orders. "That fellow has been on the force. He was standing post. Looks mighty familiar too—white stockings on two forelegs, white star on forehead. Now I wonder if that can be—here hold the reins a minute."

Going up to Skipper the man patted his nose once or twice, and then pushed the muzzle to one side. Skipper ducked and countered. He had not forgotten his boxing trick. The man turned his back and began to pace down the road. Skipper followed and picked up a riding-glove which the man dropped.

"Doyle," said the man, as he walked back to the wagon, "two years ago that was the finest horse on the force—took the blue ribbon at the Garden. Alderman Martin would give a thousand dollars for him as he stands. He has hunted the State for him. You remember Martin— Reddy Martin—who used to be on the mounted squad. Didn't you hear? An old uncle who made a fortune as a building contractor died about a year ago and left the whole pile to Reddy. He's got a fine country place up in Westchester and is in the city government. Just elected this fall. But he isn't happy because he can't find his old horse—and here's the horse."

Next day an astonished junkman stood before an empty shanty which served as a stable and feasted his eyes on a $50 bank note.

If you are ever up in Westchester County, be sure to visit the stables of Alderman P. Sarsfield Martin. Ask to see that oak-paneled box-stall with the stained-glass windows and the porcelain feed-box. You will notice a polished brass name-plate on the door bearing this inscription:

SKIPPER

You may meet the Alderman himself, wearing an English-made riding suit, loping comfortably along on a sleek bay gelding with two white forelegs and a white star on his forehead. Yes, high-priced veterinaries can cure spavin—Alderman Martin says so.

The Gift

JOHN STEINBECK

AT DAYBREAK Billy Buck emerged from the bunkhouse and stood
for a moment on the porch looking up at the sky. He was a broad,
bandy-legged little man with a walrus mustache, with square hands,
puffed and muscled on the palms. His eyes were a contemplative,
watery gray and the hair which protruded from under his Stetson hat
was spiky and weathered. Billy was still stuffing his shirt into his blue
jeans as he stood on the porch. He unbuckled his belt and tightened
it again. The belt showed, by the worn shiny places opposite each
hole, the gradual increase of Billy's middle over a period of years.
When he had seen to the weather, Billy cleared each nostril by holding its mate closed with his forefinger and blowing fiercely. Then he
walked down to the barn, rubbing his hands together. He curried
and brushed two saddle horses in the stalls, talking quietly to them
all the time; and he had hardly finished when the iron triangle
started ringing at the ranch house. Billy stuck the brush and curry-
comb together and laid them on the rail, and went up to breakfast.
His action had been so deliberate and yet so wasteless of time that he
came to the house while Mrs. Tiflin was still ringing the triangle.
She nodded her gray head to him and withdrew into the kitchen.
Billy Buck sat down on the steps, because he was a cow-hand, and it
wouldn't be fitting that he should go first into the dining-room. He
heard Mr. Tiflin in the house, stamping his feet into his boots.

The high jangling note of the triangle put the boy Jody in motion. He was only a little boy, ten years old, with hair like dusty
yellow grass and with shy polite gray eyes, and with a mouth that
worked when he thought. The triangle picked him up out of sleep.
It didn't occur to him to disobey the harsh note. He never had; no

one he knew ever had. He brushed the tangled hair out of his eyes
and skinned his nightgown off. In a moment he was dressed—blue
chambray shirt and overalls. It was late in the summer, so of course
there were no shoes to bother with. In the kitchen he waited until
his mother got from in front of the sink and went back to the stove.
Then he washed himself and brushed back his wet hair with his
fingers. His mother turned sharply on him as he left the sink. Jody
looked shyly away.

"I've got to cut your hair before long," his mother said. "Breakfast's on the table. Go on in, so Billy can come."

Jody sat at the long table which was covered with white oilcloth
washed through to the fabric in some places. The fried eggs lay in
rows on their platter. Jody took three eggs on his plate and followed
with three thick slices of crisp bacon. He carefully scraped a spot of
blood from one of the egg yolks.

Billy Buck clumped in. "That won't hurt you," Billy explained.
"That's only a sign the rooster leaves."

Jody's tall stern father came in then and Jody knew from the noise
on the floor that he was wearing boots, but he looked under the table
anyway, to make sure. His father turned off the oil lamp over the
table, for plenty of morning light now came through the windows.

Jody did not ask where his father and Billy Buck were riding that
day, but he wished he might go along. His father was a disciplinarian.
Jody obeyed him in everything without questions of any kind. Now,
Carl Tiflin sat down and reached for the egg platter.

"Got the cows ready to go, Billy?" he asked.

"In the lower corral," Billy said. "I could just as well take them in
alone."

"Sure you could. But a man needs company. Besides your throat
gets pretty dry." Carl Tiflin was jovial this morning.

Jody's mother put her head in the door. "What time do you think
to be back, Carl?"

"I can't tell. I've got to see some men in Salinas. Might be gone till
dark."

The eggs and coffee and big biscuits disappeared rapidly. Jody
followed the two men out of the house. He watched them mount
their horses and drive six old cows out of the corral and start over the
hill towards Salinas. They were going to sell the old cows to the
butcher.

When they had disappeared over the crown of the ridge Jody
walked up the hill in back of the house. The dogs trotted around the
house corner hunching their shoulders and grinning horribly with

pleasure. Jody patted their heads—Doubletree Mutt with the big thick tail and yellow eyes, and Smasher, the shepherd, who had killed a coyote and lost an ear in doing it. Smasher's one good ear stood up higher than a collie's ear should. Billy Buck said that always happened. After the frenzied greeting the dogs lowered their noses to the ground in a businesslike way and went ahead, looking back now and then to make sure that the boy was coming. They walked up through the chicken yard and saw the quail eating with the chickens. Smasher chased the chickens a little to keep in practice in case there should ever be sheep to herd. Jody continued on through the large vegetable patch where the green corn was higher than his head. The cowpumpkins were green and small yet. He went on to the sagebrush line where the cold spring ran out of its pipe and fell into a round wooden tub. He leaned over and drank close to the green mossy wood where the water tasted best. Then he turned and looked back on the ranch, on the low, whitewashed house girded with red geraniums, and on the long bunkhouse by the cypress tree where Billy Buck lived alone. Jody could see the great black kettle under the cypress tree. That was where the pigs were scalded. The sun was coming over the ridge now, glaring on the whitewash of the houses and barns, making the wet grass blaze softly. Behind him, in the tall sagebrush, the birds were scampering on the ground, making a great noise among the dry leaves; the squirrels piped shrilly on the sidehills. Jody looked along at the farm buildings. He felt an uncertainty in the air, a feeling of change and of loss and of the gain of new and unfamiliar things. Over the hillside two big black buzzards sailed low to the ground and their shadows slipped smoothly and quickly ahead of them. Some animal had died in the vicinity. Jody knew it. It might be a cow or it might be the remains of a rabbit. The buzzards overlooked nothing. Jody hated them as all decent things hate them, but they could not be hurt because they made away with carrion.

After a while the boy sauntered down hill again. The dogs had long ago given him up and gone into the brush to do things in their own way. Back through the vegetable garden he went, and he paused for a moment to smash a green muskmelon with his heel, but he was not happy about it. It was a bad thing to do, he knew perfectly well. He kicked dirt over the ruined melon to conceal it.

Back at the house his mother bent over his rough hands, inspecting his fingers and nails. It did little good to start him clean to school for too many things could happen on the way. She sighed over the black cracks on his fingers, and then gave him his books and his lunch and started him on the mile walk to school. She noticed that his mouth was working a good deal this morning.

Jody started his journey. He filled his pockets with little pieces of white quartz that lay in the road, and every so often he took a shot at a bird or at some rabbit that had stayed sunning itself in the road too long. At the crossroads over the bridge he met two friends and the three of them walked to school together, making ridiculous strides and being rather silly. School had just opened two weeks before. There was still a spirit of revolt among the pupils.

It was four o'clock in the afternoon when Jody topped the hill and looked down on the ranch again. He looked for the saddle horses, but the corral was empty. His father was not back yet. He went slowly, then, toward the afternoon chores. At the ranch house, he found his mother sitting on the porch, mending socks.

"There's two doughnuts in the kitchen for you," she said. Jody slid to the kitchen, and returned with half of one of the doughnuts already eaten and his mouth full. His mother asked him what he had learned in school that day, but she didn't listen to his doughnut-muffled answer. She interrupted, "Jody, tonight see you fill the wood-box clear full. Last night you crossed the sticks and it wasn't only about half full. Lay the sticks flat tonight. And Jody, some of the hens are hiding eggs, or else the dogs are eating them. Look about in the grass and see if you can find any nests."

Jody, still eating, went out and did his chores. He saw the quail come down to eat with the chickens when he threw out the grain. For some reason his father was proud to have them come. He never allowed any shooting near the house for fear the quail might go away.

When the wood-box was full, Jody took his twenty-two rifle up to the cold spring at the brush line. He drank again and then aimed the gun at all manner of things, at rocks, at birds on the wing, at the big black pig kettle under the cypress tree, but he didn't shoot for he had no cartridges and wouldn't have until he was twelve. If his father had seen him aim the rifle in the direction of the house, he would have put the cartridges off another year. Jody remembered this and did not point the rifle down the hill again. Two years was enough to wait for cartridges. Nearly all of his father's presents were given with reservations which hampered their value somewhat. It was good discipline.

The supper waited until dark for his father to return. When at last he came in with Billy Buck, Jody could smell the delicious brandy on their breath. Inwardly he rejoiced, for his father sometimes talked to him when he smelled of brandy, sometimes even told things he had done in the wild days when he was a boy.

After supper, Jody sat by the fireplace and his shy polite eyes sought the room corners, and he waited for his father to tell what it was he contained, for Jody knew he had news of some sort. But he was disappointed. His father pointed a stern finger at him.

"You'd better go to bed, Jody. I'm going to need you in the morning."

That wasn't so bad. Jody liked to do the things he had to do as long as they weren't routine things. He looked at the floor and his mouth worked out a question before he spoke it. "What are we going to do in the morning, kill a pig?" he asked softly.

"Never you mind. You better get to bed."

When the door was closed behind him, Jody heard his father and Billy Buck chuckling and he knew it was a joke of some kind. And later, when he lay in bed, trying to make words out of the murmurs in the other room, he heard his father protest, "But, Ruth, I didn't give much for him."

Jody heard the hoot-owls hunting mice down by the barn, and he heard a fruit tree limb tap-tapping against the house. A cow was lowing when he went to sleep.

When the triangle sounded in the morning, Jody dressed more quickly even than usual. In the kitchen, while he washed his face and combed back his hair, his mother addressed him irritably. "Don't you go out until you get a good breakfast in you."

He went into the dining-room and sat at the long white table. He took a steaming hotcake from the platter, arranged two fried eggs on it, covered them with another hotcake and squashed the whole thing with his fork.

His father and Billy Buck came in. Jody knew from the sound on the floor that both of them were wearing flat-heeled shoes, but he peered under the table to make sure. His father turned off the oil lamp, for the day had arrived, and he looked stern and disciplinary, but Billy Buck didn't look at Jody at all. He avoided the shy questioning eyes of the boy and soaked a whole piece of toast in his coffee.

Carl Tiflin said crossly, "You come with us after breakfast!"

Jody had trouble with his food then, for he felt a kind of doom in the air. After Billy had tilted his saucer and drained the coffee which had slopped into it, and had wiped his hands on his jeans, the two men stood up from the table and went out into the morning light together, and Jody respectfully followed a little behind them. He tried to keep his mind from running ahead, tried to keep it absolutely motionless.

His mother called, "Carl! Don't you let it keep him from school."

They marched past the cypress, where a singletree hung from a limb to butcher the pigs on, and past the black iron kettle, so it was not a pig killing. The sun shone over the hill and threw long, dark shadows of the trees and buildings. They crossed a stubble-field to shortcut to the barn. Jody's father unhooked the door and they went in. They had been walking toward the sun on the way down. The barn was black as night in contrast and warm from the hay and from the beasts. Jody's father moved over toward the one box stall. "Come here!" he ordered. Jody could begin to see things now. He looked into the box stall and then stepped back quickly.

A red pony colt was looking at him out of the stall. Its tense ears were forward and a light of disobedience was in its eyes. Its coat was rough and thick as an airedale's fur and its mane was long and tangled. Jody's throat collapsed in on itself and cut his breath short.

"He needs a good currying," his father said, "and if ever I hear of you not feeding him or leaving his stall dirty, I'll sell him off in a minute."

Jody couldn't bear to look at the pony's eyes any more. He gazed down at his hands for a moment, and he asked very shyly, "Mine?" No one answered him. He put his hand out toward the pony. Its gray nose came close, sniffing loudly, and then the lips drew back and the strong teeth closed on Jody's fingers. The pony shook its head up and down and seemed to laugh with amusement. Jody regarded his bruised fingers. "Well," he said with pride— "Well, I guess he can bite all right." The two men laughed, somewhat in relief. Carl Tiflin went out of the barn and walked up a sidehill to be by himself, for he was embarrassed, but Billy Buck stayed. It was easier to talk to Billy Buck. Jody asked again— "Mine?"

Billy became professional in tone. "Sure! That is, if you look out for him and break him right. I'll show you how. He's just a colt. You can't ride him for some time."

Jody put out his bruised hand again, and this time the red pony let his nose be rubbed. "I ought to have a carrot," Jody said. "Where'd we get him, Billy?"

"Bought him at a sheriff's auction," Billy explained. "A show went broke in Salinas and had debts. The sheriff was selling off their stuff."

The pony stretched out his nose and shook the forelock from his wild eyes. Jody stroked the nose a little. He said softly, "There isn't a—saddle?"

Billy Buck laughed. "I'd forgot. Come along."

In the harness room he lifted down a little saddle of red morocco leather. "It's just a show saddle," Billy Buck said disparagingly. "It isn't practical for the brush, but it was cheap at the sale."

Jody couldn't trust himself to look at the saddle either, and he couldn't speak at all. He brushed the shining red leather with his finger tips, and after a long time he said, "It'll look pretty on him though." He thought of the grandest and prettiest things he knew. "If he hasn't a name already, I think I'll call him Gabilan Mountains," he said.

Billy Buck knew how he felt. "It's a pretty long name. Why don't you just call him Gabilan? That means hawk. That would be a fine name for him." Billy felt glad. "If you will collect tail hair, I might be able to make a hair rope for you sometime. You could use it for a hackamore."

Jody wanted to go back to the box stall. "Could I lead him to school, do you think—to show the kids?"

But Billy shook his head. "He's not even halter-broke yet. We had a time getting him here. Had to almost drag him. You better be starting for school though."

"I'll bring the kids to see him here this afternoon," Jody said.

Six boys came over the hill half an hour early that afternoon, running hard, their heads down, their forearms working, their breath whistling. They swept by the house and cut across the stubble-field to the barn. And then they stood self-consciously before the pony, and then they looked at Jody with eyes in which there was a new admiration and a new respect. Before today Jody had been a boy, dressed in overalls and a blue shirt—quieter than most, even suspected of being a little cowardly. And now he was different. Out of a thousand centuries they drew the ancient admiration of the footman for the horseman. They knew instinctively that a man on a horse is spiritually as well as physically bigger than a man on foot. They knew that Jody had been miraculously lifted out of equality with them, and had been placed over them. Gabilan put his head out of the stall and sniffed them.

"Why'n't you ride him?" the boys cried. "Why'n't you braid his tail with ribbons like in the fair?" "When you going to ride him?"

Jody's courage was up. He too felt the superiority of the horseman. "He's not old enough. Nobody can ride him for a long time. I'm going to train him on the long halter. Billy Buck is going to show me how."

"Well, can't we even lead him around a little?"

"He isn't even halter-broke," Jody said. He wanted to be completely alone when he took the pony out the first time. "Come and see the saddle."

They were speechless at the red morocco saddle, completely shocked out of comment. "It isn't much use in the brush," Jody explained. "It'll look pretty on him though. Maybe I'll ride bareback when I go into the brush."

"How you going to rope a cow without a saddle horn?"

"Maybe I'll get another saddle for every day. My father might want me to help him with the stock." He let them feel the red saddle, and showed them the brass chain throat-latch on the bridle and the big brass buttons at each temple where the headstall and brow band crossed. The whole thing was too wonderful. They had to go away after a little while, and each boy, in his mind, searched among his possessions for a bribe worthy of offering in return for a ride on the red pony when the time should come.

Jody was glad when they had gone. He took brush and currycomb from the wall, took down the barrier of the box stall and stepped cautiously in. The pony's eyes glittered, and he edged around into kicking position. But Jody touched him on the shoulder and rubbed his high arched neck as he had always seen Billy Buck do, and he crooned "So-o-o Boy," in a deep voice. The pony gradually relaxed his tenseness. Jody curried and brushed until a pile of dead hair lay in the stall and until the pony's coat had taken on a deep red shine. Each time he finished he thought it might have been done better. He braided the mane into a dozen little pigtails, and he braided the forelock, and then he undid them and brushed the hair out straight again.

Jody did not hear his mother enter the barn. She was angry when she came, but when she looked in at the pony and at Jody working over him, she felt a curious pride rise up in her. "Have you forgot the wood-box?" she asked gently. "It's not far off from dark and there's not a stick of wood in the house, and the chickens aren't fed."

Jody quickly put up his tools. "I forgot, ma'am."

"Well, after this do your chores first. Then you won't forget. I expect you'll forget lots of things now if I don't keep an eye on you."

"Can I have carrots from the garden for him, ma'am?"

She had to think about that. "Oh—I guess so, if you only take the big tough ones."

"Carrots keep the coat good," he said, and again she felt the curious rush of pride.

Jody never waited for the triangle to get him out of bed after the coming of the pony. It became his habit to creep out of bed even before his mother was awake, to slip into his clothes and to go quietly down to the barn to see Gabilan. In the gray quiet mornings when the land and the brush and the houses and the trees were silver-gray and black like a photograph negative, he stole toward the barn, past the sleeping stones and the sleeping cypress tree. The turkeys, roosting in the tree out of coyotes' reach, clicked drowsily. The fields glowed with a gray frostlike light and in the dew the tracks of rabbits and of field mice stood out sharply. The good dogs came stiffly out of their little houses, hackles up and deep growls in their throats. Then they caught Jody's scent, and their stiff tails rose up and waved a greeting—Doubletree Mutt with the big thick tail, and Smasher, the incipient shepherd—then went lazily back to their warm beds.

It was a strange time and a mysterious journey, to Jody—an extension of a dream. When he first had the pony he liked to torture himself during the trip by thinking Gabilan would not be in his stall, and worse, would never have been there. And he had other delicious little self-induced pains. He thought how the rats had gnawed ragged holes in the red saddle, and how the mice had nibbled Gabilan's tail until it was stringy and thin. He usually ran the last little way to the barn. He unlatched the rusty hasp of the barn door and stepped in, and no matter how quietly he opened the door, Gabilan was always looking at him over the barrier of the box stall and Gabilan whinnied softly and stamped his front foot, and his eyes had big sparks of red fire in them like oak-wood embers.

Sometimes, if the work horses were to be used that day, Jody found Billy Buck in the barn harnessing and currying. Billy stood with him and looked long at Gabilan and he told Jody a great many things about horses. He explained that they were terribly afraid for their feet, so that one must make a practice of lifting the legs and patting the hooves and ankles to remove their terror. He told Jody how horses love conversation. He must talk to the pony all the time, and tell him the reasons for everything. Billy wasn't sure a horse could understand everything that was said to him, but it was impossible to say how much was understood. A horse never kicked up a fuss if someone he liked explained things to him. Billy could give examples, too. He had known, for instance, a horse nearly dead beat with fatigue to perk up when told it was only a little farther to his destination. And he had known a horse paralyzed with fright to come out of it when his rider told him what it was that was frightening him. While he talked in the mornings, Billy Buck cut twenty or thirty straws into neat three-inch lengths and stuck them into his hatband. Then during the whole day, if he wanted to pick his teeth or merely to chew on something, he had only to reach up for one of them.

Jody listened carefully, for he knew and the whole country knew that Billy Buck was a fine hand with horses. Billy's own horse was a stringy cayuse with a hammer head, but he nearly always won the first prizes at the stock trials. Billy could rope a steer, take a double half-hitch about the horn with his riata, and dismount, and his horse would play the steer as an angler plays a fish, keeping a tight rope until the steer was down or beaten.

Every morning, after Jody had curried and brushed the pony, he let down the barrier of the stall, and Gabilan thrust past him and raced down the barn and into the corral. Around and around he galloped, and sometimes he jumped forward and landed on stiff legs. He stood quivering, stiff ears forward, eyes rolling so that the whites showed, pretending to be frightened. At last he walked snorting to the water-trough and buried his nose in the water up to the nostrils.

Jody was proud then, for he knew that was the way to judge a horse. Poor horses only touched their lips to the water, but a fine spirited beast put his whole nose and mouth under, and only left room to breathe.

Then Jody stood and watched the pony, and he saw things he had never noticed about any other horse, the sleek, sliding flank muscles and the cords of the buttocks, which flexed like a closing fist, and the shine the sun put on the red coat. Having seen horses all his life, Jody had never looked at them very closely before. But now he noticed the moving ears which gave expression and even inflection of expression to the face. The pony talked with his ears. You could tell exactly how he felt about everything by the way his ears pointed. Sometimes they were stiff and upright and sometimes lax and sagging. They went back when he was angry or fearful, and forward when he was anxious and curious and pleased; and their exact position indicated which emotion he had.

Billy Buck kept his word. In the early fall the training began.

First there was the halter-breaking, and that was the hardest because it was the first thing. Jody held a carrot and coaxed and promised and pulled on the rope. The pony set his feet like a burro when he felt the strain. But before long he learned. Jody walked all over the range leading him. Gradually he took to dropping the rope until the pony followed him unled wherever he went.

And then came the training on the long halter. That was slower work. Jody stood in the middle of a circle, holding the long halter. He clucked with his tongue and the pony started to walk in a big circle, held in by the long rope. He clucked again to make the pony trot, and again to make him gallop. Around and around Gabilan went thundering and enjoying it immensely. Then he called, "Whoa," and the pony stopped. It was not long until Gabilan was perfect at it. But in many ways he was a bad pony. He bit Jody in the pants and stomped on Jody's feet. Now and then his ears went back and he aimed a tremendous kick at the boy. Everytime he did one of these bad things, Gabilan settled back and seemed to laugh to himself.

Billy Buck worked at the hair rope in the evenings before the fireplace. Jody collected tail hair in a bag, and he sat and watched Billy slowly constructing the rope, twisting a few hairs to make a string and rolling two strings together for a cord, and then braiding a number of cords to make the rope. Billy rolled the finished rope on the floor under his foot to make it round and hard.

The long halter work rapidly approached perfection. Jody's father watching the pony stop and start and trot and gallop, was a little bothered by it.

"He's getting to be almost a trick pony," he complained. "I don't like trick horses. It takes all the—dignity out of a horse to make him do tricks. Why, a trick horse is kind of like an actor—no dignity, no character of his own." And his father said, "I guess you better be getting him used to the saddle pretty soon."

Jody rushed for the harness-room. For some time he had been riding the saddle on a sawhorse. He changed the stirrup length over and over, and could never get it just right. Sometimes, mounted on the sawhorse in the harness-room, with collar and hames and tugs hung all about him, Jody rode out beyond the room. He carried his rifle across the pommel. He saw the fields go flying by, and he heard the beat of the galloping hoofs.

It was a ticklish job, saddling the pony the first time. Gabilan hunched and reared and threw the saddle off before the cinch could be tightened. It had to be replaced again and again until at last the pony let it stay. And the cinching was difficult, too. Day by day Jody tightened the girth a little more until at last the pony didn't mind the saddle at all.

Then there was the bridle. Billy explained how to use a stick of licorice for a bit until Gabilan was used to having something in his mouth. Billy explained, "Of course we could force-break him to everything, but he wouldn't be as good a horse if we did. He'd always be a little bit afraid, and he wouldn't mind because he wanted to."

The first time the pony wore the bridle he whipped his head about and worked his tongue against the bit until the blood oozed from the corners of his mouth. He tried to rub the headstall off on the manger. His ears pivoted about and his eyes turned red with fear and with general rambunctiousness. Jody rejoiced, for he knew that only a mean-souled horse does not resent training.

And Jody trembled when he thought of the time when he would first sit in the saddle. The pony would probably throw him off. There was no disgrace in that. The disgrace would come if he did not get right up and mount again. Sometimes he dreamed that he lay in the dirt and cried and couldn't make himself mount again. The shame of the dream lasted until the middle of the day.

Gabilan was growing fast. Already he had lost the long-leggedness of the colt; his mane was getting longer and blacker. Under the constant currying and brushing his coat lay as smooth and gleaming as orange-red lacquer. Jody oiled the hoofs and kept them carefully trimmed so they would not crack.

The hair rope was nearly finished. Jody's father gave him an old pair of spurs and bent in the side bars and cut down the strap and took up the chainlets until they fitted. And then one day Carl Tiflin said:

"The pony's growing faster than I thought. I guess you can ride him by Thanksgiving. Think you can stick on?"

"I don't know," Jody said shyly. Thanksgiving was only three weeks off. He hoped it wouldn't rain, for rain would spot the red saddle.

Gabilan knew and liked Jody by now. He nickered when Jody came across the stubble-field, and in the pasture he came running when his master whistled for him. There was always a carrot for him every time.

Billy Buck gave him riding instructions over and over. "Now when you get up there, just grab tight with your knees, and keep your hands away from the saddle, and if you get throwed, don't let that stop you. No matter how good a man is, there's always some horse can pitch him. You just climb up again before he gets to feeling smart about it. Pretty soon, he won't throw you no more, and pretty soon he *can't* throw you no more. That's the way to do it."

"I hope it don't rain before," Jody said.

"Why not? Don't want to get throwed in the mud?"

That was partly it, and also he was afraid that in the flurry of bucking Gabilan might slip and fall on him and break his leg or his hip. He had seen that happen to men before, had seen how they writhed on the ground like squashed bugs, and he was afraid of it.

He practiced on the sawhorse how he would hold the reins in his left hand and a hat in his right hand. If he kept his hands thus busy, he couldn't grab the horn if he felt himself going off. He didn't like to think of what would happen if he did grab the horn. Perhaps his father and Billy Buck would never speak to him again, they would be so ashamed. The news would get about and his mother would be ashamed too. And in the school yard—it was too awful to contemplate.

He began putting his weight in a stirrup when Gabilan was saddled, but he didn't throw his leg over the pony's back. That was forbidden until Thanksgiving.

Every afternoon he put the red saddle on the pony and cinched it tight. The pony was learning already to fill his stomach out unnaturally large while the cinching was going on, and then to let it down when the straps were fixed. Sometimes Jody led him up to the brush line and let him drink from the round green tub, and sometimes he led him up through the stubble-field to the hilltop from which it was possible to see the white town of Salinas and the geometric fields of the great valley, and the oak trees clipped by the sheep. Now and then they broke through the brush and came to little cleared circles so hedged in that the world was gone and only the sky and the circle of brush were left from the old life. Gabilan liked these trips and showed it by keeping his head very high and by quivering his nostrils with interest. When the two came back from an expedition they smelled of the sweet sage they had forced through.

Time dragged on toward Thanksgiving, but winter came fast. The clouds swept down and hung all day over the land and brushed the hilltops, and the winds blew shrilly at night. All day the dry oak

leaves drifted down from the trees until they covered the ground,
and yet the trees were unchanged.

Jody had wished it might not rain before Thanksgiving, but it
did. The brown earth turned dark and the trees glistened. The cut
ends of the stubble turned black with mildew; the haystacks grayed
from exposure to the damp, and on the roofs the moss, which had
been all summer as grey as lizards, turned a brilliant yellow-green.
During the week of rain, Jody kept the pony in the box stall out of
the dampness, except for a little time after school when he took
him out for exercise and to drink at the water-trough in the upper
corral. Not once did Gabilan get wet.

The wet weather continued until little new grass appeared. Jody
walked to school dressed in a slicker and short rubber boots. At
length one morning the sun came out brightly. Jody, at his work in
the box stall, said to Billy Buck, "Maybe I'll leave Gabilan in the
corral when I go to school today."

"Be good for him to be out in the sun," Billy assured him. "No animal likes to be cooped up too long. Your father and me are going back on the hill to clean the leaves out of the spring." Billy nodded and picked his teeth with one of his little straws.

"If the rain comes, though—" Jody suggested.

"Not likely to rain today. She's rained herself out." Billy pulled up his sleeves and snapped his arm bands. "If it comes to rain—why a little rain don't hurt a horse."

"Well, if it does come on to rain, you put him in, will you, Billy? I'm scared he might get cold so I couldn't ride him when the time comes."

"Oh sure! I'll watch out for him if we get back in time. But it won't rain today."

And so Jody, when he went to school left Gabilan standing out in the corral.

Billy Buck wasn't wrong about many things. He couldn't be. But he was wrong about the weather that day, for a little after noon the clouds pushed over the hills and the rain began to pour down. Jody heard it start on the schoolhouse roof. He considered holding up one finger for permission to go to the outhouse and, once outside, running for home to put the pony in. Punishment would be prompt both at school and at home. He gave it up and took ease from Billy's assurance that rain couldn't hurt a horse. When school was finally out, he hurried home through the dark rain. The banks at the sides of the road spouted little jets of muddy water. The rain slanted and swirled under a cold and gusty wind. Jody dog-trotted home, slopping through the gravelly mud of the road.

From the top of the ridge he could see Gabilan standing miserably in the corral. The red coat was almost black, and streaked with water. He stood head down with his rump to the rain and wind. Jody arrived running and threw open the barn door and led the wet pony in by his forelock. Then he found a gunny sack and rubbed the soaked hair and rubbed the legs and ankles. Gabilan stood patiently, but he trembled in gusts like the wind.

When he had dried the pony as well as he could, Jody went up to the house and brought hot water down to the barn and soaked the grain in it. Gabilan was not very hungry. He nibbled at the hot mash, but he was not very much interested in it, and he still shivered now and then. A little steam rose from his damp back.

It was almost dark when Billy Buck and Carl Tiflin came home. "When the rain started we put up at Ben Herche's place, and the rain never let up all afternoon," Carl Tiflin explained. Jody looked reproachfully at Billy Buck and Billy felt guilty.

"You said it wouldn't rain," Jody accused him.

Billy looked away. "It's hard to tell, this time of year," he said, but his excuse was lame. He had no right to be fallible, and he knew it.

"The pony got wet, got soaked through."

"Did you dry him off?"

"I rubbed him with a sack and I gave him hot grain."

Billy nodded in agreement.

"Do you think he'll take cold, Billy?"

"A little rain never hurt anything," Billy assured him.

Jody's father joined the conversation then and lectured the boy a little. "A horse," he said, "isn't a lap-dog kind of thing." Carl Tiflin hated weakness and sickness, and he held a violent contempt for helplessness.

Jody's mother put a platter of steaks on the table and boiled potatoes and boiled squash, which clouded the room with their steam. They sat down to eat. Carl Tiflin still grumbled about weakness put into animals and men by too much coddling.

Billy Buck felt bad about his mistake. "Did you blanket him?" he asked.

"No. I couldn't find any blanket. I laid some sacks over his back."

"We'll go down and cover him up after we eat, then." Billy felt better about it then. When Jody's father had gone in to the fire and his mother was washing dishes, Billy found and lighted a lantern. He and Jody walked through the mud to the barn. The barn was dark and warm and sweet. The horses still munched their evening hay. "You hold the lantern!" Billy ordered. And he felt the pony's legs and tested the heat of the flanks. He put his cheek against the pony's gray muzzle and then he rolled up the eyelids to look at the eyeballs and he lifted the lips to see the gums, and he put his fingers inside the ears. "He don't seem so chipper," Billy said. "I'll give him a rubdown."

Then Billy found a sack and rubbed the pony's legs violently and he rubbed the chest and the withers. Gabilan was strangely spiritless. He submitted patiently to the rubbing. At last Billy brought an old cotton comforter from the saddle-room, and threw it over the pony's back and tied it at neck and chest with string.

"Now he'll be all right in the morning," Billy said.

Jody's mother looked up when he got back to the house. "You're late up from bed," she said. She held his chin in her hard hand and brushed the tangled hair out of his eyes and she said, "Don't worry about the pony. He'll be all right. Billy's as good as any horse doctor in the country."

Jody hadn't known she could see his worry. He pulled gently away from her and knelt down in front of the fireplace until it burned his stomach. He scorched himself through and then went in to bed, but it was a hard thing to go to sleep. He awakened after what seemed a long time. The room was dark but there was a grayness in the window like that which precedes the dawn. He got up and found his overalls and searched for the legs, and then the clock in the other room struck two. He laid his clothes down and got back into bed. It was broad daylight when he awakened again. For the first time he had slept through the ringing of the triangle. He leaped up, flung on his clothes and went out of the door still buttoning his shirt. His mother looked after him for a moment and then went quietly back to her work. Her eyes were brooding and kind. Now and then her mouth smiled a little but without changing her eyes at all.

Jody ran on toward the barn. Halfway there he heard the sound he dreaded, the hollow rasping cough of a horse. He broke into a sprint then. In the barn he found Billy Buck with the pony. Billy was rubbing its legs with his strong thick hands. He looked up and smiled gaily. "He just took a little cold," Billy said. "We'll have him out of it in a couple of days."

Jody looked at the pony's face. The eyes were half closed and the lids thick and dry. In the eye corners a crust of hard mucus stuck. Gabilan's ears hung loosely sideways and his head was low. Jody put out his hand, but the pony did not move close to it. He coughed again and his whole body constricted with the effort. A little stream of thin fluid ran from his nostrils.

Jody looked back at Billy Buck. "He's awful sick, Billy."

"Just a little cold, like I said," Billy insisted. "You go get some breakfast and then go to school. I'll take care of him."

"But you might have to do something else. You might leave him."

"No, I won't. I won't leave him at all. Tomorrow's Saturday. Then you can stay with him all day." Billy had failed again, and he felt badly about it. He had to cure the pony now.

Jody walked up to the house and took his place listlessly at the table. The eggs and bacon were cold and greasy, but he didn't notice it. He ate his usual amount. He didn't even ask to stay home from school. His mother pushed his hair back when she took his plate. "Billy'll take care of the pony," she assured him.

He moped through the whole day at school. He couldn't answer any questions nor read any words. He couldn't even tell anyone the pony was sick, for that might make him sicker. And when school was finally out he started home in dread. He walked slowly and let the other boys leave him. He wished he might continue walking and never arrive at the ranch.

Billy was in the barn, as he had promised, and the pony was worse. His eyes were almost closed now, and his breath whistled shrilly past an obstruction in his nose. A film covered that part of the eyes that was visible at all. It was doubtful whether the pony could see any more. Now and then he snorted, to clear his nose, and by the action seemed to plug it tighter. Jody looked dispirited at the pony's coat. The hair lay rough and unkempt and seemed to have lost all of its old luster. Billy stood quietly beside the stall. Jody hated to ask, but he had to know.

"Billy, is he—is he going to get well?"

Billy put his fingers between the bars under the pony's jaw and felt about. "Feel here," he said and he guided Jody's fingers to a large lump under the jaw. "When that gets bigger, I'll open it up and then he'll get better."

Jody looked quickly away, for he had heard about that lump. "What is the matter with him?"

Billy didn't want to answer, but he had to. He couldn't be wrong three times. "Strangles," he said shortly, "but don't you worry about that. I'll pull him out of it. I've seen them get well when they were worse than Gabilan is. I'm going to steam him now. You can help."

"Yes," Jody said miserably. He followed Billy into the grain room and watched him make the steaming bag ready. It was a long canvas nose bag with straps to go over a horse's ears. Billy filled it one-third full of bran and then he added a couple of handfuls of dried hops. On top of the dry substance he poured a little carbolic acid and a little turpentine. "I'll be mixing it all up while you run to the house for a kettle of boiling water," Billy said.

When Jody came back with the steaming kettle, Billy buckled the straps over Gabilan's head and fitted the bag tightly around his nose. Then through a little hole in the side of the bag he poured the boiling water on the mixture. The pony started away as a cloud of strong steam rose up, but then the soothing fumes crept through his nose and into his lungs, and the sharp steam began to clear out the nasal passages. He breathed loudly. His legs trembled in an ague, and his eyes closed against the biting cloud. Billy poured in more water and kept the steam rising for fifteen minutes. At last he set down the kettle and took the bag from Gabilan's nose. The pony looked better. He breathed freely, and his eyes were open wider than they had been.

"See how good it makes him feel," Billy said. "Now we'll wrap him up in the blanket again. Maybe he'll be nearly well by morning."

"I'll stay with him tonight," Jody suggested.

"No. Don't you do it. I'll bring my blankets down here and put them in the hay. You can stay tomorrow and steam him if he needs it."

The evening was falling when they went to the house for their supper. Jody didn't even realize that someone else had fed the chickens and filled the wood-box. He walked up past the house to the dark brush line and took a drink of water from the tub. The spring water was so cold that it stung his mouth and drove a shiver through him. The sky above the hills was still light. He saw a hawk flying so high that it caught the sun on its breast and shone like a spark. Two blackbirds were driving him down the sky, glittering as they attacked their enemy. In the west, the clouds were moving in to rain again.

Jody's father didn't speak at all while the family ate supper, but after Billy Buck had taken his blankets and gone to sleep in the barn, Carl Tiflin built a high fire in the fireplace and told stories. He told about the wild man who ran naked through the country and had a tail and ears like a horse, and he told about the rabbit-cats of Moro Cojo that hopped into the trees for birds. He revived the famous Maxwell brothers who found a vein of gold and hid traces of it so carefully that they could never find it again.

Jody sat with his chin in his hands; his mouth worked nervously, and his father gradually became aware that he wasn't listening very carefully. "Isn't that funny?" he said.

Jody laughed politely and said, "Yes, sir." His father was angry and hurt, then. He didn't tell any more stories. After a while, Jody took a lantern and went down to the barn. Billy Buck was asleep in the hay, and, except that his breath rasped a little in his lungs, the pony seemed to be much better. Jody stayed a little while, running his fingers over the red rough coat, and then he took up the lantern and went back to the house. When he was in bed, his mother came into the room.

"Have you enough covers on? It's getting winter."

"Yes, ma'am."

"Well, get some rest tonight." She hesitated to go out, stood uncertainly. "The pony will be all right," she said.

Jody was tired. He went to sleep quickly and didn't awaken until dawn. The triangle sounded, and Billy Buck came up from the barn before Jody could get out of the house.

"How is he?" Jody demanded.

Billy always wolfed his breakfast. "Pretty good. I'm going to open that lump this morning. Then he'll be better maybe."

After breakfast, Billy got out his best knife, one with a needle point. He whetted the shining blade a long time on a little carborundum stone. He tried the point and the blade again and again on his calloused thumb-ball, and at last he tried it on his upper lip.

On the way to the barn, Jody noticed how the young grass was up and how the stubble was melting day by day into the new green crop of volunteer. It was a cold sunny morning.

As soon as he saw the pony, Jody knew he was worse. His eyes were closed and sealed shut with dried mucus. His head hung so low that his nose almost touched the straw of his bed. There was a little groan in each breath, a deep-seated, patient groan.

Billy lifted the weak head and made a quick slash with the knife, Jody saw the yellow pus run out. He held up the head while Billy swabbed out the wound with weak carbolic acid salve.

"Now he'll feel better," Billy assured him. "That yellow poison is what makes him sick."

Jody looked unbelieving at Billy Buck. "He's awful sick."

Billy thought a long time what to say. He nearly tossed off a careless assurance, but he saved himself in time. "Yes, he's pretty sick," he said at last. "I've seen worse ones get well. If he doesn't get pneumonia, we'll pull him through. You stay with him. If he gets worse, you can come and get me."

For a long time after Billy went away, Jody stood beside the pony, stroking him behind the ears. The pony didn't flip his head the way he had done when he was well. The groaning in his breathing was becoming more hollow.

Doubletree Mutt looked into the barn, his big tail waving provocatively, and Jody was so incensed at his health that he found a hard black clod on the floor and deliberately threw it. Doubletree Mutt went yelping away to nurse a bruised paw.

In the middle of the morning, Billy Buck came back and made another steam bag. Jody watched to see whether the pony improved this time as he had before. His breathing eased a little, but he did not raise his head.

The Saturday dragged on. Late in the afternoon Jody went to the house and brought his bedding down and made up a place to sleep in the hay. He didn't ask permission. He knew from the way his mother looked at him that she would let him do almost anything. That night he left a lantern burning on a wire over the box stall. Billy had told him to rub the pony's legs every little while.

At nine o'clock the wind sprang up and howled around the barn.

And in spite of his worry, Jody grew sleepy. He got into his blankets and went to sleep, but the breathy groans of the pony sounded in his dreams. And in his sleep he heard a crashing noise which went on and on until it awakened him. The wind was rushing through the barn. He sprang up and looked down the lane of stalls. The barn door had blown open, and the pony was gone.

He caught the lantern and ran outside into the gale, and he saw Gabilan weakly shambling away into the darkness, head down, legs working slowly and mechanically. When Jody ran up and caught him by the forelock, he allowed himself to be led back and put into his stall. His groans were louder, and a fierce whistling came from his nose. Jody didn't sleep any more then. The hissing of the pony's breath grew louder and sharper.

He was glad when Billy Buck came in at dawn. Billy looked for a time at the pony as though he had never seen him before. He felt the ears and flanks. "Jody," he said, "I've got to do something you won't want to see. You run up to the house for a while."

Jody grabbed him fiercely by the forearm. "You're not going to shoot him?"

Billy patted his hand. "No. I'm going to open a little hole in his windpipe so he can breathe. His nose is filled up. When he gets well, we'll put a little brass button in the hole for him to breathe through."

Jody couldn't have gone away if he had wanted to. It was awful to see the red hide cut, but infinitely more terrible to know it was being cut and not to see it. "I'll stay right here," he said bitterly. "You sure you got to?"

"Yes. I'm sure. If you stay, you can hold his head. If it doesn't make you sick, that is."

The fine knife came out again and was whetted again just as carefully as it had been the first time. Jody held the pony's head up and the throat taut, while Billy felt up and down for the right place. Jody sobbed once as the bright knife point disappeared into the throat. The pony plunged weakly away and then stood still, trembling violently. The blood ran thickly out and up the knife and across Billy's hand and into his shirt sleeve. The sure square hand sawed out a round hole in the flesh, and the breath came bursting out of the hole, throwing a fine spray of blood. With the rush of oxygen, the pony took a sudden strength. He lashed out with his hind feet and tried to rear, but Jody held his head down while Billy mopped the new wound with carbolic salve. It was a good job. The blood stopped flowing and the air puffed out of the hole sucked it in regularly with a little bubbling noise.

The rain brought in by the night wind began to fall on the barn roof. Then the triangle rang for breakfast. "You go up and eat while I wait," Billy said. "We've got to keep this hole from plugging up."

Jody walked slowly out of the barn. He was too dispirited to tell Billy how the barn door had blown open and let the pony out. He emerged into the wet morning and sloshed up to the house, taking a perverse pleasure in splashing through all the puddles. His mother fed him and put dry clothes on. She didn't question him. She seemed to know he couldn't answer questions. But when he was ready to go back to the barn she brought him a pan of steaming meal. "Give him this," she said.

But Jody did not take the pan. He said, "He won't eat anything," and ran out of the house. At the barn, Billy showed him how to fix a ball of cotton on a stick, with which to swab out the breathing hole when it became clogged with mucus.

Jody's father walked into the barn and stood with them in front of the stall. At length he turned to the boy. "Hadn't you better come with me? I'm going to drive over the hill." Jody shook his head. "You better come on, out of this," his father insisted.

Billy turned on him angrily. "Let him alone. It's his pony, isn't it?"

Carl Tiflin walked away without saying another word. His feelings were badly hurt.

All morning Jody kept the wound open and the air passing in and out freely. At noon the pony lay wearily on his side and stretched his nose out.

Billy came back. "If you're going to stay with him tonight, you better take a little nap," he said. Jody went absently out of the barn. The sky had cleared to a hard thin blue. Everywhere the birds were busy with worms that had come to the damp surface of the ground.

Jody walked to the brush line and sat on the edge of the mossy tub. He looked down at the house and at the old bunkhouse and at the dark cypress tree. The place was familiar, but curiously changed. It wasn't itself any more, but a frame for things that were happening. A cold wind blew out of the east now, signifying that the rain was over for a little while. At his feet Jody could see the little arms of new weeds spreading out over the ground. In the mud about the spring were thousands of quail tracks.

Doubletree Mutt came sideways and embarrassed up through the vegetable patch, and Jody, remembering how he had thrown the clod, put his arm about the dog's neck and kissed him on his wide black nose. Doubletree Mutt sat still, as though he knew some solemn thing was happening. His big tail slapped the ground gravely. Jody pulled a swollen tick out of Mutt's neck and popped it dead between his thumb-nails. It was a nasty thing. He washed his hands in the cold spring water.

Except for the steady swish of the wind, the farm was very quiet. Jody knew his mother wouldn't mind if he didn't go in to eat his lunch. After a little while he went slowly back to the barn. Mutt crept into his own little house and whined softly to himself for a long time.

Billy Buck stood up from the box and surrendered the cotton swab. The pony still lay on his side and the wound in his throat bellowed in and out. When Jody saw how dry and dead the hair looked, he knew at last that there was no hope for the pony. He had seen the dead hair before on dogs and on cows, and it was a sure sign. He sat heavily on the box and let down the barrier of the box stall. For a long time he kept his eyes on the moving wound, and at last he dozed, and the afternoon passed quickly. Just before dark his mother brought in a deep dish of stew and left it for him and went away. Jody ate a little of it, and, when it was dark, he set the lantern on the floor by the pony's head so he could watch the wound and keep it open. And he dozed again until the night child awakened him. The wind was blowing fiercely, bringing the north cold with it. Jody brought a blanket from his bed in the hay and wrapped himself in it. Gabilan's breathing was quiet at last; the hole in his throat moved gently. The owls flew through the hayloft, shrieking and looking for mice. Jody put hands down on his head and slept. In his sleep he was aware that the wind had increased. He heard it slamming about the barn.

It was daylight when he awakened. The barn door had swung open. The pony was gone. He sprang up and ran out into the morning light.

The pony's tracks were plain enough, dragging through the frost-like dew on the young grass, tired tracks with little lines between them where the hoofs had dragged. They headed for the brush line halfway up the ridge. Jody broke into a run and followed them. The sun shone on the sharp white quartz that stuck through the ground here and there. As he followed the plain trail, a shadow cut across in front of him. He looked up and saw a high circle of black buzzards, and the slowly revolving circle dropped lower and lower. The solemn birds soon disappeared over the ridge. Jody ran faster then, forced on by panic and rage. The trail entered the brush at last and followed a winding route among the tall sage bushes.

At the top of the ridge Jody was winded. He paused, puffing noisily. The blood pounded in his ears. Then he saw what he was looking for. Below, in one of the little clearings in the brush, lay the red pony. In the distance, Jody could see the legs moving slowly and convulsively. And in a circle around him stood the buzzards, waiting for the moment of death they knew so well.

Jody leaped forward and plunged down the hill. The wet ground muffled his steps and the brush hid him. When he arrived, it was all over. The first buzzard sat on the pony's head and its beak had just risen dripping with dark eye fluid. Jody plunged into the circle like a cat. The black brotherhood arose in a cloud, but the big one on the pony's head was too late. As it hopped along to take off, Jody caught its wing tip and pulled it down. It was nearly as big as he was. The free wing crashed into his face with the force of a club, but he hung on. The claws fastened on his leg and the wing elbows battered his head on either side. Jody groped blindly with his free hand. His fingers found the neck of the struggling bird. The red eyes looked into his face, calm, and fearless and fierce; the naked head turned from side to side. Then the beak opened and vomited a stream of putrefied fluid. Jody brought up his knee and fell on the great bird. He held the neck to the ground with one hand while his other found a piece of sharp white quartz. The first blow broke the beak sideways and black blood spurted from the twisted, leathery mouth corners. He struck again and missed. The red fearless eyes still looked at him, impersonal and unafraid and detached. He struck again and again, until the buzzard lay dead, until its head was a red pulp. He was still beating the dead bird when Billy Buck pulled him off and held him tightly to calm his shaking.

Carl Tiflin wiped the blood from the boy's face with a red bandana. Jody was limp and quiet now. His father moved the buzzard with his toe. "Jody," he explained, "the buzzard didn't kill the pony. Don't you know that?"

"I know it," Jody said wearily.

It was Billy Buck who was angry. He had lifted Jody in his arms, and had turned to carry him home. But he turned back on Carl Tiflin. " 'Course he knows it," Billy said furiously. "Jesus Christ! man, can't you see how he'd feel about it?"

Tzagan

CLEMENT WOOD

MIDWAY OF the mountains that bound on the northwest the demon-land of Mongolia rises the stiff peak Jagisstai. On an icy August morning a troop of wild dun horses cantered briskly along the undulating road that led from its crest to the river valley below. This was the last herd of the tarpans, the wild horses of Tatary, ancient children of the untamed steppe, who have never known bit or bridle.

At their head loped Tzagan, the white stallion, undisputed lord of the herd. He was the only white tarpan within the long memory of wild horses; the rest were dun-colored, or at most mouse-colored, with dark mane and tail and legs. Tzagan's mane and tail were shining jet, his legs a suave black; but his soft white coat was a thing new to them. Soon after he was foaled he had been recognized as a prodigy, and shielded tenderly. He had grown agile and strong, a hand taller than most and heavier in build.

Old Taiga, the Forest One, the head stallion for long cold years, grew old as the white colt matured; at last his cunning dozed. The day came when Tzagan rubbed an inquisitive white muzzle against the graying one, then drew back, to neigh out the challenge for combat. A few bitter rushes and the age-withered head horse moved aside; young Tzagan swaggered to the van of the line and gave the signal for the advance. The tarpans at once looked to the White One to lead them; and a shrewd leader he had made.

Down the rocky road from Jagisstai, with its thick crust of snow, the horses hastened. The frozen whiteness crunched under their tread; at times the icy balls that formed on their hoofs broke loose, and rolled away over the brittle surface with a sound like crackling twigs. Around the shoulders of the ridge, in and out of the descending ravines, the trail zigzagged. Squirrels chattered from the squat cedars, bullfinches flew with flaming breasts over their heads, white partridges whistled by. They passed scanty herds of bighorn and antelope, busily digging through the snow to the nutritious grasses below. To the side of the road writhed great balls of snakes; an occasional hare thumped casually away; a brown bear below giant boles of larches stared stupidly at their snow-cloudy passage.

As they reached a ravine that fed one of the headwaters of the river, Tzagan stopped abruptly, large head raised, nostrils twitching. His ears grew tense. They caught a far, faint whinny of distress, almost despair. Across the ravine his keen eyes made it out at last—a cloud of black in a grassed clearing, a winged cloud, stridently squawking. Again the pitiful whinny.

A sharp neigh from the leader and the horses swerved into a steeper path that led into the very heart of the ravine. Across fallen larches they leaped and floundered, then over a burned area beneath leafless skeletons of trees. They forded an open stream, began a stiff climb. There was no sight or sound from the grassed clearing above; but they knew what they would find there.

Long before they had neared the place other eyes discovered it. On the top bald crag of Jagisstai, all morning, had sat a living thing, hunched and huddled toward the brooding east, facing away from the shrieking devil-winds that whirled over the Siberian steppes. His far eyes could pick out the lazy sources of streams that writhed through all enchantments to the drowsy swell of the Pacific.

Had he looked north he could have seen the headwaters of the river that crept under frozen horror to the frozen Arctic. An easy day's journey to the west and he would have found a stream that made its way through the locked Caspian and more populous seas, beyond the very Pillars of Hercules. A day's travel to the south and he would have encountered water that would know the Indian Ocean, and wash at the end the final polar floes. He sat brooding above the vast highland whence all the waters of earth are fed.

Good for them that no hunted Mongols, no avenging Tatars, came upon that lone living thing huddled high upon Jagisstai. They would have fallen to their faces in the snow in holy terror. "Demon of Jagisstai!" they would have cried. "Spare us, spare us! We will build you an *obo* of branches—we will build you a tower of rocks. Spare us!" And Zaberega, the living thing, the great hunched mountain-eagle, would have turned his eyes again to the swimming horizon, and at last vaulted upward to cleave heaven.

In frigid isolation, this icy morning, he held his peak. His hooded eyes, which could see beyond what men call sight, had observed the cantering passage of the wild horses down his valley road. Now they fixed upon the stir far down the rich head-plain of the river. The great throat lifted unconsciously, the eyes blinked rapidly. What should be moving in his domain?

It had been a long time since trespassers had disputed his suzerainty. In younger days he had had to fight back full-grown hawks from the fringes of the Gobi Desert; ponderous erns, the sea-eagles from the edge of the northern ocean. He had now no rivals. And yet this stir.

As if flung by springs of steel he catapulted into the air. His wings beat upward in a long slant, then sloped in an easy spiral down toward the grassed height. As he neared the ground, they dug more savagely into the stinging air. He knew now what he had to face— that blatantly cawing cloud of black bodies. His hurled passage warmed the air as he made the last low swoop and burned his tornado way into the noisy swivet of jet wings and red beaks.

Just before he struck, a few of them saw him—a wandering Indian pie, his black beak stained crimson; a great gray shrike, larger and more murderous; an evil old chough, claws gripping the poor horse's torn flank. There was red blood too on the chough's vivid red beak —she had hardly time to open it for a sharp scream of warning, when the eagle was upon her. One slash with powerful talons—the dead bird hurtled through the air. Right and left they rose in flying panic, all the hateful flock of pies and crows, ancient foes of the eagle folk. Zaberega, the winged demon, slanted and slashed left and right, with startling activity taking bird after bird in its flight.

The last one shrieked out of vision. Tired, deeply pleased, the eagle swung slowly back and lit on the ground a score of feet from the drooping horse.

It was a tarpan mare, he saw at once—a mare with a reddish-dun coat. Her bleeding back, where the dreadful birds had troubled her, was one vast spreading sore. Zaberega knew how these cowardly killers, that hunted only in winged clouds, fastened themselves to any horse or bull whose back showed the slightest wound, and scratched and pecked at it until it was an incurable thing; how they kept at their hateful killing until at last they gorged themselves upon the splendid creature.

He preened his feathers and muttered deep in his throat.

The mare was too drooping to raise her head and see her rescuer. She stood, patiently awaiting horrid death.

Zaberega turned to make a meal of the black bodies scattered over the ground. Ah! A wounded shrike, dragging itself below the grasses.

One powerful pounce—one more foe gone. Here were glossy choughs, like feathered balls of jet with ruby beaks and feet; here were ungainly crows, glittering magpies. His curved beak tore cruelly into the warm meal.

He raised his head in sharp surprise; something drip-dripped from the beak upon a stone. Out of a dense cedar covert topping the rise broke the white head of Tzagan, the head stallion, his black mane streaming behind him. Another—a third—a dozen of the tarpans all at once appeared out of the fringing forest. Their feet clicked together; they poised uncertainly.

After a moment's scrutiny Zaberega continued his feeding.

Timidly Tzagan led the way closer. His black feet were printed deftly together, his black tail swished against his snowy coat. He neighed a salutation to the great demon-bird.

Grasping a dead chough in each claw, the eagle lifted from the grass, and flew back to the wind-bedeviled height of Jagisstai.

Tzagan's head dropped slightly. Delicately, whinnying a soft greeting, he neared the wounded one.

His sensitive eyes widened as he recognized the mare; a softer note sounded from his throat. This was Ulan, the Red One—once his favorite. She had been driven from them less than two months ago.

At the familiar whinny the mare lifted her tired head. She answered as well as she could—a feeble, discouraged response. The other horses thronged around her, exchanging their greetings. With horror they observed the evil thing on her back—the wide, bleeding wound.

A sudden unease shook Tzagan: he remembered his duty.

Head lifted, black mane stringing out on the chill wind, he trumpeted the call for the onward journey.

It was the time of the last Summer migration—you could have told that by the thinned hair of the horses. In Winter their coats were thick and soft, almost like a bear's; but as the warmer months came this fell away, until their underbodies were almost hairless, and only a sparse covering remained on back and flanks. It was now midway of the thinned season.

Again Tzagan neighed the advance.

They trotted after him, hoofs clicking on the rounded rocks.

Ulan, the red mare, started feebly to follow. She saw the herd drifting past her; she strained to keep up. The blood woke afresh on her back; her limbs would not respond to the commands of her will.

Out of the distant forest the menacing caw of shrike and chough sounded; the heavy black birds began to near the place again.

She struggled forward; a pitiful whinny died in her weakness.

Tzagan stopped, sensing the breach in the herd. He parted the others, cantering between them until he reached her side again.

As Ulan lifted her tired head to greet him, the first of the choughs flew greedily up; it lit on her unprotected flank. Her teeth showed in sickly fashion; the head sagged again. Dispiritedly her tail shook, a menace no longer.

Tzagan was different. Eyes blazing, the white head snapped at the first bird. An untasty mouthful of black feathers was his reward.

The chough flew mockingly out of reach, cawing derisive hatred.

More and more of the birds circled around Tzagan's head.

The other horses surrounded the mare again. They sought to nudge her on with them; feebly she responded. As she moved, her escort of death continued. The whole troop of horses slowed to her painful gait; several of the angered dun heads curved above her sick flanks, keeping the pies and crows at a safe aloofness. They came constantly from every direction, swirling above in a dense flock, jeering just out of reach of the snapping teeth.

At length there was grumbling among the foremost horses.

Tzagan sensed it as soon as it began. They must go forward with all speed to the northern grazing-place, the mutters told him; they had delayed too long already. He knew that his part was to direct this powerful will of his followers, or that they would choose another stallion to lead. A leader must lead, not his own way, but the way of the herd.

Again he tried to hasten Ulan's progress. The Red One drooped more and more.

The grumbling among the horses grew more open.

He could face them, and stay with the wounded mare. Let them go away without him—abandon his leadership.

No. His place was at the head of the herd.

A sharp neigh—Tzagan cantered lightly ahead. Gladly the van tarpans leaped after the flashing White One. One by one the others abandoned the hurt straggler. The birds flapped closer and closer. The last horse passed her.

Cawing discordantly, the birds came to rest upon the bleeding back. The mare's head bowed to the ground. The living death was again upon her.

The troop arrived at last at the final pass that opened to the long slope to the lower end of Lake Kosogol. Tzagan knew this demon country well—this land of sliding sand-demons. There were constant fallen larch-trees, that must be circled cautiously; underneath these, even below clear stretches of the tuft, were miry swamps—still, hidden pools of putrefying water, where a horse might sink and never rise again. The swamp snakes rustled beside them; a long red fox swayed on his haunches and barked mockingly.

The road turned upward. There were no more quagmires, but instead a path along the top of a precipice, paved with cobbles and small stones that rolled deceptively from under their feet, and threatened to throw them over the great split in the hills. At times the very road melted away beneath them, in great ugly slides of stone and sand; it was all they could do to leap to scrambling safety, when one of these unexpectedly opened under their very way.

A small army of goldfinches whistled past the cautious steps of the tarpans. A white ermine snaked close to the ground across their path. In the willows below they could see a drove of wild camels munching phlegmatically. A flock of cranes cut between them and the sun.

Unnoticing, the horses continued this last rise.

Ah! The fringing valley at the head of the Kosogol in full sight! Now for a wild gallop down the ultimate slope to the rich grazing below.

But Tzagan stopped uncertainly. His feet lifted and dropped in perplexity. Here—before him—the old way, but altered. A vast cuplike depression sliced across the path—a wide new slide. Above the road were sharp gray rocks, steep and hard to climb; these curved in a great horseshoe to the firm path more than a hundred yards ahead. Sagging below this was the queer sink of sand and stone, with gray rocks again at its lower left-end and the precipice beyond that. Trees sprawled in ungainly fashion upon it; several lay on their sides, torn, impotent roots whitening in the air. It was all strange, all new.

Behind him crowded the others, eager to get down to the lush grass below. The foremost horses nudged him speculatively.

Circle around the top?

But they might be injured in the wild, rocky scramble.

Go back a few miles, and cross above?

The nudges grew more definite. He made up his mind to try it.

One tentative hoof went forward, then another. It seemed firm enough.

Cautiously he began to make his way across it.

The sliding demon heaved abruptly beneath him. His front legs slipped in to the hock, then to the knee; he felt the ground yield below his back feet. He tried to leap aside; the viscid sand held. He was moving, at increasing speed, toward the top of the abyss.

He became acutely aware of the other horses. A young stallion was a length below, at his right; behind his left flank was a third one, the Wood Mouse, a clever, timid tarpan, named also from his color. Tzagan tried to leap forward, and gained a doubtful yard. At the same moment, he sensed the Wood Mouse's backward spring to safety. A second afterward Tzagan heard the despairing sound as the stallion below, in a vain effort to leap out of the sand, stumbled over upon his side. A quick glimpse out of the corner of his eye showed the thrashing legs, the anguished head, as the quickening masses of sand and rock began to cover him with hissing clatter.

Tzagan thrust all power into his legs and sprang. Almost out of the depths. His front hoofs struck a stone; he leaped again—and into deeper sand, sliding ever more rapidly. Again, again he tried.

He was tiring now; it took all of his energy to remain upright. Far behind he caught the troubled whinnies of the rest of the troop. There were choked sounds below him.

He had veered around now, and faced down-hill. In full view was the body of the lowest stallion, desperately floundering beneath its crushing load of sliding death. The distance between them increased rapidly.

Tzagan's feet were poised together below him as well as could be. The treacherous sand was well above his knees. If he could only remain upright until the bottom was reached, and then leap free.

This hope fled swiftly. He saw the last despairing heave as the lowest horse was rolled over the edge of the precipice. He heard the dreadful clamor of the rocky mass pouring in a cataract over the sheer edge of the great clove—the sound of tree-boughs crackling and breaking as the stallion's body ricocheted to death among them.

Queerly enough, his part of the slide was more sluggish than that to the right. Ahead, he could see where the stream turned before him, avoiding the obstruction of gray rocks. If he could reach them——!

Cautiously he began to work himself farther to the left in order to be swung as close to the stones as possible. They were a kind of rock wall, that made the slide veer away to the right and narrowed its lower end. In his eagerness he nearly lost his footing. A great rock bounded across his shoulder; he shivered in pain. Desperately he steadied himself upon his feet; the inevitable tug of the sand dragged him again to the right.

Here—right at him—hardly four feet away—the gray rocks. One desperate dive with his legs, all his power pushing into the yielding mass. He felt himself lifting out of it. One wild second spring—he hurled himself sideways against the gray crags. A leg tripped on the nearest rock. He fell, rolling over twice. Against an uptilted slab of stone he came to rest. Just beyond this gaped the final drop of a thousand feet.

Weakly he pulled himself up, legs trembling from exertion and excitement. Over the edge his glazed eyes peered. The stallion below was out of sight. The sandslide poured by, dropping deafeningly into the void. Far below the screaming caw of chough and pie.

So near to death—and now so far from it!

Skirting the left end of the slide, he set out painfully up the rocky wall that had meant such amazing salvation. As he stepped his shoulder stung. There was a damp feeling, a drip on the rocks when he paused to rest. He sniffed at it—it was the red water that comes when the skin is broken. Shaking his head clear, he neighed once toward the top of the hill, and continued on his way.

At the far end of the wide curve at the top, he came upon the others. In their eyes was fear, that might easily turn into panic as they watched his approach. This could not be Tzagan, who had disappeared in the rumbling death!

He whinnied reassuringly.

Their white muzzles smelled of him; their warm tongues licked the wounded shoulder.

Back with his own again!

He resumed the lead, and took up the march down to the grazing-ground beside the lake.

Out of the woods he heard the harsh chatter of rook and chough. At first he did not heed it; evidently they had found some new victim. Over the backs of the horses they flew and slanted until they had reached the head of the line.

Suddenly he felt a sharp pain on his shoulder. One of the birds had dashed against him, ripping with red beak at the red wound.

Viciously Tzagan snapped back.

The chough veered away.

From the other side a second one slashed at him.

Thoroughly infuriated, he champed back. The other horses aided in this.

More slowly than the first stages of their journey, they came down to the grassy ground at the head of the lake.

The horses lowered their muzzles for the ample grazing.

But Tzagan, the White One, found it impossible to crop the sweet, soft food. The ominous birds circled slashingly around his head, ever more and more of them. His full energy was needed to deal with them.

Then began dreadful days and nights for Tzagan.

Again and again, that first afternoon, he sought to lower his head, to nibble at the delicate grass. Each time half a dozen of the winged murderers seized the moment to stab into the living flesh. They were always at him. Evening found him unfed, wearied, pain-racked.

It was a little better after the sun had gone. At least he could doze.

Toward morning he dispiritedly cropped at the nearer grass, which the herd had already gone over. Dawn came all too quickly, and with it again the flying menace.

That day and that night—the next day, the next night—endless days, endless nights—passed in the same horrid fashion. The wound was worse now and spreading—that he knew. At night he ate as best as he could, but his strength was no longer up to that of the rest of the herd.

He was still regarded as leader. But long ago he had dropped back toward the rear, weakly proud that he could keep pace with the poorest of the cantering hoofs. The other horses did what they could to aid him; but they must eat sometimes, and the devil-birds never rested.

Day by day it grew harder to keep up. The day came when he was last in the line. Far ahead the Wood Mouse was leading. There had been no battle with the formal change of headship; Tzagan was too ill to dispute his sick abdication.

The cloud of winged death never left him, from the thin bud of dawn to the blankness of night. Even in day-bright moonlight a few overgreedy birds stayed to plague him. Only in the scant black hours was he his own at last; and he was too tired and drowsy to eat much at this time.

The day came when the last mare in the line loped away, and Tzagan could not follow. The birds descended in a jubilant cloud upon him, tearing at his very life.

He backed against some trees, snapping with all his vigor at the menacing claws. The low boughs were partial protection; without this they would leech to his very back. With sick despair he heard the thud of the last hoofs dying away in the distance.

Alone—abandoned.

His thought was all of Ulan, the red mare. By now, long ago dead, on the grassed clearing below Jagisstai, the peak of the demon. Pictures of her dreadful plight bewilderingly passed over him, strangely blurred and altered. He seemed to be the red mare, torn to death.

A faint wave of denial swept over him. At least he could still slash with his tail and snap with his teeth.

His blows grew feebler and feebler.

It was only a matter of how long he could hold out. There would come a time when he could not.

Day after hideous day he stood, backed against the screen of trees, fighting back the hovering death that gave him no moment's rest. The evil hordes were always upon him; their evil odors pained his sensitive nostrils. Harder and harder the effort to snap back; it had been many days since he had eaten a full meal. And food was life.

He crept out in the black of night and cropped what herbage he could. One morning dawn came before he knew it; he was still far from the trees. The hordes of slaughter gathered unexpectedly. A killing half day he snapped back, keeping them away as best he could. His legs trembled from the pain of the vast hurt, extending now across his shoulders and almost to his tail.

Noon came, and tiring afternoon. His head rose slower each time; ever more feebly he fought away the tearing death.

Suddenly his body stiffened with strange hope. He sensed a stir of deliverance.

Out of the menacing air it came—the whir of great beating wings, the cyclone breath of passage, as the demon-bird, Zaberega, swept down among the cowardly killers. The great pinions fanned his back as they swept over him. He felt spasmodic clutchings as the birds, too late, sought to rise. Right and left Tzagan saw bodies fall amid cawing screams of terror. The eagle slew a score before the last of the enemies had made a panicky escape.

For the first time in weeks Tzagan knew life that was not torn by the talons of death.

The trees. He must reach them before the killers returned. He started his trembling journey; Zaberega, as if understanding that his presence was relief, drifted beside, pouncing upon the foolhardy shrike or chough that ventured out again.

The trees were hardly a hundred yards away now. One satisfied, menacing scream, and Tzagan heard the great wings thrash the air as the demon-bird soared off to his lone peak.

At once he grasped what this might mean. Glazed eyes fastened to the distant trees; he sought to master and hasten his weak steps.

The rooks and pies cawed their summons. Closer, closer, came the sound.

Desperately he pushed forward. Worn knees suddenly betrayed him; he staggered sideways, and fell heavily, his chin striking a projecting stone. The tired body rested a moment on the old earth. It was so easy to give up, to die. Now as well as later. He was tired, tired.

A piercing pain in his shoulder—the winged fiends again! Inflamed eyes hardened to terrible determination. He pulled up to his feet and set off at a feeble canter for the last hope of life.

The rooks and pies dashed against his face, ripped his back, clung to him like evil river-leeches. This time he did not fight them away; all energy must be saved for the final yards. Before him the trees. And, more than that—he blinked his eyes painfully to make sure that they were not deceiving him—more than that, a cave—a hollowed opening below a great rock—a slight cave, hardly his height. It might mean shelter. With every ounce of reserve in his body, he held his legs to the torturing canter. Death tore at his life. He stood this, determined to make the shelter, or die.

He made it.

Here—just before him—the scooped-out place, barely higher than his neck. With despairing briskness he slued his body around and began to back in. The birds, realizing that their prey was trying to escape, screeched and shrieked. The low top of the cave-way struck the birds clinging above his tail, and rasped them off. Sharp, burning pains shot through him at their last wild clawings. Farther and farther in he pushed; he could feel the living body of one bird caught between his sore back and the cave's top. He arched his body; the bird, breath squeezed out, slid past his flanks to the ground. Vengeful hoofs ground it into the soil.

He was entirely within it now but for his head. There was no more room. The birds whizzed back viciously, seeking to tear his face. Summoning what little strength was left, he snapped at their approaching threat and kept them off. There was at least no wound on his face that they could claw.

It was late afternoon. Until after dark the magpies and crows massed in front of the cave entrance, waiting for him to come out. There was one especial chough, an old fellow, larger than the rest, gleaming jet body contrasting bravely with scarlet beak and scarlet feet, that planted himself on the ground right before Tzagan's face. The baleful bird eyes, below a feather torn rakishly awry, watched for some sign of weakening. If he could wait, the old chough seemed to say, so could they.

At last the sun drowsed below the hills. The chill vacancy of night strode eerily over the basin. One by one the birds flopped away.

He was all alone.

His legs gave; he sagged forward to his knees. His head collapsed to the half-frozen ground. His eyes closed.

After a half-hour's rest he managed to rise again upon his shivering legs. Step by step he staggered out of the cave. Every instant he expected the birds to hurl their punishing beaks upon him. No; black night was his protection. By some dim supersense he knew that the moon would rise after a few hours. He must make the most of this short space; the terrors might return in the false dawn of moonlight.

Just beyond the cave's mouth commenced the grass. Hungrily his weary lips crunched the succulent stems. At length he had his fill. Not far to the left, he remembered, there was a stream. Quietly he trudged over and drank. He did not go farther; if there was to be life for him, it lay in that cave; he must always be within reach of it.

At last the moon washed the sky gray. Guzzling another drink, he cropped his way back to the hollow scooped below the big rock, senses alert for the onrush of the birds.

They did not come.

For a few hours he dozed; then he ate again, before the gray promise of dawn brought back the jeering enemies.

Day after day passed the same way. A few of the birds tired of the long wait; there was one day when only half a dozen stayed with him; evidently the rest had found a slaughtered prey near by. The next day most of them were back again. Always just below his nose squatted the old black chough, one feather still rakishly awry, gleaming scarlet beak waiting for scarlet food.

One morning Tzagan was slow in returning to the cave. The birds came at him before he reached it, tearing him. As he backed wildly in, the big chough, with the feather aslant, flew in ahead and sought to claw him from behind. With firm assurance the horse closed up the opening with his body. Methodically he kicked backwards, once —twice—thrice. Ah! On the third kick he felt his hoof strike something yielding, squirming. One horrid scream of anguish. His hoofs danced the body of the would-be murderer into the rocks. White throat lifted, black mane tossing as it had not for days, he neighed victory—victory! Here was one enemy who would not plague him again.

After that the birds were more careful. There was more than one morning, when he was tardy in his return, that several tore the wounds open again. Never as bad as at first, however. Day by day he grew stronger, more able to travel; day by day the birds grew more doubtful as to this meal that had once seemed within their very beaks.

More than six weeks passed. The Winter chill came into the air. There would come a day when the tarpan troop would return up the grassy bank of the lake and seek again the southern fields beyond Jagisstai. Meanwhile, below the healing wound the Winter hairs, thick and soft, like the covering of a bear, were pushing their way. The hour came when he knew there was no more open wound—only healing scabs. The hour came when the last of these dropped away, and he was whole again.

But still the crows and choughs waited; still Tzagan was unwilling or afraid to come out, so used had he become to this imprisonment from the threat of clawed day.

It was a morning in late October when the horse's nose wrinkled at an unexpected odor upon the wind out of the brooding east. His ears pricked up, his senses sharpened acutely.

In scattering alarm the black birds rose. Some flew away, others settled a short distance away, in cawing uncertainty.

Down the wind came the sound of faint neighings. Tzagan, strangely excited, pranced up and down in the narrow caveway.

Across the grassy plain he saw them at last—the tarpan herd, the wild horses, with the Wood Mouse dancing along in the lead.

He took two or three uncertain steps forward. He was out in the sunshine of day for the first time in two months. Speculatively the crows observed him: one or two flung themselves upon his twitching flanks and sought to bury their beaks in the thick matted hair. His teeth clicked vigorously at them; they jawed out of sight into the far woodlands.

The horses loped ever closer.

Alone, before the cave, the white tarpan stood.

There was a sudden whinnying from the front ranks. A hundred feet from him they came to a stop; intent doubt was on their faces. A sudden noise and they would have wheeled and galloped off in veritable panic. A white tarpan! There had never been but one; and he was dead long ago, pestered to his death by the punishing birds.

He neighed the old greeting.

There was an answering neigh, half joyful, half unbelieving.

Delicately he stepped out. The sun shone on his bright black mane and tail, on his shining black legs; it spangled on the tangled mat of thick white hair covering the rest of his body. He came to a stop ten feet away from the Wood Mouse.

Threateningly the darker stallion raised his head; a red glaze came across his eyes. He approached the stranger, menace in his bearing.

Tzagan did not move. The other turned, and neighed the command for all to fall in and resume the journey.

Out of the sky came the far whir of great wings. Black against its brazen deeps, they could see the high blur of Zaberega, the demon-bird, returning to his aerie on the crest of Jagisstai. The sight of the familiar eagle brought back to the Wood Mouse remembrance of those days when he was only a follower and the White One the leader. The great wings passed out of sight. The dark stallion eyed the other in some perplexity.

Cruelly Tzagan held his eye until the usurper looked down at the ground. Then, lifting his throat, until the wind sprayed out his mane like a black pennon of victory, the White One trumpeted the call to advance. A bit sullenly, the Wood Mouse ranged himself behind the old leader, so strangely returned to them. A sudden clatter—the clicking hoofs struck the pebbles of the way again—a swirl of dust.

Up the long road the herd of wild horses cantered, with Tzagan, the White One, back with his own again.

Valiant Lady

J. C. BENRODT

So you go to the races? You form one of the amazing multitude who follow the Sport of Kings and deadbeats, and all the varied kinds of people in between. Perhaps the siren call of "easy money," the thrill of a close-fought finish, the love of a satin-coated thoroughbred, the performance of a social duty, brings you there. Whichever it is, there is one thing I do know, and that is that you who see the gigantic stage, set with its tens of thousands close-packed in colossal grand-stands, its glorious flowers, its great green stretches where the cream of the equine world sob their hearts out in a game where only the superlative survive, know little of the work and the thought and the hopes and the fears of that band of men who produce the four-legged stars you come to see do battle for fame and fortune.

Well, I'll try to tell you why I go to races. I'll tell you how I, an owner-trainer who loves a thoroughbred, feel from the time I go with a few hard-won shekels to some famous sale ring, to the moment that my colors flash into sight where the field is bunching far up the home stretch for that heart-stirring, heart-breaking run to a little white line on a little black board, and the eagle eye of a judge from whose decision there is no appeal. And if you love a thoroughbred horse, if you *really* love them, you can read this, and if you don't— well, read something else, because you won't be interested, and you wouldn't understand.

They've come from the four corners of a dozen beautiful pasture lands, from the studs of men who have studied the production of the ultimate in horses for generations. Each of these soft-eyed babies could tell you that his, or her, blood lines could be traced exactly to equine heroes who came from their desert homes to Merrie England, along with the fashions Charles the First made *à la mode*. Believe

me! And some of them could speak of ancestors who cropped the
grass of Devon when Henry the Eighth displayed his Catholic taste
in harems.

A little nervous, more than a trifle frightened, they have come
from their lovely homes to this noisy, terrifying saleyard, so that you
who have burned the midnight oil studying pedigrees may choose
and buy a champion. If you can. Yes, indeed! *If* you can!

Hundreds of them, all well-bred, all beautiful, or nearly all, but
only a meagre handful who will ever become that miracle of speed
and courage and stamina that will fling their names in flaunting
banners across the sporting pages of a continent.

For days you study them. Hour after hour, you tramp from stable
to stable, comparing, measuring, concentrating, and, curiously
enough, it is only at night-time that you know you're weary. Then,
just a few hours before the auctioneer will call the babies forth to
face whatever the future may hold for them, you open the door of a
box you have not yet entered, and there, in a corner, stands a baby
filly. Now for weeks a colt has been in your mind. You are almost
Chinese in your ironclad preference for the male of the species, but
here is one little lady you feel you must really have a word with. She
is too beautiful to pass by, as you have passed by so many of her sex,
because you want a colt. A dark bay, this one—perfect from the
points of her tiny black-tipped ears to her almost equally tiny feet. A
glorious example of what hundreds of years of careful breeding can
produce.

A long five minutes you study her intently, while she gazes fear-
lessly and just as intently back at you with her soft dark eyes. There
is no fear in those eyes—just a quiet curiosity. Marvellous, you say;
small, yes, but still—marvellously perfect, and she will grow—just a
baby. But you want a colt, not a filly, and then, just as you turn to go,
she takes a step toward you. She is curious, or perhaps Fortune smiles,
and you stop and call her softly—encouragingly. She comes and lays
her muzzle in your out-flung hand, and then, as she stretches her
glistening neck, her lovely head comes to rest against your own hard
face, and so, for a moment, for you and for her, the world stands still.
And then—well, and then believe me or, as Mr. Ripley says, believe
me not, in the quiet of that stable you think you hear a tiny voice
say "Buy *me!* Never mind that colt. Buy *me!*" And instantly you
tell her, "All right baby, I'll buy you if I have to bust the bank-roll
wide open." And that's a promise! Weeks of study, weeks of tramping, weeks of indecision. Then finality! Just by chance—just like that!

So you go to the ring, and you wait for her, when for weeks you've thought you were going to that ring to wait for a colt, and never did lover wait for sweetheart more anxiously.

You look round those hundreds of intent faces. You study that close-packed amphitheatre. Tier on tier of keen-eyed men—prince and pauper, stable boy and lord of a million acres, cheek by jowl, shoulder to shoulder, but horsemen all, come to buy a champion *if* they can. Always that "if" in racing! Will they see what you have seen? How many of them will have picked that soft-eyed filly waiting in her stall for her turn to face the play of Fortune's wheel? Where will the fall of the auctioneer's hammer send her? What sort of a master will guide her destiny? Well, you made a promise, so you know where she'll go, if the bank-roll will stand it—if some lord of a million acres doesn't make your meagre shekels look like the change he uses for car-fare. What if they bid a figure you can't come up to? But she's very small. Oh yes, of course, that's your chance—she's *very* small.

Well then, here she comes, head held proudly like the tiny princess she is, little hoofs hardly seem to touch the velvet turf she steps upon. Eyes wide with bewilderment as she faces that crowded circle of quiet-faced men.

The auctioneer's voice drones on and on. Her father did this, her mother that, her brother did this, her sister that. The recounting of the miracles of her forbears comes to an end, eventually the courteous question is asked, "And now, gentlemen, what am I bid?"

And an optimist says "One hundred guineas," and the race is on. Once again Fortune smiles. "Three hundred and fifty," someone calls, and instantly you snap back "Three hundred and seventy-five," and there is silence. It's all you've got to spend on her. It isn't much, I know, but you don't own a million acres. The time will come when you'll spend ten times as much for just one horse, but you don't know that then. Quietly you pray that no one says "four hundred," and then, after what seems to *you* to be intolerable aeons of time, that hammer falls, and she belongs to you. Her attendant leads her back to a stall where you are waiting to praise her and pat her, and tell her that everything is O.K. now. And she puts her head in your arms, and rests it there, which is by way of saying, "Thank you, Master, thank you very much indeed."

A small boy, who must lose her now, says sadly, "I've looked after her, Mister, since she was knee-high to a grasshopper. You'll take care of her?" And you say, "Sure, son, sure, I'll take care of her, never doubt it."

There is so much to do from that time on. Floats, ships, attendants to take her on the ocean voyage which will bring her to the dockside at which you wait so anxiously. There has been a cyclone. The papers tell you that the ship on which she travels, tied in a narrow stall deep in a stinking hold, is laboring in a welter of furious seas and howling gales. The Storm Gods chose an awkward time to rave and rant. Two days ago those tumbling seas were calm. Has she been hurt? You've paid a man to guard her well. Has he done the job you paid him for? Well, you'll soon know.

Out of an evil-smelling hold she comes, slung in a crate high above the ship that carried her. Winches rattle, raucous voices spill commands, the crate lands at your feet, and from it, very tired, very sick and *very* frightened, steps your tiny filly. Wide dark eyes seek yours in that bedlam of shouting stevedores, rattling winches, snarling motors, and your voice is very soft, and your hand is very gentle, as you tell her that she's home now, that everything at last is as it should be. Then, after you've rattled and bumped through a great city in a gigantic vehicle they call a float but which has precious little "float" about it, she is "home." A cool, quiet stable, knee-deep in straw, water, food, and your foreman's voice: "Sure, Boss, she's beautiful, but small, strike me, *very* small!"

And you say, "Sure! Her grandfather won two Ascot Gold Cups, and her grandmother won the Oaks, and she'll grow."

Then knowing hands probe and delve as the "stable" looks her over, and heads are shaken, and "too small" they say, even if her grandmother won the Oaks with nineteen flaming stone.

Just for a moment you feel a tiny doubt. Perhaps a colt would have been better. There was that one from Star Sapphire, and then you look again at the weary little mite you've gone to so much trouble to get and—shrug your shoulders. Your foreman's eyes have never left you, and he says suddenly, "To hell with them, Boss. They wouldn't know a racehorse from a Rocky Mountain goat, but me—well, I'll be looking after *her* myself." And this, you know, is honor in excelsis.

"She'll grow," you've said. Oh, yes, you've said it so many times, but she doesn't grow. And she doesn't eat, and she doesn't do any of the things you have figured on. Instead she becomes very ill. You try everything you know—uselessly. That tiny horse is very sick indeed. So you call in the vets to help you. They come, examine, question, shake their head. No constitution—colitis, that dread disease—possibly had it for months—probably never race—certainly not "early." Still they'll do the best they can. And you know they will, even if their bills are never paid. That's racing. And you'll do *your* best too. Disappointing? Oh, sure!

Away in the distance a dream, something or other to do with the

Gimcrack Stakes—just a dream—a long way off now—a *very* long way off. Horses bunched at the turn for that battle down that long home stretch. The thunder of the multitude. A name on the lips of thousands in one long roar of sound—your filly's name as she battles with the favorite at that vital furlong pole for mastery, and gains it, goes on, spreadeagles the cream of her age—flashes past that little white line against its little black board, and that judge from whose decision there is no appeal—lengths to the good! Oh, sure! Just a dream, especially with a weary little horse, despondent and sick, asking to be petted and helped—not trained and harried about for a race a bare six months away.

Her breeder comes to Sydney. A sportsman, this. He hears the vet's report and—offers you another horse if you care to send her back. He will give you that Star Sapphire colt you like so much in her place. You go into your filly's box to say good-bye, and you go when no one else can see you, because it isn't an easy thing to do. I mean easy to say good-bye. And then Fortune, who must take care of all horsemen, if they are ever to own a *race* horse, smiles again. With that little head pressed against yours, you just can't do it, and so that night, you tell the quiet man who bred her that you'll "carry on."

You go to work. Day after day, week after week, month after month, the treatment continues. But that little filly is very close to those Happy Hunting Grounds to which all good horses go, before she turns the corner. You do just exactly what those clever vets have ordered—special diet, cunning medicines, warmth, care, kindness. Oh, yes, lots of kindness. You feed a race horse oats, or you feed it nitrogenous food of some sort. You have to. No alternative. But you can't feed this filly oats, nor nitrogenous food of any kind. It's pure poison to her with the malady she has.

Three months go by—a coat like polished copper is beginning to glisten again. Symptoms are favorable. You try your first feed of oats. A very small feed of grain, mixed with a very large feed of hope. She eats them, and with no ill effects, praise be. No recurrence of the malady she seems to have overcome. Well, if she can eat oats, you can train her. Gimcrack Stakes—three months away. You don't like early two-year-old racing, but that was the race you dreamed about for this little lady, because she's pitched and balanced to go like greased lightning, and she's bred to stay. Perhaps, if you're *very* careful, you can go far enough to let *her* tell *you* what to do. She'll tell you, never doubt it, if you've sense enough to know her language.

And so now it's work in earnest, but work you love. Your little horse thrives under it. Five in the morning until ten at night, your foreman watches, massages, feeds, exercises, does the thousand and one things one does when a horse is set to win a race. And in the case of this filly, two or three things that are not usually included.

And then one day, with the Gimcrack Stakes six weeks away, you decide to let her "run down a furlong." Ah, folks, *there* is a day for you. When, after months of preparation, you bring out the old stopwatch and prepare to learn your fate. Can she run a furlong in twelve seconds? Can she—or will she, as nine out of ten do, take longer? Can she, by some miracle, break twelve with her heavy irons on? Well, well, you'll see in the morning. And if she, as the racing argot has it, "takes a week," there isn't anything that you can do about it—no, not a thing!

And so, when the older horses have departed, and the trainers have gone where all good trainers go at breakfast time, when the sun has chased the frost away, you stand, timer in hand, and watch your filly canter gaily to the mark, and breaking away like a flash, run in a blur of speed to a furlong pole. You click your watch, and peek at it, and then, startled, you look again, and you say, "Well, I'll be ——!" and you suddenly remember that you almost went back on a promise made, in all good faith, to a little horse with black-tipped ears, and that you nearly sent her home for something out of Star Sapphire. Perhaps it's the wind that makes you shiver.

Your watch, which is a perfectly good watch, tells the story. Your filly, in working shoes, carrying 8.10, and allowed to please herself, flashed over that furlong in eleven seconds and two-fifths, and that, you know, isn't galloping—that, as so many years of trying has so amply taught you, is simply flying! So who can blame you if you start to dream again?

Two weeks go by, and daily your baby horse grows stronger, bigger, faster. Did I say faster? Yes, faster, because one fine morning you take her far from prying eyes, and on a track where once years ago a crack sprinter in racing shoes ran two in twenty-three and three-quarters, but on which no horse since has done so well, your filly, in working shoes, flashes over that same two furlongs in twenty-three and *one*-quarter, and then you know that if she runs true to pedigree, and gets an even break in the race you've set her for, she will be very hard to beat indeed. Oh, very hard!

That evening you go to a great friend who loves to make thousands grow where only one thousand was before, and you tell him, imploring secrecy, that you've got a filly big as a minute, beautiful as a sculptor's dream, faster than chain lightning, and game as an

Australian bull-dog ant. And he says, as a doctor will say to his patient, soothingly, quietly, "Sure, Jim, I know. Have a drink." But
you persist, and eventually he becomes enthusiastic, and forecasts
that the noble brotherhood of the Ring are due for an outsize dose
of sackcloth and ashes, and a notable lack of that legendary fruit of
which the resting-place is that equally legendary sideboard!

Then he wants to know of her training. How many four furlong
sprints with the pressure on? And you say "None at all. Absolutely
none at all." And he laughs, and suggests that you talk of other
things, and that's that. You speak nervously of heredity, of the values
in pace work, half pace, strong three-quarter pace, of ancestry. You
talk in vain. Just over your shoulder when you came into his study,
Fortune beckoned him: Fortune who, in the last analysis, governs
every little thing there is in racing. Fortune had gone from that
room before you left.

The great day grows closer. There are barrier trials now, and daily
the young ones who have been "tried" and who have survived their
early preparation thus far (so many don't) spring into flashing life
from behind tapes as the starter calls.

Then one day there is a mighty gathering of babies at the official
two-year-old trials, and heat after heat thunder down a lightning fast
track under racing conditions. Of the colts and the fillies, the fair
sex take all honors. Two of them run four furlongs in forty-eight
seconds, and that evening their names get headlines, and you know
you'll have opponents worthy of your steel, which is as it should be.
At the trials, someone who knows you have a young one too, asks
you where your filly is, and you say, "Having her breakfast, I suppose," and he shakes his head. "Great practice this, Jim," he remarks; "learns them race conditions." "Sure," you say. "They're
fine. I know other ways." He grins. "You've quaint ideas, Jim—how's
dancing, or is it skating, nowadays?" You leave it at that!

Ten days before the race, you send your own baby out "tipped"
and with her chosen horseman in silks and satins, in the saddle. And
where the world doesn't see, she beats seven others similarly
equipped, flying like a little bay meteor over three furlongs from
the barrier, and then the crack little horseman on her back has to fight
like a tiger to stop her running three furlongs more at that same
terrific pace. Bred to stay? Oh, sure. I told you that. Or didn't I?
That dream is getting closer now!

And from then on? Well, no more gallops, no more strain. Just
potter about, with a bit of strong three-quarter pace work here and
there. Massage, good food, kindness—oh yes, plenty of that. You say

she's fit, your friends say you're crazy, your foreman grunts. So what? So someone's crazy! Maybe it's you! You have the courage of your convictions in the racing game—when you've got convictions. So often you just don't know, and neither does anyone else!

But in an education that has encompassed most things, one thing remains to be done. Have you, who watch the babies run, ever thought of their ordeal when first they see the milling thousands, hear the roar of the ring, become part of that electric atmosphere that is the race-course? Stage-fright, fear, anxiety, bewilderment, leave many a baby horse half beaten long before the starter's voice sends them thundering away.

And so that she may get used to it, you take your filly to the races —to a meeting where voices bellow, and strangers come to gaze at her. Where men in red coats on white horses canter by, and all the ordered pandemonium of the Sport of Kings surrounds her.

You take your colt too. Oh, yes, you have a colt, with a coat like a cloak of burnished brass, and the disposition of a Pirate King.

She takes it well. You parade them both, and your friends come in dozens to see them, and long and loud are the praises for your golden-coated colt, and long and pregnant are the silences that follow your humble suggestion that the filly is lovely too.

"Oh, yes," they say, if they say anything at all, "rather small though—a mite miserable—go for a couple like a scalded cat—but that colt! Now, Mister, *there's* a racehorse!" And the colt, with his burnished copper coat, and his disposition of a swaggering buccaneer, stands high in the air with his front feet pawing at a point yards above your head, and sends his shrill clear reply over ring and paddock: "Boy, you've said a mouthful!" But what he doesn't tell them is that the little lady no one cares for could give him a stone and a start and a beating any time you like to call the tune!

And *you* don't tell them either, because you are a little sad, and a wee bit puzzled. Can't they see your lovely filly, or is it *your* eyes that cannot see her imperfections? "Beauty is in the eye of the beholder." Well, maybe so—maybe so.

Then among the curious ones who wander past, a young "man about town" stops long enough to remark, "A fine colt," and then, turning to where your little horse is standing in her scarlet silken sheet, and her spotless bandages, with the brass and leather of her head collar gleaming, because proud hands have worked for hours so that her "ensemble" may be perfect, the gentleman remarks, "Don't think much of her," and your foreman, fed to the teeth, and because he is a little sad too, snarls savagely, "Mister, which end of her do *you* think kicks?"

Well, you take them home, and then, presently, lo and behold, the Great Day dawns. That day you dreamed about six long months ago. A dream that, before evening falls again, will have shattered into the oblivion of painful memories, or triumphed into the miracle of a *fait accompli*. That's a day, my racegoing friends, that is "just another day" to you. But for me! Oh, well, I'll try to tell you.

Coffee that morning was hot and strong, and newspapers, race papers, and tipsters' sheets made the bed covering. All that ocean of type that sums up the discoveries of that colossal espionage system that delves with the eye of an eagle, the sagacity of a fox, and the tenacity of a weasel, into the chances of the thoroughbred horse, and out of that multitude of forecasts not one gives your horse a chance! No—not even a place chance, and you think suddenly of that song you sang when you marched to war—"They're all out of step but Jim!" And then you remember that it was *Jim* who was out of step and *your* name is Jim.

A hurried toilet, a red and white tie, your racing colors. She'll carry them, so you'll carry them too. Then to the stable in a car that must wonder if you think you're Malcolm Campbell. Your foreman's grunted greeting (he's "strung up" too, though woe betide you if you say so!), the rhythmic swing of his brush massaging muscles like fluid steel beneath a satin coat, that changes in places into little pools of light as a shaft of early morning sun finds her. A velvet muzzle that spares a moment to caress your cheek, before it buries itself in sweet-smelling food. Lips that move with that curious rotary motion, jaws that grind with the even steadiness of a metronome—sweet music to the trainer's ears on race day—I'll say it is.

Dark eyes are clear, untroubled. Under those enormous hot poultice bandages, you know her legs are clean and cool and, best of all, under your enquiring finger-tips, her heart beats strong and true, 38–39, maybe 40 to the minute. That marvellous muscle from which comes all those things, you know she's got. Well, little filly, I've done my best, and those who have helped me have done their best, and now—well, now, it's up to *you!*

The rhythmic swing of that brush goes on and on and on. How many thousand hours has he swung a brush like that? How many years has he hissed sibilantly like a disturbed snake, as is the way of all horsemen with a brush? How much of it was worth while? Ask him! He wouldn't know what you were talking about. It was *all*

worth while from his point of view. Were they not all Thoroughbred? They're born and bred that way in racing.

Hours go by, and eventually you stand with your small horse, in a
big stall, with a hundred other horses in a long line of stalls on either
side of you. The clamor of the racecourse envelops you, and you wish
time wouldn't drag so. A famous horse is stabled next your own, and
hundreds come to look him over. You step aside so that they can see
your filly too. But they don't gesticulate, and they don't admire.
They just walk away, and never look in your direction. After all,
who are you, and who is your filly? Just one of twenty-one babies
entered in an early Classic, some of whom can run half a mile in
forty-eight, which is worthy of note. But what can that little one
run? Well, nobody knows. Not even you know, though you *think*
you do. Hardly any one ever heard her name. Well, in a little while
now, they'll fling her name in banner type across the sporting pages
of a nation—well, *maybe* they will!

Gradually your world grows smaller until the whole of it is con-
centrated in just one small baby horse. The gamble of the barrier
draw has given you nine marbles. Not so bad. From the nearby ring
an enormous bellow calls your horse at twenty to one. A week ago,

that would have seemed philanthropy—almost *lese-majesté*. Now, on the brink of the Great Ordeal, you're not so sure. But you know the ladies will back her—with a name like that—oh, sure they will! And you'll back her—with what you've got. She won't be friendless! Twenty to one. It's a bonny price, and they say Shylock sired the bookmaker breed. My goodness gracious! Twenty to one!

The parade is on. Twenty-one babies in their flaunting colors. Your jockey comes—smart, capable, cool. You wonder at his coolness. Thank heaven *you* don't have to ride her. Now you know what courage is! Look at her—calm, unflurried—and *she* knows just as well as *you* know that she's on the threshold of a hard, tough battle. *How* does she know? Bred in her, of course, and in most of those like her, over hundreds of years. How about your own courage? Well, maybe the less said about that, just now, the better. *You* don't need any; you just have to sit and watch!

A pat on a glossy neck, a last word to the jockey and your voice is hard. "No whip, Bill, no spurs. Let her do it herself. She'll fight it out—bred that way." And his merry, smiling answer, "Don't worry, Boss. She's home and hosed. Go put the mortgage on her."

You don't. You couldn't, even if you had a mortgage. Curiously money doesn't seem to matter now. Only one thing matters. You flee to a spot high in a towering grandstand, as far from folk as possible, and through your glasses in the far distance you pick up a huddle of horses who wheel and dive and change in a kaleidoscope of brilliant color.

And then your entire world narrows down to just one thing. Gone are the crowds, gone the tumult and the shouting, gone any vestige of consciousness of anything or anyone except that distant mass wheeling and diving like a flock of gulls at a five strand barrier. If you breathe, you don't know it, and you pray for just one thing. That she'll get away when the starter calls, and that she won't be asked to break her heart chasing a field that stole a march on her. That your dream won't go west in a split second of faulty judgment.

You can't see her colors in that shifting huddle. The day is dull, the visibility poor, but you know suddenly that they're off, and then I'll *swear* you do not breath at all. Your glasses range forward, then backward over that flying field. You can't find her, but two horses on the rails obscure one on the outside of them. Perhaps *she's* running there outside of those you see so plainly. Then a quarter of a mile away, they swing for home. Desperately your glasses range from the head of that flying field to the tail of it, and back again. A misty rain has blurred your vision so that the blazing colors the jockeys carry are vague and almost indecipherable. You are conscious of a sense of unbearable urgency. You've got to find her! You've *got* to! Then suddenly you freeze into complete immobility. *That* must be her. There just outside of the chestnut on the rails, is a blood-red bay, with a great white blaze. Going like the wind. *That's* her! Then you're dreaming again.

Horses bunched at the turn for their battle down that long home stretch—the thunder of the multitude—a name on the lips of thousands in one long roar of sound. Your filly's name, as she battles with the favorite at that vital furlong pole for mastery, and gains it, goes on, spreadeagles the cream of her age—flashes past that little white line against its little black board, and that judge from whose decision there is no appeal—lengths to the good!

Then suddenly you realize that it's a dream come true, and that that little filly trotting back on dainty feet, black-tipped ears pricked on lovely little head—belongs to you!!

And her name, folks—oh, yes, I forgot to tell you: GAY ROMANCE.

. . . . .

Owned and trained by the Author, Gay Romance won the Gimcrack Stakes at Randwick in 1937. Later she became a matron at the stud.

Storm Winds

R. J. ROCKLIN

THE first big gust of wind slammed the garage doors against the sides of the shop. It struck cool against the sweat-spots on Ben Redmon's coveralls, but he was hardly aware of the change in temperature. Without looking at the woman, he would have known she had gone to the street and looked at the sky. Twice before she had done the same thing while he was working on her Model A.

Ben closed the hood on the car and glanced through the rear window. Halfway toward the horizon, the afternoon sun had turned to a smoky orange. Flat, dark clouds hung close to it, their tops tinged with a thin frosting of the same color.

Becky, his wife, came in from the garden. The sun at her back put her deep-set eyes and straight nose in shadow while the hair piled on top of her head turned more to gold than it was. Without speaking, she looked through the door of the stable that Ben had built against the garage for the horses. Ben could see the frost gather over her eyes as the black outlaw neighed heavily and jockeyed against his stall.

Ben wiped his oily hands on a piece of burlap sacking and put the tools away. *Won't she ever learn what's so fascinating about horses?* he thought. *Has she ever tried? Has she ever let them nuzzle in her pocket for sugar? Can't she see them laughing when they're happy, and brooding when they're sad?*

When Ben had brought Becky to Newtonsville, he had hoped she would understand his love of horses. But more than anything, Ben had wanted her to understand the enormous amount of faith and trust they placed in the human being. . . .

Ben started the car and backed it out of the garage.

"The fan-belt was slipping a little, Mrs. Latham," he told the woman. He climbed out and looked at the sky. "They going to get your wheat in?"

"I don't know." Carrie Latham's face became more tired. Defeat was apparent in the roundness of her shoulders. She counted the money into Ben's hand slowly. Ben felt sorry for her when she added: "They're still at Lee Evans' place."

Ben watched her turn the corner, then briskly walked back into the garage.

"Becky," he said, "don't fix any supper for me. I've got to get those horses ready for the storm. And you better tighten up the hen-house and close the windows in the house before it hits."

"Storm?" Becky echoed quickly. Ben was surprised. This was the first time in months that she didn't have some comment to make when he mentioned the horses. He was surprised, too, at the anxiety that so suddenly had gathered on her face. Ben thought he detected a note of false confidence when she added: "You mean that we're going to have a shower?"

"Shower? Hardly that." Ben was amused. "There'll be some rain probably; but from the signs, I'd say it'll be mostly wind, with lightning and thunder."

Becky shivered as if she were suddenly cold. "It doesn't look like a storm."

"See that sun?" Ben pointed through the rear window. "And listen to Walker's cows. They don't moo like that except when they're scared. The horses aren't cutting up just for fun, either. Lord, I hope Leah doesn't pick tonight to throw her colt."

Ben picked up a board and started toward the stable. For a minute he thought Becky was going to follow him, but then her slow steps on the walk came to him, and finally the slam of the screen door. Ben was more disappointed than he wanted to admit. He had been hoping she would suggest that she help him with the horses. . . .

Sonny Boy, the Peavine stallion, danced toward the rear of his stall when Ben climbed across the manger to nail the board across the opening in Leah's box.

He finished the job just as Doc Miller, the veterinarian who sometimes doubled on the human side when a physician wasn't handy, stuck his head into the stable.

"How's that mare?" Doc asked.

"Doc, you don't think she'd foal tonight,"—Ben frowned,—"do you?"

Doc stuck his thumb in the lower buttonhole of his coat and

laughed. "My boy, I only help 'em when they're ready. I don't tell 'em when they should or they shouldn't. Wish I could. I'd get a sight more sleep."

Ben looked worried. "She's four days overdue already."

"Well. . . . Walker wants me to look at one of his cows. If she shows any signs, you better send George or somebody after me. If I see George, I'll send him over."

Ben worked in the stable until after nightfall. By that time the wind was slapping at the shaggy-barked maples in the front yard. As Ben came out of the barn, he could hear the squeaking of the hinges on the sign over the grocery across the street. For a little while he stood and watched a whirling finger of wheat-dust and tree-leaves race across Newtonsville's only junction of roads.

Ben debated about leaving the horses. Already they were jockeying against the stable walls. Easter, the excitable sorrel gelding, neighed full-throated. The black outlaw, Rodney, rapped his heels against the boards of his stall. Cricket was adding her bit to the confusion too. Only the stallion and Leah seemed to be taking it easy, although Ben expected Sonny Boy to explode without notice.

In the kitchen, Ben's boots left a trail of prints on Becky's clean linoleum, but he wasn't aware of them. After hanging up his jacket, he started to build a fire in the stove, but a wave of heat from the parlor swayed him against it. He made a sandwich from left-overs and stepped up into the parlor.

Something about Becky huddled in her print-covered chair struck him as being skittish. Ben decided that he wouldn't say anything to her about the horses. But soon he forgot the resolution.

"Now let's pray that Leah holds on to her colt," he said between bites, "and that the others decide to be good little horses."

Becky put the nail of her thumb between her teeth and looked at the fire.

"Sometimes I think you wish you were married to a horse," she said.

"Shucks, honey, I thought I was." Ben was provoked at himself for breaking his promise to himself. Before Becky could draw back, he leaned over and kissed her. "I took one look at your eyes, and knew you were a thoroughbred if I ever saw one. Never would have married you without that look."

"I'm not a horse," Becky cried. "I'm *not*, do you understand, Ben! I'm *not*."

Ben stopped chewing, surprised. "What's got into you, Becky? You're as jittery as Rodney tonight. Are you afraid of storms?"

Ben continued to stare at his wife as Becky picked up one of his socks from the untouched pile in her lap and shoved a burned-out light-bulb into the toe. For a while her fingers steadied, but soon she dropped the socks and the bulb into the basket beside her chair.

Over the voice of the rising storm, Ben heard Sonny Boy's squeal join the others.

"There goes the stallion," he said. "Now if only Leah—"

"Can't you talk about something else? Isn't there anything else in the world that interests you?" Becky pushed herself out of the chair and pulled her housecoat tighter. She looked up at the ceiling as if she expected it to cave in. "If you didn't want the colt, why did you breed her?"

"Even horses have the right to motherhood," Ben answered slowly; he found it difficult to keep his voice under control.

Ben felt greatly relieved when a small tapping of knuckles on the door interrupted what might have been an argument.

"That's probably George," he said. "You don't mind if I bring him in, do you?"

"Must you?" Becky answered. "I don't feel like having servants in the house tonight."

"Servant?" Ben flared at last. "I've never considered George anything but a friend, and I've known him all my life."

"Never mind, I'll leave." With a feeling of guilt Ben watched her slim back as she swept into the bedroom. Somehow he could never make up his mind who was wrong.

Ben opened the door. "Come on in out of the cold, George. Doc send you over?"

An old Negro, his cap held close to his chest, stood framed against the back-drop of the town behind him. White-ringed eyes gleamed, and his lips pulled back hugely from his teeth.

George was as much a fixture in Newtonsville as any of the buildings. With his shaggy white head peering below his hat, and his sciatica as obvious as a pair of rusty hinges, he limped through town, a willing object for all the children's practical jokes.

"I knocked at the back door, but you folks didn't hear, I s'pect," he said shyly as he limped in.

"You use the front door any time, George," Ben answered.

George was pleased. "She's a bad one, sure 'nough," he commented. The old Negro pointed his thumb over his shoulder at the storm. "You gonna have trouble with them horses, sure. I've never seen a night like this."

"They've got me tired out already." Ben lowered himself into

Becky's chair and motioned to George to bring another up to the fire. "All of them are feeling the storm except Leah. Hope she stays that way."

"That Leah," the Negro said with an admiring shake of his head, "she got class, that ol' lady is. Leah for a mammy an' Sonny Boy for a pappy? Shooie, that colt, he gonna be a real humdinger!"

Ben let himself relax in the chair. The fire, the tempest, and George's comfortable horse talk—all of it added to make his eyelids heavier.

"Think I'll breed Cricket in the spring," he yawned.

"Shooie, Mistuh Ben," George scoffed, "that Cricket too short for any good colt out o' her. That mare—why, shucks now, you aint gonna breed that mare, is you?"

Ben laughed. "I think I will, George. I think somebody bred her too young. That'll stunt the best of them."

There was no warning as suddenly thunder and lightning struck. Every timber in the house strained against itself. In the barn the horses squealed and pounded their stalls. The noise brought Ben to his feet.

"Go on, George," he urged the Negro. "I'll be right out. And for God's sake, keep the stallion away from Leah. He'll kill her if he gets into her stall."

Ben shoved George through the door, then turned and groped for his jacket in the dark. He was halfway out when Becky opened her door.

Ben came back and switched on the light. Becky's face was knotted. Her eyes were wide, and stains on her cheeks told him she had been crying.

"What's wrong, Becky?"

"I'm afraid." Her voice was low. "Can't George take care of the horses by himself?"

"They're too much for one person, Becky," Ben said as gently as he knew how. "Get something else on, and come out to the barn with us, why don't you?"

"Horses! The horses always come first!" Becky looked at the window where a branch of a maple scraped against the glass. "I'm your wife. Doesn't that mean anything?"

"Becky, listen: It isn't that. Have you ever seen horses during a storm? I can't let them go through that alone. They don't know any better. They can't reason. But you can, Becky. Don't you see?" Ben knew she didn't. He dropped his hands to his side and turned to the door. "I wish you'd come along."

He hurried out into the grip of the wind, with Becky standing in the middle of the floor looking after him. Above the storm, he heard George yelling: "Down, Sonny, come down, you damn' fool!"

Ben saw the stallion standing on hindlegs amid shattered boards, his white-stockinged forelegs slashing at the Negro's head. Flattened ears almost touched the new pine ceiling. His eyes were white-ringed circles of fear.

"George, take Easter." And Ben grabbed the stallion's lead rope and vaulted into the manger. Again the horse reared, nostrils distended and velvet lips pulled back from his teeth.

Ben crashed into the sidewalls to evade the flailing hoofs. Then he propelled himself under the colt and reached up between his legs for the chin-strap. For a fraction of a second Sonny Boy's full weight rested on his shoulder, but Ben twisted away and dropped his own weight on the halter.

"Now take it easy, you lop-eared mutt, or I'll put you behind a plow." Ben quickly shortened the lead rope and tied it to what was left of the manger. Affectionate insults and Ben's hands on his rippling neck muscles soon had the stallion chewing a mouthful of hay.

Ben turned to see how George was doing with the sorrel, but found Becky staring at him from the doorway.

"He's a handful," he said, trying to show her by the tone of his voice that he was glad she was there. When she didn't speak, but stood looking at the ceiling as another series of thunderclaps shook the barn, he added: "Stand with Leah, Becky."

He heard her walk through the layer of hay and seed in the long walk in front of the stalls. "What am I supposed to do?" she asked after a while.

"Just talk. Pet her. Do anything to let her know you're there to see that nothing happens to her." Ben went on stroking the stallion's neck, because he didn't know how else to give Becky reassurance.

At first weakly, then getting stronger, he heard her repeating the Lord's Prayer. Ben felt humble, then. As she stood there soothing the mare, she seemed like a child to him.

"You all right, George?" he called gruffly. When he received no answer, Ben peered through the slats, and saw the darky holding his hat to his chest, his shaggy head bent.

Outside the barn, Ben heard an automobile pull up and stop. The barn door opened; the farmer closed it against the wind.

"Evenin', folks," he rumbled. The man was heavily clothed, and solid and short. "Gosh dang, I'd say you had your hands full enough here! How're you, Mrs. Redmon?"

Ben slid out of the stallion's stall. "Everything all right at your place, Lee?"

"Yeah. Blanche and the kids got the stock restin'," Lee Evans said. "But Guy Latham's in a jam. Ever'body's wheat's in but his'n. An' 'less I miss my guess, this wind's goin' to turn to rain 'fore morning. If it does, that crop aint goin' to be worth the powder to blow it into the next county."

Ben remembered the look on Carrie Latham's face when she had come for the car that afternoon. This would mean more privation, more hoping, more scheming. "Can we get it in tonight?"

"Bunch o' the men are down there now," Evans shrugged. His blunt fingers twisted a strand of hay into a knot while his eyes studied the drooping head of the pregnant chestnut. "You got a sick mare there, Ben. She in foal?"

"I'm afraid it'll happen any minute," Ben nodded. Leah's head was sagging. She appeared to be trying to cough, but her attempt stopped halfway and resulted in an obvious strain. Although another thunderclap sent the horses into nervous steps, the mare was oblivious to the noise.

"Well—" Ben watched the mare closely. "George—" Then suddenly reaching a decision, he said: "George, you get Doc Miller. Run, now. Becky, Doc'll be here soon, and—"

"You don't hafta come, Ben," Evans broke in. "You aint farmin'. I just saw your light—"

Evans stopped talking. He knew by the way Ben and Becky looked at each other that anything he said wouldn't be heard.

"You'll be all right?" It was hard to tell if Ben asked a question or made a statement.

If Becky had turned and faced him, if she had said something, Ben would have stayed. He turned and kicked at the matted hay and walked to the door.

"I'll come back the minute the wheat's in, Becky," he said. Ben went out into the storm, remembering how fragile and small she looked facing the horses.

Evans started the car. "You never know, Ben," he said with a brief moment of clairvoyance. "Sometimes you're right, sometimes you're wrong. But you never know for sure."

The path to the wheatfields wound through heavily barbed briars that clutched against their clothes. Distant shadows of trees along the creek flagged uniformly before the press of the wind. They too were rocked by its heady insistence.

Evans went on, and Ben approached a dark-shaped wagon where a single man was trying to load and arrange the bundles of wheat by himself. In the yellow light from the lantern, Ben recognized a farmer from around Cozzadale.

"I'll throw 'em up," Ben shouted.

The farmer paused and peered and waved a greeting. "Aint this a night?" he gasped. "The women-folk're feeding the thresher up at the barn."

Ben walked slowly down the row of bundled grain, lifting and throwing, then bending for another bundle. In other rows he could

see other teams of horses and men moving against the bulk of wheat-filled acres.

As fast as Ben loaded a wagon, it moved off toward the glow over the hill where Guy Latham's portable Delco system lighted up the yard. Through the hours, wisps of wheat and dust cut into his face and seeped into his clothes. Muscles ached. His bare hands felt as if powdered glass had been rubbed into them.

Another series of rumblings started at the horizon as another wagon drew up. Then, like the initial charge of a fireworks display, a canopy of light teased the darkness overhead and died, only to come to life again in a multi-fingered aurora that dashed downward and hit the earth's atmosphere with a ground-shaking jar.

All around him, Ben saw men straighten up as the accompanying thunder rolled and buffeted the earth. Over the hill, they saw the light from the barn flash out.

"That one did some damage," Ben heard someone shout. Men gathered together in loose circles, their weary glances pointed toward the hill.

Ben was startled out of his short lethargy as he heard a voice calling from the hill. "Doc Miller! Is Doc Miller down there? Get Doc up to the house! Quick!"

A drop of rain hit Ben's hand and ran down between his fingers. "Is Doc Miller here?" he yelled to the man on the wagon. The driver leaned down close to Ben's ear.

"He's with the other crowd that's working toward us."

Ben ran through the wheat-stubble. Behind him groups broke and dashed after him. *"If George couldn't find Doc— Surely, Becky will be all right,"* Ben consoled himself. . . .

By the time Ben arrived in the yard, several automobiles had converged their lights on the house. Ben looked for Doc Miller but couldn't find him. He did see a group of women standing together, some crying, others talking in soft voices.

"Oh, it's awful," one of them moaned to Ben. "The big sycamore fell on the kitchen where Carrie was cooking. It caved the roof in, and Carrie's under it."

From the barn, Guy Latham, his white hair flowing wildly in the wind, dashed toward the house, carrying with supernatural strength a lengthy four-by-four. Ben ran after him.

The tree, its huge mass of leaves and boughs resting in the wreckage of the kitchen with paradoxical serenity, was splintered off halfway up the bole. Ben saw Latham thrust at the tree without making it budge. Around him some of the women milled, their indecision and helplessness apparent in their hand-wringing and crying.

"Get the timber under it more, Guy!" Ben yelled. He put his own shoulder to the beam. The soft earth sucked at his boots as the tree trembled and ground against the remnants of the kitchen.

"Raise it a little more," someone shouted from under the rustling foliage. Ben recognized Lee Evans' rumbling voice.

Beside him, Guy Latham worked soundlessly. Ben knew that as long as he lived he would never forget what he saw on the old man's face. There was despair so deep his eyes were numb particles of ice. And his very silence was a deep well, the bottom of which no man could see.

As the other men arrived, their shoulders and other timbers hoisted the fallen giant from the kitchen.

"Hold it," Evans called. "I can get her out now."

Ben heard rain falling in the leaves as the timber burrowed into his shoulder. Evans kicked his way out of the kitchen with Carrie Latham lying limp in his arms. They let the tree drop back, and some of the men helped Lee carry the woman around to the front part of the house.

"There's Doc," someone said. Ben ran toward him.

"George get ahold of you, Doc?"

"George?" Miller continued to hurry toward the house. "No. See if you can find some barrel-staves. I may need temporary splints."

Dozens of different pictures reeled through Ben's mind. Becky's face, white and frightened, telling him she was afraid of the storm. The stallion on his hindlegs. George, and the limp in his right leg.

Ben swung his foot against the barrel at the side of the house under the rain-spout and leaped back as the water sloshed through the caving-in of the staves. He thrust a handful of the slats into a woman's arms with instructions to see that Miller got them.

Just then the front door opened, and Ben saw Miller push Guy into the rain. Ben ran to the old man.

"I've got to go, Guy," he told him. "Becky's alone with the horses."

Awareness had begun to return to the old man's face for the first time since Ben had come over the hill. Guy looked at his calloused hands and then at the house, and his lips trembled.

"The wheat's in, Guy," Ben said.

Latham shook his head. "That doesn't matter. I've got Carrie to think of. I never did before, much. I've always thought of the crops and the stock, but never much about her."

"She'll be all right," Ben tried to reassure him. "Doc'll have her fixed up good as new."

Latham's eyes smiled a little as they searched Ben's face. "Don't ever put anything before your wife, son. I hope God will spare Carrie long enough to let me make it all up to her. Go on, Ben. Hurry home. Becky needs you more than I do."

Ben started running over the hill to the path that led to the road amid a steadily increasing rain that slowed down the pace of the wind. Tired, his boots heavy with mud, he fought through the briars.

From a bend in the road he could see a light in the barn. Even though it appeared weak, he took courage from the fact that it still burned. He jerked at the door and dashed in.

Two pairs of eyes laughed at his dishevelment, black hair plastered to his forehead, wet clothes, his wide eyes and worried mouth. He looked from one to the other, and suddenly felt an interminable tiredness creep over him, and a feeling that he had reached a haven of rest.

"Shooie, Mistuh Ben," George grinned, "we-uns sure got a colt what is a humdinger. That ol' lady, she done herself proud."

Becky sat on a pile of hay in the stall. Her piled-up hair had slipped over one side of her face, and across her cheek was a smear of dirt. She held a nippled bottle to the mouth of the colt whose head rested in her lap. Leah tried to burrow past the blanket Becky had wrapped around the colt. Becky laughed at the mare's anxiety.

"You all right, Becky?" Ben was afraid to move for fear the whole picture might be only a dream.

"Of course I'm all right," Becky smiled. "George couldn't find Doctor Miller, so we played midwife, didn't we, George?"

"Yes ma'am, we did sure 'nough." The old Negro grinned hugely. "Miz Becky say I'm godfather to that rascal."

Ben continued to stare at his wife. Becky's face became motionless, but her eyes were filled with a light that bathed Ben with love and understanding.

Ben climbed into Leah's stall and sat down beside Becky. He knew that it wasn't necessary to say all the things he had intended telling her. Somehow he was sure that Becky knew.

"What've we got?" he laughed. "A boy or girl?"

Before Becky could answer, the colt shook off the blanket and struggled to his feet. Leah nickered, and rubbed her muzzle against his wet, furry hide.

"Ben, Ben, what a fool I've been!" Becky clasped and unclasped her hands in her lap. "But I'm not any more. Now I can see why you love them so. They're so big, and yet they're so helpless. Leah had such a hard time of it and all I could think of was to make it as easy as I could for her."

George limped away from Leah's stall, grinning foolishly. "You's a daddy now," he whispered in Sonny Boy's ear. He sneaked another look into Leah's stall, then turned quickly away as the stallion nickered.

"Now just what you laughing at, you little devil, huh?" George demanded. "You mind your own business 'fore I bust you one."

Sonny Boy pulled back his lips, then changed his mind and fell to searching for tidbits in the hay.

My Friend Flicka

MARY O'HARA

WHEN Ken opened his eyes next morning and looked out he saw that the house was wrapped in fog. There had been no rain at all since the day a week ago when the wind had torn the "sprinkling system" to pieces and blown all the tattered clouds away. That was the day he had found Flicka. And it had been terribly hot since then. They had hardly been able to stand the sun out on the terrace. They had gone swimming in the pool every day. On the hills, the grass was turning to soft tan.

Now there were clouds and they had closed down. After a severe hot spell there often came a heavy fog, or hail, or even snow.

Standing at the window, Ken could hardly see the pines on the Hill opposite. He wondered if his father would go after the yearlings in such a fog as this—they wouldn't be able to see them; but at breakfast McLaughlin said there would be no change of plans. It was just a big cloud that had settled down over the ranch—it would lift and fall—perhaps up on Saddle Back it would be clear.

They mounted and rode out.

The fog lay in the folds of the hills. Here and there a bare summit was in sunshine, then a little farther on, came a smother of cottony white that soaked the four riders to the skin and hung rows of moonstones on the whiskers of the horses.

It was hard to keep track of each other. Suddenly Ken was lost—the others had vanished. He reined in Shorty and sat listening. The clouds and mist rolled around him. He felt as if he were alone in the world.

A bluebird, color of the deep blue wild delphinium that dots the plains, became interested in him, and perched on a bush near by; and as he started Shorty forward again, the bluebird followed along, hopping from bush to bush.

287

The boy rode slowly, not knowing in which direction to go. Then, hearing shouts, he touched heels to Shorty and cantered, and suddenly came out of the fog and saw his father and Tim and Ross.

"There they are!" said McLaughlin, pointing down over the curve of the hill. They rode forward and Ken could see the yearlings standing bunched at the bottom, looking up, wondering who was coming. Then a huge coil of fog swirled over them and they were lost to sight again.

McLaughlin told them to circle around, spread out fanwise on the far side of the colts, and then gently bear down on them so they would start towards the ranch. If the colts once got running in this fog, he said, there'd be no chance of catching them.

The plan worked well; the yearlings were not so frisky as usual, and allowed themselves to be driven in the right direction. It was only when they were on the County Road, and near the gate where Howard was watching, that Ken, whose eyes had been scanning the bunch, as they appeared and disappeared in the fog, realized that Flicka was missing.

McLaughlin noticed it at the same moment, and as Ken rode toward his father, McLaughlin turned to him and said, "She's not in the bunch."

They sat in silence a few moments while McLaughlin planned the next step. The yearlings, dispirited by the fog, nibbled languidly at the grass by the roadside. McLaughlin looked at the Saddle Back and Ken looked too, the passionate desire in his heart reaching out to pierce the fog and the hillside and see where Flicka had hidden herself away. Had she been with the bunch when they first were found? Had she stolen away through the fog? Or hadn't she been there in the beginning? Had she run away from the ranch entirely, after her bad experience a week ago? Or—and this thought made his heart drop sickeningly—had she perhaps died of the hurts she had received when she broke out of the corral and was lying stark and riddled with ants and crawling things on the breast of one of those hills?

McLaughlin looked grim. "Lone wolf—like her mother," he said. "Never with the gang. I might have known it."

Ken remembered what the Colonel had said about the Lone Wolf type—it wasn't good to be that way.

"Well, we'll drive the yearlings back up," said Rob finally. "No chance of finding her alone. If they happen to pass anywhere near her, she's likely to join them."

They drove the yearlings back. Once over the first hill, the colts got running and soon were out of sight. The fog closed down again so that Ken pulled up, unable to see where he was going, unable to see his father, or Ross or Tim.

He sat listening, astonished that the sound of their hoofs had been wiped out so completely. Again he seemed alone in the world.

The fog lifted in front of him and showed him that he stood at the brink of a sharp drop, almost a precipice, though not very deep. It led down into a semi-circular pocket on the hillside which was fed by a spring; there was a clump of young cottonwoods, and a great bank of clover dotted with small yellow blossoms.

In the midst of the clover stood Flicka, quietly feasting. She had seen him before he saw her and was watching him, her head up, clover sticking out of both sides of her mouth, her jaws going busily.

At sight of her, Ken was incapable of either thought or action.

Suddenly from behind him in the fog, he heard his father's low voice, "Don't move—"

"How'd she get in there?'" said Tim.

"She scrambled down this bank. And she could scramble up again, if we weren't here. I think we've got her," said McLaughlin.

"Other side of that pocket the ground drops twenty feet sheer," said Tim. "She can't go down there."

Flicka had stopped chewing. There were still stalks of clover sticking out between her jaws, but her head was up and her ears pricked, listening, and there was a tautness and tension in her whole body.

Ken found himself trembling too.

"How're you going to catch her, Dad?" he asked in a low voice.

"I kin snag her from here," said Ross, and in the same breath McLaughlin answered, "Ross can rope her. Might as well rope her here as in the corral. We'll spread out in a semicircle above this bank. She can't get up past us, and she can't get down."

They took their positions and Ross lifted his rope off the horn of his saddle.

Ahead of them, far down below the pocket, the yearlings were running. A whinny or two drifted up, and the sound of their hoofs, muffled by the fog.

Flicka heard them too. Suddenly she was aware of danger. She leaped out of the clover to the edge of the precipice which fell away down the mountainside toward where the yearlings were running. But it was too steep and too high. She came straight up on her hind legs with a neigh of terror, and whirled back toward the bank down which she had slid to reach the pocket. But on the crest of it, looming uncannily in the fog, were four black figures—she screamed, and ran around the base of the bank.

Ken heard Ross's rope sing. It snaked out just as Flicka dove into the bank of clover. Stumbling, she went down and for a moment was lost to view.

"Goldarn—" said Ross, hauling in his rope, while Flicka floundered up and again circled her small prison, hurling herself at every point, only to realize that there was no way out.

She stood over the precipice, poised in despair and frantic longing. There drifted up the sound of the colts running below. Flicka trembled and strained over the brink—a perfect target for Ross, and he whirled his lariat again. It made a vicious whine.

Ken longed for the filly to escape the noose—yet he longed for her capture. Flicka reared up, her delicate forefeet beat the air, then she leaped out; and Ross's rope fell short again as McLaughlin said, "I expected that. She's like all the rest of them."

Flicka went down like a diver. She hit the ground with her legs folded under her, then rolled and bounced the rest of the way. It was exactly like the bronco that had climbed over the side of the truck and rolled down the forty-foot bank; and in silence the four watchers sat in their saddles waiting to see what would happen when she hit bottom—Ken already thinking of the Winchester, and the way the crack of it had echoed back from the hills.

Flicka lit, it seemed, on four steel springs that tossed her up and sent her flying down the mountainside—perfection of speed and power and action. A hot sweat bathed Ken from head to foot, and he began to laugh, half choking—

The wind roared down and swept up the fog, and it went bounding away over the hills, leaving trailing streamers of white in the gullies, and coverlets of cotton around the bushes. Way below, they could see Flicka galloping toward the yearlings. In a moment she joined them, and then there was just a many colored blur of moving shapes, with a fierce sun blazing down, striking sparks of light off their glossy coats.

"Get going!" shouted McLaughlin. "Get around behind them. They're on the run now, and it's cleared—keep them running, and we may get them all in together, before they stop. Tim, you take the short way back to the gate and help Howard turn them and get them through."

Tim shot off toward the County Road and the other three riders galloped down and around the mountain until they were at the back of the band of yearlings. Shouting and yelling and spurring their mounts, they kept the colts running, circling them around toward the ranch until they had them on the County Road.

Way ahead, Ken could see Tim and Howard at the gate, blocking the road. The yearlings were bearing down on them. Now McLaughlin slowed up, and began to call, "Whoa, whoa—" and the pace decreased. Often enough the yearlings had swept down that road and through the gate and down to the corrals. It was the pathway to oats, and hay, and shelter from winter storms—would they take it now? Flicka was with them—right in the middle—if they went, would she go too?

It was all over almost before Ken could draw a breath. The yearlings turned at the gate, swept through, went down to the corrals on a dead run, and through the gates that Gus had opened.

Flicka was caught again.

Mindful that she had clawed her way out when she was corraled before, McLaughlin determined to keep her in the main corral into which the stable door opened. It had eight-foot walls of aspen poles. The rest of the yearlings must be manoeuvered away from her.

Now that the fog had gone, the sun was scorching, and horses and men alike were soaked with sweat before the chasing was over and, one after the other, the yearlings had been driven into the other corral, and Flicka was alone.

She knew that her solitude meant danger, and that she was singled out for some special disaster. She ran frantically to the high fence through which she could see the other ponies standing, and reared and clawed at the poles; she screamed, whirled, circled the corral first in one direction, and then the other. And while McLaughlin and Ross were discussing the advisability of roping her, she suddenly espied the dark hole which was the open upper half of the stable door, and dove through it. McLaughlin rushed to close it, and she was caught—safely imprisoned in the stable.

The rest of the colts were driven away, and Ken stood outside the stable, listening to the wild hoofs beating, the screams, the crashes. His Flicka within there—close at hand—imprisoned. He was shaking. He felt a desperate desire to quiet her somehow, to *tell her*. If she only knew how he loved her, that there was nothing to be afraid of, that they were going to be friends—

Ross shook his head with a one-sided grin. "Sure a wild one," he said, coiling his lariat.

"Plumb loco," said Tim briefly.

McLaughlin said, "We'll leave her to think it over. After dinner, we'll come up and feed and water her and do a little work with her."

But when they went up after dinner, there was no Flicka in the barn. One of the windows above the manger was broken, and the manger was full of pieces of glass.

Staring at it, McLaughlin gave a short laugh. He looked at Ken.

"She climbed into the manger—see? Stood on the feed box, beat the glass out with her front hoofs and climbed through."

The window opened into the Six Foot Pasture. Near it was a wagonload of hay. When they went around the back of the stable to see where she had gone they found her between the stable and the hay wagon, eating.

At their approach, she leaped away, then headed east across the pasture.

"If she's like her mother," said Rob "she'll go right through the wire."

"Ay bet she'll go over," said Gus. "She yumps like a deer."

"No horse can jump that," said McLaughlin.

Ken said nothing because he could not speak. It was the most terrible moment of his life. He watched Flicka racing toward the eastern wire.

A few rods from it, she swerved, turned and raced diagonally south.

"It turned her! it turned her!" cried Ken, almost sobbing. It was the first sign of hope for Flicka. "Oh, Dad, she has got sense, she has! She has!"

Flicka turned again as she met the southern boundary of the pasture, again at the northern; she avoided the barn. Without abating anything of her whirlwind speed, following a precise, accurate calculation, and turning each time on a dime, she investigated every possibility. Then, seeing that there was no hope, she raced south towards the range where she had spent her life, gathered herself, and rose to the impossible leap.

Each of the men watching had the impulse to cover his eyes, and Ken gave a howl of despair.

Twenty yards of fence came down with her as she hurled herself through. Caught on the upper strands, she turned a complete somersault, landing on her back, her four legs dragging the wires down on top of her, and tangling herself in them beyond hope of escape.

"Damn the wire!" cursed McLaughlin. "If I could afford decent fences—"

Ken followed the men miserably as they walked to the filly. They stood in a circle watching while she kicked and fought and thrashed until the wire was tightly wound and tangled about her, piercing and tearing her flesh and hide. At last she was unconscious, streams of blood running on her golden coat, and pools of crimson widening on the grass beneath her.

With the wire cutters which Gus always carried in the hip pocket of his overalls, he cut the wire away; and they drew her into the pas-

ture, repaired the fence, placed hay, a box of oats, and a tub of water near her, and called it a day.

"I doubt if she pulls out of it," said McLaughlin briefly. "But it's just as well. If it hadn't been this way it would have been another. A loco horse isn't worth a damn."

Ken lay on the grass behind Flicka. One little brown hand was on her back, smoothing it, pressing softly, caressing. The other hand supported his head. His feet hung over her.

His throat felt dry; his lips were like paper.

After a long while he whispered, "I didn't mean to kill you, Flicka—"

Howard came to sit with him, quiet and respectful as is proper in the presence of grief or mourning.

"Gee! Highboy was never like that," he said.

Ken made no answer to this. His eyes were on Flicka, watching her slow breathing. He had often seen horses down and unconscious. Badly cut with wire, too—they got well. Flicka could get well.

"Gosh! She's about as bad as Rocket," said Howard cheerfully.

Ken raised his head scowling. "Rocket! That old black hellion!"

"Well, Flicka's her child, isn't she?"

"She's Banner's child too—"

There were many air-tight compartments in Ken's mind. Rocket —now that she had come to a bad end—had conveniently gone into one of them.

After a moment Howard said, "We haven't given our colts their workout today." He pulled up his knees and clasped his hands around them.

Ken said nothing.

"We're supposed to, you know—we gotta," said Howard. "Dad'll be sore at us if we don't."

"I don't want to leave her," said Ken, and his voice was strange and thin.

Howard was sympathetically silent. Then he said, "I could do your two for you, Ken—"

Ken looked up gratefully. "Would you, Howard? Gee—that'd be keen—"

"Sure I'll do all of 'em, and you can stay here with Flicka."

"Thanks." Ken put his head down on his hand again, and the other hand smoothed and patted the filly's neck.

"Gee, she was pretty," said Howard, sighing.

"What d'ya mean—*was!*" snapped Ken. "You mean she *is*—she's beautiful."

"I meant when she was running back there," said Howard hastily.

Ken made no reply. It was true. Flicka floating across the ravines was something quite different from the inert mass lying on the ground, her belly rounded up into a mound, her neck weak and collapsed on the grass, her head stretched out, homely and senseless.

"Just think," said Howard, "you could have had any one of the other yearlings. And I guess by this time, it would have been half tamed down there in the corral—probably tied to the post."

As Ken still kept silent, Howard got slowly to his feet. "Well, I guess I might as well go and do the colts," he said, and walked away. At a little distance he turned. "If Mother goes for the mail, do you want to go along?"

Ken shook his head.

When Howard was out of sight, Ken kneeled up and looked Flicka all over. He had never thought that, as soon as this, he would have been close enough to pat her, to caress her, to hold and examine her. He felt a passion of possession. Sick and half destroyed as she was, she was his own, and his heart was bursting with love of her. He smoothed her all over. He arranged her mane in more orderly fashion; he tried to straighten her head.

"You're mine now, Flicka," he whispered.

He counted her wounds. The two worst were a deep cut above the right rear hock, and a long gash in her chest that ran down into the muscle of the foreleg. Besides those, she was snagged with three-cornered tears through which the flesh pushed out, and laced with cuts and scratches with blood drying on them in rows of little black beads.

Ken wondered if the two bad cuts ought to be sewn up. He thought of Doc Hicks, and then remembered what his Dad had said: "You cost me money every time you turn around." No—Gus might do it— Gus was pretty good at sewing up animals. But Dad said best thing of all is usually to let them alone. They heal up. There was Sultan, hit by an automobile out on the highway; it knocked him down and took a big piece of flesh out of his chest and left the flap of skin hanging loose—and it all healed up of itself and you could only tell where the wound had been by the hair's being a different length.

The cut in Flicka's hind leg was awfully deep—

He put his head down against her and whispered again, "Oh, Flicka—I didn't mean to kill you."

After a few moments, "Oh, get well—get well—*get well*—"

And again, "Flicka, don't be so wild. *Be all right,* Flicka—"

Gus came out to him carrying a can of black grease.

"De Boss tole me to put some of dis grease on de filly's cuts, Ken—it helps heal 'em up."

Together they went over her carefully, putting a smear of the grease wherever they could reach a wound.

Gus stood looking down at the boy.

"D'you think she'll get well, Gus?"

"She might, Ken. I seen plenty horses hurt as bad as dot, and dey yust as good as ever."

"Dad said—" But Ken's voice failed him when he remembered that his father had said she might as well die, because she was loco anyway.

The Swede stood a moment, his pale blue eyes, transparent and spiritual, looking kindly down at the boy; then he went on down to the barn.

Every trace of fog and mist had vanished, and the sun was blazing hot. Sweltering, Ken got up to take a drink of water from the bucket left for Flicka. Then, carrying handfuls of water in his small cupped hands, he poured it on her mouth. Flicka did not move, and once again Ken took his place behind her, his hand on her neck, his lips whispering to her.

After a while his head sank in exhaustion to the ground. . . .

A roaring gale roused him and he looked up to see racing black clouds forming into a line. Blasts of cold wind struck down at the earth and sucked up leaves, twigs, tumbleweeds, in whorls like small cyclones.

From the black line in the sky, a fine icy mist sheeted down, and suddenly there came an appalling explosion of thunder. The world blazed and shuddered with lightning. High overhead was a noise like the shrieking of trumpets and trombones. The particles of fine icy mist beating down grew larger; they began to dance and bounce on the ground like little peas—like marbles—like ping-pong balls—

They beat upon Ken through his thin shirt and whipped his bare head and face. He kneeled up, leaning over Flicka, protecting her head with his folded arms. The hailstones were like ping-pong balls —like billiard balls—like little hard apples—like bigger apples— and suddenly, here and there, they fell as big as tennis balls, bouncing on the ground, rolling along, splitting on the rocks.

One hit Ken on the side of the face and a thin line of blood slid down his cheek with the water.

Running like a hare, under a pall of darkness, the storm fled east-
ward, beating the grass flat upon the hills. Then, in the wake of the
darkness and the screaming wind and hail, a clear silver light shown
out, and the grass rose up again, every blade shimmering.

Watching Flicka, Ken sat back on his heels and sighed. She had not
moved.

A rainbow, like a giant compass, drew a half circle of bright color
around the ranch. And off to one side, there was a vertical blur of
fire hanging, left over from the storm.

Ken lay down again close behind Flicka and put his cheek against
the soft tangle of her mane.

When evening came, and Nell had called Ken and had taken
him by the hand and led him away, Flicka still lay without moving.
Gently the darkness folded down over her. She was alone, except for
the creatures of the sky—the heavenly bodies that wheeled over her;
the two Bears, circling around the North Star; the cluster of little
Sisters clinging together as if they held their arms wrapped around
each other; the eagle, Aquila, that waited till nearly midnight before
his great hidden wings lifted him above the horizon; and right overhead, an eye as bright as a blue diamond beaming down, the beautiful star, Vega.

Less alive than they, and dark under their brilliance, the motionless body of Flicka lay on the blood-stained grass, earth-bound and
fatal, every breath she drew a costly victory.

Toward morning, a half moon rode in the zenith.

A single, sharp, yapping bark broke the silence. Another answered,
then another and another—tentative, questioning cries that presently became long quavering howls. The sharp pixie faces of a pack
of coyotes pointed at the moon, and the howls trembled up through
their long, tight-stretched throats and open, pulsating jaws. Each little prairie-wolf was allowed a solo, at first timid and wondering, then
gathering force and impudence. Then they joined with each other
and at last the troop was in full, yammering chorus, capering and
malicious and thumbing noses and filling the air with sounds that
raise the hair on human heads and put every animal on the alert.

Flicka came back to consciousness with a deep, shuddering sigh.
She lifted her head and rolled over on her belly, drawing her legs
under her a little. Resting so, she turned her head and listened. The
yammer rose and fell. It was a familiar sound, she had heard it since
she was born. The pack was across the stream on the edge of the
woods beyond.

All at once, Flicka gathered herself, made a sudden, plunging effort, and gained her feet. It was not good for a filly to be helpless on the ground with a pack of coyotes near by. She stood swaying, her legs splayed out weakly, her head low and dizzy. It was minutes before balance came to her, and while she waited for it her nostrils flared, smelling water. *Water!* How near was it? Could she get to it?

She saw the tub and presently walked unsteadily over to it put her lips in and drank. New life and strength poured into her. She paused, lifting her muzzle and mouthed the cold water, freshening her tongue and throat. She drank deeply again, then raised her head higher and stood with her neck turned, listening to the coyotes, until the sounds subsided, hesitated, died away.

She stood over the tub a long time. The pack yammered again, but the sound was like an echo, artless and hollow with distance, a mile away. They had gone across the valley for hunting.

A faint luminousness appeared over the earth and a lemon-colored light in the east. One by one the stars drew back, and the pale, innocent blue of the early-morning sky closed over them.

By the time Ken reached Flicka in the morning, she had finished the water, eaten some of the oats, and was standing broadside to the level sunlight, gathering in every ultraviolet ray, every infrared, for the healing and the recreation her battered body needed.

Northwind

HERBERT RAVENEL SASS

It was in the days when Moytoy of Tellequo was High Chief of the
Cherokee nation that the wild chestnut stallion known afterward as
Northwind left the savannahs of the Choctaw country and travelled
to the Overhills of the Cherokees. He made this long journey because
the Choctaw horse-hunters had been pressing him hard. A rumor had
run through the tribe, started perhaps by some learned conjurer or
medicine man, that the tall, long-maned chestnut stallion who was
king of the wild horse herds was descended from the famous steed
which the Prince Soto rode when, many years before, he led his
Spaniards through the Choctaw lands far into the Mississippi wilderness and perished there.

This rumor sharpened the eagerness of the younger braves, for it
was well known that Soto's horse had magic in him. That spring they
hunted the wild stallion more persistently than ever; and at last,
taking two sorrel mares with him, he struck northeastward, seeking
safer pastures.

He did not find them in the Overhills, as the Cherokees called the
high Smokies and the Blue Ridge where they lived and hunted. At
dawn one May morning, as he lay on a bed of fresh sweet-scented
grass near the middle of a natural pasture known as Long Meadow,
a warning came to him. He raised his head high and sniffed the air,
then jumped nimbly to his feet. For a half minute, however, he did
not rouse the two mares lying on either side of him; and they, if they
were aware of his movement, were content to await his signal.

He gave the signal presently, and the mares rose, their ears
pricked, their nostrils quivering. A light breeze blew across the
meadow from the north. The stallion faced south, for his sensitive
nose told him that no foeman was approaching from the opposite
direction. He knew that his ears had not deceived him and that the

299

sound which he had heard was near at hand. But he did not know
the exact quarter from which the sound had come; and though his
large eyes were well adapted to the dim light, nowhere could he
discern that sinister weaving movement of the tall, close-growing
grass which would reveal the stealthy approach of bear or puma. So,
for some minutes, he waited motionless, his head held high, every
faculty keyed to the utmost.

Twenty yards away down the wind Corane the Raven, young warrior of the Cherokees, crouching low in the grass, watched the wild
stallion eagerly. Himself invisible, he could see his quarry more and
more plainly as the light grew stronger; and he knew already that the
wits of this slim, long-maned chestnut horse, which had come over
the mountains from the west, were worthy of his beauty and strength.
With all his art—and the Raven prided himself on his skill as a still-
hunter—and with all the conditions in his favor, he had been baffled.
Having located the beds of the wild horses, he had left his own horse,
Manito-Kinibic, at the edge of the woods and had crept through the
grass as furtively as a lynx. But his approach had been detected when
he was yet five lance-lengths distant, and since then the stallion had
made no false move, had committed no error of judgment.

Corane the Raven knew the wild horses well. Most of them were
small and wiry, already approaching the mustang type of later years;
but in those early days, before inbreeding had proceeded very far,
an occasional stallion still revealed unmistakably the fine qualities of
blooded forebears. From his hiding place in the grass the young
warrior, naked except for a light loincloth of deer-hide, studied the
great chestnut carefully, thoughtfully, marvelling at the lithe sym-
metry of his powerful but beautifully moulded form, admiring his
coolness and steadiness in the face of danger. The stallion showed no
sign of fear. He did not fidget or caper nervously. Only his head
moved slowly back and forth, while with all his powers of sight,
scent, and hearing he strove to locate the precise spot where his
enemy was lurking.

Then Raven smiled in approval; and presently he applied a test
of another kind.

With his long spear he pushed the grass stems in front of him,
causing the tops of the tall blades to quiver and wave. The movement was slight; yet even in the pale morning light the wild horse
saw it. He watched the spot intently for some moments. Then he
moved slowly and cautiously forward, the mares following in his
tracks. He moved neither toward the danger nor away from it. Instead, he circled it, and the Raven realized at once what the stallion's
purpose was. He intended to get down wind from the suspected spot,

so that his nose could tell him whether an enemy hid there, and if so, what kind of enemy it was.

The young warrior waited, curious to see the outcome. Suddenly the stallion's head jerked upward. He was well down the wind now and a puff of air had filled his nostrils with the man-scent. A moment he stood at gaze; and in that moment one of the mares caught the tell-tale scent, snorted with terror and bolted at full speed. Close behind her raced the other mare; while the stallion, wheeling gracefully, followed at a slower pace, his eyes searching the grassy plain ahead.

The Raven had risen to his feet and stood in plain view, but the chestnut stallion scarcely glanced at him again. He was no longer a menace. Of greater importance now were other dangers unknown, invisible, yet possibly imminent.

The natural meadows of lush grass and maiden cane were perilous places for the unwary. In them the puma set his ambush; there the black bear often lurked; hidden in that dense cover, the Indian horse-hunter sometimes waited with their snares. The mares, in a frenzy of panic, were beyond their protector's control. Their nostrils full of the man-smell, they had forgotten all other perils. But the stallion had not forgotten. Before the mares had run fifty yards the thing that he feared happened.

Out of the grass a black bulk heaved upward, reared high with huge hairy arms outspread, fell forward with a deep grunting roar on the haunch of the foremost mare. Screaming like a mad thing, the mare reeled, staggered and went down. In a fraction of a second she was on her feet again, but the big mountain black bear, hurling himself on her hindquarters, crushed them to the ground.

Corane the Raven, racing forward at the sound of the mare's frenzied scream, was near enough to see part of what happened. He saw the wild stallion rear to his utmost height and come down with battering forefeet on the bear's back. He heard the stallion's loud squeal of fury, the bear's hoarse grunt of rage and pain. Next moment the mare was up again and running for her life, the stallion cantering easily behind her.

When the Raven reached the spot, the bear had vanished; and the young Indian, marvelling at what he had seen, ran toward the woods-edge where his swift roan, Manito-Kinibic, awaited him.

In this way began the chase of the chestnut stallion—Northwind, as he was afterward known—that long hunt which Corane the Raven made long ago, even before the time of Atta-Lullu-Kulla the Wise. It was Dunmore the trader who first brought down from the Overhills the story of that hunt and told it one night in Nick Rounder's tavern in Charles Town. Dunmore had it from the Raven himself; and the Raven was known among the white traders and hunters as a truthful man. But he was known also as a man of few words, while Dunmore, great hunter and famous Indian fighter though he was, had a tongue more fluent than a play-actor's.

So it was probably Dunmore who put color into the story, and undoubtedly his quick brain, well warmed with rum that night in the tavern, filled in many details. The tale appealed to him, for he was a lover of horses; and this story of the feud between Northwind, the wild stallion, and Manito-Kinibic, the Raven's roan, concerned two horses which were paladins of their kind.

For the hunt which began that morning in Long Meadow became in large measure a contest between these two. It happened that the Raven had returned not long before from a peace mission to the Choctaws, and while in their country he had heard of the wonderful wild horse which was said to have in him the blood of the Prince Soto's steed and which had vanished from the savannahs after defying all attempts to capture him. In the Overhills wild horses were rare. When the Raven found the tracks of three of them near Long Meadow about sunset one May day, he thought it worth while to sleep that night near the meadow's edge and have a look at the horses in the morning.

So at dawn he had tried to stalk them in their beds; and the moment he saw the wild stallion rise from his sleeping place in the grass he knew that the great chestnut horse of which the Choctaws had spoken stood before him. That morning in Long Meadow he knew also that he could not rest until he had taken this matchless wild horse for his own.

It would be a long hunt, for the stallion would not linger in the Overhills. Small bands of wild horses occasionally crossed the mountains from the west, and always these migrating bands travelled fast, pausing only to feed. Yet, though the hunt might carry him far, Corane the Raven, as he ran swiftly across Long Meadow toward the woods-edge where he had left Manito-Kinibic, had little doubt as to its issue. This wild stallion was a great horse, beautiful, swift and strong—by far the finest wild horse that the Raven had ever seen. But there was one other that was his equal in all things except beauty; and that other was Manito-Kinibic, the Raven's roan.

There was no chief of the Cherokees, the Creeks, or the Choctaws who had a horse that could match Manito-Kinibic. His like had never been known in the Overhills. Dunmore the trader had seen him and had wondered whence he came; for though the Raven had

taken him from the Chickasaws, whose country lay west of the mountains, it was plain that this big-boned burly roan was not of the
Western or Southern wild breed, while his name, which in the white
man's tongue meant Rattlesnake, had to Dunmore's ear a Northern
sound.

Thick-bodied, wide-headed, short-maned, heavy-eared, Manito-
Kinibic was almost grotesquely ugly; yet in his very ugliness there
was a sinister, almost reptilian fascination, heightened by the metal-
lic sheen of his red-speckled coat, the odd flatness of his head, and
the fixed stony glare of his small, deep-set eyes. No warrior of the
Cherokees except the Raven could ride him. Few could even approach him, for his temper was as arrogant as that of the royal ser-
pent for which he was named.

There lurked in him, too, a craftiness recalling the subtle cunning
which the red men attributed to the rattlesnake and because of which
they venerated the king of serpents almost as a god; and with this
craftiness he harbored a savage hatred of the wild creatures which the
Indians hunted, so that on the hunt he was even more eager, even
more relentless than his rider. It was the Raven's boast that Manito-
Kinibic could follow a trail which would baffle many a red hunter;
that he could scent game at a greater distance than the wolf; that his
ears were as keen as those of the deer; that he was as crafty as the fox
and as ruthless as the weasel; and that he feared no wild beast of the
forest, not even the puma himself.

Such was the horse that Corane the Raven rode on his long hunt.
From the beginning of that hunt until its end Manito-Kinibic
seemed to live for one thing only—the capture of the wild stallion
whose scent he snuffed for the first time that morning in Long
Meadow after the wild horse's encounter with the bear.

A few minutes after that encounter, the Raven had reached the
woods-edge where he had left the big roan, had vaulted upon his
back and, riding as swiftly as was prudent through the tall grass and
beds of maiden cane, had struck the trail of the three wild horses near
the spot where they had passed from the meadow at its lower end
into the woods.

The trail was plain to the eye. The scent was strong where the
wild horses had brushed through the rank grass. From that moment
Manito-Kinibic knew what game it was that his rider hunted; and in
that moment all the strange smouldering hatred of his nature was
focused upon the wild stallion which, as his nose told him, had passed
that way with one or two mares.

Manito-Kinibic leaped forward with long bounds, his nostrils dilated, his ears flattened against his head. Corane the Raven, smiling

grimly, let him go. It might be true, as the Choctaws believed, that the wild stallion was sprung from the mighty horse of the Prince Soto himself. But surely this huge implacable horse that now followed on the wild one's trail must have in his veins the blood of the great black steed which the Evil Spirit bestrode when he stood, wrapped in cloud, on the bare summit of Younaguska peak and hurled those awful arrows of his that flashed like lightning.

Northwind, the chestnut stallion, had passed within sight of Younaguska, highest of the Balsams, which men in these days call Caney Fork Bald; but that sombre mountain lay far behind him now, for he had crossed both the main ranges of the mountain bulwark and had begun to descend the eastern slope of the second and lesser range. From Long Meadow he led his mares southeastward at a steady gait, following in general the trend of the valleys and the downward-sloping ridges. The injured mare, though her haunch was raw and bloody where the bear's claws had raked it, kept pace with her companions; and the three travelled fast, pausing only once or twice to drink at some cold, clear, hemlock-shaded stream.

For the most part their course carried them through a virgin forest of oak, chestnut, hickory, and other broad-leaved trees, clothing the ridges, the slopes, and most of the valleys. Occasionally the stallion chose his own way, though as a rule he followed the narrow trails made by the deer; but when in the early forenoon he found a broader path through the woods, well-marked and evidently often used, he turned into it unhesitatingly and followed it without swerving. The wild horse of the southwestern savannahs recognized this path at once. It was one of the highways of the buffalo herds, a road trodden deep and hard through many centuries by thousands of hoofs.

The buffalo were far less abundant now on the eastern side of the mountains. Although the white men's settlements were still confined to a strip along the coast, white hunters sometimes penetrated the foothills and white traders encouraged the taking of pelts. The deer still abounded in almost incredible numbers, but the eastern buffalo herds were withdrawing gradually across the Appalachians. Small droves, however, still ranged the eastern foothills and kept open the deep-worn paths; and the main buffalo roads across the mountain barrier, wider than the narrow buffalo ruts of the western plains, were still highways for wild creatures of many kinds. It was one of these main roads that the chestnut stallion and his mares were following; a road which would lead them with many windings down from the mountains into the hills and through the hills to the broad belt of rolling lands beyond which lay the swamps and savannahs of the Atlantic plain.

All that forenoon the Raven trailed his quarry. Both to the roan stallion and to his rider the trail was a plain one; and when the tracks of the wild horses turned into the buffalo path, the Raven knew that he had only to follow that highway through the woods. With a guttural word he restrained Manito-Kinibic's savage eagerness. So long as the wild horses kept to the buffalo road the task of following them would be simple. The Raven preferred that for the present the chestnut stallion should not know that we was pursued.

Half a bowshot ahead of the young warrior a troop of white-tails crossed the path, following a deer trail leading down the slope to a laurel-bordered stream. Once, at a greater distance, he saw a puma come out of the woods into the path, sit for a moment on its haunches, then vanish at a bound into the forest on the other side. Again and again wild turkeys ran into the woods on either hand, seldom taking wing; and with monotonous regularity ruffed grouse rose a few paces in front of him and whirred swiftly away.

About noon he killed a cock grouse in the path, pinning the bird to the ground with a light cane arrow tipped with bone; and he had scarcely remounted when around a curve of the path appeared the shaggy bulk of a huge buffalo bull. A moment the great beast stood motionless, blinking in astonishment, his massive head hanging low. Then, with surprising nimbleness, he turned and darted around the bend of the trail.

The Raven heard the stamping and trampling of many hoofs and gave Manito-Kinibic his head. The roan bounded forward and almost in an instant reached the bend of the path. At a word from his rider he halted; and the Raven, quivering with excitement, gazed with shining eyes upon a spectacle which sent the blood leaping through his veins—a herd of twenty buffalo pouring out of the path, crowding and jostling one another as they streamed down the mountainside through the woods, following a deer trail which crossed the buffalo road almost at right angles. Twice the young warrior bent his bow and drew the shaft to the head; and twice he lowered his weapon, unwilling to kill game which he must leave to the wolves.

Afternoon came and still the Raven rode on through the teeming mountain forest, following the deep-worn highway which the migrating herds through unknown centuries had carved across the Overhills. More keenly than ever now his eyes searched the path ahead. The wild stallion and his mares had probably grazed abundantly in Long Meadow before their early-morning rest had been interrupted;

but by this time they should be hungry again, for since leaving Long Meadow they had not stopped to feed. Wherever the Raven saw the forest open a little ahead of him so that grass grew under the far-spaced trees, he halted and listened carefully. Before long in one of these grassy places he should find the three wild horses grazing, and he wished to avoid frightening them.

The path, which heretofore had wound around the mountain shoulders, dipped suddenly into a deep gorge-like valley at the bottom of which a torrent roared. The forest here was close and dark. The wild horses would not halt in this valley, for there was no grass to be had; and for a time the Raven relaxed his vigilance, letting his eyes stray from the path ahead.

From a tall hemlock on the mountainside a wild gobbler took wing, sailing obliquely across the valley, and the Raven saw an eagle, which had been perching on a dead tulip poplar, launch himself forward in swift pursuit. The young brave turned on his horse's back, gazing upward over his shoulder, eagerly watching the chase.

Without warning, Manito-Kinibic reared, swerved to the right and plunged forward. His rider, taken utterly by surprise, lurched perilously, yet somehow kept his seat. For an instant, as Manito-Kinibic reared again, the Raven saw a sinewy naked arm raised above a hideous grinning face daubed with vermilion and black. Steel-fingered hands clutched the Raven's leg; on the other side another hand clawed at his thigh. Out from the thicket into the path ahead leaped three more warriors, feathered and plumed with eagle-tails and hawk-wings, striped and mottled with the red and black paint of war. More dreadful than the hunting cry of the puma, the shrill war-whoop of the Muskogee split the air.

But for Manito-Kinibic the Rattlesnake, the chase of the chestnut stallion would have ended then. But the Muskogee war party which waylaid Corane the Raven in the pass, hoping to take him alive for slavery or torture, failed to reckon with the temper and strength of the mighty roan.

In an instant Manito-Kinibic had become a rearing, snorting fury, a raging devil of battering hoofs and gleaming teeth. The Raven saw one Muskogee go down before the plunging roan stallion. He saw another whose shoulder was red with something that was not war paint. He saw the three warriors in the path ahead leap for their lives into the thicket as Manito-Kinibic charged down upon them. Bending low on his horse's neck, he heard an arrow speed over him and, a half-second later, another arrow. Then, remembering that he was the son of a war captain, he rose erect, looked back, and flourishing

the hand which still held his bow and spear, hurled at his enemies the Cherokee whoop of triumph.

Thenceforward for a time the Raven watched the path behind
rather than the path ahead. The war parties of the Muskogee were
often mounted, and the young Cherokee thought it likely that this
party had horses concealed in the thickets near the path. They would
probably pursue him, but with Manito-Kinibic under him he was
safe. Yet for a while he gave the sure-footed roan his head, racing
onward as swiftly as the uneven surface of the trail allowed. So it
happened that he was driven by necessity into doing the thing which
he had intended to avoid.

A mile beyond the scene of the ambush the valley widened. Here,
encircled by forested heights, lay a level, sun-bathed meadow, sweet
with clover and wild pea vine. Northwind and his mares had travelled far and fast. Urged on by his restless eagerness to get out of the
dark, forbidding mountains, perhaps impelled, too, by some mysterious premonition of danger, the great chestnut horse had permitted
no halt for food. In this beautiful vivid-green oasis in the wilderness
of woods he halted at last.

The meadow was dotted with grazing deer. Clearly no enemy
lurked there. With a joyful whinny Northwind turned aside from
the path and led his consorts to the feast.

A half-hour later, an instant before the wariest of the white-tails
had caught the warning sound, the wild stallion raised his head suddenly, listened intently for a moment, then, with a peremptory summons to the mares, trotted slowly with high head and tail toward the
lower end of the meadow. Because wild creatures do not ordinarily
rush headlong through the forest, he miscalculated the speed of the
intruder whose hoofbeats he had heard. He was still near the middle
of the meadow, while the mares, loath to leave the clover beds, were
far behind him, when he saw the Raven on Manito-Kinibic dash out
of the woods.

The young brave heard the wild stallion's snort of surprise, saw
him leap forward and race for the buffalo path, while the mares
wheeled and galloped off to the left. In long, beautiful bounds the
stallion skimmed over the grass to the meadow's lower end where
the path reentered the forest. There he disappeared amid the trees.

The damage having been done, the Raven let Manito-Kinibic do
his best for two or three miles. But the wild horse ran like the north
wind which blows across the summit of Unaka Kanoos. It was then
that the Raven named him, in honor of that north wind which is the
swiftest and keenest of all the winds of the mountains. Until his

rider checked him, Manito-Kinibic ran a good race. But they saw the
wild stallion no more that day.

Even among the Cherokees, great hunters and marvelously skillful
trackers, it was considered a noteworthy thing that Corane the Raven
and Manito-Kinibic the Rattlesnake were able to follow the trail of
the chestnut stallion all the way from the eastern slope of the Overhills to the Low Country of the Atlantic coast, more than two hundred miles as the white man reckons distance. Certain circumstances
aided the pursuers. Nearly always Northwind kept to the game paths.
Until he was well out of the mountains he followed the buffalo road.
For many miles through the upper foothills he used the narrow paths
trodden out by the deer. Always he chose those paths which led him
south or southeast, following the slope of the land.

When he passed from the foothills into the rolling country where
the forest was more open and where many prairie-meadows lay em-
bosomed in the woods, the Raven's problem was somewhat harder;
and in the Low Country of the coastal plain, so utterly unlike his
mountain home, there were moments when the young warrior saw
defeat staring him in the face. Yet it was evident that the wild stallion himself was not at home in this land of dense cypress swamps
and towering pinewoods, of vast canebrakes and wide wastes of
rushes, of dark sluggish rivers winding silently through moss-draped
mysterious forests.

If this was the land which some deep-seated instinct had impelled
him to seek, it was evidently not what he had expected it to be—not
a land like that which he had known westward of the mountains. It
was rich beyond measure, affording pasturage of numerous kinds.
But in many respects it was strange to him, and his first night within
its borders taught him that it bristled with dangers.

He rested that night near the end of a long woods-prairie or open
savannah close to a tall canebrake bordering a great swamp. In the
late afternoon he had grazed in the savannah amid herds of deer and
flocks of tall gray cranes. The air was melodious with the songs of
numberless birds. Over him, as he cropped the grass, passed many
wild turkeys coming in from the woods to their roosts in the giant
pines of the swamp. Around the margins of a marshy pond scores of
graceful milk-white egrets walked to and fro amid hundreds of
smaller herons of darker plumage. To the stallion it seemed that he
had come to a land of plenty and of peace where no enemies lurked.

The night revealed his mistake. The swamp rang with the cries
and roars of hunting beasts and with the long-drawn resonant bel-
lowings of great alligators—a fearful chorus of the wilderness such

as he had never heard before. Twice he saw round fiery eyes glaring at him out of the darkness. Once his nose told him that near at hand in the canebrake a puma was passing along one of the winding pathways through the canes. Sleep was impossible; yet, the night being very black, he judged it unsafe to move, fearing to run upon an invisible enemy. He spent the long hours standing, tense and rigid, his senses strained to the utmost, expecting each moment to feel the fangs or claws of some unknown foe.

How long the chestnut stallion remained in the wild swamp region of the Low Country cannot be told. Probably not long, for while food was abundant, the perils were too many. Nor can it be related how he avoided those perils and found his way at last to the edge of the wide salt marshes between the Low Country mainland and the barrier islands along the sea. Day after day Corane the Raven and Manito-Kinibic the Rattlesnake followed him in his wanderings; and day after day the Raven, patient with the long patience of his race, held fast to the resolution which he had formed at the beginning— the resolution not to attempt the capture of the wild stallion until the time should be fully ripe.

He had to wait long for that time, but in one respect fortune favored the young warrior. Except for the Muskogee ambush in the mountain pass, he suffered no interference at the hands of man and, indeed, saw scarcely a human face between the Overhills and the coast. Even when he had reached the white men's country—where, however, the settlements were still small and sparse—the wild horse's fear of human enemies kept both himself and his pursuers out of man's way. The spot where the long chase had its ending was as lonely as the remotest wilderness.

To Northwind, after his long journey, that spot seemed a paradise. To Corane the Raven, viewing it cautiously from the cover of the woods about noon of a warm cloudless June day, it seemed to combine all the conditions essential for his success. A dry level meadow carpeted with short thick grass and shaped like a broad spearhead lay between a converging river and creek which came together at the meadow's lower end. There, and for some distance along the shore, the land sloped sharply to the river, forming a little bluff about ten feet in height; while beyond the river lay vast marshes stretching for miles toward the hazy line of woods on the barrier isles.

The Raven took in these things at a glance; noted, too, with satisfaction that here and there in the meadow stood clumps of some dense, stiff-branched bush of a kind unknown in the mountains. Then, well pleased, his plan complete to the smallest detail, he let his eyes rest again upon that feature of the scene which was the most important and most gratifying of all.

Almost in the center of the meadow stood Northwind, the wild stallion, alert, arrogant, confident, a picture of lithe, clean-cut beauty and perfectly proportioned strength. But he no longer stood alone. Just beyond him grazed five mares, all of them bays and all of them of one size and build. The Raven knew at once that they were not wild horses and he surmised that they were strays from the white men's stock. But it mattered little whence they had come. The essential fact was that Northwind had taken them as his own, had become their master and protector.

Two hours before midnight, when the moon, almost at the full, swung high above the marshes beyond the river and the grassy expanse of the meadow was bathed in ghostly light, the Raven led Manito-Kinibic from his hiding place in the woods to the edge of the open. There the young brave halted. The big roan, his nostrils tingling with a scent which set his blood on fire, needed no word of instruction. He knew his part and would play it perfectly. Quivering with eagerness, yet too well trained to give way to the fury that possessed him, Manito-Kinibic moved out into the meadow at a slow walk, his hoofs making no sound.

The Raven waited until the roan had become a dim uncertain shape in the moonlight. Then, crouching low, the Indian stole to the nearest bush-clump, thence to another isolated thicket, and thence by a roundabout course to a third. He was halfway down the meadow when he heard the wild stallion's challenge and knew that Manito-Kinibic's keen nose had led the roan straight to his goal. Bending close to the ground, sometimes creeping on all fours, sometimes crawling like a snake, the Raven moved from bush-clump to bush-clump toward the sound.

A fresh breeze blew from the sea across the marshes. The wild stallion, resting with his mares near the meadow's lower end where the creek and river joined, could neither smell nor hear an enemy approaching from the direction of the woods. Manito-Kinibic was scarcely fifty paces distant when Northwind saw him.

A moment the wild horse stood at gaze, his muscles tense for the long leap which would launch him forward in swift flight. Then fear passed out of him and fury took its place. A glance had shown him what the intruder was—a lone stallion, riderless, unaccompanied by man, roaming at will and evidently seeking the bay mares. Loud and shrill rang Northwind's challenge. Instantly he charged his foe.

Manito-Kinibic the Rattlesnake was a veteran of many battles.

The fiercest battle of his career was the one which he fought that night in the moonlit meadow where the long chase of the chestnut stallion had its end. Northwind, too, had conquered many rivals to make good his mastery of the wild horse herds; but never before had he faced an antagonist as formidable as the burly roan. With Manito-Kinibic lay the advantage of size and weight; with the wild horse the advantage of quickness and agility. In courage neither surpassed the other. In cunning each was the other's match.

Almost at once they took each other's measure and, despite their fury, fought with instinctive skill, each striving to utilize to the ut-most those powers in which he excelled. After his first whirlwind charge, Northwind did not charge again. He knew after that first onset that he must not hurl himself recklessly against the roan's weight and bulk. This was an enemy too big to be overwhelmed; he must be cut to pieces with slashing hoofs and torn to ribbons with ripping, raking teeth. Hence the wild stallion whirled and circled, feinted and reared, dashed in and leaped clean again, like a skillful rapier-man whose opponent wields a broadsword—and wields it well.

For Manito-Kinibic was no blundering bruiser whose sole reliance was his strength. He, too, fought with cunning and skill, manœu-vring with a lightness which belied his bulk, parrying and thrusting with an adroitness not much inferior to that of his opponent. But, ap-parently realizing the advantage which his weight gave him, he strove from the first for close quarters. Furiously, incessantly he forced the fighting, seeking to grip and hold his elusive enemy, rear-ing high to crush the wild horse with his battering hoofs, plunging forward with all his weight to drive his mighty shoulder against his foe and hurl him to the ground.

It was a fight too furious to last long. A stallion's hoofs and teeth are fearful weapons. A few minutes more must have brought a bloody end to the battle, though no man can say what that end would have been. Suddenly from a bush-clump a shadow darted, sped lightly across the grass, and vanished in a tuft of tall weeds. Northwind did not see it because it was behind him. If Manito-Kinibic saw it, he gave no sign.

The battling stallions wheeled and reared, biting and plunging, striking with their forefeet, thrusting, parrying, feinting. Once more the roan hurled himself forward, his small eyes gleaming red, his teeth bared, his heavy hoofs stabbing the air; and once more his slim, long-maned opponent, light as a dancer, lithe as a panther, whirled aside, escaping destruction by an inch.

Again, as they fenced for an opening, rearing high, snorting and squealing, the wild horse's back was turned to the clump of weeds; and again the shadow darted forward, swiftly, noiselessly, gliding over the turf.

The next moment Corane the Raven crouched close behind the chestnut stallion. A half-second more, and he had swung his rawhide thong with the skill for which he was famous. Then, with a shout, he leaped for Manito-Kinibic's head.

Northwind was down. He lay on his side, motionless as a dead thing. The rawhide thong, weighted at its ends, was wrapped around his hind legs, binding them tightly together. The greatest miracle

was not the skill with which the Raven had thrown his snare. More wonderful still was the quelling of Manito-Kinibic's battle-fury, the swiftness with which his master brought the raging roan under control. Yet this was merely the result of teaching, of long, painstaking instruction. Corane the Raven, the most successful horse-hunter among the Cherokees, owed his success partly to the peculiar methods which he employed and partly to the perfect training of his famous roan.

Manito-Kinibic, his neck and shoulders bloody, his flanks heaving, stood quietly, gazing down at his fallen foe with eyes in which the fire of hatred still glowed; but Northwind, his silky sides streaked with red, lay inert, inanimate, seeming scarcely to breathe. He offered no resistance as the Raven with deft fingers slipped a strong hobble around the slim forelegs and made it fast above each fetlock.

There was no terror, no fierceness in the wild horse's large eyes. Instead they seemed singularly calm and soft, as though the brain behind them were lulled with a vision of places far away and days long ago.

Yet, if the chestnut stallion, a prisoner at last, dreamed of some green, daisy-sprinkled forest-prairie beyond the mountains, the dream passed quickly. Presently the Raven removed the thong which had held Northwind's hind legs helpless; and instantly the wild horse came to life, panic-stricken, furious, frantic for his freedom.

For a moment he thought himself free. His hind legs were no longer bound. The hobble around his forelegs bound them only loosely. With a snort he heaved upward and leaped away in mad flight—only to pitch headlong to the ground with a force which almost drove the breath from his body. Up he scrambled once more and down again he plunged as his fettered forelegs crumpled under him. Five times he rose and five times he fell before he seemed to realize his helplessness.

For several minutes, then, he lay utterly still. The Raven had remounted Manito-Kinibic. The wild horse could not escape; yet it was well to be prepared for whatever might happen. The ordeal might be over in an hour, or, on the other hand, many hours might pass before Northwind's spirit was broken.

At last he struggled to his feet. The Raven circled him on the roan, watching him keenly. The captive's frenzy seemed to have passed. He was cooler now, steadier on his legs. Sudden anxiety which was almost panic gripped the young Indian. He recalled that once he had seen a hobbled wild horse travel a distance of half a bow-shot in short labored bounds before falling; and in a flash he had become aware of a danger hitherto unrealized.

Quickly he slipped from Manito-Kinibic's back and approached Northwind from behind, uncoiling the weighted rawhide thong which he had removed from the wild stallion's hind legs. He would snare those hind legs again and thus make certain of his captive.

By a margin of moments he was too late. Northwind wheeled, bounded forward, and this time he did not fall. He had learned what not one hobbled wild horse in a thousand ever discovered—that while a leap of normal length would throw him every time, he could travel at least a little distance at fair speed if his leaps were very short.

Another bound he made, another and another—stiff-legged, labored, heartbreaking—keeping his balance by a miracle. He was more than halfway to the river's edge when the hobble threw him, and though he fell heavily, almost in an instant he was on his feet again, bounding onward as before.

On the very verge of the low bluff, the Raven, who had remounted as quickly as possible, drove Manito-Kinibic against the chestnut's flank in a last attempt to turn or throw him. Reeling from the blow, Northwind staggered on the brink. Then, rallying his strength for a supreme effort, he plunged sideways down the steep slope, and the water closed over him.

Some say he was drowned. The Raven never saw him again, though the moon shone brightly on the river. But the water is very deep beside that bluff, and there the ebb tide is very strong and swift. It might have borne him quickly beyond the Indian's vision; and since the hobble allowed his forelegs some freedom of action, he might have made shift to swim.

At any rate, when Dunmore the trader told the story of the chestnut stallion that night in Nick Rounder's tavern, an old seafaring man, who was present, pricked up his ears and asked the trader certain questions. Then, with a great show of wonder and a string of sailor's oaths, he spun a queer yarn.

One midnight, he said, while his ship lay at anchor in a rivermouth between two barrier islands, the lookout sighted a big chestnut horse coming down the river with the tide. They manned a boat, got a rope over the horse's head and towed him to the sandy island shore. He seemed almost exhausted, his neck and shoulders were cut and bruised, and how he had come into the river was a mystery, since his forelegs were hobbled. They could not take the horse aboard their vessel; so, after cutting the hobble, they left him lying on the beach, apparently more dead than alive. They expected to see his body there in the morning, but when they weighed anchor at sunrise he was gone.

Dunmore believed the old man's story; but others held that he had invented the tale on the spur of the moment, in the hope that the trader would stand him a noggin of rum. However that may be, an odd legend exists today on the barrier islands of the Carolina coast.

The story runs that the slim wiry ponies of those islands, rovers of the beaches and marsh flats, have in their veins the blood of De Soto's Andalusian horses abandoned nearly four centuries ago in the Mississippi wilderness six hundred miles away, beyond the mountains.

It seems a fantastic legend; yet the river in which Northwind made his last desperate bid for freedom passes quickly to the sea between two of those barrier isles.

The Horse and His Rider

AESOP

(As retold by Beth Brown)

A SOLDIER once had a horse of whom he took the greatest care. All through the war, as they fought together, the soldier groomed him every day and fed him every night with the best of hay and oats. He combed his mane. He cleaned his stall and spread it with sweet hay. And the horse served his master as well as his master served him.

Then the war came to a close and the soldier went home with his horse.

Here was played another tune. The man gave his beast the worst of food. He made him carry great loads of brick. He never groomed him or spread sweet hay in his stall. The horse grew thin and weary and old.

Then the war broke out again and the soldier made haste to return to the battlefield. He climbed into his clanking coat of mail and leaped upon the horse. The weight of his master proved too much for the poor, broken-down beast and he fell to the ground in a heap.

He told his master: "You can no longer ride me to the battlefield. You will have to go there on foot, for you have turned me from a Horse into an Ass and I can never again turn from an Ass into a Horse."

DAMAGE IS SLOW TO MEND.

The Chariot Race

LEW WALLACE

(from BEN-HUR)

WHEN the dash for position began, Ben-Hur, as we have seen, was on the extreme left of the six. For a moment, like the others, he was half blinded by the light in the arena; yet he managed to catch sight of his antagonists and divine their purpose. At Messala, who was more than an antagonist to him, he gave one searching look. The air of passionless hauteur characteristic of the fine patrician face was there as of old, and so was the Italian beauty, which the helmet rather increased; but more—it may have been a jealous fancy, or the effect of the brassy shadow in which the features were at the moment cast, still the Israelite thought he saw the soul of the man as through a glass, darkly: cruel, cunning, desperate; not so excited as determined—a soul in a tension of watchfulness and fierce resolve.

In a time not longer than was required to turn to his four again, Ben-Hur felt his own resolution harden to a like temper. At whatever cost, at all hazards, he would humble this enemy! Prize, friends, wagers, honor—everything that can be thought of as a possible interest in the race was lost in the one deliberate purpose. Regard for life even should not hold him back. Yet there was no passion, on his part; no blinding rush of heated blood from heart to brain, and back again; no impulse to fling himself upon Fortune: he did not believe in Fortune; far otherwise. He had his plan, and, confiding in himself, he settled to the task never more observant, never more capable. The air about him seemed aglow with a renewed and perfect transparency.

When not half-way across the arena, he saw that Messala's rush would, if there was no collision, and the rope fell, give him the wall; that the rope would fall, he ceased as soon to doubt; and, further, it came to him, a sudden, flash-like insight, that Messala knew it was

318

to be let drop at the last moment (prearrangement with the editor could safely reach that point in the contest) ; and it suggested, what more Roman-like than for the official to lend himself to a country-man who, besides being so popular, had also so much at stake? There could be no other accounting for the confidence with which Messala pushed his four forward the instant his competitors were prudentially checking their fours in front of the obstruction—no other except madness.

It is one thing to see a necessity and another to act upon it. Ben-Hur yielded the wall for the time.

The rope fell, and all the fours but his sprang into the course un-der urgency of voice and lash. He drew head to the right, and, with all the speed of his Arabs, darted across the trails of his opponents, the angle of movement being such as to lose the least time and gain the greatest possible advance. So, while the spectators were shivering at the Athenian's mishap, and the Sidonian, Byzantine, and Corin-thian were striving, with such skill as they possessed, to avoid in-volvement in the ruin, Ben-Hur swept around and took the course neck and neck with Messala, though on the outside. The marvellous skill shown in making the change thus from the extreme left across to the right without appreciable loss did not fail the sharp eyes upon the benches: the Circus seemed to rock and rock again with pro-longed applause. Then Esther clasped her hands in glad surprise; then Sanballat, smiling, offered his hundred sestertii a second time without a taker; and then the Romans began to doubt, thinking Messala might have found an equal, if not a master, and that in an Israelite!

And now, racing together side by side, a narrow interval between them, the two neared the second goal.

The pedestal of the three pillars there, viewed from the west, was a stone wall in the form of a half-circle, around which the course and opposite balcony were bent in exact parallelism. Making this turn was considered in all respects the most telling test of a charioteer; it was, in fact, the very feat in which Orestes failed. As an involuntary admission of interest on the part of the spectators, a hush fell over all the Circus, so that for the first time in the race the rattle and clang of the cars plunging after the tugging steeds were distinctly heard. Then, it would seem, Messala observed Ben-Hur, and recognized him; and at once the audacity of the man flamed out in an astonish-ing manner.

"Down Eros, up Mars!" he shouted, whirling his lash with prac-tised hand. "Down Eros, up Mars!" he repeated, and caught the well-doing Arabs of Ben-Hur a cut the like of which they had never known.

The blow was seen in every quarter, and the amazement was universal. The silence deepened; up on the benches behind the consul the boldest held his breath, waiting for the outcome. Only a moment thus: then, involuntarily, down from the balcony, as thunder falls, burst the indignant cry of the people.

The four sprang forward affrighted. No hand had ever been laid upon them except in love; they had been nurtured ever so tenderly; and as they grew, their confidence in man became a lesson to men beautiful to see. What should such dainty natures do under such indignity but leap as from death?

Forward they sprang as with one impulse, and forward leaped the car. Past question, every experience is serviceable to us. Where got Ben-Hur the large hand and mighty grip which helped him now so well? Where but from the oar with which so long he fought the sea? And what was this spring of the floor under his feet to the dizzy, eccentric lurch with which in the old time the trembling ship yielded to the beat of staggering billows, drunk with their power? So he kept his place, and gave the four free rein, and called to them in soothing voice, trying merely to guide them round the dangerous turn; and before the fever of the people began to abate he had back the mastery. Nor that only: on approaching the first goal, he was again side by side with Messala, bearing with him the sympathy and admiration of every one not a Roman. So clearly was the feeling shown, so vigorous its manifestation, that Messala, with all his boldness, felt it unsafe to trifle further.

As the cars whirled round the goal, Esther caught sight of Ben-Hur's face—a little pale, a little higher raised, otherwise calm, even placid.

Immediately a man climbed on the entablature at the west end of the division wall, and took down one of the conical wooden balls. A dolphin on the east entablature was taken down at the same time.

In like manner, the second ball and second dolphin disappeared.

And then the third ball and third dolphin.

Three rounds concluded: still Messala held the inside position; still Ben-Hur moved with him side by side; still the other competitors followed as before. The contest began to have the appearance of one of the double races which became so popular in Rome during the later Cæsarean period—Messala and Ben-Hur in the first, the Corinthian, Sidonian, and Byzantine in the second. Meantime the ushers succeeded in returning the multitude to their seats, though the clamor continued to run the rounds, keeping, as it were, even pace with the rivals in the course below.

In the fifth round the Sidonian succeeded in getting a place outside Ben-Hur, but lost it directly.

The sixth round was entered upon without change of relative position.

Gradually the speed had been quickened—gradually the blood of the competitors warmed with the work. Men and beasts seemed to know alike that the final crisis was near, bringing the time for the winner to assert himself.

The interest which from the beginning had centred chiefly in the struggle between the Roman and the Jew, with an intense and general sympathy for the latter, was fast changing to anxiety on his account. On all the benches the spectators bent forward motionless, except as their faces turned following the contestants. Ilderim quitted combing his beard, and Esther forgot her fears.

"A hundred sestertii on the Jew!" cried Sanballat to the Romans under the consul's awning.

There was no reply.

"A talent—or five talents, or ten; choose ye!"

He shook his tablets at them defiantly.

"I will take thy sestertii," answered a Roman youth, preparing to write.

"Do not so," interposed a friend.

"Why?"

"Messala hath reached his utmost speed. See him lean over his chariot-rim, the reins loose as flying ribbons. Look then at the Jew."

The first one looked.

"By Hercules!" he replied, his countenance falling. "The dog throws all his weight on the bits. I see, I see! If the gods help not our friend, he will be run away with by the Israelite. No, not yet. Look! Jove with us, Jove with us!"

The cry, swelled by every Latin tongue, shook the *velaria* over the consul's head.

If it were true that Messala had attained his utmost speed, the effort was with effect; slowly but certainly he was beginning to forge ahead. His horses were running with their heads low down; from the balcony their bodies appeared actually to skim the earth; their nostrils showed blood-red in expansion; their eyes seemed straining in their sockets. Certainly the good steeds were doing their best! How long could they keep the pace? It was but the commencement of the sixth round. On they dashed. As they neared the second goal, Ben-Hur turned in behind the Roman's car.

The joy of the Messala faction reached its bound: they screamed and howled, and tossed their colors; and Sanballat filled his tablets with wagers of their tendering.

Malluch, in the lower gallery over the Gate of Triumph, found it hard to keep his cheer. He had cherished the vague hint dropped to him by Ben-Hur of something to happen in the turning of the western pillars. It was the fifth round, yet the something had not come; and he had said to himself, the sixth will bring it; but, lo! Ben-Hur was hardly holding a place at the tail of his enemy's car.

Over in the east end, Simonides' party held their peace. The merchant's head was bent low. Ilderim tugged at his beard, and dropped his brows till there was nothing of his eyes but an occasional sparkle of light. Esther scarcely breathed. Iras alone appeared glad.

Along the home-stretch—sixth round—Messala leading, next him Ben-Hur, and so close it was the old story:

> "First flew Eumelus on Pheretian steeds;
> With those of Tros bold Diomed succeeds;
> Close on Eumelus' back they puff the wind,
> And seem just mounting on his car behind;
> Full on his neck he feels the sultry breeze,
> And, hovering o'er, their stretching shadow sees."

Thus, to the first goal, and round it. Messala, fearful of losing his place, hugged the stony wall with perilous clasp; a foot to the left, and he had been dashed to pieces; yet, when the turn was finished, no man, looking at the wheel-tracks of the two cars, could have said, here went Messala, there the Jew. They left but one trace behind them.

As they whirled by, Esther saw Ben-Hur's face again, and it was whiter than before.

Simonides, shrewder than Esther, said to Ilderim, the moment the rivals turned into the course: "I am no judge, good sheik, if Ben-Hur be not about to execute some design. His face hath that look."

To which Ilderim answered: "Saw you how clean they were and fresh? By the splendor of God, friend, they have not been running! But now watch!"

One ball and one dolphin remained on the entablatures; and all the people drew a long breath, for the beginning of the end was at hand.

First, the Sidonian gave the scourge to his four, and, smarting with fear and pain, they dashed desperately forward, promising for a brief time to go to the front. The effort ended in promise. Next, the Byzantine and Corinthian each made the trial with like result, after which they were practically out of the race. Thereupon, with a readiness perfectly explicable, all the factions except the Romans joined hope in Ben-Hur, and openly indulged their feeling.

"Ben-Hur! Ben-Hur!" they shouted, and the blent voices of the many rolled overwhelmingly against the consular stand.

From the benches above him as he passed, the favor descended in fierce injunctions.

"Speed thee, Jew!"

"Take the wall now!"

"On! loose the Arabs! Give them rein and scourge!"

"Let him not have the turn on thee again. Now or never!"

Over the balustrade they stooped low, stretching their hands imploringly to him.

Either he did not hear, or could not do better, for half-way round the course and he was still following; at the second goal even still no change!

And now, to make the turn, Messala began to draw in his left-hand steeds, an act which necessarily slackened their speed. His spirit was high; more than one altar was richer of his vows; the Roman genius was still president. On the three pillars only six hundred feet away were fame, increase of fortune, promotions, and a triumph ineffably sweetened by hate, all in store for him! That moment Malluch, in the gallery, saw Ben-Hur lean forward over his Arabs, and give them the reins. Out flew the many-folded lash in his hand; over the backs of the startled steeds it writhed and hissed, and hissed and writhed again and again, and though it fell not, there were both sting and menace in its quick report; and as the man passed thus from quiet to resistless action, his face suffused, his eyes gleaming, along the reins he seemed to flash his will; and instantly not one, but the four as one, answered with a leap that landed them alongside the Roman's car. Messala, on the perilous edge of the goal, heard, but dared not look to see what the awakening portended. From the people he received no sign. Above the noises of the race there was but one voice, and that was Ben-Hur's. In the old Aramaic, as the sheik himself, he called to the Arabs:

"On, Atair! On, Rigel! What, Antares! dost thou linger now? Good horse—oho, Aldebaran! I hear them singing in the tents. I hear the children singing and the women—singing of the stars, of

Atair, Antares, Rigel, Aldebaran, victory!—and the song will never end. Well done! Home to-morrow, under the black tent—home! On, Antares! The tribe is waiting for us, and the master is waiting! 'Tis done! 'tis done! Ha, ha! We have overthrown the proud. The hand that smote us is in the dust. Ours the glory! Ha, ha!—steady! The work is done—soho! Rest!"

There had never been anything of the kind more simple; seldom anything so instantaneous.

At the moment chosen for the dash, Messala was moving in a circle round the goal. To pass him, Ben-Hur had to cross the track, and good strategy required the movement to be in a forward direction; that is, on a like circle limited to the least possible increase. The thousands on the benches understood it all: they saw the signal given—the magnificent response; the four close outside Messala's

outer wheel, Ben-Hur's inner wheel behind the other's car—all this they saw. Then they heard a crash loud enough to send a thrill through the Circus, and, quicker than thought, out over the course a spray of shining white-and-yellow flinders flew. Down on its right side toppled the bed of the Roman's chariot. There was a rebound as of the axle hitting the hard earth; another and another; then the car went to pieces; and Messala, entangled in the reins, pitched forward headlong.

To increase the horror of the sight by making death certain, the Sidonian, who had the wall next behind, could not stop or turn out. Into the wreck full speed he drove; then over the Roman, and into the latter's four, all mad with fear. Presently, out of the turmoil, the fighting of horses, the resound of blows, the murky cloud of dust and sand, he crawled, in time to see the Corinthian and Byzan-

tine go on down the course after Ben-Hur, who had not been an instant delayed.

The people arose, and leaped upon the benches, and shouted and screamed. Those who looked that way caught glimpses of Messala, now under the trampling of the fours, now under the abandoned cars. He was still; they thought him dead; but far the greater number followed Ben-Hur in his career. They had not seen the cunning touch of the reins by which, turning a little to the left, he caught Messala's wheel with the iron-shod point of his axle, and crushed it; but they had seen the transformation of the man, and themselves felt the heat and glow of his spirit, the heroic resolution, the maddening energy of action with which, by look, word, and gesture, he so suddenly inspired his Arabs. And such running! It was rather the long leaping of lions in harness; but for the lumbering chariot, it seemed the four were flying. When the Byzantine and Corinthian were half-way down the course, Ben-Hur turned the first goal.

And the race was WON!

The consul arose; the people shouted themselves hoarse; the editor came down from his seat, and crowned the victors. . . .

And the day was over.

Maudie Tom, Jockey

GLADYS HASTY CARROLL

OVERNIGHT a great white placard had appeared on the blackboard at the corner of the village street. Pictures of horses were pasted all over it, and there was printing at the bottom. Maudie Tom, crouched low on Bess's back, stared at it for a long time. Then she tugged on her reins and cantered into the bustling, crowded square.

She was a strange figure among the thronging summer guests of the little town. College-girl waitresses, off duty for a few hours, hopped on bare pink feet toward the beach, pulling off blue-and-scarlet coolie coats as they went. Ladies in soft-colored cotton dresses wandered in and out among the little gift-shops. Clean, brown children stood in sun-suits before the big show-window which revealed a gigantic candy machine in operation. Men in milk-white clothes strolled about, puffing expertly at fragrant cigars. People laughed and skipped and called across from one corner to another, and drank cloudy brown and rosy sodas from tall glasses. But Maudie Tom rode grim and dark and silent through the carnival of summer; a big, bony girl with ragged black hair, blue overalls, and a secure seat on her vicious, prancing horse.

When she attempted to draw up before the post-office, the beast flung her head about and leaped forward. Maudie Tom sawed economically but inexorably at the ugly, uplifted mouth.

"Stand, will you!" said Maudie Tom. "Hey, Bill!"

A man leaning against a building thrust his hat up from his eyes and looked at her. There was no friendliness between them—only recognition and a certain similarity of feature.

"They going to have the races again, ain't they?" called Maudie Tom, steady hands on the reins.

"Sure. What do you care?"

"When they going to have them?"

"Labor Day, of course."

"When's that?" persisted Maudie Tom. "You know I can't tell."

The man shifted his position and figured silently. Neither face had altered even faintly in expression.

"A week from Monday, that is," said the man.

Maudie Tom jerked on the reins. The horse had sagged in sleep and now awoke more irritable than ever. She reared slightly. Maudie Tom sat tight.

"How's Pa?" asked the man.

"Oh, he's all right," said Maudie Tom, laconically.

A group of girls walking with linked arms down the boardwalk watched her gallop away. "How she can ride!" one of them said.

"I always wonder what goes on inside her head," another added.

"Hasn't she a marvelous build, though!" said a third. "Sinewy as an Indian."

Maudie Tom had seen them from the corner of her eye, their crisp piqué dresses, their smooth hair knotted at their necks, but she did not know what they said of her. She only imagined, and imagining soon made her mouth grow hard with bitterness and sulking. She sat forward and urged her mount with a boot-heel sharp on a red hind quarter.

"We'll show them, you old fool of a horse," she growled, "come a week from Monday."

Fourteen years and a half ago, one December, Maudie Tom, the lighthouse keeper's daughter, had been born in the small, snugly built house on the island a half-mile off the coast. A storm raged at the time; the strip of water between the island and the mainland was too rough for doctors to cross. The mother died, but the baby lived, and was named Maudie Tom—nobody knew why.

She grew up on the island with her father and a lazy, surly brother who appeared occasionally, when no more convivial roof would shelter him. She drank goat's milk and ate hen's eggs; she ran in the sun and grew as big and strong as a boy. The room where she slept looked out on the water, across the path of the signal-light; she learned to trim the lamp herself. Fogs drifted in, storms blew out of the northeast. She heard distress signals, saw rocket flares, once made coffee for a rescued crew. Sometimes she lay all day on a shelf rock that nobody knew of but herself. Gray gulls dipped and soared; her fingers played with wet, dark-green seaweed; wind could not reach her; it grew warm, and she slept.

When she was nine, officials came to ask if she had been sent to school. She had not. The officials pursed their lips and shook their heads.

"She's got an aunt," her father said, "up to Portland. She can go up there to get her schooling. I been meaning to send her right along. A young one ain't much these days without an education."

But Maudie Tom was well past ten before she went, and then she stayed only two weeks. She did not like Portland. She could not find her way about; her aunt, and the teacher, too, had whipped her. She ran away home, and her father slapped her on the shoulder and they laughed together. When the officials came again, faintly sea-sick from their brief boat-ride across the choppy sea, her father said that Maudie Tom was fourteen. It was not true, but she was large for her age, and after a fourteenth birthday education was not compulsory in Maine. Maudie Tom had come back to the island, and she meant to stay. It was part of her, and she loved it as she loved no other thing.

Her father, in his glee, bought her a horse and built a stable for it beside their little boat-house on the mainland. Nearly every day when the weather was fine she rowed over, with short, rapid movements of her strong dark arms, and mounted Bess, to tear away through the village and up into the rocky, pine-covered hills, her hair blowing back in the wind, and salt water dripping off her boots. But she was not happy.

She was not happy because of the city people who came every summer. She saw perfumed women who looked to her like the brisk, neat little Portland teacher who had struck her with a ruler seven times on the hand. She saw men who lay, clean and smiling, on the sands, reading newspapers. Little children played games together— games that Maudie Tom had never played. But it seemed to her that more than half the people she saw in the village, summertimes, were girls of fourteen and fifteen. Even in the dead of winter, when storm winds rocked her bed, she could see the faces of the girls who came to the Cape in summer. Laughing, faces with small, sunburned noses and cool, appraising eyes. She could see their figures in bathing-suits, or in dresses that were sometimes rumpled but never soiled. She remembered the books and magazines old Aunt Maggie Dennis, from the fisher colony, found in their rooms when she cleaned the cottages at the end of the season. They had pictures, all of girls, and all beautiful. In the winter nights she thought of them.

"I hate them kids," thought Maudie Tom.

She did not hate them for being so different from herself, but only because of the opinion she imagined they had of her.

"They ain't so much," she told herself. "I can do a lot of things they can't. I'd like to see them ride a horse like me."

Two years ago the summer people had inaugurated the Labor Day races. Horses were bought and a community stable built. It was a friendly sport. Men practised on the beach before breakfast, advising one another, admiring all the mounts. There were two girl riders among them, one in a brown leather jacket and tweed knickers, the other in a scarlet jockey-suit with an absurd little visored cap. Maudie Tom had not gone across to town on the previous Labor Days, but she had seen the horses and their riders from her steps, where she sat ominously dour.

"I could beat them," jeered Maudie Tom, "even if Bess balked, the old fool of a horse."

This year she meant to try. It had taken a tremendous amount of self-persuasion, for she feared these summer visitors as much as she envied and hated them.

The horses came, and a fine, rich scent of well-kept horse-flesh made Bess lift her upper lip and prance and neigh.

"Never mind being so friendly," scolded Maudie Tom. "You've got them all to beat in the races!"

Now the poster had appeared, spattered with the heads of handsome horses and decorated with the complete outline of a beautiful bay mare at full stride, her neck stretched out in ecstasy of effort. It was time for the trial.

"You ain't got so much looks," said Maudie Tom, buckling a strap about Bess's head, "but looks ain't everything."

Still, she trimmed the mane and tail of her mount on Labor Day morning. She brushed the straight back, rubbed down the wide, veined flanks and bulging joints, and even tied a bit of dirty ribbon on the thick black forelock. Maudie Tom herself wore a clean dress from the store—a cheap little print with the wild, glaring figures usually seen in smocks, which became her wonderfully well.

It was a cool, bright, windy day. Maudie Tom and Bess went out into the sun together, down along the coast, through the town, and up to the beach where the races were held. Men already stood about with flags and pistols; other horses had arrived, stepping high with dainty legs, twitching pleasurably with every thunderous crash of rolling breakers.

"I want to get into the races," said Maudie Tom to a man who held an open book.

"You want—"

He broke off and stepped aside to address another man. Only members of the Jockey Club were expected for the races, but

Maudie Tom did not know this. Women and girls and children were approaching from all directions. The two girl jockeys, one in blue and white this year, and one in yellow leather, stared curiously.

"All right, miss," said the man of the note-book, returning. "Glad to have you. What's your name?"

"Maudie Tom."

"Maud— Well, what else?"

"I don't— Oh, Tibbetts."

"Maud Tibbetts. And the horse?"

"Huh?"

"The horse's name?"

"Bess."

"All right, Miss Tibbetts. We start the trial heats in about half an hour. I'll let you know when you're listed. Stand just over there, will you, Miss Tibbetts?"

The recurrence of "Miss Tibbetts" annoyed Maudie Tom. She sat, big and glowering, on the folded blanket which served her as a saddle. When the other two girl jockeys came up with proffered sugar, both horse and rider waited with suspicion. Maudie Tom did not speak, and Bess snapped at their fingers.

"Ouch," said the girl in blue and white. She smiled at Maudie Tom. "Unfriendly beast you have."

"Leave her alone; she's all right," growled Maudie Tom.

Inside her another prouder, more fiercely wretched voice was saying: "You can leave me alone, too. You needn't try to make out you're so much. I'm going to beat you!"

What she was thinking showed in her face. The girls drew away. "Whew!" exclaimed one. "Isn't she marvelous, though? What wouldn't Miss Kincaid make out of her if she had a chance? That girl's got stuff!" And the other said: "She's a lot of pluck to turn up here with that beast. She fascinates me." But Maudie Tom did not hear what they said. She only saw their incredulous, faintly injured faces, and the curls escaping under their caps.

A broad, white strip of hard sand, the race-track, divided the two streams of onlookers.

Nine horses were entered. The officials divided them into three groups for the trial heats, and Bess was number two of the first. A man with snow-white hair and pink cheeks pinned a great "2" on Maudie Tom's back. She headed Bess into line, her heart pounding under the huge flowers stamped on her dress. On one side of her was a grinning boy on a young sorrel horse, and on the other the leather-jacketed girl, riding a steed which looked as swift as ever Lochinvar's was. Both riders smiled at Maudie Tom and waved to friends on the side-lines, but Maudie Tom did not smile back and she had no friends to wave to. She crouched low on Bess's high, unlovely back.

The pistol cracked. The horses leaped forward. At the sound Bess had pawed the air in nervousness and bad temper, and set out a length behind the others. Her gait was awkward and gangling. She threw out her feet like brown spray to each side of her step. She kicked her hind left ankle with her right and left a trail of blood in the sand. The other horses ran swift and straight, tails lifted, manes flying, noses in the air. But the girl in yellow leather let her mount break from his smooth trot into a gallop, and so was disqualified. The

boy who grinned so engagingly was riding for the first time in a race; he did not know where to bear his weight or when to urge his horse. Maudie Tom rode like a part of Bess—two big, bony, untamed things together, the girl's face close to the corded red neck, her voice quick with unintelligible sounds, her boot-heel a sharp, firm pressure. The red horse beat the sorrel by half a length.

"Two!" yelled the judges in good-humored amazement. What of their blooded stables now.

"Good!" cried the boy.

"Splendid!" sang out the yellow-jacketed girl, cantering up. "What *riding!* Simply magnificent!"

Clapping ran along the lines. To the summer people these races added a charming interest to their last day. Having the picturesque daughter of the lighthouse keeper entered gave new color to a familiar excitement. They rather hoped she would win the finals, and they clapped and smiled encouragement.

Maudie Tom scarcely looked at them. She was now one of the three best. She had won the first race!

"You wait. I'll show you something yet," she told them under her breath. "You think you know it all."

Her heart thumped as if it would tear through her breast. She dismounted, led Bess far up the beach, and made her walk in the salt water, to cleanse the wounded ankle. The sound of other pistol-shots and more clapping reached them. When they returned, the girl in blue and white, on a coal-black mare, and a fat, little baldheaded man on a fiery gray horse, had won the two other races. They sat waiting, a Number One and a Number Two. Some one changed Maudie Tom's number to a "3."

"You got to do it," choked Maudie Tom. "You got it, you old fool of a horse! You got to win!"

But she could not win—it was absurd! Dusky Dart was four years old, daughter of His Majesty, and had done six furlongs in 1:15 many times. Gray Skies was a three year old with a pedigree that filled a pigeonhole. Bess was twenty, if a day—badly built, untrained, and nobody had ever dreamed of recording her parentage.

The pistol cracked—they were off! Maudie Tom rode as an eagle flies; her hair blew back, and her strong body held itself as light as a feather. But Dusky Dart went past and Gray Skies' tail flicked Bess's nose. The crowd roared, the breakers boiled and foamed, the tape broke—with Dusky Dart the winner, the blue-and-white girl on her back. Gray Skies had been a three-quarter length behind. Maudie Tom let Bess into a walk twenty paces back.

The white-haired, pink-faced man tied blue ribbons on Dusky Dart's mane and tail. Blue sky, blue water, blue ribbons, and laughter. Maudie Tom thought she could not bear it.

"Get up," she breathed in Bess's ear. "Get out of here before that leg goes lame. Get up!"

They galloped off together, as if making an escape. She heard hoofs behind, and urged Bess faster.

"Go on, you!"

But again Dusky Dart proved the better horse. The girl in blue and white overtook Maudie Tom and crossed before her, so that she had to stop.

"Where are you going?" she asked. She, too, had straight hair, but it was yellow, and her cheeks were soft. "You must come back and get your ribbon."

"Ribbon?" echoed Maudie Tom dully.

"Yes, the green one. Third prize, you know. Come on."

The girl in blue and white reached for Bess's rein and turned her around. They rode back together, side by side.

"I'm Carolyn Kincaid" the girl said. "I think you're marvelous. I'd give anything in the world if I could ride the way you do."

Maudie Tom lifted her head and looked full at Carolyn. Her eyes were asking. She did not think she could have heard rightly.

"You live over at the lighthouse, don't you?" asked the other.

Maudie Tom nodded.

"Do you stay there all the time?"

Maudie Tom nodded again.

"Because I'm going to live here with my aunt until at least November. I'm supposed to stay outdoors a lot. My aunt's a teacher, but she's taking a leave of absence. I wonder—you know, you don't have to say you will—but I wonder if you'd want to teach me more about riding while I'm here. Would you?"

Maudie Tom swallowed. She wanted to speak, but she could think of no words to use. Finally she nodded once more.

Carolyn bounced up and down in glee.

"Oh, good! And listen, will you take me over to the island some time?"

This time Maudie Tom managed, "Sure!"

"Really? What fun! Do you know, I'm beginning to be *glad* I'm staying. You must come and meet my aunt. About my riding-lessons —we'll want to pay you, of course. Or—is there anything you want to learn that we could teach you?"

"Teach me?" said Maudie Tom with a comical, confidential movement of her eyebrows. "I don't know anything!"

They reached the judges, and the white-haired man replaced Bess's dirty ribbon with crisp green ones. He stroked the thin old nose and spoke gently. Bess did not snap at him, but looked up softly out of wondering, chastened eyes.

Colt of Destiny

ALIDA MALKUS

PROLOGUE: *Part One*
The Feral Foal

IT was within the first two hours of their halt that it happened. The encampment was in its deepest sleep. The sentry had passed by, had noted that even the horses slept, had heard no sounds other than the snoring and stirring that arose from the bivouac of some two hundred and fifty men, and nearly as many animals.

Darkness, deep and beautiful, lay over the desert. In the blackness of the night sky the stars were magnificent; but none noted their splendor. One hundred bold cuirassed adventurers and their Indian guides slept the sleep of exhaustion.

For days they had plodded across the hot dry sands of this desert land of Tiguex, following Coronado's brave captain, the fair-bearded Don Pedro de Alvarado, in the daring and ill-fated expedition of this year of Our Lord 1540. They had found no water that day, and the heat had been intense. But now a light breeze drifted down from the mountains, rattling the dry lance of the Spanish saber, and chafing the mesquite branches with a gentle whisper. Less a breeze it seemed, than a moving in of cooler air, as the warm breath of day continued to rise from the heated sandy plain.

Yet it brought, however faintly, a hint of water, a promise of a thirst-quenching mountain pool, to the widened velvet nostrils of the Arab mare, Tamiri; a Quhaylah mare, Tamiri, brought all the way from the deserts of Arabia to this New World.

A sharp shudder passed over her. Instinct told her she must get away, up there in the hills that rose from the desert's edge, find the water for which she was in such desperate need, and find a place for the young that moved so strongly within her. Her time was coming; she would foal in a few hours.

And her young would never be able to keep up the pace of this train of humans. Instinct told her that also. What she could not know was that the foal would have been carried in a sling along the march by these same humans, until it was strong enough to run beside its dam. But if she did not have water she would not have milk. This, too, she knew through her deep, age-old wisdom.

Men appeared to have no thought for themselves, no need for rest or water. Her master, the boy she loved—he was a man. Often she had smelled the scent of deadly fatigue on the boy, and of fear, and she would stop, hoping that he would mount again—for he had spared her during the journey over the desert, and she had carried only her finely tooled saddle and blanket, while he had walked— and she felt the urge to carry him away to water and to rest.

She herself had been smelling water from time to time for the last twenty-four hours. But always the train pressed on, though no enemy pursued. Usually, like the other horses, she understood tacitly and accepted the will of her master, even though death might result.

But now the mare was concerned with life, and must flee death. She must escape. Yet here she was, tied to a deep-driven stake, the leather cord around her neck fastened tightly to it, while the boy clutched the tether in the middle. A sudden pain swept her; she had traveled far today. She pawed at the stake, as if to uproot it. Her teeth clenched upon its notched end, and gnawed upon it.

It was a hard, smooth-surfaced stake; but pain and fear as strong as thirst gave her added strength. Her teeth caught in the notch that held the cord. The wood splintered. She reared back and felt the tether yield.

Her teeth closed around the knotted circlet, trying to bite through it, to pull it off. It would move no further. In a sudden spasm she bit again at the side of the stake. Again it splintered, and tore her lip. The needlelike pain made her jerk back sharply, tossing up her head. Another piece of the stake was in her teeth, together with the knotted end of the rope. She dropped them on the ground, sniffing at the broken point of the stake which had hurt her, at the rope lying loose there, at her young master.

The boy Jaime lay with his face to the stars. It was at this moment that the sentry passed, observed the mare standing beside the young Otero, her head drooping above him. The soldier passed on. Gently Tamiri breathed on the boy's hand, on the clenched fingers. They opened, and the unconscious Jaime turned on his side, leaving the reata loose upon the ground.

In a moment she was gone, heading into the wind, down which there came again the whispering promise of water. Swiftly over the rising mesa—her feet, her very being, knew such country as this—and she was loping along the base of the foothills, following the cool air that poured from innumerable gullies leading down from the mountains.

Up one of these quebradas she finally turned, following its pebbly stream bed, twisting, turning, further and further. And up, until the sand was damp, then wet, and her short quick ears caught the drip, drip of water above. But there the way was blocked by a pile of rock. Slipping, scrambling, Tamiri won her way up the rugged slope to one side, and stepping delicately over the rocks came down to a tiny pool in the center of a level smooth place. Muzzle deep in the cool water, she drank; slowly, not too deeply.

Beside the pool was an overhanging ledge, beneath it the sand was still warm. Here she stopped.

With the rising sun, a strange and pretty sight would have been revealed had any been there to see. The golden sorrel stood nuzzling a lovely little creature that lay beside her on the warm sand, its wide dark eyes regarding with gentle curiosity the light of a new world. And well might that new world have regarded with wonder this first-born foal of Tamiri, the Arab mare—the first-born horse upon this land. For here, since millenniums long past, no horse had been foaled. Then, through Pleistocene ages, herds of prehistoric horses, short, big-headed and pot bellied, had roamed the Western plains.

The foal's long legs were folded beneath it, and though it panted slightly, its head was held strongly erect. It was of a pale creamy color, that blended with the sand of the grotto floor. Its lips were black, and so was the inside of its mouth as it yawned. When Tamiri had examined him carefully, from his small velvety ears to the wavy little plume of his tail, she turned her attention from her son to the cliffside, where the first green shoots of spring grew near the dripping rock.

She hobbled over, for she had hurt her foot on the rocks the night before, and pulled eagerly at them—ate and drank until her strength was restored. After a while she nudged her baby to its feet. The foal was hungry now, and somewhat weak. He struggled to keep his four legs at the proper angle. In a moment he found what he needed and bunted his mother happily.

Down on the desert a dust storm had blown up, shutting away the caravan train as it started slowly for the hills. Here the mare and her foal were above the dust clouds and the air was clear and sunny —an excellent place. Nothing could leap down from above upon Tamiri or her foal, sheltered by the ledge as they were; and the rocky wall surrounding this hidden spot was so steep and so smooth that not even a mountain lion could descend it. The only entrance was from below, by the path over which the mare had scrambled.

Water trickled down from melting snow high above, clear and delicious. She would remain right here until the foal was ready to venture forth and until her foot was healed. Here she felt secure; and in her delight in this foal Tamiri had temporarily forgotten her young master Jaime. But perhaps deep in her consciousness she half-expected him to find her, to appear in this hideaway at any moment. She would have been very happy, and proud, to display her foal.

She had really loved the boy Jaime Otero. She knew the very sound of his name. He had tended her carefully on the long march up across deserts and over mountain passes and along river beds, on the way from Mexico. He had walked beside her, had rubbed her down whenever they halted on the march, and would even have carried her saddle if that had been necessary.

The tall fair captain whom they called Alvarado, and others of the train, came often to see her and to admire her. She was prized and loved, and this she knew.

Now an impulse moved her to pick her way back down over the rocks. She did not descend into the narrow canyon bed up which she had come, but sought higher ground, climbing limpingly up to a cliff from which she could see out over the plain spread below.

The dust of the desert had settled, and far in the distance the mare could see the last of the horse train winding its way toward these very mountains. She lifted her head to catch the breeze, her nostrils widened, a low nicker rumbled in her throat, died away. She watched until the last horseman disappeared from view.

Then she turned and swiftly made her way back to her aerie. In a few moments she was once more nuzzling her foal.

Within her consciousness lay the impulse to follow the train—later on. But as the days passed this impulse faded, and her contentment grew. Here was water, green shoots along the waterway, the sun warmer each day, the nights less cold. In the black of the night she kept close to the rock under the ledge. By day the little foal drew strength from the sun, panting gently as he rested with feet folded under him, his crimpy tail flicking off an occasional insect. He might have been a part of the white rock and the creamy sand.

He stood up only when he wanted milk, which was frequently. By the end of the fourth day he was quite firm on his legs, if unexpected in his movements. When he was three weeks old it rained, a heavy downpour. The little fellow was standing out from under the ledge and was terrified. What was this? His mother pushed him in under their shelter and made him lie down close to her so that she could warm him from the sudden chill in that high air. Spring had come, nevertheless.

And with spring, danger stalked their hideaway. In the night the hideous scream of the mountain lion echoed down the canyon, hungry after the lean winter, baffled. For while it was true that no creature could either climb down or leap down upon them, yet their nearness frightened the foal, and Tamiri was nervous, ever on the alert.

She suspected dangers of which she had no real knowledge. And in the dark of the night, at times, she saw eyes peering down at her from the cliff top. Once a bear cub tumbled over a precipice into the canyon below their spring, and she smelled death. But before their paradise could be tainted, great birds came and carried the small creature away.

Tamiri did not want to leave the foal for long, even in this safe nook, but she was forced to descend farther and farther down the canyon in search of food. Favoring her foot, and stepping with caution, she would hobble over the stones, her small hoofs finding foothold where those of a heavier-footed horse would have slipped clumsily.

The desire to descend to the plains grew; they must have space to run. But the foal was six weeks old before she could coax him over the stones. The last few feet were a sheer jump.

This achieved, he trotted along beside her down the narrow, sandy bed; in the beginning he would not cross the rocky places. His tiny hoofs slipped on the rounded stones. But patiently the mare encouraged him. They must get down to where she could find graze.

All this time the leather reata had trailed from her neck. It was a great nuisance. Sometimes she bit at it for minutes on end, where it hung beneath her head. One day she stepped on the trailing thong, somehow it got caught between the rocks, and there she was, held fast.

Backing up to the end of the tether she reared suddenly, pulling it taut. It stretched, but did not break. Angry now, and determined to be rid of the thing, Tamiri plunged forward; the wretched reata snapped just below her neck, where she had been chewing at it and weakening it. After that she became used to having the throng around her throat and it stayed there for more than a year, until a stallion bit it off.

Now, free from the dragging tether, she led the wandering foal down to the plain below, a different place indeed, from the dry and dusty desert she had crossed weeks before. Little pools of water from a heavy rain during the night sparkled in the morning sun. The mesquite was fragrant with its dainty green leaves.

There was no sign of man, nor of other horses, no scent or tracks to remind her of the company she had left. And yet now memory stirred her strongly, and she turned back toward the mountain, looking for a way to cross. But there seemed in the shimmering light of day to be only a great blue barrier raised before her.

Yet it had been in this direction that the train, together with her young master and the others, had been headed. Not at last she missed him.

But Tamiri did not yet know this terrain, and she could not by instinct know which of the canyons might prove to be a pass. The way was hard for her baby when it led up over rock. So, while the foal grew stronger, they lived on the plain, though often at night they heard the howl of wolves. But grazing was plentiful, and during the rainy season there were always little pools to drink from, while the desert flowered with stretches of white poppies and bright cactus blooms. By night Tamiri chose low hollows where they bedded down, the mare watching while the foal slept.

She worked her way gradually along the skirts of the mountain until they came at last to the end of the spur. The rainy season had ended; summer was growing hot and dry. Now the desert was deep in powdered dust, for there had been no rain in days. Again she must find water. Instinct led her around the foothills, down across a mesa to the far green of trees, and the scent of a river. A wide and muddy river—she had found her way back to the valley of the Rio Grande.

Had she turned north she would have come upon the encampment of the Spanish, and she and her foal would undoubtedly have been discovered. But this was a good place, grass and plenty of water. The river was high.

Still swollen with the last rains in the mountains, there was a swift current and the sands were treacherous. But Tamiri and the colt, for he was no longer the unsure foal, remained along the banks in the golden-leafed cottonwood groves. The colt grew stronger and more beautiful. His mother paced him along the riverbank, paced him and raced him. He was six months old.

One day a Queres Indian boy from one of the pueblos saw them capering in the grove. He was fascinated. Here were two of these creatures about which the braves told in the kivas at night by the red firelight. Such animals had been brought into the land by the bearded white men, whom they carried upon their backs, running with the burden swift as the wind across the plains. His people had killed a number of these white men, and also their animals.

The boy was hunting. He was a good shot, and also he had a fine new bow and flint-tipped arrows. Now he fitted one to the bow and drew careful aim on the colt. It was too small yet to carry a man, but what a trophy! It would probably taste like deer, and how he would be praised. Then suddenly it occurred to him, and he held the arrow without letting it fly, this creature could grow, could carry a man like the wind; where a deer could not. Why kill him?

Keeping down wind, slipping behind trees and shrubbery, he crept carefully up on the mare and her colt, where they ran in the sun along the riverbank, stopping now and again to crop a special herb or leaf which the mare wished the colt to know and eat. But good a stalker as he was, the boy could not get near them. They frisked along, always just beyond. Had he only known it, Tamiri would have stopped, would have come forward, had she seen man standing still. She had not forgotten, and the rope, it still dangled from her neck, ready to grasp.

But at length the boy went away, back to his village. That night in the kiva he told what he had seen; some believed and some thought he was trying to gain importance. But one of the younger hunters of his clan said he too had seen such creatures with his own eyes in another valley. The white men who had come over the mountains in the spring of the year had brought many of them. He drew a picture of a horse on the kiva floor.

Yes, an old cacique nodded, that was the animal, the same he himself had seen when bearded white men came to the terraced town of Zuñi; the people of Zuñi had captured a number of these creatures and had slain them when they were unable to ride them. Some of the Acomans had captured several with their young unborn, that very summer, and had ridden them away in swift escape, never stopping. But the animals had died under them, and one had thrown its rider, and escaped. He thought none remained.

It was decided that before dawn next morning a party of hunters would go where the boy led. They would capture the mother and its young. Fate, however, kept the mare from such a destiny; for the red men were cruel to animals, being used only to wild creatures, which they hunted and killed for meat or slew as enemies. They would ride the mare to death, the young brave knew, and the colt too, long before it had its growth.

The young brave decided that he would go secretly to the encampment of the white men and tell them of the horse and her young. They had been kind to him, the white men, had given him a fine sharp knife and talked kindly to him through their Pima interpreters on the other side of the mountain. Now they were encamped up the valley, at a place which they called Bernalillo. It was thus that the Spaniards learned Tamiri had survived, and her colt with her.

At sundown on that same day Tamiri and the colt had stood at the river brink drinking. The river bed was by now half dry and only in the center did a swift current run, roiling up the yellow 'dobe soil. While Tamiri drank, her head down, the colt ventured out a bit too far, and stepping off suddenly into deep water, found himself struggling in the current and whickered in dismay.

The mare plunged instantly into the water, swam around beside him and tried to push him over and back to the bank they had just left. But the current was too swift, the weight of the mud-freighted water irresistible, and they were carried along with it. The colt struggled valiantly, encouraged by his mother's example. Tamiri saw that a spit of sand reached out into the winding channel ahead, within a few feet of the main current, although on the opposite side of the river.

Dropping back behind the colt, she guided him with her head toward the far shore. Some time later she shoved him, with a mighty effort, up onto a quaking bank. Their feet sank in, but they were able to gain the solid shore beyond. They were safe. And from a distant dune a roan stallion, whose graying flanks had once been a rich bay, watched the mare and her colt wind cautiously up between the hills.

Prologue: *Part Two*
The Roan Stallion

The torn ears of the old roan pricked forward, the claw-scarred hide quivered along his flanks, his nostrils dilated redly. He could not see well, but he could smell, and the breeze bore to him a scent which for long had not met his nostrils, accustomed only to the sun-drenched plains, or to the unwelcome stench of coyote or mountain lion.

A rumbling nicker vibrated in his chest. The mare kept steadily on. Restraining the wild scream which tore at his throat, the stallion plunged down the bluff on which he had been standing, sliding on rump and hocks to meet her. Tail high, he trotted briskly down the gully and emerged upon the river flats.

But where were the mare and her colt? He could not see them. They had disappeared. A screaming call broke from him as he wheeled, looking, then, now with nose to earth, now throwing up his head to test the air.

Tamiri had led the colt quickly away from the riverbank and had already taken refuge in a willow-filled wash. She heard the stallion scream, and left off nuzzling her colt. Wheeling in front of him, she faced outward; he was getting to the stage where, before too long, he would be in danger from a stallion.

The roan came plunging up the sandy arroyo; he stopped short opposite the clumps of willow and cottonwood where Tamiri hid and whinnied to her. But she would not come out, and if he had come any nearer she would have turned tail and let fly with her heels. Presently he stopped his high-tailing back and forth and waited meekly. All night they stayed in the scrub thicket, but with dawn Tamiri led the way back down out of the arroyo to the river to drink. The roan followed at a respectful distance. He knew very well his presence was unwelcome to a mare with a young colt.

But gradually the old stallion ventured closer; he grazed near them as they wandered south along the river valley. It was colder now at night. Autumn was coming. Frost lay in the blue shadows until the sun got around to them and dried it up. From the beginning Tamiri had taught the colt to remain wherever she left him, and this saved them all one crisp autumn day when the cream-colored colt napped in the sun in a hidden nest of dry grasses. As Tamiri grazed on the mesa above, suddenly the sound of pounding hoofs— for long they had not heard the sound of hoofs other than their own —came up from the plain, and two flying horses appeared, ridden bareback by two copper-skinned young hunters of the Pueblos.

The riders saw Tamiri and turned toward her. They rode madly, pressed their horses cruelly; having sighted Tamiri, they intended to capture her. But being down wind, she smelled the sweat of the lathered horses, and, filled with fear, stampeded, yet still would never have escaped among the winding gullies and ascending foot-hills if it had not been for the roan. He knew the country and herded her to a safe spot, hidden from view. The colt, at this stage, could never have kept up with them, and both he and Tamiri would have suffered capture. One of the horses ridden by the Pueblos was raced to its death.

Well after dark the roan led the way back down to where Tamiri had left her colt, and by the light of the moon he headed them both back to the foothills. In a sheltered canyon they found fresh pastures. The old stallion knew the canyon well. He knew the whole Jemez range country. One of a whole corral of horses driven off by the Zuñi when Coronado first reached their land almost a year ago, he had been ridden away bareback across desert and valley toward the mountains, following the mares willingly.

But he had repeatedly thrown the braves who mounted him, had killed one, so that finally they fled from him in terror. The red men would have killed him, but he escaped, his flanks torn with pursuing arrows, his heart with rage and hatred of the red men. Thereafter he lived a wild, precarious existence, largely in the hills, where the bear and the mountain lion stalked him, while on the plains the wolves and coyotes annoyed him in packs. He grew into a formidable

fighter who relied not solely on his speed but on his teeth and hoofs as well. His ears were torn with wild cat encounters, his flanks scarred with the furrows of bear claws. His temper was bitter and in his loneliness he grew both wiser and more vicious.

During the winter he had herded away a mare stolen away from Coronado by the people of the terraced town of Zuñi, and they had roamed mesa and valley, but in the spring she was heavy, and she had met her death, alone, in the quicksands along the river. The roan never knew what became of her, and all during the fall he kept returning to the river valley where, about midsummer, he had last seen her.

When he saw Tamiri, his delight could scarcely be expressed. He would stop and paw the ground before her, and whinny pleadingly. But it was not until her colt was attacked by a mountain lion, and the roan fought it off in a bitter battle, that Tamiri finally accepted him.

It happened thus. Cropping their way farther and farther up into the mountains, they reached a sheltered meadow, green as an emerald. Here they remained, making it their own. Tamiri continued the education of her son, pacing him round and round the meadow in the swinging, tireless stride that she herself had learned, tied to a camel in her own coltish days. Mother and son possessed an unusually deep affection for each other. Here, too, they were confident and at ease, while the roan grazed watchfully from a vantage point at one end of the little upland valley.

At sunrise one morning Tamiri led the way to the rockbound pool at the canyon's head, and she and the colt lowered their muzzles to drink the icy snow water. They had grown overconfident, for not far above them a great beast, long and tawny, crouched unseen among the rocks. The pale coat of the colt, his obvious youth, marked him to the mountain cat. The mother did not seem too formidable, and the hungry hunter had had no experience with such an animal—another kind of deer probably, without horns or antlers that could prod or pierce.

He crept noiselessly, belly-flat, over the rocks. Twitching from side to side as he made ready for the spring, he leaped down directly at the colt. At that instant Tamiri lifted her head, and as suddenly the colt raised his, and saw the moving shadow darken the stream, the shadow that was imminent death, and shied away from it with one of those sudden, awkward-seeming movements of a colt.

The lion missed, although one claw caught the youngster's velvety foreflank, leaving a scarlet wound from neck to foreleg. A scream of pained surprise broke from him; he stood trembling, rooted to the

spot as the lithe body sailed by. Tamiri plunged forward as the giant
cat crouched to spring again, while the terrified colt backed swiftly
away to the sheer wall inclosing the pool.

Rising up on her hind legs, Tamiri came down with close-planted
hoofs upon the lion's forequarters, but although the blow was a terrible one he turned like a streak of lightning and clawed her belly.
The mare's shrill neigh of pain and fear reached the roan stallion—
it had all happened in the few moments that he grazed with his
head in the other direction—and he came thundering down the
meadow.

Tamiri reared, pawing the air between the lion and the colt,
circling around the crouching creature, flailing at it, the punishment in her hoofs menacing enough to demand the lion's entire
attention, but not sufficiently so to stop it, and again it sprang. But
just as suddenly the stallion's hoofs came down with almost crushing
force on its back while the old roan's teeth tore into the lean, steel-
muscled flank.

The fight was now between the two, the veteran stallion, survivor
of many disciplining journeys and many fights, and the great cat, in
its predatory prime. The stallion was heavier, cleverer, and an experienced fighter, but the lion was lithe, could spring and cling, with
a murderous weapon in each claw. Blood stained the pale sand,
crimsoned the pool, the earth was torn up. The cat was of a sudden at
the roan's throat, and hung there, clawing at his belly with all four
feet, while the roan tore impotently at the neck of his assailant.

They would have fought to the death, of one or both, but now
Tamiri sprang forward, and whirling around let fly with her hind
hoofs and all her force at the lion's back. Again and again she kicked.
The lion could no longer endure the punishment; he let go, his ribs,
his back, broken. The enraged and bleeding stallion finished him
off, while Tamiri pushed the trembling colt away from the boxed-in
pool and into the safe center of the meadow, where she nosed him
all around and licked his wound.

The roan came slowly over the meadow to her, all the fight gone
out of him, and stood dejectedly before her, blood streaming from
his throat and belly. Timidly Tamiri approached him, her muzzle
touched his, she licked his wounds.

The roan was some time in recovering from the fight. They went
down from the high meadow and lived on the flanks of the foothills
where they could see for miles in every direction. But the roan had
learned to live in this wild country, while the red hunters he feared
had been avoided so successfully that they had never laid eyes on him

since his escape. Battle-scarred veteran that he was, the fire of his youth had not yet been quenched, and instead of going off alone into the hills to die when his time came, fate had led him forth to guide Tamiri and the colt.

They recovered from the fight quickly enough, although they too were to carry their scars to the end of their days. The colt was never to forget this introduction to the perils of their life. They spent the winter on the wide plains west of the river which the Spaniards called the Rio Grande. The roan knew this country too, and where to find pasture in the arid, painted desert lands.

By spring the colt was a handsome yearling, a tall, leggy creature, and Tamiri was carrying another foal. The roan guarded her devotedly, never letting her out of his sight, and continually edging between her and her first-born. The cream coat of the colt seemed almost silvery in the sun, as did his tail, which was now pluming out. He still lingered near his mother, and would race toward her from across the wide plains, nosing her affectionately and with whinnies of delight. As the months rolled by he was well on the way to becoming the splendid, full-grown animal of his prime, longer-legged than his dam, longer of barrel. His sire had been uncommonly tall for an Arab.

The lessons learned from the old roan were to stand him in good stead, and well it was that he had them, for now the roan, in a last burst of the fire of his youth, and with the bitter spirit of his lonely life, had grown jealous of the half-grown horse. The old stallion was snappish; his caution and his suspicion increased. He could no longer see nor run as well as he had before the fight with the mountain lion, which had seriously impaired his strength. But he had taught Tamiri and her son all he knew—how to sidestep the coiled rattlesnake and stamp him out, how to outwit a starveling, desperate pack of coyotes, how to avoid poisonous weeds when the spring rains first brought the deserts into bloom. Now he was losing his sense of smell, also, but more serious was the loss of sight. It was this which brought him to his end at last.

Tamiri had been striding over the mesas in the long steady camel trot of her youth, following the flashing plume of the two-year-old as it whisked in the sunlight across the plain. The colt could jump and took with ease ever wider arroyos as they came. Tamiri was never so good a jumper at any time, and racing up to the very edge of an arroyo she veered suddenly, shying from the leap, and went on down a slope by which she could detour around the jump.

The roan came heavily along behind her, but facing the sun as he was he could not see, and coming to the edge of the arroyo he plunged over. He fell on his head, breaking his neck, and died instantly. Tamiri mourned over him until sundown, but the colt avoided death. Thereafter he and his mother ranged alone. The Arab who had owned his mother would have claimed her offspring with pride; a white or cream stallion was ever to be desired in the desert, for he could not easily be seen against the sands.

The people of the terraced city on the rock, the Acomans, saw him racing across the desert below, however, and said it was the ghost of the horses of the Spaniards, the horses which their young men had stolen and ridden to death. Word traveled among the Pueblos, and was told half a century later, when finally the Acoma penol was won, and the sky city surrendered to the siege of the Spanish. The white horse the Acomans saw was "El Espiritu" of the horses and riders they had killed, indeed. And so the Pueblo people continued to call any white horse "El Espiritu," and to avoid it.

Tamiri's second foal saw the light that next spring. Up until almost the time of its coming, El Espiritu followed after his mother, until she drove him away, pushing him with her head, gently at first, and finally with an unmistakable kick. For the colt was now a grown horse; not fully grown, lean, but tall as he ever would be, a splendid two-year-old colt, an animal of unusual intelligence, speed, and beauty. The followers of Alvarado, who had heard of the cream-colored horse, looked up and down the river valley to try to find him. But the brave Alvarado himself was killed that summer of the year 1541, and the two friars left among the Zuñi by Coronado were killed also during the following year, and thereafter many years passed before the Spaniards ventured up into the land of the Pueblos again.

But meanwhile Tamiri's progeny flourished, finding the most fertile valleys, the best pastures. The settlers who years later came up into the valley of the Rio Grande and the Upper Pecos under de Sosa in the year 1591 heard of a band of wild horses and hunted for them. Yet, needing mounts as they did, no expedition ever succeeded in finding any. But whenever in the years that followed a mare foaled a creamy white colt, or a sorrel and cream piebald, it was attributed to the mysterious stallion.

For the story of the lost Tamiri and her foal was recalled by the Pueblos, and the tale told and retold. Truth to tell, El Espiritu ranged far and wide. As the years rolled on he gathered together a little band. His colts succeeded him, sometimes stealing a newcomer when more settlers came into the land, bringing with them more horseflesh. Bold and tireless, El Espiritu roamed the West until he died. He was seen, over the years, here, there, and five hundred miles distant. He became a legend.

Long before this, however, as the years passed, the Quhaylah mare had reached her thirty-fourth birthday. Thus it was that on a sultry late afternoon, just at sunset, a golden-colored mare was found standing just outside the walls of a mission in this New Mexico. Father Xavier approached her slowly, spoke softly. The mare was very shy, yet gentle. She was old, he saw, yet about to drop a colt. She had been a beautiful animal. Now he saw that she was hurt, and he led her beneath a stable roof and bedded her down on fresh wild hay. He gave her water, and she drank gratefully. During the night she whinnied several times and was answered by a distant neighing. The good brother had gladly started from his bed to tend this poor creature, a valuable animal, who had undoubtedly strayed from some one of Coronado's expeditions and become lost in the hills; or perhaps had been stolen.

The mare was breathing heavily as the night wore on. Hearing a horse's nicker just outside, Brother Xavier looked up and saw beyond the wall in the clear moonlight a spectral white horse trotting back and forth. The friar took a halter and went cautiously out. If he could catch this splendid creature, perhaps they could keep him here at the mission. It would be an acquisition of wealth and usefulness.

But the phantom horse trotted swiftly out of reach. After many futile attempts to approach him, Brother Xavier returned to the stable. He had spent more time than he realized, and now he found a newborn filly foal lying in the hay, a beautiful cream and sorrel piebald, golden-hued, like her dam, with black lips and nostrils. But Brother Xavier regarded her with sorrow; he would have to raise her on burro's milk, for her mother lay dead.

Brother Xavier was good with animals, but he could not have saved the mare, he thought, for she had indeed been sorely injured. She must have borne several foals in her lifetime.

Tamiri had indeed borne many, and they were to travel far, and serve both the red man and the white. As for El Espiritu, many a foal inherited the special stamina and intelligence drawn from Tamiri, as well as the ability to survive which the stallion had acquired in this New World.

Corkran of Clamstretch

JOHN BIGGS, JR.

THIS is a record of genius. I saw him for the first time as he lay beneath an apple tree, endeavoring by muscular twitchings of his upper lip to grab an apple which lay just beyond the reach of his long black nose. Indisputably it was a game which he played, and he ordered it by set rules of his own devising. It was fundamental that he could not move his body, but he might crane or stretch his neck to any impossible posture. I climbed the paddock fence, and moved the apple an inch toward him. He looked at me reproachfully, but seized it none the less, and devouring it with a single crunching bite, rose to his feet and proceeded inscrutably to stare.

He was a dumpy little horse, resembling a small fat businessman, and as soon to be suspected of immortal speed as a stockbroker of a sonnet. His torso was a rotund little barrel. From this his legs, heavy and muscular, stuck out at odd angles. A lean neck rose from the mass, and upon this was plastered a head, many sizes too large, which looked as if it had been thrown at him from a distance and had inadvertently stuck.

His gaze mellowed and he regarded me more leniently. A faint smile began to wreath his lips; the smile expanded to soundless tittering. At last, in looking at me he fairly laughed. This I considered impolite and told him so. He listened courteously, but made no comment other than raising a quizzical hoof. He walked around me and looked carefully at my reverse side. This satisfied him. He returned to the apple tree, yawned broadly, and lay down. Richard Thomas Corkran was at rest.

Tentatively I offered him apples, but his ennui was not to be dispelled. Finally, he slept the sleep of a good and honest horse. I retired to the fence lest I disturb the sacred slumbers.

Genius is an unutterable thing. It is a spark flying from no visible flame. It is an excitement of the soul; it is a terrific motivation. It is a vapor that splits the rock of reality.

Richard Thomas Corkran was a strange rhapsody of speed. He was without circumstance, without explanation. No great family had crossed a bar sinister upon his unknown escutcheon. His fathers were indistinguishable clods of work. At the time of his first race his sides were galled from plough harness. Literally he was self-made.

He was possessed of an iron will and intelligence. Consummately he understood his metier; never did his greatness overwhelm him. He remained unmoved, his attitude the epitome of a successful business. Yet he was capable of a cold and dignified fury. Always was it merited, but he worked himself to it, for he had found it to be an efficient symbol. A balanced quietness was his attitude upon the track, and from it he never deviated. He raced without the slightest enthusiasm or excitation. Icy imperturbability marked his technique—an imperturbability that was unaffected. From the tips of his tiny hoofs to his absurd head he was polite, both to his rivals, whom he scorned, and his attendants, whom he considered unworthy of notice, and this politeness proceeded from his conscious known superiority.

One thing of all things aroused his wrath, hot and sincere. He considered himself a free agent; any molestation of this right caused anger to boil within him. The hours of his business were those which he spent upon the track; at all other times he came and went as he pleased. He would permit no officious infringement upon his leisure. As to his racing, it was indomitably his own. He considered all human aid simply cooperation. If it became direction, no matter how tactfully suggested, he was done. He would not move a hoof toward the track's end. In his maiden race, a whip had been laid, solely as an incentive, upon his muscular little thighs. Richard Thomas Corkran had slid to a stop with stiffened forefeet and, without heat or expression, but with icy malevolence, had kicked his sulky to fragments of wood and steel. Thereafter his driver, by iron order, sat braced to the sulky, and with loose reins simply fulfilled the requirements of rule. The race and the trotting of it were solely Richard Thomas Corkran's.

It was five o'clock when they came to arouse him, and this partook of a stately, ordered ceremony. There were five men in all, and I presume that he would not have deigned to rise for less. Down the field in careful formation they advanced. First came the head trainer, magnificently unencumbered by blanket, sponge, or currycomb, the veritable master of the bed-chamber, and flanking him, his subalterns, two graceful yellow boys—this touch exotic—carrying combs and skin-brushes; next came two buckets, marked with the white initials R.T.C., and then his *own* blanket, plaid-striped, refulgent, the one slight vulgarity necessary to all genius. Last of all was a small white dog, like an animated washrag, propelling itself forward with staccato bounds and barks.

The process halted; the dog continued forward, and barked malevolently in the ear of recumbent greatness, which responded with a slow opening of its left eye. The long thin neck rose from the ground at a right angle and surveyed the halted host. Richard Thomas Corkran got to his feet and shook his rotund little body. He stood waiting.

As they combed and brushed him, he moved no muscle, but placidly chewed a succession of straws that hung pendulous from his lower lip. It was a gesture nonchalant. At length his black coat was sleeked and glossed. The head trainer stepped forward and felt his chest, his hocks, and pasterns. This he endured with kindness, and inspection over, trotted toward the watering trough, preceded, however, by the white dog. Pleasurably he played with the water, drinking but little. He blew through his nostrils, causing white bubbles to rise and burst through the turmoil of the surface. The light, finely made racing harness was then put upon him and adjusted perfectly to each of his expanding muscles, and last the blanket, strapped and belted, making him look like a fat plaid-cowled monk. The gate was now opened, and he walked gravely from the paddock. Behind him streamed his acolytes in meek procession. Heralding him was the wooly dog. Last was his sulky, wheeled by a Negro boy. Past the judge's house he plodded, and I saw the old jurist rise from the porch to greet him.

The discovery of Richard Thomas Corkran, and his relation to Judge Coleman, a famous county story, deserves record.

At dusk one summer evening Judge Coleman, exercising a favorite mare, herself of note, had, on the Clamstretch, come upon a son of a neighboring farmer, atop the height of an old-fashioned racing sulky, a wooden affair with high shaking wheels. Beneath this relic, for the sulky jutted out almost over his rump, careened an odd little horse, looking in the darkness, so says the judge, like a small, black mouse.

"I'll race you, Tommy," said the judge jokingly to the boy.

"Done," was the reply, and the little horse moved up to the mare's nose.

"Take a handicap, Tommy," said the judge, amused by the boy's confidence.

"*You* take the handicap, Judge," said the boy, and the judge, fearful of hurting the boy's feelings, walked his mare some ten yards to the front.

"*Now!*" shouted the boy, and the judge heard with amazement the strong, unbelievably quick beat of the little horse's hoofs as he struck to his stride through the white dust of the road. Past the striving mare he went as if she were haltered to the ground. Three times was this astounding performance repeated, while the straining nostrils of the mare grew red with effort.

The judge pulled to the side of the road.

"What do you use that horse for?" he asked.

"For ploughin'," replied the boy, and he was near tears with pride and rage. "I have to use him for ploughin'."

"What do you call him?" went on the judge.

"Richard Thomas Corkran," replied the boy. "After grandpop."

Then and there, for an adequate price, Richard Thomas Corkran changed hands, and the judge that night, examining him by the light of a stable-lantern, discovered the marks of plough-galls upon his flanks.

No attempt was made to teach R.T.C. to race; none was ever needed. When the time came for a race he plodded to the track, and from thence to the starting point, and thereafter at some time favorable to himself he commenced to trot. No agitation of spectators or contesting horses, no jockeying of driver might shake his icy imperturbability, his utter calm. The race done and won, he returned at a walk to his paddock. In two years upon the Grand Circuit he had never missed a meeting nor ever lost a race.

With something of awe I watched him as he passed between the high stone posts of the judge's entrance gate and entered the Clamstretch.

This road is a long white ribbon which runs from the Porter Ferry to the hills. Its crown is covered with clamshells beaten to a soft imponderable dust, and from this it is known as the Clamstretch. It is agreed by county racing authorities that from the centre of the ferry gate to the old Weldin Oak is a perfect half mile, and a horse that covers that distance under two minutes is worthy of notice. Richard Thomas Corkran, when the humor was upon him, had trotted the exact half mile in one minute and five seconds.

It is a county saying that colts the day they are born are instructed by their mother mares in the trotting of the Clamstretch.

Beneath the old Weldin Oak and lining the road are rough wooden benches, and before them the ground had been worn bare and hard by many feet. At the side of the road sways a decrepit whitewashed stand, as high as a man's chest and with two cracker-boxes for steps. This is the official stand of the judge of the course when such a formality is necessary.

The customs of the Clamstretch have grown up with time, and are as unbending as bronze. It is decreed that Judge Coleman shall be the ruling authority of the meeting, that the time of trotting shall be from twilight to darkness, and that there shall be as much racing as the light permits.

First the horsemen gather and solemnly trot practice heats, each driver carefully keeping his animal from showing its true worth, though the exact record of each is known to all. Then with stable boys at the horses' heads, they collect in little groups about the oak, and with tobacco, portentous silences, and great gravity lay careful bets. But with the entrance of the judge comes drama.

He minces across the bare space before the oak and nods gravely to each friend. From an interior pocket of his immaculate gray coat he draws a small black book, the official record of the Clamstretch. In this book he enters the contesting horses, the names of the owners, and the bets. This finished, the four horsemen selected for the first race pass to the road, briefly inspect their gear, climb to the sulkies, sit magnificently upon the outstretched tails of their horses, and with whips at point, drive slowly toward the gate of the ferry lodge.

The noise of the hoofs dies to abrupt silence as the contestants jockey for position at the start, broken by the sudden thunder of the race. Puffs of white dust, hanging low over the road, rise beneath the drumming hooffs; strained red nostrils flash across the finish. Comes the stentorian voice of the announcer, giving the winner and the time. Gradually the soft light fades; the last race is ended; the judge bids the company a grave good night, and the red point of his cigar disappears in the gloom of the meadow.

There are many names great in the history of racing, whose owners have trotted the broad white road and have been duly inscribed in the black book. From Barnett and Barnetta B., from Almanzer and the Bohemia Girl forever from R.T.C., the time of the Clamstretch is set, and it is a point of honor between horse and man that when a great king falls he is brought back to trot his last from the lodge gate to the Weldin Oak. From Clamstretch to Clamstretch, is the saying.

I have often witnessed the custom of the Clamstretch, and this time

I entered upon it inconspicuously in the magnificent wake of Richard Thomas Corkran. Upon the bare meadow, around the old oak as a nucleus, were gathered many horses. A wild roan mare led the group, a young untried creature, who kicked and squealed in a nervousness that turned from sudden anger to helpless quaking. A Negro at her head, a shining black hand upon her bit, soothed and quieted her with honey upon his tongue and a sturdy desire to thump her in his heart. Her owner, a bewhiskered farmer, stood just beyond the range of her flying heels and looked at her with dismay.

"Now, pettie," he kept saying. "Now, pettie, that ain't no way to behave. That ain't no way."

A hilarious group of friends, in a half circle behind him, ridiculed his attempts at reconciliation.

"She ain't your pettie," they shouted. "She's some other feller's. . . . Maybe she ain't got none at all. . . . Give her hell, Jim. . . . Soft stuff's no dope."

A large horse, piebald and pretty, looking as if he had been purchased in a toy store, stood next to the virago. Her nervousness was apparently communicated to him, for occasionally he would back and rear. At these times, he raised clouds of dust, which sifted gently over the field, causing a shiver to run down the line of waiting horses.

"Keep 'em horses still," shouted the Negro boys. "Hold onto 'em."

One giant black, a colossal hand upon the muzzle of his horse, a mare as dainty and graceful as a fawn, threw out his great chest with pride.

"My lady's a lady," he crooned softly as the other horses stamped and grew restive. "My lady's a lady." The pretty creature looked at him with wide brown eyes, and shook her head as if softly denying.

An animal at the end of the line held my attention. His hide was the color of running bronze. His head might have been struck for one of the horses of Time, the nostrils flaring and intense, the eyes wild with hint of action. He looked as if he might run with the whirlwind, be bitted to a comet's orbit, and triumph. Sacrilege, it seemed, when I learned that he had never won a race, was quite lacking in the heart that creates a great horse. In him nature was superbly bluffing.

Richard Thomas Corkran stood at some distance from the rank and file. Boredom was unutterably upon him. He seemed looking for a place to lie down and continue his interrupted slumbers, and to be restrained only by the fear that he might be considered *gauche*. Truly there was nothing in which he might be honestly interested. No horse present could give him even the beginnings of a race.

His heaviest work had been done upon the grand circuit in the spring
and early summer. Vacation and leisure possessed him for this day
at least. True, upon the next day he was to trot a race which was,
perhaps, the most important of his career. Now, through the courtesy of the judge, he was the *pièce de résistance,* the staple, of the
evening. At the end of the racing he would trot a heat in solitary
grandeur—one heat, not more, and this heat would be preparation for tomorrow's test. Two horses, strategically placed over the
straight half mile, would pace him, but they would have as little to
do with his trotting as the distance posts upon the track. A little knot
of men, gaping and solemn, had already gathered about him, inter-
preting his every bored motion as proof positive of his phenomenal
speed. He accepted this as his due and was in no manner affected
by it.

The men, as always, interested me. A few were professional
horsemen, so marked and moulded. They were calm persons, who
spoke without gesture or facial expression. Thought flowed soundlessly behind their shrewd eyes. Their attitude was one of continual
weighing and balancing of mighty points.

The rest were prosperous farmers, country gentlemen, or honest
artisans from the nearby village, all pleasure-bent. The regalia of
those who were to drive, or hoped to drive, was unique. They
seemed to express their personalities best through high black boots,
striped trousers, and flaming calico shirts. The climacteric pinnacle
was usually reached with an inherited racing cap, scarlet, ochre,
brown, yellow, plaid.

Twilight cupped the world, seeming to grant a hush to earth.
The road took on a new whiteness, the meadow gradually darken-
ing, touched by the night and the brooding quietness that comes
as the sun goes down.

The first race came to a close—a torrent of young horses. The wild-
eyed virago was among them, and she won by a prodigious stretching
of the neck. Thereat, totally unable to withstand triumph, she
bucked and squealed, dragging her sulky, that tormenting appendage,
behind her.

"Shure, it's temperamental she is," said a Scotch-Irish farmer
standing beside me. "But she might have walked in on her hands and
won."

The spectacle was dramatic. There was a flurry of horse and man
as a race was called, a rushing to the track's edge by the spectators,
a happy bustling of self-important officials. From the knots of excited humanity emerged the horses, the drivers with their whips at
trail beneath their elbows, their eyes self-consciously upon the

ground. Slender sulkies, goassamer-wheeled, were pulled out, tested by heavy thumpings, and attached. Carefully the reins were bitted, run back through the guide-rings, and the drivers swung themselves up. The final touch was the arranging of the horse's tail, and here technique differed. A good driver must sit upon his horse's tail. This is beyond question. The mooted point is whether he shall do so spread or flat. Authority as usual holds both sides. Richard Thomas Corkran absolutely dissenting, for he would allow no one to sit on his tail but himself.

The horses dwindle to specks upon the long white road. The sound of hoofs dies to faint pulsing in the ears, a shadow of sound. Silence follows, breathless, expectant, broken by the clarion of the start.

The rhythm becomes a rhapsody of pounding hoofs, quick-timed, staccato. A black swirl up the road falls to detail of straining bodies. A roar crescendos to high shreds of sound as they flash across the finish. A second of tense silence—pandemonium.

Three races of three heats each were trotted. Darkness was drifting down upon us as the last was finished, and Richard Thomas Corkran walked out upon the track.

His small black body blent with the semidarkness, rendering him almost indistinguishable. The crowd followed him across the track. There was no preparation, no ceremony. The small figure plodded into the graying distance. His pace was scarcely above a walk. He might have been a plough-horse returning from a day of labor. The spectators drew back to the road's edge.

The twilight deepened. We waited in silence. A faint drum of hoofs sounded down the wind. Sharper, swifter, it grew. A black line split the darkness, lengthening so quickly as to vanquish eyesight. There was an incredible twinkling of legs as he passed me, a glimpse of square-set methodical shoulders, which moved with the drive of pistons, of a free-floating tail spread to the rushing scythe of air. He finished.

Carefully he stopped, not too sharply lest he strain himself. He turned and plodded toward the oak, where hung his blanket, and as its folds fell upon him he returned to peaceful contemplation.

Came the voice of the announcer, a hoarse bellow through the gloom—"*Ti-i-me by the ha-a-alf. O-o-one-five-an'-two-fi-i-ifths!!*" A roar of applause broke to scattered clapping. Relaxation from the tension expressed itself in laughter, jest, and play. The crowd prepared to go home. The Clamstretch was for that day done.

After dinner Judge Coleman, whose guest I was, and myself walked down the close-cropped green to the paddock fence. A moon had risen, bathing the land in clear pale yellow. Within the paddock and beneath his apple tree lay Richard Thomas Corkran. He rested upon his side, his small torso rising and falling gently with the even flow of his breath. From his upper lip protruded a straw which moved gently as the air was expelled from his nostrils. Untroubled by thoughts of tomorrow's race, he was again sound asleep.

The next morning I saw him leave his paddock for the fair grounds. A large truck, whose side just disclosed the upper edge of his rotund, barrelled little body, held him, his three attendants, and his staccato, white and woolly dog. His placid eye fell upon me as he passed, and I saluted and followed him.

The site of the State Fair was a great fenced field upon the outskirts of a nearby city. Upon one side towered a huge grandstand, facing a broad and dusty half-mile track. In the gigantic oval, thus formed, was a smaller ring, tanbarked and barricaded, used at times as a horse-show ring, across a corner of which was now built a small, precarious wooden platform, where vaudeville teams disported themselves in a bedlam of sound for the free edification of the multitude.

On the outside of the oval of track stretched the Midway, in parlance "Mighty," a herd of tents and rough-board shacks, a staggering line, running to a quiet Negro graveyard, overgrown with yellow grass and flecked with the gray of forgotten tombstones.

Toward the city in larger tents and squat, unsided buildings were the farming exhibits, and between these and the outer road the racing stables, flanking a hard-beaten square, in whose center leaned a rusty pump, dry for years and used as a hitching post. Beyond, in a multiplicity of stalls and sties and bins, uncovered to the air, were huge and blooded bulls, monster hogs, and high-crowing, cackling fowl.

Over the wide field hung a haze of dust that stung the nostrils and soaked into the skin, causing a gray change.

I entered through a choked gate into which people streamed as a river banks against a bulwark, a confusion of carriages and cars, walking women with toddling children, red and blue balloons swaying between the ground and the gateposts, flying bits of straw and dust, howling hawkers: a high-pitched excitation of mob.

As I passed through the wooden arch came the sleek backs of racing-horses, surging toward the eight's posts, and the wild foreground of waving arms as the spectators beat against the rail.

The crowd was a sluggish, slow-moving monster that proceeded with sudden aimless stoppings. It was impossible to change or alter its spasmodic pace. It rippled into every corner of the field; it ran over fences and beat down barricades. It possessed an attribute of quicksilver in that it could never be gathered or held.

Its sound was a great crushing. It winnowed the grass beneath its feet, and the beaten odor came freshly to my nostrils. It surged over itself and spun slowly back. It never seemed to break or detach itself into individuals. Its tentacles might loop and cling to various protuberances, but its black bulk moved ever on.

I wandered through the maze of exhibits, stopping and listening where I would. The broad river of crowd divided to smaller eddies that swirled endlessly within and between the long rows of building and tents.

I passed glittering rows of farming machinery, red-painted, sturdy, clawed feet hooked into the ground. This bushy-bearded farmers tenderly fingered, and fought bitingly and ungrammatically with one another as to its merits.

A small tractor crawled upon its belly through the mud, and struggled and puffed its way over impossible obstacles. It was followed by

a hysterical herd of small boys, who miraculously escaped destruction under its iron treads.

I crossed the square where the lean, cowled racing-horses were led patiently back and forth by the stable boys. Always the crowd was with me, beating its endless, monotonous forward path. I grew to hate it, longed to tear apart its slow viscosity, to sweep it away and clear the earth.

Inside the buildings I passed between endless counters piled high with pyramids of jelly, saw the broad smiles of the presiding housewives, smelt brown loaves of prize bread. Baskets of huge fruit were allotted place, red apples succulent and glowing, fuzzy peaches white and yellow. The presiding deity of the place—the veritable mother of all food—I found in the center of the shack. Her function was the creation of pie, and this of itself seemed to me sufficient. She was a large woman, red-faced, red-handed, and without a curve to her body. She was composed of but two straight lines, and between these lay her solid ample self. Her round fat arms were bare to the

elbow and white with flour. On the table before her was an incalcu-
lable area of pie crust, which she kneaded and powdered and cut with
deft and stubby fingers. Behind her was a huge charcoal range upon
which uncountable pies cooked, and around her were infinite bat-
talions of pies, tremendous legions of pies, gigantic field-armies of
pies. Exaggeration itself fell faint.

Before her, in the consummation of a new miracle, fed the multitude. All men they were, and they ate steadily, unemotionally, as if
they might eat eternally. They went from pie to pie to pie. They
never ceased, even to wipe their lips. They never stopped to speak.
They selected their next pie before they had eaten their last, and
reached for it automatically. It was a spectacle so vast as to possess
grandeur. Such a woman and such men might have created the world
and devoured it in a day.

Around the eaters stood their wives—certainly none could have
dared be sweethearts—gaping with that curious feminine lack of understanding—awed but unreasonable—at such prodigies of feeding.

I came next upon monster hogs, buried deep in the straw. Grunt-
ingly they lifted their battleship bulks and waddled to the walls of
the pen in response to the pointed sticks of small boys. The air was
permeated with animal odor, occasionally split by the fresh smell of
cooking pastry and pungent aromatic spices.

With the Midway, sturdy respectability changed to blowsy, tar-
nished sin. Gaudy placards in primal colors bellied with the wind.
All appeal was sensual, to grotesquerie or chance. From the tent of
the "Circassian Syrian Dancing Girls" came the beat of a tom-tom,
like that of a heavy pulse. Squarely in the passageway a three-shell
merchant had placed his light table and was busily at work.

"Step up, ladies!" he called. "Step up, gents. Th' li'l pea against
the world! Match it an' y' win! You take a chance every day. When
yer born you take a chance, when you marry you take a chance,
when you die you take an awful chance. Match me! Match me!
Match me!"

His fingers moved like the dartings of a snake's tongue. The tiny
pea appeared and disappeared.

"You lost! Poor girl. She lost her quarter. The Lord knows how
she got it. Time tells an' you ain't old yet . . . !"

Beyond, outside a larger tent, sat a mountainous woman, a tiny
fringed ballet skirt overhanging her mammoth legs. She was like some
giant jellied organism. To the crowd which gapingly surrounded her
she addressed a continual tittering monologue.

"Step up here, baby. . . . Come up, lady! No, I ain't particular
even if I am fat. . . . I don't care who looks at me. I'm a lady, I am.

Hell, yes! See that man over there?" She swung a monster finger toward a barker. "He keeps me up here. . . . Sure, he does! You jest let me down an' at him—I'll do him in—I can make twelve of him!"

Further on the crowd clustered thickly around a small tank, from the end of which rose a tall ladder topped by a tiny platform. So high was the ladder that it seemed to melt into a single line. As I watched, a young man climbed upon the edge of the tank. He grimaced and bowed to the crowd.

He stripped off a beflowered green bathrobe, disclosing a body as sleek as a wet seal's, and like a slender black monkey, climbed the ladder. Reaching the platform, he posed with outstretched arms. The crowd stiffly craned their necks.

At the side of the tank appeared another man with a flat, pock-marked face. There ensued an extraordinary dialogue.

"Leopold Benofoski!" shouted the man beside the tank to him in the air. "Is there any last word that you would like to leave your wife and family?"

"No," shouted the man upon the platform.

"Leopold Benofoski!" shouted the interlocutor. "Are you pre-pared to meet your fate?"

"Yes," said the young man.

"Then dive!" shouted the other. "—And God be with you!" He hid his face with a prodigious gesture of despair.

The young man drew back his arms until he was like a tightened bow. For a second he poised upon tensed legs, then, like a plummet, dropped from the edge of the platform. Incredibly, swiftly he flashed down. I caught the glint of his white legs as he hit the water, a high splash, and he had drawn himself out of the other side. A grimace of shining teeth, and he was gone. The crowd, unmoved, went sluggishly on.

Slowly I worked myself through the area before the grandstand, where the crowd was thickest. There had been an accident upon the track: a young horse, "breaking" because of the hard path worn in the finely combed dirt between the turnstiles of the fence and the grandstand, had reared and flung its forelegs into the air. A debacle had followed as the animals close in the ruck had plunged into the leader. Three drivers had been thrown into a thresh of horses. Splin-tered sulkies and broken shafts lay in the debris, hazed by the cloud of dust. One horse, maddened with fear, had run squealing on, not to be stopped until it had completed the mile. One driver was badly injured.

This had had its effect on the crowd. An uneasy ripple ran across the grandstand. There was a tinge of hysteria in the movement, a desire to clutch and shiver. As time passed, the tension heightened. In the official's stand I saw the small, staid figure of the judge, peering alertly at the frightened multitude. Then came a consultation of bent heads, and his hand swung up to the cord of the starting bell. The flat clang, for the bell was muffled, beat into the turbulence. A gradual quiet fell.

There followed the announcement of the curtailment of the program to the immediate race of Richard Thomas Corkran.

I cut my way swiftly through the crowd, back to the stables, for I desired to see the little horse leave the paddock.

I found him firmly braced up on stocky legs as they bound his anklets. His refulgent blanket drooped over his rotund torso, and from the striped folds emerged the long, grotesque neck and the absurd hobbyhorse head. As I approached he eyed me with droll appreciation, for I seemed always subtly to please him.

As the last anklet was buckled he shook himself. It was methodical testing to see that he was entirely in place. Satisfied, he took a few short steps forward, carefully balancing his weight so that no muscle might be strained. At this juncture the white dog, apparently just released from captivity, bounced forward like a lively rubber ball. Fierce was his attack upon the nose of Richard Thomas Corkran. Devious were his advancings and retreatings. Quietly did the little horse receive this adulation. Again he shook himself.

Now was the spider-web tracery of harness put upon him, the silvered racing-bridle and the long thin bit. The blanket readjusted, the paddock-gate was opened, and with the small, white dog surging before him, his attendants following, he plodded toward the arena.

As he emerged into the crowd there beat upon him a roar of sound. Like a great wave it ran down the field and re-echoed back. Through the path that opened out before him he slowly went, unnoticing and grave. He entered the weighing ring.

Courteously he stood as his blanket was removed, and he stood bared to the gaze of the three inspecting officials. Then the slender spider-wheeled sulky was pulled up and attached. Suddenly I saw his head lift: the contesting horse had entered the arena.

He was like a legged arrow, a magnificent, straight-lined dart. Thin to the point of emanciation, the bones of his body moved like supple reeds beneath a lustrous skin. Lightly muscled was he, tenuous skeins at his wrists and hocks. He looked as if he might drift before the wind.

He was very nervous. There was a continual thin white line across his nostrils as his high chest took air. A rippling shiver ran through him.

Richard Thomas Corkran was the first to leave the ring. Never had he taken his eyes from his opponent. His small, black muzzle remained fixed, imperturbable. Slowly he plodded out upon the track.

The flat sound of the bell, calling the race, drifted down from above my head. As I fought my way to the rail, the roar of the crowd rose to frenzy. The horses were going by the official's stand to the starting post.

The challenger went first, his curved neck pulling against the bit, his gait a drifting, a slithering stride. After him came Richard Thomas Corkran, a tiny, methodical figure. His head was down. I could see the sulky move gently forward under his easy step.

As they reached the post and turned, the tumult died away to a clear and appalling silence. Glancing up the rail, I saw the heads of the crowd leaning forward in motionless expectation.

For an instant they hung unmoving at the post. Then the challenger seemed to lift himself in the air, his forefeet struck out in the beginning of his stride, for Richard Thomas Corkran, without warning, had begun to *trot*.

They swept down toward the thin steel wire that overhung the track at the start. In breathless silence they passed, and I heard the shouted—"*Go!*"

Like a dream of immeasurable transiency, they vanished at the turn. I heard the staccato beat of hoofs as they went down the backstretch.

The crowd had turned. To the rail beside me leaped a man, balancing himself like a bird.

"He's ahead!" he shouted wildly. "He's ahead!—ahead!"

I swept him from the fence and climbed upon it myself. Above the bodies of the crowd at the far side of the track I saw two plunging heads. For a second only were they visible. Again they vanished.

They came down the stretch in silence, the spectators standing as though struck into stone. At the three-eights post they seemed to be equal, but as they drew down the track I saw that the challenger led by a fraction of a foot. His flying hoofs seemed never to strike the ground. He was like some advancing shadow of incredible swiftness.

Richard Thomas Corkran raced with all that was in him. His small legs moved like pistons in perfected cadence.

As the challenger passed I could hear the talking of the driver, low-pitched, tense, driving his horse to a frenzy of effort.

"Boy! Boy! Boy! Let him have it! Let him have it! Take it from him. I'm tellin' you. Go it! Go it! Go it!"

Richard Thomas Corkran's driver sat braced to his sulky, the reins loose upon the horse's back. I caught a glimpse of his grim, strained face above the dust of the advance.

Again there was the wild beating of hoofs up the back of the track. "He's gotta do it now. He can't lose! He can't lose!"

At the seven-eighths post the crowd thrust out its arms and began to implore. The waving arms leaped down with the striving horses. The challenger was ahead by yards. His red nostrils flared to the wind. Never had I seen such trotting!

He came under the wire in a great plunge, his driver madly whipping him. Richard Thomas Corkran was defeated!

For seconds the crowd hung mute, seemingly afraid to move or speak. Then from the edge of the grandstand came a single shout. It grew and ran around the field, swelling to an uninterrupted roar that seemed to split itself against the heavens—a tribute to the victor, a greater tribute to the vanquished!

Richard Thomas Corkran plodded slowly around the track to the paddock gates. His head was down as before, and his rotund little body moved steadily onward. At the gates he halted and waited as the winner was led through before him. Then he gravely followed and disappeared into the crowd.

He had met triumph with boredom; he met defeat, as a great gentleman should, with quiet courtesy and good humor. There was nothing of disdain or bitterness upon his small, black muzzle; Richard Thomas Corkran passed to the gods of horse as he had come, imperturbable, alert, sublimely sensible. But in his passing his tiny hoofs were shod with drama. Departing greatness may ask no more!

I saw him later in the paddock. His white, woolly dog was stilled; a Negro rubber sobbed as he held a washing bucket. The little horse stood by himself, his feet as ever firm upon the ground, untouched, unmoved, and quietly resting. The thoughts that he possessed he kept, as always, to himself. I bowed my head and turned away.

The Pacing Mustang

ERNEST THOMPSON SETON

Jo CALONE threw down his saddle on the dusty ground, turned his horses loose, and went clanking into the ranch-house.

"Nigh about chuck time?" he asked.

"Seventeen minutes," said the cook glancing at the Waterbury, with the air of a train-starter, though this show of precision had never yet been justifid by events.

"How's things on the Perico?" said Jo's pard.

"Hotter'n hinges," said Jo. "Cattle seem O.K.; lots of calves.

"I seen that bunch o' mustangs that waters at Antelope Springs; couple o' colts along; one little dark one, a fair dandy; a born pacer. I run them a mile or two, and he led the bunch, an' never broke his pace. Cut loose, an' pushed them jest for fun, an' darned if I could make him break."

"You didn't have no reefreshments along?" said Scarth, incredulously.

"That's all right, Scarth. You had to crawl on our last bet, an' you'll get another chance soon as you're man enough."

"Chuck," shouted the cook, and the subject was dropped. Next day the scene of the roundup was changed, and the mustangs were forgotten.

A year later the same corner of New Mexico was worked over by the roundup, and again the mustang bunch was seen. The dark colt was now a black yearling, with thin, clean legs and glossy flanks; and more than one of the boys saw with his own eyes this oddity—the mustang was a born pacer.

Jo was along, and the idea now struck him that that colt was worth having. To an Easterner this thought may not seem startling or

367

original, but in the West, where an unbroken horse is worth $5, and where an ordinary saddle-horse is worth $15 or $20, the idea of a wild mustang being desirable property does not occur to the average cowboy, for mustangs are hard to catch, and when caught are merely wild animal prisoners, perfectly useless and untamable to the last. Not a few of the cattle-owners make a point of shooting all mustangs at sight, for they are not only useless cumberers of the feeding-grounds, but commonly lead away domestic horses, which soon take to the wild life and are thenceforth lost.

Wild Jo Calone knew a 'bronk right down to subsoil.' "I never seen a white that wasn't soft, nor a chestnut that wasn't nervous, nor a bay that wasn't good if broke right, nor a black that wasn't hard as nails, an' full of the old Harry. All a black bronk wants is claws to be wus'n Daniel's hull outfit of lions."

Since then a mustang is worthless vermin, and a black mustang ten times worse than worthless, Jo's pard "didn't see no sense in Jo's wantin' to corral the yearling," as he now seemed intent on doing. But Jo got no chance to try that year.

He was only a cow-puncher on $25 a month, and tied to hours. Like most of the boys, he always looked forward to having a ranch and an outfit of his own. His brand, the hogpen, of sinister suggestion, was already registered at Santa Fé, but of horned stock it was borne by a single old cow, so as to give him a legal right to put his brand on any maverick (or unbranded animal) he might chance to find.

Yet each fall, when paid off, Jo could not resist the temptation to go to town with the boys and have a good time 'while the stuff held out.' So that his property consisted of little more than his saddle, his bed, and his old cow. He kept on hoping to make a strike that would leave him well fixed with a fair start, and when the thought came that the Black Mustang was his mascot, he only needed a chance to 'make the try.'

The roundup circled down to the Canadian River, and back in the fall by the Don Carlos Hills, and Jo saw no more of the Pacer, though he heard of him from many quarters, for the colt, now a vigorous, young horse, rising three, was beginning to be talked of.

Antelope Springs is in the middle of a great level plain. When the water is high it spreads into a small lake with a belt of sedge around it; when it is low there is a wide flat of black mud, glistening white with alkali in places, and the spring a water-hole in the middle. It has no flow or outlet and yet is fairly good water, the only drinking-place for many miles.

This flat, or prairie as it would be called farther north, was the favorite feeding-ground of the Black Stallion, but it was also the pasture of many herds of range horses and cattle. Chiefly interested was the 'L cross F' outfit. Foster, the manager and part owner, was a man of enterprise. He believed it would pay to handle a better class of cattle and horses on the range, and one of his ventures was ten half-blooded mares, tall, clean-limbed, deer-eyed creatures, that made the scrub cow-ponies look like pitiful starvelings of some degenerate and quite different species.

One of these was kept stabled for use, but the nine, after the weaning of their colts, managed to get away and wandered off on the range.

A horse has a fine instinct for the road to the best feed, and the nine mares drifted, of course, to the prairie of Antelope Springs, twenty miles to the southward. And when, later that summer Foster went to round them up, he found the nine indeed, but with them and guarding them with an air of more than mere comradeship was a coal-black stallion, prancing around and rounding up the bunch like an expert, his jet-black coat a vivid contrast to the golden hides of his harem.

The mares were gentle, and would have been easily driven homeward but for a new and unexpected thing. The Black Stallion became greatly aroused. He seemed to inspire them too with his wildness, and flying this way and that way drove the whole band at full gallop where he would. Away they went, and the little cow-ponies that carried the men were easily left behind.

This was maddening, and both men at last drew their guns and sought a chance to drop that 'blasted stallion.' But no chance came that was not 9 to 1 of dropping one of the mares. A long day of manœuvring made no change. The Pacer, for it was he, kept his family together and disappeared among the southern sand-hills. The cattlemen on their jaded ponies set out for home with the poor satisfaction of vowing vengeance for their failure on the superb cause of it.

One of the most aggravating parts of it was that one or two experiences like this would surely make the mares as wild as the Mustang, and there seemed to be no way of saving them from it.

Scientists differ on the power of beauty and prowess to attract female admiration among the lower animals, but whether it is admiration or the prowess itself, it is certain that a wild animal of uncommon gifts soon wins a large following from the harems of his rivals. And the great Black Horse, with his inky mane and tail and his green-lighted eyes, ranged through all that region and added to his following from many bands till not less than a score of mares were in his 'bunch.' Most were merely humble cow-ponies turned out to range, but the nine great mares were there, a striking group by themselves. According to all reports, this bunch was always kept rounded up and guarded with such energy and jealousy that a mare, once in it, was a lost animal so far as man was concerned, and the ranchmen realized soon that they had gotten on the range a mustang that was doing them more harm than all other sources of loss put together.

II

It was December, 1893. I was new in the country, and was setting out from the ranch-house on the Pinavetitos, to go with a wagon to the Canadian River. As I was leaving, Foster finished his remark by: "And if you get a chance to draw a bead on that accursed mustang, don't fail to drop him in his tracks."

This was the first I had heard of him, and as I rode along I gathered from Burns, my guide, the history that has been given. I was full of curiosity to see the famous three-year-old, and was not a little disappointed on the second day when we came to the prairie on Antelope Springs and saw no sign of the Pacer or his band.

But on the next day, as we crossed the Alamosa Arroyo, and were rising to the rolling prairie again, Jack Burns, who was riding on ahead, suddenly dropped flat on the neck of his horse, and swung back to me in the wagon, saying:

"Get out your rifle, here's that —— stallion."

I seized my rifle, and hurried forward to a view over the prairie ridge. In the hollow below was a band of horses, and there at one end was the Great Black Mustang. He had heard some sound of our approach, and was not unsuspicious of danger. There he stood with head and tail erect, and nostrils wide, an image of horse perfection and beauty, as noble an animal as ever ranged the plains, and the mere notion of turning that magnificent creature into a mass of carrion was horrible. In spite of Jack's exhortation to 'shoot quick,' I delayed, and threw open the breach, whereupon he, always hot and hasty, swore at my slowness, growled, 'Gi' me that gun,' and as he seized it I turned the muzzle up, and *accidentally* the gun went off.

Instantly the herd below was all alarm, the great black leader snorted and neighed and dashed about. And the mares bunched, and away all went in a rumble of hoofs, and a cloud of dust.

The Stallion careered now on this side, now on that, and kept his eye on all and led and drove them far away. As long as I could see I watched, and never once did he break his pace.

Jack made Western remarks about me and my gun, as well as that mustang, but I rejoiced in the Pacer's strength and beauty, and not for all the mares in the bunch would I have harmed his glossy hide.

III

There are several ways of capturing wild horses. One is by creasing—that is, grazing the animal's nape with a rifle-ball so that he is stunned long enough for hobbling.

"Yes! I seen about a hundred necks broke trying it, but I never seen a mustang creased yet," was Wild Jo's critical remark.

Sometimes, if the shape of the country abets it, the herd can be driven into a corral; sometimes with extra fine mounts they can be run down, but by far the commonest way, paradoxical as it may seem, is to *walk* them down.

The fame of the Stallion that never was known to gallop was spreading. Extraordinary stories were told of his gait, his speed, and his wind, and when old Montgomery of the 'triangle-bar' outfit came out plump at Well's Hotel in Clayton, and in presence of witnesses said he'd give one thousand dollars cash for him safe in a box-car, providing the stories were true, a dozen young cow-punchers were eager to cut loose and win the purse, as soon as present engagements were up. But Wild Jo had had his eye on this very deal for quite a while; there was no time to lose, so ignoring present contracts he rustled all night to raise the necessary equipment for the game.

By straining his already overstrained credit, and taxing the already overtaxed generosity of his friends, he got together an expedition consisting of twenty good saddle-horses, a mess-wagon, and a fortnight's stuff for three men—himself, his 'pard,' Charley, and the cook.

Then they set out from Clayton, with the avowed intention of walking down the wonderfully swift wild horse. The third day they arrived at Antelope Springs, and as it was about noon they were not surprised to see the black Pacer marching down to drink with all his band behind him. Jo kept out of sight until the wild horses each and all had drunk their fill, for a thirsty animal always travels better than one laden with water.

Jo then rode quietly forward. The Pacer took alarm at half a mile, and led his band away out of sight on the soapweed mesa to the southeast. Jo followed at a gallop till he once more sighted them, then came back and instructed the cook, who was also teamster, to make for Alamosa Arroyo in the south. Then away to the southeast he went after the mustangs. After a mile or two he once more sighted them, and walked his horse quietly till so near that they again took alarm and circled away to the south. An hour's trot, not on the trail, but cutting across to where they ought to go, brought Jo again in close sight. Again he walked quietly toward the herd, and again there was the alarm and flight. And so they passed the afternoon, but circled ever more and more to the south, so that when the sun was low they were, as Jo had expected, not far from Alamosa Arroyo. The band was again close at hand, and Jo, after starting them off, rode to the wagon, while his pard, who had been taking it easy, took up the slow chase on a fresh horse.

After supper the wagon moved on to the upper ford of the Alamosa, as arranged, and there camped for the night.

Meanwhile, Charley followed the herd. They had not run so far as at first, for their pursuer made no sign of attack, and they were getting used to his company. They were more easily found, as the shadows fell, on account of a snow-white mare that was in the bunch. A young moon in the sky now gave some help, and relying on his horse to choose the path, Charley kept him quietly walking after the herd, represented by that ghost-white mare, till they were lost in the night. He then got off, unsaddled and picketed his horse, and in his blanket quickly went to sleep.

At the first streak of dawn he was up, and within a short half-mile, thanks to the snowy mare, he found the band. At his approach, the shrill neigh of the Pacer bugled his troop into a flying squad. But on the first mesa they stopped, and faced about to see what this persistent follower was, and what he wanted. For a moment or so they stood against the sky to gaze, and then deciding that he knew him as well as he wished to, that black meteor flung his mane on the wind, and led off at his tireless, even swing, while the mares came streaming after.

Away they went, circling now to the west, and after several repetitions of this same play, flying, following, and overtaking, and flying again, they passed, near noon, the old Apache look-out, Buffalo Bluff. And here, on watch, was Jo. A long thin column of smoke told Charley to come to camp, and with a flashing pocket-mirror he made response.

Jo, freshly mounted, rode across, and again took up the chase, and back came Charley to camp to eat and rest, and then move on up stream.

All that day Jo followed, and managed, when it was needed, that the herd should keep the great circle, of which the wagon cut a small chord. At sundown he came to Verde Crossing, and there was Charley with a fresh horse and food, and Jo went on in the same calm, dogged way. All the evening he followed, and far into the night, for the wild herd was now getting somewhat used to the presence of the harmless strangers, and were more easily followed; moreover, they were tiring out with perpetual travelling. They were no longer in the good grass country, they were not grain-fed like the horses on their track, and above all, the slight but continuous nervous tension was surely telling. It spoiled their appetites, but made them very thirsty. They were allowed, and as far as possible encouraged, to drink deeply at every chance. The effect of large quantities of water on a running animal is well known; it tends to stiffen the limbs and spoil the wind. Jo carefully guarded his own horse against such excess, and both he and his horse were fresh when they camped that night on the trail of the jaded mustangs.

At dawn he found them easily close at hand, and though they ran at first they did not go far before they dropped into a walk. The battle seemed nearly won now, for the chief difficulty in the 'walk-down' is to keep track of the herd the first two or three days when they are fresh.

All that morning Jo kept in sight, generally in close sight, of the band. About ten o'clock, Charley relieved him near José Peak and that day the mustangs walked only a quarter of a mile ahead with much less spirit than the day before and circled now more north again. At night Charley was supplied with a fresh horse and followed as before.

Next day the mustangs walked with heads held low, and in spite of the efforts of the Black Pacer at times they were less than a hundred yards ahead of their pursuer.

The fourth and fifth days passed the same way, and now the herd was nearly back to Antelope Springs. So far all had come out as expected. The chase had been in a great circle with the wagon following a lesser circle. The wild herd was back to its starting-point, worn out; and the hunters were back, fresh and on fresh horses. The herd was kept from drinking till late in the afternoon and then driven to the Springs to swell themselves with a perfect water gorge. Now was the chance for the skilful ropers on the grain-fed horses to close in, for the sudden heavy drink was ruination, almost paralysis, of wind and limb, and it would be easy to rope and hobble them one by one.

There was only one weak spot in the programme, the Black Stallion, the cause of the hunt, seemed made of iron, that ceaseless swinging pace seemed as swift and vigorous now as on the morning when the chase began. Up and down he went rounding up the herd and urging them on by voice and example to escape. But they were played out. The old white mare that had been such help in sighting them at night, had dropped out hours ago, dead beat. The half-bloods seemed to be losing all fear of the horsemen, the band was clearly in Jo's power. But the one who was the prize of all the hunt seemed just as far as ever out of reach.

Here was a puzzle. Jo's comrades knew him well and would not have been surprised to see him in a sudden rage attempt to shoot the Stallion down. But Jo had no such mind. During that long week of following he had watched the horse all day at speed and never once had he seen him gallop.

The horseman's adoration of a noble horse had grown and grown, till now he would as soon have thought of shooting his best mount as firing on that splendid beast.

Jo even asked himself whether he would take the handsome sum that was offered for the prize. Such an animal would be a fortune in himself to sire a race of pacers for the track.

But the prize was still at large—the time had come to finish up the hunt. Jo's finest mount was caught. She was a mare of Eastern blood, but raised on the plains. She never would have come into Jo's possession but for a curious weakness. The loco is a poisonous weed that grows in these regions. Most stock will not touch it; but sometimes an animal tries it and becomes addicted to it. It acts somewhat like morphine, but the animal, though sane for long intervals, has always a passion for the herb and finally dies mad. A beast with the craze is said to be locoed. And Jo's best mount had a wild gleam in her eye that to an expert told the tale.

But she was swift and strong and Jo chose her for the grand finish of the chase. It would have been an easy matter now to rope the mares, but was no longer necessary. They could be separated from their black leader and driven home to the corral. But that leader still had the look of untamed strength. Jo, rejoicing in a worthy foe, went bounding forth to try the odds. The lasso was flung on the ground and trailed to take out every kink, and gathered as he rode into neatest coils across his left palm. Then putting on the spur the first time in that chase he rode straight for the Stallion a quarter of a mile beyond. Away he went, and away went Jo, each at his best, while the fagged-out mares scattered right and left and let them pass. Straight across the open plain the fresh horse went at its hardest gallop, and the Stallion, leading off, still kept his start and kept his famous swing.

It was incredible, and Jo put on more spur and shouted to his horse, which fairly flew, but shortened up the space between by not a single inch. For the Black One whirled across the flat and up and passed a soapweed mesa and down across a sandy treacherous plain, then over a grassy stretch where prairie dogs barked, then hid below, and on came Jo, but there to see, could he believe his eyes, the Stallion's start grown longer still, and Jo began to curse his luck, and urge and spur his horse until the poor uncertain brute got into such a state of nervous fright, her eyes began to roll, she wildly shook her head from side to side, no longer picked her ground—a badger-hole received her foot and down she went, and Jo went flying to the earth. Though badly bruised, he gained his feet and tried to mount his crazy beast. But she, poor brute, was done for—her off fore-leg hung loose.

There was but one thing to do. Jo loosed the cinch, put Lightfoot out of pain, and carried back the saddle to the camp. While the Pacer steamed away till lost to view.

This was not quite defeat, for all the mares were manageable now, and Jo and Charley drove them carefully to the 'L cross F' corral and claimed a good reward. But Jo was more than ever bound to own the Stallion. He had seen what stuff he was made of, he prized him more and more, and only sought to strike some better plan to catch him.

IV

The cook on that trip was Bates—Mr. Thomas Bates, he called himself at the post-office where he regularly went for the letters and remittance which never came. Old Tom Turkeytrack, the boys called him, from his cattle-brand, which he said was on record at Denver, and which, according to his story, was also borne by countless beef and saddle stock on the plains of the unknown North.

When asked to join the trip as a partner, Bates made some sarcastic remarks about horses not fetching $12 a dozen, which had been literally true within the year, and he preferred to go on a very meagre salary. But no one who once saw the Pacer going had failed to catch the craze. Turkeytrack experienced the usual change of heart. He now wanted to own that mustang. How this was to be brought about he did not clearly see till one day there called at the ranch that had 'secured his services,' as he put it, one, Bill Smith, more usually known as Horseshoe Billy, from his cattle-brand. While the excellent fresh beef and bread and the vile coffee, dried peaches and molasses were being consumed, he of the horseshoe remarked, in tones which percolated through a huge stop-gap of bread:

"Wall, I seen that thar Pacer to-day, nigh enough to put a plait in his tail."

"What, you didn't shoot?"

"No, but I come mighty near it."

"Don't you be led into no sich foolishness," said a 'double-bar H' cow-puncher at the other end of the table. "I calc'late that maverick 'ill carry my brand before the moon changes."

"You'll have to be pretty spry or you'll find a 'triangle dot' on his weather side when you get there."

"Where did you run acrost him?"

"Wall, it was like this; I was riding the flat by Antelope Springs and I sees a lump on the dry mud inside the rush belt. I knowed I never seen that before, so rides up, thinking it might be some of our stock, an' seen it was a horse lying plumb flat. The wind was blowing like —— from him to me, so I rides up close and seen it was the Pacer, dead as a mackerel. Still, he didn't look swelled or cut, and there wa'n't no smell, an' I didn't know what to think till I seen his ear twitch off a fly and then I knowed he was sleeping. I git down me rope and coils it, and seen it was old and pretty shaky in spots, and me saddle a single cinch, an' me pony about 700 again a 1,200 lbs. stallion, an' I sez to meself, sez I: ' 'Tain't no use, I'll only break me cinch and git throwed an' lose me saddle.' So I hits the saddle-horn a crack with the hondu, and I wish't you'd a seen that mustang. He lept six foot in the air an' snorted like he was shunting cars. His eyes fairly bugged out an' he lighted out lickety split for California, and he orter be there about now if he kep' on like he started—and I swear he never made a break the hull trip."

The story was not quite so consecutive as given here. It was much punctuated by present engrossments, and from first to last was more or less infiltrated through the necessaries of life, for Bill was a healthy young man without a trace of false shame. But the account was complete and everyone believed it, for Billy was known to be

reliable. Of all those who heard, old Turkeytrack talked the least
and probably thought the most, for it gave him a new idea.

During his after-dinner pipe he studied it out and deciding that
he could not go it alone, he took Horseshoe Billy into his council
and the result was a partnership in a new venture to capture the
Pacer; that is, the $5,000 that was now said to be the offer for him
safe in a box-car.

Antelope Springs was still the usual watering-place of the Pacer.
The water being low left a broad belt of dry black mud between the
sedge and the spring. At two places this belt was broken by a well-
marked trail made by the animals coming to drink. Horses and wild
animals usually kept to these trails, though the horned cattle had no
hesitation in taking a short cut through the sedge.

In the most used of these trails the two men set to work with
shovels and digged a pit 15 feet long, 6 feet wide and 7 feet deep. It
was a hard twenty hours work for them as it had to be completed
between the Mustang's drinks, and it began to be very damp work
before it was finished. With poles, brush, and earth it was then
cleverly covered over and concealed. And the men went to a distance
and hid in pits made for the purpose.

About noon the Pacer came, alone now since the capture of his
band. The trail on the opposite side of the mud belt was little used,
and old Tom, by throwing some fresh rushes across it, expected to
make sure that the Stallion would enter by the other, if indeed he
should by any caprice try to come by the unusual path.

What sleepless angel is it watches over and cares for the wild animals? In spite of all reasons to take the usual path, the Pacer came
along the other. The suspicious-looking rushes did not stop him;
he walked calmly to the water and drank. There was only one way
now to prevent utter failure; when he lowered his head for the second draft which horses always take, Bates and Smith quit their holes
and ran swiftly toward the trail behind him, and when he raised
his proud head Smith sent a revolver-shot into the ground behind
him.

Away went the Pacer at his famous gait straight to the trap. Another second and he would be into it. Already he is on the trail, and
already they feel they have him, but the Angel of the wild things is
with him, that incomprehensible warning comes, and with one
mighty bound he clears the fifteen feet of treacherous ground and
spurns the earth as he fades away unharmed, never again to visit
Antelope Springs by either of the beaten paths.

V

Wild Jo never lacked energy. He meant to catch that Mustang, and when he learned that others were bestirring themselves for the same purpose he at once set about trying the best untried plan he knew—the plan by which the coyote catches the fleeter jackrabbit, and the mounted Indian the far swifter antelope—the old plan of the relay chase.

The Canadian River on the south, its affluent, the Piñavetitos Arroyo, on the northeast, and the Don Carlos Hills with the Ute Creek Cañon on the west, formed a sixty-mile triangle that was the range of the Pacer. It was believed that he never went outside this, and at all times Antelope Springs was his headquarters. Jo knew this country well, all the water-holes and cañon crossings as well as the ways of the Pacer.

If he could have gotten fifty good horses he could have posted them to advantage so as to cover all points, but twenty mounts and five good riders were all that proved available.

The horses, grain-fed for two weeks before, were sent on ahead; each man was instructed now to play his part and sent to his post the day before the race. On the day of the start Jo with his wagon drove to the plain of Antelope Springs and, camping far off in a little draw, waited.

At last he came, that coal-black Horse, out from the sand-hills at the south, alone as always now, and walked calmly down to the Springs and circled quite around it to sniff for any hidden foe. Then he approached where there was no trail at all and drank.

Jo watched and wished he would drink a hogshead. But the moment that he turned and sought the grass Jo spurred his steed. The Pacer heard the hoofs, then saw the running horse, and did not want a nearer view but led away. Across the flat he went down to the south, and kept the famous swinging gait that made his start grow longer. Now through the sandy dunes he went, and steadying to an even pace he gained considerably and Jo's too-laden horse plunged through the sand and sinking fetlock deep, he lost at every bound. Then came a level stretch where the runner seemed to gain, and then a long decline where Jo's horse dared not run his best, so lost again at every step.

But on they went, and Jo spared neither spur nor quirt. A mile— a mile—and another mile, and the far-off rock at Arriba loomed up ahead.

And there Jo knew fresh mounts were held, and on they dashed.

But the night-black mane out level on the breeze ahead was gaining
more and more.

Arriba Cañon reached at last, the watcher stood aside, for it was
not wished to turn the race, and the Stallion passed—dashed down,
across and up the slope, with that unbroken pace, the only one he
knew.

And Jo came bounding on his foaming steed, and leaped on the
waiting mount, then urged him down the slope and up upon the
track, and on the upland once more drove in the spurs, and raced
and raced, and raced, but not a single inch he gained.

Ga-lump, ga-lump, ga-lump with measured beat he went—an
hour—an hour, and another hour—Arroyo Alamosa just ahead
with fresh relays, and Jo yelled at his horse and pushed him on and
on. Straight for the place the Black One made, but on the last two
miles some strange foreboding turned him to the left, and Jo fore-
saw escape in this, and pushed his jaded mount at any cost to head
him off, and hard as they had raced this was the hardest race of all,
with gasps for breath and leather squeaks at every straining bound.
Then cutting right across, Jo seemed to gain, and drawing his gun
he fired shot after shot to toss the dust, and so turned the Stallion's
head and forced him back to take the crossing to the right.

Down they went. The Stallion crossed and Jo sprang to the
ground. His horse was done, for thirty miles had passed in the last
stretch, and Jo himself was worn out. His eyes were burnt with
flying alkali dust. He was half blind so he motioned to his 'pard'
to "go ahead and keep him straight for Alamosa ford."

Out shot the rider on a strong, fresh steed, and away they went—
up and down on the rolling plain—the Black Horse flecked with
snowy foam. His heaving ribs and noisy breath showed what he
felt—but on and on he went.

And Tom on Ginger seemed to gain, then lose and lose, when in
an hour the long decline of Alamosa came. And there a freshly
mounted lad took up the chase and turned it west, and on they went
past towns of prairie dogs, through soapweed tracts and cactus
brakes by scores, and pricked and wrenched rode on. With dust and
sweat the Black was now a dappled brown, but still he stepped the
same. Young Carrington, who followed, had hurt his steed by pushing at the very start, and spurred and urged him now to cut across
a gulch at which the Pacer shied. Just one misstep and down they
went.

The boy escaped, but the pony lies there yet, and the wild Black
Horse kept on.

This was close to old Gallego's ranch where Jo himself had cut across refreshed to push the chase. Within thirty minutes he was again scorching the Pacer's trail.

Far in the west the Carlos Hills were seen, and there Jo knew fresh men and mounts were waiting, and that way the indomitable rider tried to turn the race, but by a sudden whim, of the inner warning born perhaps—the Pacer turned. Sharp to the north he went, and Jo, the skilful wrangler, rode and rode and yelled and tossed the dust with shots, but down a gulch the wild black meteor streamed and Jo could only follow. Then came the hardest race of all; Jo, cruel to the Mustang, was crueller to his mount and to himself. The sun was hot, the scorching plain was dim in shimmering heat, his eyes and lips were burnt with sand and salt, and yet the chase sped on. The only chance to win would be if he could drive the Mustang back to Big Arroyo Crossing. Now almost for the first time he saw signs of weakening in the Black. His mane and tail were not just quite so high, and his short half mile of start was down by more than half, but still he stayed ahead and paced and paced and paced.

An hour and another hour, and still they went the same. But they turned again, and night was near when Big Arroyo ford was reached —fully twenty miles. But Jo was game, he seized the waiting horse. The one he left went gasping to the stream and gorged himself with water till he died.

Then Jo held back in hopes the foaming Black would drink. But he was wise; he gulped a single gulp, splashed through the stream and then passed on with Jo at speed behind him. And when they last were seen the Black was on ahead just out of reach and Jo's horse bounding on.

It was morning when Jo came to camp on foot. His tale was briefly told:—eight horses dead—five men worn out—the matchless Pacer safe and free.

" 'Tain't possible; it can't be done. Sorry I didn't bore his hellish carcass through when I had the chance," said Jo, and gave it up.

VI

Old Turkeytrack was cook on this trip. He had watched the chase with as much interest as anyone, and when it failed he grinned into the pot and said: "That mustang's mine unless I'm a darned fool." Then falling back on Scripture for a precedent, as was his habit, he still addressed the pot:

"Reckon the Philistines tried to run Samson down and they got done up, an' would a stayed done ony for a nat'ral weakness on his part. An' Adam would a loafed in Eden yit ony for a leetle failing which we all onderstand. An' it aint $5000 I'll take for him nuther."

Much persecution had made the Pacer wilder than ever. But it did not drive him away from Antelope Springs. That was the only drinking-place with absolutely no shelter for a mile on every side to hide an enemy. Here he came almost every day about noon, and after thoroughly spying the land approached to drink.

His had been a lonely life all winter since the capture of his harem, and of this old Turkeytrack was fully aware. The old cook's chum had a nice little brown mare which he judged would serve his ends, and taking a pair of the strongest hobbles, a spade, a spare lasso, and a stout post he mounted the mare and rode away to the famous Springs.

A few antelope skimmed over the plain before him in the early freshness of the day. Cattle were lying about in groups, and the loud, sweet song of the prairie lark was heard on every side. For the bright snowless winter of the mesas was gone and the springtime was at hand. The grass was greening and all nature seemed turning to thoughts of love.

It was in the air, and when the little brown mare was picketed out to graze she raised her nose from time to time to pour forth a long shrill whinny that surely was her song, if song she had, of love.

Old Turkeytrack studied the wind and the lay of the land. There was the pit he had labored at, now opened and filled with water that was rank with drowned prairie dogs and mice. Here was the new trail the animals were forced to make by the pit. He selected a sedgy clump near some smooth, grassy ground, and first firmly sunk the post, then dug a hole large enough to hide in, and spread his blanket in it. He shortened up the little mare's tether, till she could scarcely move; then on the ground between he spread his open lasso, tying the long end to the post, then covered the rope with dust and grass, and went into his hiding-place.

About noon, after long waiting, the amorous whinny of the mare was answered from the high ground, away to the west, and there, black against the sky, was the famous Mustang.

Down he came at that long swinging gait, but grown crafty with much pursuit, he often stopped to gaze and whinny, and got answer that surely touched his heart. Nearer he came again to call, then took alarm, and paced all around in a great circle to try the wind for his foes, and seemed in doubt. The Angel whispered "Don't go."

But the brown mare called again. He circled nearer still, and neighed once more, and got reply that seemed to quell all fears, and set his heart aglow.

Nearer still he pranced, till he touched Solly's nose with his own, and finding her as responsive as he well could wish, thrust aside all thoughts of danger, and abandoned himself to the delight of conquest, until, as he pranced around, his hind legs for a moment stood within the evil circle of the rope. One deft sharp twitch, the noose flew tight, and he was caught.

A snort of terror and a bound in the air gave Tom the chance to add the double hitch. The loop flashed up the line, and snake-like bound those mighty hoofs.

Terror lent speed and double strength for a moment, but the end of the rope was reached, and down he went a captive, a hopeless prisoner at last. Old Tom's ugly, little crooked form sprang from the pit to complete the mastering of the great glorious creature whose mighty strength had proved as nothing when matched with the wits of a little old man. With snorts and desperate bounds of awful force the great beast dashed and struggled to be free; but all in vain. The rope was strong.

The second lasso was deftly swung, and the forefeet caught, and then with a skilful move the feet were drawn together, and down went the raging Pacer to lie a moment later 'hog-tied' and helpless on the ground. There he struggled till worn out, sobbing great convulsive sobs while tears ran down his cheeks.

Tom stood by and watched, but a strange revulsion of feeling came over the old cow-puncher. He trembled nervously from head to foot, as he had not done since he roped his first steer, and for a while could do nothing but gaze on his tremendous prisoner. But the feeling soon passed away. He saddled Delilah, and taking the second lasso, roped the great horse about the neck, and left the mare to hold the Stallion's head, while he put on the hobbles. This was soon done, and sure of him now old Bates was about to loose the ropes, but on a sudden thought he stopped. He had quite forgotten, and had come unprepared for something of importance. In Western law the Mustang was the property of the first man to mark him with his brand; how was this to be done with the nearest branding-iron twenty miles away?

Old Tom went to his mare, took up her hoofs one at a time, and examined each shoe. Yes! one was a little loose; he pushed and pried it with the spade, and got it off. Buffalo chips and kindred fuel were plentiful about the plain, so a fire was quickly made, and he soon had one arm of the horse-shoe red hot, then holding the other wrapped in his sock he rudely sketched on the left shoulder of the helpless mustang a turkeytrack, his brand, the first time really that it had ever been used. The Pacer shuddered as the hot iron seared his flesh, but it was quickly done, and the famous Mustang Stallion was a maverick no more.

Now all there was to do was to take him home. The ropes were loosed, the Mustang felt himself freed, thought he was free, and sprang to his feet only to fall as soon as he tried to take a stride. His forefeet were strongly tied together, his only possible gait a shuffling walk, or else a desperate labored bounding with feet so unnaturally held that within a few yards he was inevitably thrown each time he tried to break away. Tom on the light pony headed him off again and again, and by dint of driving, threatening, and manœuvring, contrived to force his foaming, crazy captive northward toward the Piñavetitos Cañon. But the wild horse would not drive, would not give in. With snorts of terror or of rage and maddest bounds, he tried and tried to get away. It was one long cruel fight; his glossy sides were thick with dark foam, and the foam was stained with blood. Countless hard falls and exhaustion that a long day's chase was powerless to produce were telling on him; his straining bounds first this way and then that, were not now quite so strong, and the spray he snorted as he gasped was half a spray of blood. But his captor, relentless, masterful and cool, still forced him on. Down the slope toward the cañon they had come, every yard a fight, and now they were at the head of the draw that took the trail down to the only crossing of the cañon, the northmost limit of the Pacer's ancient range.

From this the first corral and ranch-house were in sight. The man rejoiced, but the Mustang gathered his remaining strength for one more desperate dash. Up, up the grassy slope from the trail he went, defied the swinging, slashing rope and the gunshot fired in air, in vain attempt to turn his frenzied course. Up, up and on, above the sheerest cliff he dashed then sprang away into the vacant air, down—down—two hundred downward feet to fall, and land upon the rocks below, a lifeless wreck—but free.

The Pinto Horse

CHARLES ELLIOTT PERKINS

IN THE spring of '88, "Patch" was running a band of Oregon mares in the Bull Mountains of Southern Montana. The Bull Mountains are a range of high and broken hills, sparsely covered with jack pine, and heavily grassed in the open parks, with springs at the coulee heads; an ideal winter range for horses. On the south, the country falls away in lessening grassy ridges twenty miles to the Yellowstone. To the north, it drops more steeply to the Mussel Shell Flats.

In those days, the country north of the Yellowstone had not been restocked after the terrible winter of '86; the range was all open to the Canadian line, and the native grass grew in its natural abundance. From May to November the mares were divided into two bands, one which ranged south to the Yellowstone, the other to the north of the Bull Mountain hills. Each spring, the Honorable William Spencer Fitzhenry Wantage, third son of the Earl of Palmadime, brought up from his ranch on Powder River the thoroughbred stallions that were to run with the mares; each November he came for them. In the meantime, all Patch had to do was to ride each morning from his cabin in the foothills, locate his mares, count them, and once a week cross over to the other side of the hills to see that his assistant, Mr. "Slippery Bill" Weston, and the mares that he looked after were in good order. It was a pleasant life; twice a week the Billings stage left the mail in a tin box on the Yellowstone Trail, and once a month Patch hooked up his mule and drove into Billings for supplies. That trip took three days, and always Patch came back strapped but happy.

In the autumn, when the stallions had gone back to Powder River, the horses of both bands were brought together to the corrals at the head of Big Coulee, the weanlings branded, the geldings that were to be broken cut out and turned into the saddle-horse pasture, and the balance of the herd turned loose again to winter in the hills.

Range horses know the seasons as well as man, and they know their range as no man ever knows it. They know the pockets where the Northers never strike; they know where the warm springs are that never freeze; and they know which ridges are exposed to the Chinooks—warm winds that melt the snow. The range horse loves its native range as no other animal loves its home, and will return to it hundreds of miles, if it has the chance. Especially is this true of mares, which never forget the range where their first foal is dropped. Once a mare has foaled, she will spend the rest of her life within a radius of a few miles, if there is enough feed and water.

The first autumn and winter that Patch had the Oregon mares, he spent all the days and many freezing nights riding to turn them back in their drift toward the West.

When Patch and the Honorable William Spencer Fitzhenry Wantage, who owned a half interest in the horses, were bringing the mares from Oregon, their regular pack horse went lame and they caught what seemed a quiet mare to pack in its place. They haltered the mare and tied her to a tree, packed on her their bedding and cook outfit, and then, as she seemed frightened by the pack sheet, the Honorable, thinking to get her used to it, tied one end to the front of the pack saddle and, with a corner of the other end in each hand, stood behind her and gave it a flap. The result was electric. The mare broke away and dashed down the road, the loose sheet flying and flapping above her like a cloud. The first thing she struck was the band of mares, which scattered far and wide; the next thing she ran into was a herd of beef being driven to the railroad; these stampeded like the mares. There were two drummers driving out from town, with a pair, in a top buggy. The flying mare met them head on. The team jackknifed, broke the pole and a drummer's leg, and disappeared like the beef steers and the mares, while she pursued her unhallowed course into town, wrecked a mounted pageant of the Knights of Columbus, threw the Grand Knight through the plate-glass window of the Masonic Hall, and finally fell down herself in the public square.

Patch and the Honorable William Spencer Fitzhenry Wantage spent the next two days rounding up all of the scattered mares that they could find. Twelve they never got, and of these, nine eventually found their way back from Montana to the range in

Oregon where they were foaled, *eight hundred miles away,* swimming the Snake River to get there.

So Patch was looking after the band of mares on the Bull Mountain range, when, one morning in June, he rode out to locate them, and to see if Stowaway, the thoroughbred stallion which had begun his first season on the range a month before, was all right. Over the grassy ridges he jogged, whistling "Garryowen," while the larks, out of sight above, poured down a stream of song. He had found the band the day before and knew, if nothing had disturbed them, he would find them again a few miles further on toward the Yellowstone. Sure enough, when he was still two miles away, he saw them feeding on a little flat along the Cottonwood. But before he reached them, crossing a dry wash, he came upon Stowaway, covered with blood and carrying all the marks of battle, too lame and sore to climb out of the shallow gully into which he had staggered.

Patch knew it meant that some range stallion had found the band, nearly killed Stowaway, and taken them for himself. That must be seen to. He kicked his pony into a gallop, but before he had come within one hundred yards of the grazing mares, a black and white spotted stallion came snorting out to meet him. Indian, thought Patch, escaped from some band of Crows off their reservation south of the Yellowstone, or else a wanderer driven from some herd of Crow horses which had smelled the mares from miles across the river and come over to get a harem of his own. On came the pinto stallion, ears back, mouth open, until, within twenty yards, Patch untied his slicker and swung it around his head. The wild horse slid to a stop, stamped, snorted and trotted back to the mares.

It was lucky for him that the cowboy feared Indians might be camped nearby, or a bullet from his forty-five would have ended the career of that spotted Don Juan there and then, for thoroughbred stallions were scarcer on the Montana Range than feathered frogs, and Patch was mad; it would take Stowaway weeks to get over his beating. What was to be done? He could not shoot the pinto. For, though the Indians were peaceful enough at home, they did not leave their reservation unless they were up to some mischief; and in killing a lone cowboy, and stealing his horse and guns, there would be no risk of discovery in that unsettled country. There was nothing for it but to start the mares quietly up the creek toward the corrals, twelve miles away at the winter camp at the Big Coulee; the wild stallion would go with them, and, once started, Patch knew that they would head straight for the corrals where they were regularly

salted. So, with one eye over his shoulder in case of an Indian surprise, he worked his way to the lower side of the herd, careful to keep below the rim of the encircling hills.

The Indian stallion dashed to and fro, snorting, always between Patch and the mares, but the flying slicker kept him from attacking the saddle horse, and gradually the cowboy got near enough to turn one grazing mare and then another, until he had the whole band slowly walking up the creek. For a mile they strolled on, feeding as they went, and then, as they got far enough away so that the dust would not be noticed, Patch crowded the last ones until they began to jog and then to gallop. After another mile he knew he had them fully roused and that they would not stop or turn until they got to the corrals.

Then Patch pulled up and watched them out of sight—the wild stallion turned to snort and stamp once more before he disappeared after the mares. The cowboy loped back down the creek, and cutting across to where Stowaway was still standing in the dry wash, dropped his rope over the stallion's head and started with him to the home camp; but the battered horse went slowly, and it was midafternoon when Patch left him in the shade of some alders half a mile from the corrals. There, as he hoped, he found the mares, some licking salt, some rolling in the dust, the pinto stallion just inside the gate. Patch knew that the only way to get rid of him was to scare him so badly that he would go back to his own range, and to do that he would have to catch him. He could not keep the mares in the corral; there was no feed, and if the stallion were not badly scared, he would stay in the broken country nearby and wait until the mares came out. Patch slipped off his horse and crept nearer; the stallion did not wind him, and he got within ten yards, screened by some chokeberry bushes.

Then with a yell he started. The wild horse saw him the fraction of a second too late, and the heavy gate slammed in his face as he reared against it. The rest was simple; the pinto was roped, thrown, and hog-tied, and a lard pail full of stones, the top wired on, tied to his tail. The mares were penned in the second corral, the gate thrown open, the tie-ropes loosed, and the terrified stallion crashed off down the draw, the lard pail banging at his hocks.

That night, thirty miles to the south, the sleeping Indians on the Little Horn clutched each other in terror, and their frightened ponies scattered to the hills.

The Seeing Eye

WILL JAMES

IT's worse than tough for anyone to be blind but I don't think it's as tough for an indoor born and raised person as it is for one whose life is with the all out-of-doors the most of his life from childhood on. The outdoor man misses his freedom to roam over the hills and the sight of 'em ever changing. A canary would die outside his cage but a free-born eagle would dwindle away inside of one.

Dane Gruger was very much of an out-of-door man. He was born on a little ranch along a creek bottom, in the heart of the cow country, growed up with it to be a good cowboy, then, like with his dad, went on in the cow business. A railroad went through the lower part of the ranch but stations and little towns was over twenty miles away either way.

He had a nice little spread when I went to work for him, was married and had two boys who done some of the riding. I'd been riding for Dane for quite a few days before I knew he was blind, not totally blind, but, as his boys told me, he couldn't see any further than his outstretched hand, and that was blurred. He couldn't read, not even big print, with any kind of glasses so he never wore any.

That's what fooled me, and he could look you "right square in the eye" while talking to you. What was more, he'd go straight down to the corral, catching his horse, saddle him and ride away like any man with full sight. The thing I first noticed and wondered at was that he never rode with us, and after the boys told me, I could understand. It was that he'd be of no use out on the range and away from the ranch.

Dane had been blind a few years when I came there and he'd of

390

course got to know every foot of the ten miles which the ranch covered on the creek bottom before it happened. The ranch itself was one to two miles wide in some places and taking in some brakes. The whole of that was fenced and cross-fenced into pastures and hay lands, and Dane knew to within an inch when he came to every fence, gate or creek crossing. He knew how many head of cattle or horses might be in each pasture, how all was faring, when some broke out or some broke in, and where. He could find bogged cattle, cow with young calf needing help, and know everything that went well or wrong with what stock would be held on the ranch.

He of course seldom could do much towards helping whatever stock needed it or fix the holes he found in the fences, but when he'd get back to the ranch house he could easy tell the boys when there was anything wrong, and the exact spot where, in which field or pasture, how far from which side of the creek or what fence and what all the trouble might be. It would then be up to the boys to set things to rights, and after Dane's description of the spot it was easy found.

During the time I was with that little outfit I got to know Dane pretty well, well enough to see that I don't think he could of lived if he hadn't been able to do what he was doing. He was so full of life and gumption and so appreciating of all around him that he could feel, hear and breathe in. I'd sometimes see him hold his horse to a standstill while he only listened to birds or the faraway bellering of cattle, even to the yapping of prairie dogs which most cowboys would rather not hear the sound of.

To take him away from all that, the open air, the feel of his saddle and horse under him and set him on a chair to do nothing but sit and babble and think, would of brought a quick end to him.

With the riding he done he felt satisfied he was doing something worth doing instead of just plain riding. He wouldn't of cared for that, and fact was he well took the place of an average rider.

But he had mighty good help in the work he was doing, and that was the two horses he used, for they was both as well trained to his wants and care as the dogs that's used nowadays to lead the blind and which are called "The Seeing Eye."

Dane had the advantage of the man with the dog, for he didn't have to walk and use a cane at every step. He rode, and he had more confidence in his horses' every step than he had in his own, even if he could of seen well. As horses do, they naturally sensed every foot of the earth under 'em without ever looking down at it, during sunlight, darkness or under drifted snow.

Riding into clumps of willows or thickets which the creek bottoms had much of, either of the two horses was careful to pick out a wide enough trail through so their rider wouldn't get scratched or brushed off. If they come to a place where the brush was too thick and Dane was wanting to go through that certain thicket, the ponies, regardless of his wants, would turn back for a ways and look for a better opening. Dane never argued with 'em at such times. He would just sort of head 'em where he wanted to go and they'd do the rest to pick out the best way there.

Them horses was still young when I got to that outfit, seven and eight years of age, and would be fit at least twenty years more with the little riding and good care they was getting. Dane's boys had broke 'em especially for their dad's use that way and they'd done a fine job of it.

One of the horses, a gray of about a thousand pounds, was called Little Eagle. That little horse never missed a thing in sight or sound. With his training, the rustling of the brush close by would make him investigate and learn the cause before leaving that spot. Dane would know by his actions whether it was a new-born calf that had been hid or some cow in distress. It was the same at the boggy places along the creek or alkali swamps. If Little Eagle rode right on around and without stopping, Dane knew all was well. If he stopped at any certain spot, bowed his neck and snorted low, then Dane knew that some horse or cow was in trouble. Keeping his hand on Little Eagle's neck, he'd have him go on, and by the bend of that horse's neck as he went, like pointing, Dane could tell the exact location of where that animal was that was in trouble, or whatever it was that was wrong.

Sometimes, Little Eagle would line out on a trot, of his own accord and as though there was something needed looking into right away. At times he'd even break into a lope, and then Dane wouldn't know what to expect, whether it was stock breaking through a fence, milling around an animal that was down, or what. But most always it would be when a bunch of stock, horses or cattle would be stringing out in a single file, maybe going to water or some other part of the pasture.

At such times, Little Eagle would get just close enough to the stock so Dane could count 'em by the sounds of the hoofs going by, a near impossible thing to do for a man that can see, but Dane got so he could do it and get a mighty close count on what stock was in each pasture that way. Close enough so he could tell if any had got out or others got in.

With the horses in the pastures, there was bells on the leaders of every bunch and some on one of every little bunch that sort of held together and separate from others. Dane knew by the sound of every bell which bunch it was and about how many there would be to each. The boys kept him posted on that every time they'd run a bunch in for some reason or other. Not many horses was ever kept under fence, but there was quite a few of the pure-bred cattle for the upbreeding of the outside herds.

At this work of keeping tab on stock, Little Eagle was a cowboy by himself. With his natural intellect so developed as to what was wanted of him, he could near tell of what stock was wanted or not and where they belonged. The proof of that was when he turned a bunch of cattle out of a hayfield one time, and other times, and drove 'em to the gate of the field where they'd broke out of, circled around 'em when the gate was reached and went to it for Dane to open. He then drove the cattle through, none got away, not from Little Eagle, and Dane would always prepare to ride at such times, for if any did try to break away, Little Eagle would be right on their tail to bring 'em back, and for a blind man, not knowing when his horse is going to break into a sudden run, stop or turn, that's kind of hard riding, on a good cowhorse.

About all Dane would have to go by most of the time was the feel of the top muscles on Little Eagle's neck, and he got to know by them about the same as like language to him. With one hand most always on them muscles, he felt what the horse seen. Tenseness, wonder, danger, fear, relaxation and about all that a human feels at the sight of different things. Places, dangerous or smooth, trouble or peace.

Them top muscles told him more, and more plainly than if another rider had been riding constantly alongside of him and telling him right along of what he seen. That was another reason why Dane liked to ride alone. He felt more at ease, no confusion, and wasn't putting anybody out of their way by talking and describing when they maybe wouldn't feel like it.

And them two horses of Dane's, they not only took him wherever he wanted to go but never overlooked any work that needed to be done. They took it onto themselves to look for work which, being they always felt so good, was like play to them. Dane knew it when such times come and he then would let 'em go as they chose.

Neither of the horses would of course go out by themselves without a rider and do that work. They wouldn't of been interested doing that without Dane's company. What's more, they couldn't have opened the gates that had to be gone through, and besides they wasn't wanted to do that. They was to be the company of Dane and with him in whatever he wanted to do.

Dane's other horse was a trim bay about the same size as Little Eagle, and even though just as good, he had different ways about him. He was called Ferret, and a ferret he was for digging up and finding out things, like a cow with new-born calf or mare with colt, and he was even better than Little Eagle for finding holes in fences or where some was down.

All that came under the special training the boys had given him and Little Eagle, and if it wasn't for automobiles these days, such as them would be mighty valuable companions in the city, even more useful in the streets than the dog is, for the horse would soon know where his rider would want to go after being ridden such places a few times.

Unlike most horses, it wasn't these two's nature to keep wanting to turn back to the ranch (home) when Dane would ride 'em away, and they wouldn't turn back until they knew the ride was over and it was time to. Sometimes Dane wouldn't show up for the noon meal, and that was all right with the ponies too, for he'd often get off 'em and let 'em graze with reins dragging. There was no danger of either of them ever leaving Dane, for they seemed as attached to him as any dog could be to his master.

It was the same way with Dane for them, and he had more confidence in their trueness and senses than most humans have in one another.

A mighty good test and surprising outcome of that came one day as a powerful big cloudburst hit above the ranch a ways and left Dane acrost the creek from home. The creek had turned into churning wild waters the size of a big river in a few minutes, half a mile wide in some places and licking up close to the higher land where the ranch buildings and corrals was.

It kept on a-raining hard after the cloudburst had fell and it didn't act like it was going to let up for some time, and the wide river wouldn't be down to creek size or safe to cross, at least not for a day or so.

The noise of the rushing water was a-plenty to let Dane know of the cloudburst. It had come with a sudden roar and without a drop of warning, and Dane's horse, he was riding Little Eagle that day, plainly let him know the danger of the wide stretch of swirling fast waters. It wasn't the danger of the water only but uprooted trees and all kinds of heavy timber speeding along would make the crossing more than dangerous, not only dangerous but it would about mean certain death.

Little Eagle would of tackled the swollen waters or anything Dane would of wanted him to, but Dane knew a whole lot better than to make that wise horse go where he didn't want to, any time.

Dane could tell by the noise, and riding to the edge of the water and the location where he was how wide the body of wild water was. He knew that the stock could keep out of reach of it on either side without being jammed against the fences, but he got worried about the ranch, wondering if the waters had got up to the buildings. He worried too about his family worrying about him, and maybe try to find and get to him.

That worrying got him to figuring on ways of getting back. He sure couldn't stay where he was until the waters went down, not if he could help it. It wouldn't be comfortable being out so long in the heavy rain either, even if he did have his slicker on, and it wouldn't do to try to go to the neighbor's ranch which was some fifteen miles away. He doubted if he could find it anyway, for it was acrost a bunch of rolling hills, nothing to go by, and Little Eagle wouldn't know that *there* would be where Dane would be wanting him to go. Besides, there was the thought of his family worrying so about him and maybe risking their lives in trying to find him.

He'd just have to get home, somehow, and it was at the thought of his neighbor's ranch and picturing the distance and country to it in his mind that he thought of the railroad, for he would of had to cross it to get there, and then, thinking of the railroad, the thought came of the trestle crossing along it and over the creek. Maybe he could make that. That would be sort of a dangerous crossing too, but the more he thought of it the more he figured it worth taking the chances of trying. That was the only way of his getting on the other side of the high waters and back to the ranch.

The railroad and trestle was only about half a mile from where he now was and that made it all the more tempting to try. So, after thinking it over in every way, including the fact that he'd be taking chances with losing his horse also, he finally decided to take the chance, at the risk of both himself and his horse, that is if his horse seen it might be safe enough. He felt it had to be done and it could be done, and there went to show his faith and confidence in that Little Eagle horse of his.

And that confidence sure wasn't misplaced, for a cooler-headed, brainier horse never was.

There was two fences to cross to get to the railroad and trestle, and it wasn't at all necessary to go through gates to get there, for the swollen waters with jamming timbers had laid the fence down for quite a ways on both sides of the wide river, some of the wire strands to break and snap and coil all directions.

A strand of barbed wire, even if flat to the ground, is a mighty dangerous thing to ride over, for a horse might pick it up with a hoof and, as most horses will scare, draw their hind legs up under 'em and act up. The result might be a wicked sawing wire cut at the joint of the hock, cutting veins and tendons and often crippling a horse for life. In such cases the rider is also very apt to get tangled up in the wire, for that wicked stuff seems to have the ways of the tentacles of a devilfish at such times.

Loose wire laying around on the ground is the cowboys' worst fear, especially so with Dane, for, as he couldn't see, it was many times more threatening as he rode most every day from one fenced-in field to the other. But the confidence he had in his two cool-headed ponies relieved him of most all his fear of the dangerous barbed wire, and either one of 'em would stop and snort a little at the sight of a broken strand coiled to the ground. Dane knew what that meant and it laways brought a chill to his spine. He'd get down off his saddle, feel around carefully in front of his horse, and usually the threatening coil would be found to within a foot or so of his horse's nose. The coil would then be pulled and fastened to the fence, to stay until a ranch hand who, with team and buckboard, would make the rounds of all fences every few months, done a general fixing of 'em.

It's too bad barbed wire *has* to be used for fences. It has butchered and killed many good horses, and some riders. But barbed wire is about the only kind of fence that will hold cattle, most of the time, and when there has to be many long miles of it, even with the smaller ranches, that's about the only kind of fence that can be afforded or used. Cattle (even the wildest) seldom get a scratch by it, even in breaking through a four-strand fence of it, or going over it while it's loose and coiled on the ground, for they don't get rattled when in wire as a horse does, and they hold their hind legs straight back when going through, while with the horse he draws 'em under him instead and goes to tearing around.

Both Little Eagle and Ferret had been well trained against scaring and fighting wire if they ever got into it, also trained not to get into it, and stop whenever coming to some that was loose on the ground. That training had been done with a rope and a piece of smooth wire at one end, and being they was naturally cool-headed they soon learned all the tricks of the wire and how to behave when they come near any of that coiled on the ground.

There was many such coils as the flood waters rampaged along the creek bottom, and as Dane headed Little Eagle towards the railroad and trestle he then let him pick his own way through and around the two fence entanglements on the way there, along the edge of the rushing water.

Little Eagle done considerable winding around and careful stepping as he came to the fences that had been snapped and washed to scattering, dangerous strands over the field. Dane gave him his time, let him go as he chose, and finally the roar of the waters against the high banks by the trestle came to his ears. It sounded as though it was near up to the trestle, which he knew was plenty high, and that gave him a good idea of what a cloudburst it had been.

He then got mighty dubious about trying to cross the trestle, for it was a long one, there was no railing of any kind on the sides, and part of it might be under water or even washed away. There was some of the flood water in the ditch alongside the railroad grade and it wasn't so many feet up it to the track level.

Riding between the rails a short ways he come to where the trestle begin and there he stopped Little Eagle. The swirling waters made a mighty roar right there, and how he wished he could of been able to see then, more than any time since his blindness had overtook him.

Getting off Little Eagle there, he felt his way along to the first ties to the trestle, of the space between each, which was about five inches, and just right for Little Eagle's small hoofs to slip in between, Dane thought. One such a slip would mean a broken leg, and the horse would have to be shot right there, to lay between the rails. The rider would be mighty likely to go over the side of the trestle, too.

Dane hardly had any fear for himself, but he did have for Little Eagle. Not that he feared he would put a foot between the ties, for that little horse was too wise, cool-headed and careful to do anything like that, Dane knew. What worried him most was if the trestle was still up and above water all the way acrost. There would be no turning back, for in turning is when Little Eagle would be mighty liable to slip a hoof between the ties. The rain had let up but the wind was blowing hard and the tarred ties was slippery as soaped glass.

It all struck Dane as fool recklessness to try to cross on that long and narrow trestle at such a time, but he felt he should try, and to settle his dubiousness he now left it to Little Eagle and his good sense as to whether to tackle it or not.

If he went, he would *ride* him across, not try to crawl, feel his way and lead him, for in leading the horse he wouldn't be apt to pay as much attention to his footing and to nosing every dangerous step he made. Besides, Dane kind of felt that if Little Eagle should go over the side he'd go with him.

So, getting into the saddle again, he let Little Eagle stand for a spell, at the same time letting him know that he wanted to cross the trestle, for him to size it up and see if it could be done. It was up to him, and the little gray well understood.

It might sound unbelievable, but a good sensible horse and rider have a sort of feel-language which is mighty plain between 'em, and when comes a particular dangerous spot the two can discuss the possibilities of getting over or acrost it as well as two humans can, and even better, for the horse has the instinct which the human lacks. He can tell danger where the human can't, and the same with the safety.

It was that way with Little Eagle and Dane, only even more so, because as Little Eagle, like Ferret, had been trained to realize Dane's affliction, cater and sort of take care of him, they was always watchful. Then with Dane's affection and care for them, talking to 'em and treating 'em like the true pardners they was, there was an understanding and trust between man and horse that's seldom seen between man and man.

Sitting in his saddle with his hand on Little Eagle's neck, the two "discussed" the dangerous situation ahead in such a way that the loud roar of the water foaming by and under the trestle didn't interfere any with the decision that was to come.

There was a tenseness in the top muscles of Little Eagle's neck as he looked over the scary, narrow, steel-ribboned trail ahead, nervous at the so careful investigation, that all sure didn't look well. But he'd now left it all to Little Eagle's judgment, and as Dane had about expected he'd be against trying, Little Eagle, still all tense and quivering some, planted one foot on the first tie, and crouching a bit, all nerves and muscles steady, started on the way of the dangerous crossing.

Every step by step from the first seemed like a long minute to Dane. The brave little horse, his nose close to the ties, at the same time looking ahead, was mighty careful how he placed each front foot, and sure that the hind one would come up to the exact same place afterwards, right where that front one had been. He didn't just plank his hoof and go on, but felt for a sure footing on the wet and slippery tarred ties before putting any weight on it and making another step. Something like a mountain climber feeling and making sure of his every hold while going on with his climbing.

The start wasn't the worst of the crossing. That begin to come as they went further along and nearer to the center. There, with the strong wind blowing broadside of 'em, the swift waters churning, sounding like to the level of the slippery ties, would seem about scary enough to chill the marrow in any being. But there was more piled onto that, for as they neared the center it begin to tremble and sway as if by earth tremors. This was by the high rushing waters swirling around the tall and now submerged supporting timbers.

Little Eagle's step wasn't so sure then, and as careful as he was there come a few times when he slipped, and a time or two when a hoof went down between the ties, leaving him to stand on three shaking legs until he got his hoof up and on footing again.

With most any other horse it would of been the end of him and his rider right then. As it was, Little Eagle went on, like a tightrope walker, with every muscle at work. And Dane, riding mighty light on him, his heart up his throat at every slip or loss of footing, done his best not to get off balance but help him that way when he thought he could.

If the shaking, trembling and swaying of the trestle had been steady, it would of been less scary and some easier, but along with the strong vibrations of the trestle there'd sometimes come a big uprooted tree to smash into it at a forty-mile speed. There'd be a quiver all along the trestle at the impact. It would sway and bend dangerously, to ship back again as the tree would be washed under and on.

Such goings on would jar Little Eagle's footing to where he'd again slip a hoof between the ties, and Dane would pray, sometimes cuss a little. But the way Little Eagle handled his feet and every part of himself, sometimes on the tip of his toes, the sides of his hoofs and even to his knees, he somehow managed to keep right side up.

Good thing, Dane thought, that the horse wasn't shod, for shoes without sharp calks would have been much worse than none on the slippery ties. As it was, and being his shoes had been pulled off only a couple of days before to ease his feet some between shoeings, his hoofs was sharp at the edges and toe, and that give him more chance.

The scary and most dangerous part of the trestle was reached, the center, and it was a good thing may be that Dane couldn't see while

Little Eagle sort of juggled himself over that part, for the trestle had been under repair and some of the old ties had been taken away in places, to later be replaced by new ones; but where each tie had been taken away that left an opening of near two feet wide. Mighty scary for Little Eagle too, but he eased over them gaps without Dane knowing.

Dane felt as though it was long weary miles and took about that much time to finally get past the center and most dangerous part of the five-hundred-yard trestle, for them five hundred yards put more wear on him during that time than five hundred miles would of.

And he was far from near safe going as yet, for he'd just passed center and the trestle was still doing some tall trembling and dangerous weaving, when, as bad and spooky as things already was, there come the sound of still worse fear and danger, and Dane's heart stood still. It was a train whistle he'd heard above the roar of the waters. It sounded like the train was coming his way, facing him, and there'd sure be no chance for him to turn and make it back, for he'd crossed over half of the trestle, the worst part, and going back would take a long time.

All the dangers and fears piling together now, instead of exciting Dane, seemed to cool and steady him, like having to face the worst and make the best of it. He rode right on towards the coming train.

He knew from memory that the railroad run a straight line to the trestle, that there was no railroad crossing nor other reason for the engineer to blow his whistle, unless it was for him, himself. Then it came to him that the engineer must of seen him on the trestle and would sure stop his train, if he could.

Standing up in his stirrups, he raised his big black hat high as he could and waved it from side to side as a signal for the engineer to stop his train. Surely they could see that black hat of his and realize the predicament he was in. That getting off the trestle would mean almost certain death.

But the train sounded like it was coming right on, and at that Dane wondered if may be it was coming too fast to be able to stop. He got a little panicky then, and for a second he was about to turn Little Eagle off the trestle and swim for it. It would of been a long and risky swim, maybe carried for miles down country before they could of reached either bank, and it would of taken more than luck to've succeeded. But if they'd got bowled over by some tree trunk and went down the churning waters, that would be better,

Dane thought, than to have Little Eagle smashed to smithereens by the locomotive. He had no thought for himself.

About the only thing that made him take a bigger chance and ride on some more was that he knew that the whole train and its crew would be doomed before it got halfway on the trestle, and what if it was a passenger train?

At that thought he had no more fear of Little Eagle keeping his footing on the trestle. His fear now went for the many lives there might be on the train, and he sort of went wild and to waving his big black hat all the more in trying to warn of the danger.

But he didn't put on no such action as to unbalance the little gray in any way. He still felt and helped with his every careful step, and then there got to be a prayer with each one, like with the beads of the Rosary.

He rubbed his moist eyes and also prayed he could see, now of all times and if only just for this once, and then the train whistle blew again, so close this time that it sounded like it was on the trestle, like coming on, and being mighty near to him. Dane had done his best, and now was his last and only chance to save Little Eagle and himself, by sliding off the trestle. He wiped his eyes like as though to better see, and went to reining Little Eagle off the side of the trestle. But to his surprise, Little Eagle wouldn't respond to the rein. It was the first time excepting amongst the thick brush or bad creek crossings that horse had ever went against his wishes that way. But this was now very different, and puzzled, he tried him again and again, with no effect, and then, all at once, *he could see.*

Myself and one of Dane's boys had been riding, looking for Dane soon after the cloudburst hit, and seeing the stopped passenger train with the many people gathered by the engine, we high-loped towards it, there to get the surprise of seeing Dane on Little Eagle on the trestle and carefully making each and every dangerous step towards us and solid ground.

We seen we sure couldn't be of no use to the little gray nor Dane, only maybe a hindrance, and being there was only a little ways more, we held our horses and watched. Looking on the length of the trestle we noticed that only the rails and ties showed above the high water, there was quite a bend in it from the swift and powerful pressure and the rails and ties was leaning, like threatening to break loose at any time.

How the little horse and Dane ever made it, with the strong wind, slippery ties and all a-weaving, was beyond us. So was it with the passengers who stood with gaping mouths and tense watching. What if they'd known that the rider had been blind while he made the dangerous crossing?

And as the engineer went on to tell the spellbound passengers how that man and horse on the trestle had saved all their lives, they was more than thankful, for, as the heavy cloudburst had come so sudden and hit in one spot, there'd been no report of it, and, as the engineer said, he might of drove onto the trestle a ways before knowing. Then it would of been too late.

But Little Eagle was the one who played the biggest part in stopping what would have been a terrible happening. He was the one who decided to make the dangerous crossing, the one who had to use his head and hoofs with all his skill and power, also the one who at the last of the stretch would not heed Dane's pull on the reins to slide off the trestle. His first time not to do as he was wanted to. He'd disobeyed and had saved another life. He'd been "The Seeing Eye."

The fuss over with as Dane finally rode up on solid ground and near the engine, we then was the ones due for a big surprise. For Dane *spotted* us out from the crowd, and smiling, rode straight for us and looked us both "square in the eye."

The shock and years he lived crossing that trestle, then the puzzling over Little Eagle not wanting to turn at the touch of the rein had done the trick, had brought his sight back.

After that day, Little Eagle and Ferret was sort of neglected, neglected knee deep in clover, amongst good shade and where clear spring water run. The seeing eyes was partly closed in contentment.

Gypsy

BETH BROWN

HER NAME was Gypsy. Her eyes were brown. Her legs were long. Her neck was short. She stood fifteen hands high and her tail was docked. But Pop Moses, the milkman, was as proud of his horse as if she were a Derby winner.

Early each morning, Pop and Gypsy would climb the long hill to bring the new day to the door. They came without fail, in all sorts of weather, so the hotel guests would be sure to have their quota of healthful refreshment.

Of course, everyone knew Mr. Jolly's Hotel for Dogs. The original charter had specified that only dogs would be boarded. But cats soon appeared on the scene and the charter was changed to include them. At times, Mr. Jolly wondered whether he could meet the mounting milk bill. Just the same, he would not stint on the table or give notice to any of his many non-paying boarders.

The hotel also boarded a parrot, among other strange strays on its roster. But, then, Mr. Jolly himself was somewhat fey.

Years ago, as a postman in Brooklyn, he had tramped along the streets—the straight streets and the crooked streets—walking through autumn into winter and out of winter into spring—and out of spring into summer—the seasons beside him at his left—and a dream beside him at his right. And that dream was to retire some day to a place in the country where he could make a heaven on earth for those beloved and those unloved—those adopted and those abandoned. And in his dream, the latchstring was out for them all and the friendly hotel for the friendless became a reality.

The roving country road suddenly turned right, and there it was at the top of the hill—an old white house framed in a white picket fence and hung like a painting against the blue sky.

Mr. Jolly, pink, plump and placid, stood knee-deep in the tall autumn grass at the roadside, watching Sam, his assistant, swing the new sign into place and fasten it to the iron rod beside the open gate. His heart skipped a beat as he stepped back to read the imposing inscription:

HOTEL FOR DOGS AND CATS
JOSEPH J. JOLLY, PROPRIETOR

"There! It won't come loose now."

"I hope it's not too tight. I want it to swing with the wind."

Sam gave the sign a smart tap with his hammer. "How's that?"

"It swings!"

"I'll say it swings!"

"Do you think you can get it to sing?"

Sam turned the rod like a weather vane. Now the sign made the wind its companion. "Listen to it!"

Mr. Jolly listened enraptured. "It sings."

"Anything else you want it to do?"

"Yes, Sam. I want it to speak to every homeless stray in America. I want it to say *Welcome to Jolly's Hotel.*"

"The print is big enough. A blind dog could read it a mile away."

"That's good!"

"Here comes a customer," announced Sam.

"It's Gypsy!"

"Yes, and she's going a mile a minute!"

"Wonder what's up?"

"What in the world are they doing out at this hour of the day?"

"Look! They're turning in here!"

"Here comes Gypsy!" announced Mister Farley, the parrot, from his vantage point on the weather vane where he sat like a sea captain holding down his bridge. "Foul weather ahead!" he called down below. "All hands on deck!"

The cats came running from all directions and took up their positions on the top step of the porch like a lot of curious old women hungry for a choice cut of gossip. They sat with their tails curled primly around their front paws—their eyes agog at the strange proceedings that were taking place on the grounds below.

The dogs now joined them. They came more slowly, reluctant to leave behind them the series of holes they had been digging the length and the breadth of the lawn.

"Pop's on the rampage!" declared Lord Byron. "Look at the way he's cutting up our lawn!"

Pop drove past the door—between the trees—down to the river—then up again to the top of the slope. Here he pulled up with all the flourish of a coach-and-four on a mission of life and death.

"We're here! This is it!"

Gypsy agreed with a neigh.

Mr. Jolly and Sam, the house guests *en masse* at their heels, came streaming over the lawn.

"What do you mean by driving past the door?" greeted Mr. Jolly good-humoredly. "Good thing you missed all those holes!"

"You'd think you were going to a steeple-chase!" grumbled Sam, lifting the broken limb of a tree.

"We're in trouble," announced Pop. He tied the reins around the whip in the whip's socket and climbed down out of the wagon. "We're in trouble on account of Gypsy—"

He straightened her big straw hat that had fallen over one eye. He gave her a wisp of hay to chew, and chewed on one himself.

Sam tapped his forehead knowingly. Pop's trouble was deeper than the migraine headaches of which he was always complaining.

"How do you feel, Pop?" inquired Mr. Jolly.

"Never felt worse!"

"Can we be of help?"

"We're beyond help!"

Pop was mad. That was plain to see. His fists were clenched. His eyes flashed fire. His Adam's apple churned up and down, choking the words in his throat.

"Didn't get your cream this morning, did you—or your milk either?"

"No," replied Sam. "First time that's ever happened—"

"Well, it won't be the last!" declared Pop hotly. "Them and their new-fangled notions!"

"Here, have a seat!" Mr. Jolly invited, removing the tools from the wheelbarrow. "Now, out with it! What is it?"

"It's the milk company." Pop snorted his disdain. "They've decided to motorize the route—and give me an automobile. Mr. Slocum, the President—"

"An automobile!"

"You mean to deliver the milk?"

"Why, it'll turn to buttermilk!"

"It'll do worse than that! First thing you know, I'll be delivering milk in a Greyhound bus! Might as well fly it now by plane as take the cars off later!"

Mr. Jolly did his best to console him. He sided indignantly with Pop and argued against the company.

"It's either take it or leave it—" Pop concluded drearily, "and I got to make a living. I got to stay with the job—"

"But what about Gypsy?"

"Gypsy!" Pop was aroused all over again. "What do you suppose they planned doing to Gypsy?"

"Retire her, of course. She deserves it." Mr. Jolly's recommendation was made in all earnestness. "The Government takes care of its people when they turn sixty-five. No reason it shouldn't do the same for its horses when they get too old to work."

"You mean pension her off—an old-age pension for Gypsy?"

"That's right! What's wrong with the idea?" And now Mr. Jolly was launched on one of his favorite themes. "Some day they'll pass a bill that will speak in the cause of all God's loving creatures who cannot speak for themselves." He paused, looked out on the river and beyond the river to the blue. "Yes, Pop. Some day man will face His Maker out there—and beside him will be standing the dog he kicked down here in the world below. St. Peter will say: Can't let this man in. And the dog will say: Then I'm not coming in either!"

"And how," inquired Pop, enchanted in spite of himself, "is St. Peter going to finally settle it?"

"It won't be the man taking the dog into Heaven. Yes, more likely, the dog will be taking the man!"

"He sure tells some tall ones, don't he!" declared Sam, "even if he has to reach up to Heaven to get them!"

"Wait till Mr. Slocum meets up with St. Peter! Pension her off indeed! He was all for sending her off to the boneyard to make glue. But I soon nipped that in the bud!" Vehemently: "Gypsy belongs to me, thank God! I bid for her and I bought her!"

"Well, you got a bargain—no matter what you paid." Mr. Jolly gave Gypsy a pat to mark his complete approval.

Sam was more practical. "Now that you got her—where is she going to live?"

"Well—" and now Pop moved more cautiously. "I figured Gypsy might like stopping at a hotel for a spell—"

Mr. Jolly caught the point at once. Sam lagged some distance behind, taking slow, careful steps in his mind in order to fathom Pop's meaning. A frown began to form on the dark brown face.

"Didn't know there was hotels for horses—"

"How about this place? Ain't it a hotel?"

"Sure. But we ain't in business for horses. We don't keep nothing here but dogs and cats. And we got our hands full with them!"

"Any rule against horses? Any reason for not taking them in?"

"Well—" Mr. Jolly was weakening. "We've never done it before. It sort of sets a precedent—"

Sam was amazed at his easy surrender. "Don't you know what this means? We'll have to change the charter all over again. And what about our sign?"

"Just add a horse," said Pop. He chuckled. "Hotel For Horses. Now there's an idea!"

"So now it's horses!" Sam leaped to his feet. "Horses!"

"Wait a minute, Sam."

"No! I ain't waiting—not for a horse! First thing I know, we'll have goats moving in. Next thing I know, you'll be taking in elephants. You'll be making a zoo out of this hotel—and I'll be a nursemaid to snakes. No, thank you! Me for New York. I'm going to hunt me a train back home. I didn't know when I was well off. Them was the good old days. Say goodbye, Whitey." Sam picked up his five-toed, one-eyed, moth-eaten cat. "You're going back with me!"

Mr. Jolly waited for the storm to subside. The storm subsided. He feigned surprise to find that the clouds had rolled away only to leave Sam standing exactly where he stood before. "I thought you were gone—"

"You know why I'm here."

"Why?"

"You owe me money."

Pop stepped in between them as self-appointed referee.

"How much?"

"One year's back salary—"

"How much is that?"

"He gets a dollar a year—" Now Mr. Jolly again wheeled on Sam. "How about what you owe me? There's the garage rent for that jalopy of yours—"

"How about the two bucks for that watch of mine you got in hock—"

"That makes three dollars all together." Pop offered to pay it. "Here—"

"No. Let him go to the till and get it!"

Sam stood his ground. "You know darn well there's nothing in the till." He rattled his pockets. A jingle sounded.

"So you've been holding out on me, have you? Pockets full of money and me without a cent!"

"I got fourteen coppers. Them's the fourteen coppers I brought when I come here. It's all I got in the world." He paused for emphasis, then succumbed as usual to the dictates of his heart. "But if you want them—they're yours!"

"I'm not asking you for your money, Sam. All I want from you is one kind word for Gypsy."

"I got nothing against her—personally. It's just the idea of having a horse around."

"You're being rude, Sam, positively rude! The least we can do is to listen to Pop's proposition. It won't cost us anything to look into the business of housing a horse." He rose from the stump, where he had been squatting with Queenie, the dog, on his lap, assumed his most professional manner, and began on a global tour of Gypsy. First he circled around her. Then he stepped back and regarded the view from the rear.

Sam followed the proceedings out of suspicious black eyes. He was visibly torn between an ardent wish to leave and as ardent a wish to remain. It was no easy task to tear himself bodily away from a technical, microscopic study of the horse which was now taking place in the rostrum.

"How do you wash a horse?" Mr. Jolly was asking of Pop.

"Wash her?" Pop fell companionably into step beside him.

"You can't wash her in the tub the way we do the dogs, that's certain." Mr. Jolly closed one eye, the better to judge Gypsy's dimensions. "I suppose we could turn on the hose—"

"There's always the river," said Sam from the sidelines. "And you *could* leave her out in the rain!"

"I'd drop around with her curry comb—"

"Hmm. That settles that!" Mr. Jolly studied the next high hurdle. "What does a horse eat?"

"Oh! That's easy! Oats, mostly—grass when it's green—and her hat, if you let her have it! You won't have to mow the lawn—not with Gypsy around. She'll do that little job for you—"

"Yeah," said Sam with a mirthless chuckle. "She'll do the weeding, too."

"If you decide to take her in," promised Pop, "I'd provide her fodder—" He threw a baleful look at Sam. "Oats for life—and straw for bedding! How's that?"

"Bedding?" echoed Mr. Jolly, and he stopped dead in his tracks. "We can't let her sleep in the dining room. She'd take up too much space. We can't make her bed in the cellar—that's where we keep the coal. No, she can't sleep inside the house, that's sure."

"How about outside?" suggested Pop. "Gypsy's used to all sorts of weather. Just turn her loose in the back lot—and she'll be as happy as a lark."

Sam threw a thought from the sidelines. "How about putting her up in a circus tent?" he gibed. "She ought to fit in that!"

"No, it's not practical," declared Mr. Jolly, turning again to Pop. "There's a stiff wind blowing off the river. We'd wake up some morning and find Gypsy sailing out of sight with the tent wrapped round her neck—"

"You see, Mr. Jolly," decided Sam with unmistakable finality. "It's like I said before. You can't let Gypsy come in here. Why, there ain't even room on the Register!"

The talk subsided into silence. The three men sat there studying this Trojan horse that had come into their midst. Gypsy posed a problem that required a great deal of thought.

She seemed a little tired now—weighed down by more than the wooden shafts that bound her and the reins that held her. All at once the fancy straw hat no longer looked becoming on the old brown face. She stood as if in a courtroom facing the members of a jury. She had served this jury—through day and night—through sun and storm—sometimes fed and sometimes starved—sometimes wet and hungry and left outdoors all night—sometimes hot and thirsty and left in the sun all day. She had been bought and sold on an auction block. And now Pop was deserting her.

Even the guests were sorrowful. The cats and the dogs gathered around the old horse like mourners at a wake.

Hobo, with Candy beside him, stood gazing at Gypsy out of moist, sympathetic eyes.

"I hope they let you stay."

"I'd like to stay. There's no place I'd rather spend my last days than here at Jolly's Hotel."

She looked longingly at the house with its friendly, old-fashioned face. She looked longingly at the river. She knew the river and she loved its song. She knew these trees and this earth and this universe sweet with life given into man's keeping. Man was God on earth—a God who sometimes betrayed his trust to his own beneficent Father.

Now Candy was making a comment. "If all you eat is grass, it shouldn't cost much to feed you."

"I always thought that a horse ate steak—" remarked Queenie.

"Oh, no," said Gypsy. "I'm strictly a vegetarian."

"What's a vegetarian?"

"I don't eat anything that has a soul."

"Hasn't grass got a soul?" inquired Tuesday, the frolicsome black-and-white kitten.

"Yes," volunteered Lord Byron, "but it's of a low vibration."

"I don't know about vibration," declared Gypsy. "I just know I like grass."

"I like the stars," said Wednesday.

"I don't blame you. There's nothing as friendly as a star when you have to work at night."

"Astronomy," mused Lord Byron. "Now there's a subject I want to pursue."

"Me for the big dipper—when it's brimming over with cream!"

Now Monday poked her inquisitive nose into Gypsy's private life. "What do you do when you go to bed?"

"What do you mean—what do I do?"

"Well, do you stand up or sit down when you go to sleep? Do you lie on your back? Do you snore?"

Gypsy chuckled good-naturedly. "What do you do, little Monday?"

"I don't remember. I just fall asleep, I guess."

"Me, too," said Gypsy.

"Was Gypsy always your name?" queried Friday.

"Did you always haul a milk wagon?" inquired Wednesday.

"No, I started life as a show horse. A rodeo brought me to New York. I was something to see—in those days—and it cost a ticket to see me. Then the big event was over and so was my Wild West life. I left uptown through the back door and was taken downtown to the horse market."

"What a way to finish up!"

"Yes, I thought I was finished. But I was only starting on a new way of life. A hansom cab owner bought me. I stood outside the Plaza after that and hauled a shiny cab. The tall silk hat didn't always mean that my new masters were kind. But I was luckier than the other hansom cab horses. I only changed owners four times."

"I've had a dozen masters," recalled Candy. "Go on, Gypsy."

"Well, then business dropped off—the ranks were thinned out— and I was slated for the discard again. This time, I was auctioned off at the stables down on 24th Street. This time, Pop bid for me."

"I bet you were blue."

"Yes, till I got to know Pop." Gypsy paused. "He was so good to me I had to pinch myself to see if I were dreaming."

"Where did you pinch yourself, Gypsy? Show me!"

"Now, Tuesday!" And Monday boxed her on the ear.

"Don't mind them, Gypsy. That goes on all the time."

"Where was I?"

"You were saying how good Pop's been to you."

"Oh, yes. Pop bedded me down with nice clean straw. He looked after my hoofs when they needed it—and after my soul when it needed it." Passionately: "That's why it hurts to say good-bye. You know, when you've been with the same man as long as I have you get to love that man!"

Pop was saying the same thing about Gypsy.

"You know, when you've been with the same horse as long as I have you get to love that horse!"

"I don't doubt it," agreed Mr. Jolly.

"I owe a lot to Gypsy. You see, I never had a dog. I never had a wife—or a home. I was always mighty lonesome. I was lonesome till I met Gypsy."

"That's how I feel about Queenie."

"I toted Whitey a lot of miles before I got her home—"

"I don't know about Queenie—or Whitey either. But you can talk to a horse. A horse knows what you're saying—"

"Same as a dog?"

"Same as a cat?"

"Same—and yet different. Horses can count, you know. They can waltz. They can do almost anything but write out a check—"

"They can't nab burglars—"

"They can't catch mice—"

"They can love you to beat Old Harry!" Mr. Jolly was saying.

"Yes, and they can save your life!" added Pop. "I owe my life to Gypsy!"

"You don't say!"

"Sure enough?" Sam's belligerent manner softened imperceptibly.

"Sure enough! You're looking square at the proof! There's the horse and here's the man!"

"Tell us about it. What happened?"

Pop leaned back in the wheelbarrow and launched upon his story.

"You see, after she got to know the route, I could go to sleep on the way home. I could trust myself to her. Well, we started back for the stable one night as usual. I fell asleep as usual. When I woke up, there was Gypsy—standing still like she was made of stone. I called to her to get moving. But she refused to obey. Then I lost my temper and used the whip on her—"

"I bet that did it!" from Sam. "That made her pick up and go!"

"No," corrected Pop. "It didn't make her go. It only made me madder. I got down in the dark—and grabbed hold of the reins. It was raining hard. I was soaked clean through. I looked to see what the trouble could be—and what do you think it was?"

"Wouldn't know—"

"The bridge was down," said Pop. "It had gone in the night— swept away by the freshet. I would have drowned in the river—and taken Gypsy with me!" Pop came to his feet. He put an arm around Gypsy. "Don't tell me a horse can't think or love and look after you. I couldn't begin to tell you what Gypsy's meant to me—"

Sam held Whitey very close. "They sure fill your heart for you, don't they?"

"There ain't much room left when I put Gypsy inside."

"That's why your heart is so big."

"I once knew a man who had a pet flea," came the contribution from Sam.

"Oh, Sam!"

"Sure enough! He had a flea circus. Fooled you that time, didn't I?" And Sam leaned back to enjoy his own hearty laughter.

"I wish Gypsy was a cat!" pronounced Pop.

"I wish Sam would change his mind about Gypsy," observed Mr. Jolly.

The two studied Sam with surreptitious glances. But Sam, still unrelenting, sat stolid on his stump.

Mr. Jolly suddenly decided to try a ruse. He lifted his voice and let the wind carry it so Sam could not help but hear it.

"You see, Pop, if it's a choice between Gypsy and Sam—there's only one thing to do. Sam's been my best friend ever since we first met over at the post office. He wouldn't let me down. I couldn't let him down. Sorry to have to refuse you. But I've decided against Gypsy—"

"All right, Gypsy." Pop was resigned. "Off to the glue factory for you. Let's go!" He made a move toward the milk wagon.

"Just a minute!" Sam leaped to his feet. "What's wrong with boarding Gypsy? We could use a horse around here!"

"Why, Sam!"

"If she ain't staying—I ain't staying. You heard me! I'm going back to New York."

"Wait a minute, Sam!" Mr. Jolly pretended to turn to Pop for support. "Wait a minute, Pop. There's some sort of mix-up here."

Now Sam was slapping Gypsy on the rump. "If only you had a kennel of your own."

"Is that all?" echoed Mr. Jolly. "A kennel, eh?" An idea seemed to have struck him. "Give me a hand with these wheels," he ordered Pop.

"What for?"

"Never mind asking questions. Just do as you're told! Come on, Sam. Over here with that good right hook of yours."

"Why, sure, Joe. Anything you say, Joe. What do you want us to do?"

"Take the wheels off the wagon."

"What!"

"You heard me."

"All of them?"

"All of them."

Pop Moses had not bargained for such concerted frenzy. Besides, it was a hot afternoon. But at last the wheels were off. The shafts were down. The wagon rested on the ground.

Mr. Jolly walked dramatically to the door—flung it open, stepped back, and called to Gypsy.

"Gypsy!"

Gypsy went straight to the opening as if she had been rehearsed in the scene.

It was not easy getting through the door. She had a good deal of trouble with her rear end. Then her tail refused to fit inside. But finally she made it. The view from the window was worth it. She stuck out her head—faced her audience with a pleased expression—and neighed at the top of her lungs.

"Looks kind of uncomfortable if you ask me—"

"Reminds me of a lady trying to fit a size nine foot into a size six shoe!"

And now Mr. Jolly was saying: "We'll send for Ole to build an extension to take care of those hind quarters of hers—"

And now Pop was saying: "He better raise the roof a bit and put in a casement window—"

And now Sam was streaking back from the lobby with the hotel register in one hand and a paint pot in the other. "First it was dogs," he pronounced. "Then it was cats. Now we'll be boarding horses. Here! You change the sign. I'm busy."

"What in the world are you doing?" asked Mr. Jolly.

Sam was thrusting the book under Gypsy's nose. He opened it up and showed her the place on the empty page that he had reserved for her name.

"Sign right here—on the dotted line," he instructed her.

"Are you sure you want her?"

"Sure!" said Sam.

"After all," observed Mr. Jolly, "she spent her whole life riding outside that wagon of hers. It's high time she came in!"